D1445443

Deep in the Heart

Sharon Oard Warner

DEEP
in the
HEART

THE DIAL PRESS

Published by
The Dial Press
Random House, Inc.
1540 Broadway
New York, New York 10036

Library of Congress Cataloging-in-Publication Data

Warner, Sharon Oard.
Deep in the heart / Sharon Oard Warner.
p.   cm.
ISBN 0-385-32006-X
1. Women—Texas—Austin—Fiction.   2. Pro-choice movement—
Fiction.   3. Pro-life movement—Fiction.   4. Austin (Tex.)—
Fiction.   5. Abortion—Fiction.   I. Title.

PS3573.A7675 D44 2000
813'.54—dc21
99-089403

Book design by Francesca Belanger

Manufactured in the United States of America.
Published simultaneously in Canada.

April 2000

10 9 8 7 6 5 4 3 2 1
BVG

For my father, Eugene Edwin Oard,
and
in memory of my mother-in-law,
Janet Sanford Warner

Part

I

Chapter 1

PENNY SAT ON A SLAT-BACKED CHAIR in the dappled light of her grandmother's kitchen and tried not to move. Haircuts made her fidgety, always had. Today, only the heat kept her still. The air was so warm and close that Mattie had left the back door ajar, and the black bodies of flies buzzed and bumped against the screen. From next door, Penny could hear the shrieking laughter of children, two toddlers, a black-haired boy and girl, born so close together they were often mistaken for twins. Only children could tolerate such heat, she thought. Outside, the late-afternoon sun was unrelenting, bearing down on streets and yellowing lawns all over Austin, baking the tops of people's heads. They were in the midst of a Texas fall, which meant July was running right through September.

The haircut was a ritual both knew by heart. For as long as Penny could remember, they'd been doing it this same way—the two of them under the kitchen window, Penny wearing a thin towel around her shoulders, Mattie wielding scissors with long gray blades and chipped black handles. These were the same shears Mattie used to clip coupons and articles from the newspaper, to snip lengths of yarn and prune unwieldy houseplants. Once every few months, she put them to work cutting the wispy brown hair on her granddaughter's head. Usually, the haircut turned out just fine; usually they had a nice chat. But not today. Today, Mattie was meddling in Penny's love life, or in her potential love life. Penny didn't really have a love life, not yet, anyway, but her grandmother was seeing to that. Her grandmother saw to everything, or tried to.

"He's going to ask you out," Mattie was saying. "Praise the Lord!"

Neither of them bothered to use his name, no need to do so. They knew so few men, and the others, as far as Penny could recall, were all either married or dead. That left Dr. Bill, their minister, who was surely twenty years Penny's senior. He might look young, but he'd lived a whole life, and if the rumors were accurate, as many as two or three. "A long and checkered past," some said, whereas Penny, at age twenty-three, had no past at all. Surely, she thought, their conversations would be very one-sided.

"How do you know he's going to ask me out?" she sputtered, shifting her legs slightly but not slightly enough. The carpet of newspapers rustled under her feet, and Penny could feel her grandmother frowning down at the top of her head.

"Stop squirming," Mattie said. "You want me to get this right, don't you?" The papers rustled again. Now she would be standing back, admiring what she'd done so far.

"How do you know?" Penny tried again.

"I know because he told me so. Let me concentrate." Penny knew what that meant—if she persisted, the haircut might go mysteriously wrong. It had happened before. They lapsed into silence, and, dazed by the heat, Penny closed her eyes and dozed a little. She'd been out in the sun all day, rushing from her service van to the shade of porches, carrying bouquets of flowers that threatened to droop on her, clouds of balloons that hung limply in the heavy air. Usually, she was greeted with smiles, sometimes even squeals of joy, but today no one had acted especially happy to see her. They'd quickly thanked her, shut their doors abruptly, and sent her on her way with a short blast of refrigerated air.

"Wake up, Penny!" Mattie gave her granddaughter a quick pinch on the cheek, then knelt behind the chair and began snipping along the hairline, coming so close that her breath cooled the hot, damp skin of

Penny's neck. The blades of the scissors opened and closed, a tiny creak followed by a louder click, a familiar and comforting sound.

"Just a trim," Penny reminded her. Then, hesitantly: "Don't you think he's too old for me?"

"I certainly do not!" Mattie replied. "He's still a young man where it counts: young enough to play with children, mow the yard, make a decent living. Old enough to have his wits about him." She clipped a little more. "Too old?" she repeated, as though the very idea were preposterous.

Ever since Mattie had nursed Dr. Bill through the chicken pox, she'd been protective and possessive of him. About a year back, the illness had swept through the Sunday school classroom before knocking Dr. Bill flat on his back. Adult cases were always more severe than children's, or so Mattie said. Dr. Bill's had been worse than most; a secondary infection had set in. The older women in the church had taken turns nursing him, making sure he swallowed his antibiotics, preparing his oatmeal baths, swabbing his "poor body" with salve. Mattie had organized the shifts and spent a night or two sleeping on his living room couch. Afterward, Dr. Bill had taken to calling her his "ministering angel."

Before he got sick, Mattie had been skeptical of their new minister. All sorts of gossip had preceded him: Some swore he'd been a country DJ over in Shreveport, others that he'd spent time in jail, been a hippie, jumped out of helicopters over Vietnam. Mattie pooh-poohed all that. Her objections had to do with the content of his Sunday morning sermons, which were too much psychologizing and not enough preaching for her tastes. "The man can't decide if he's Oral Roberts or Dr. Ruth," she'd complained. But his illness had cured her. "No one is closer to God," she'd told Penny, "than one who has strayed and found his way back."

Now Mattie placed a hand on either side of Penny's head, adjusting it to suit her. As a child, Penny had loved this part, the way her grandmother's hands had covered her ears, creating the roar of an ocean in the quiet room. "Look straight ahead," Mattie instructed. Careful not to move her head, Penny shifted her eyes and studied the shadow of the mimosa, which spread itself across the counter and far wall, thick branches and feathery fronds that shuddered in the slightest breeze. Once or twice in the past, she'd lugged the kitchen chair out to the patio and convinced her grandmother to set up shop outside. But Mattie had complained of the sun on her back and the chatter of the mockingbird that perched in the live oak by Penny's garage apartment. "If that bird shrieks again," she'd said, "I'm liable to cut your ear off." Mattie was startle-prone; Penny couldn't deny that.

Fortunately, she'd put down the scissors and was combing out Penny's bangs when the knock came, a loud rapping on the wooden frame of the screen door. Mattie squinted and peered through the screen before smiling and waving with the large brown comb. "Come in, Henry!" she called. Penny twisted about in time to see their next-door neighbor duck his dark head inside.

"Afternoon," he greeted them, going on to explain that his son had tossed a toy into the tree. None of them could shake it out. "Can I borrow your ladder?" he asked.

"Out in the garage," Mattie replied. "It's unlocked. Help yourself."

"Sure appreciate it," he replied.

Penny shifted uncomfortably. "Grandmother," she began, but Mattie placed a heavy palm on the top of her head and kept it there until Henry was gone. He was a small wiry man. Penny told herself that, in all likelihood, the ladder would bear his weight. Still, it was a rickety, rotten thing, missing a rung, and older than Penny was. She didn't trust it, and she was so slight people often mistook her for a teenager. "I don't think that ladder is safe," she finished.

"Of course it is," her grandmother snapped. "It's been serving us for years and years. . . ." The words died away, and when Penny looked up, her grandmother was facing the window. Mattie's deep-set eyes were lost in shadow, but a bar of light shone across her long, thin nose and over a stretch of delicate cheekbone, a bit sunken now that she was into her fifties. Her hair was pure white, had been for years. Now and again, Esther from church would sidle up to Penny and slyly ask about that head of hair. "It's beautiful," she whispered, "but it sure don't look natural." Mattie maintained she'd come by it naturally, not that it was anybody's business. She kept it clipped short and trimmed around a pair of small ears that curled inward, like tender flowers.

"Grandmother," Penny said softly. "Are you all right?"

Mattie nodded absently, then slowly turned her head and blinked, as though returning from a great distance. Finally, she gazed down at Penny, twisted her lips into a smile, and dropped the comb on the table. "I nearly forgot," she said, and disappeared into the living room, returning with a rectangular mailing box in the crook of one arm and a blue envelope in her other hand. Penny recognized the familiar loopy handwriting, the scrawled letters that took up most of the available space. Something from her mother.

"Came in the mail this morning," Mattie said, dropping the envelope into Penny's lap. "This box must be your birthday present." The present was good and late, nearly a month now, which was just like Delia. Mattie gave it a quick shake before slipping it onto the breakfast table. "Take it with you when you leave."

The envelope was square, the paper nubby, the blue a bit watery, like the sky on a hot day. Penny turned it over in her hands and traced a finger over her name, *Penelope Reed.* "Go on and open it," Mattie directed. "I've already read mine."

The invitation was printed on the same pale blue paper, and when Penny pulled it from the envelope, a sheet of tissue slipped out with it. There was nothing hippie or New Age about this wedding invitation, no pressed flowers or prayers from an Indian guru. This one was on the up and up, marriage American style. Delia Angeline Reed to wed Dwayne Hanson. Saturday, November 5, at the United Methodist Church in Houston, Texas. Penny was studying the details when Mattie spoke: "*To every thing there is a season, and a time to every purpose under heaven.*"

The scripture was familiar, of course, but Penny had no idea what it meant in the here and now. As usual, Mattie was being cryptic. "Maybe the third time's a charm," Penny offered in response, not sure what else to say. Delia had been married twice before, short, unhappy unions she rarely mentioned.

Mattie took up the scissors. "In this case," she said, "I think it will be."

"Really?" Penny was surprised to hear her say so. "Do you think you'll go?"

No reply. Mattie got busy trimming, and Penny knew better than to repeat her question. She was never sure how to talk to her grandmother

about Delia, how to walk the line between her mother and her grandmother without straying into one or the other's territory. Any neutral
ground went unmarked and, as far as Penny could tell, was liable to
shift from one day to the next. The only certainty was this: Mattie had
a grudge against her daughter the size of the Lone Star State. Penny
didn't begin to understand it, but she had to live with it nonetheless.
The blades of the scissors opened and closed, the rhythm picking up as
her grandmother shaped the hair on top, holding it between her fingers, snipping faster and faster. Penny tensed, certain Mattie was getting carried away. After all, she hadn't much hair to begin with. "Just a
trim," she said again.

"I know, I know," her grandmother replied. In another minute, she
declared the haircut finished and handed her granddaughter a mirror.
"How's that?"

Dutifully, Penny held it up. Sure enough, her hair was shorter than
she'd wanted. Much shorter. Even her reflection was diminished now,
her face a bit more pinched than it had been moments before. Much as
she'd enjoyed the ritual, she disliked the results, which made of her a
baby bird, all head and open beak. No point in saying so, though,
because Mattie would only pout for days. "Great!" she said lightly, and
held still yet again while her grandmother brushed the hair from her
shoulders and swept around her feet.

Chapter 2

CARL SOLACE STUDIED HIS WIFE, Hannah, in the rearview mirror. She was perched in the middle of the backseat, her narrow lap filled with their bulky cocker spaniel, Neil—head, chest, and front paws—all of him that would fit. Several times since they'd left the house, Hannah had tried to heave the whole of him into her arms, but Neil was simply too big for that. Now she had her arms wrapped tightly around the dog's chest, forcing him to crane his neck for a glimpse out the window. That can't possibly be comfortable, Carl thought, as he pulled the Blazer into the left-hand turn lane, not for either of them. Why doesn't she let him go, let him press his nose to the glass, see whatever he can still see?

"I wish you were sitting in front with me," he complained. "I feel ridiculous."

"Neil's scared, Carl," Hannah explained again. "He knows we're going to the vet's."

"How would he know where we're going?" Carl asked. "He rides by himself in the backseat all the time and is perfectly happy."

The truth was, he wanted his wife next to him, despite her bad mood, which had stalled instead of blowing over, settling in for the entire week. Maybe more than a week, now that he thought about it.

He glanced again in the mirror. Today, Hannah wore her red hair plaited down her back, and as she shifted her weight, the heavy braid slid across her shoulder and hung, ropelike, over one breast. She braided her hair on the weekends, and it gave her a tomboy look Carl had always been fond of. His wife was beautiful—all milky skin and long limbs—the most beautiful woman he'd ever known. For him, the fact of their marriage was proof of the world's bewildering bounty. Now he took note of Hannah's pink lips turned down in a slight frown. She looked preoccupied, though with what he didn't know. More than Neil, he thought.

Neil's situation hadn't changed, really, though they had been up with him at 2 A.M. last night when he'd walked into a wall and woke them with his wild yelping. This morning, Hannah had called the vet, insisting on an appointment. "I want to bring him in today," he'd heard her say more than once. Carl doubted they would accomplish anything, but no matter the futility of the errand or his wife's unhappiness, he still felt pleasure in being with her, in riding in the same car, going to the same place, a long Saturday afternoon stretching out before them. The sun shone brightly through the windshield of the Blazer, a hot September day made tolerable by air-conditioning.

In front of him, a long line of cars arced through the intersection, all making the same left-hand turn onto Lamar, all racing to get through before the green arrow disappeared. His turn. Carl pressed his foot to the gas and accelerated into the turn, zipping through the intersection without so much as a honk of protest. "Wow, this car will pick up and go, Hannah!" Carl called back to her.

"I knew you'd like it if you'd just get behind the wheel."

Hannah's cherry-red Blazer was several months old, but Carl had refused to drive it until now. From the first moment he'd laid eyes on the damn thing, everything about it had irritated him: the fact that she'd bought it on a whim, without consulting either him or *Consumer Reports*; the fact that it was actually a small bus, and she was a solitary soul who went nearly everywhere alone; the fact that it was red, a car color he'd always associated with single women. Nearly twenty years of marriage, and here he was, still puzzling over his wife's behavior. Shouldn't he know her better by now? Shouldn't he be able to predict her unpredictability or, at the very least, cease to worry over it?

They were late for their appointment at the animal clinic. Only scattered seats were available in the waiting room, and Carl was forced to take one across the room from his wife and dog. Neil sat on the floor in front of Hannah, haunches resting on her white sneakers, wet black nose sniffing the air around him, smell the only pleasure left to him now. In the last year, Neil had suffered through two surgeries for cataracts. Even so, his eyes were milky. When they fixed on Carl now, it seemed more accident than anything else. Little wonder that he ran into walls in the middle of the night.

Hannah had gotten out of bed first. He'd felt her roll off the mattress, then heard the slap of her bare feet on the hardwood floor. From somewhere in the house came a distant yelping. Neil's in pain, he thought, but he couldn't manage to drag himself from bed. Not for the longest. Finally, he staggered down the hall and found them in the kitchen, Hannah hunched on the red tile floor, cradling Neil and singing an off-key lullaby. She'd looked so lovely, that brilliant red hair streaming across her chest and down over Neil, the dog's weight pulling the neck of her sleep shirt over one milky shoulder. "What's wrong?" he'd asked. Neil had looked fine, a little befuddled maybe, but no worse for wear. Hannah had ignored the question, just gone on singing, as though Carl weren't in the room, as though all of it were his fault, the inbreeding of cocker spaniels, the aging process, the idiocy of veterinarians, the slickness of the tile floor. Or maybe he was wrong; maybe she hadn't been thinking of him at all.

Now he watched his wife studying the shelves of overpriced supplies: bags of Science Diet piled against the wall, collars and leashes in every shade of the rainbow. Likely she'd want to buy Neil something before they left, spend a little more money they didn't have. Hannah enjoyed buying things; the mere act of exchanging cash for objects seemed to make her feel better. Carl made a mental note to lead her out the other door.

The squat assistant with braces called Neil's name fairly quickly, raising their hopes, only to whisk them into another smaller room to wait. The vet showed up a half hour later, mumbling apologies, and after a brief examination pronounced Neil completely blind. Nothing else they could do, he said. "Is that all?" Carl didn't intend sarcasm, but he couldn't believe this was the expert opinion they'd been waiting for. Surely, they should hear something they didn't already know. He looked from Neil to the vet, whose gaze was on Hannah. She was grasping the edge of the examining table, her eyes squeezed shut, which made the emerging lines on her face more pronounced. She wouldn't have liked to see herself this way. Hannah was thirty-nine and a half and had always looked younger than her years. She still did. Her face had the sheen of porcelain sculpture, pure and fine. But porcelain didn't age, at least not the way Hannah would. Just last week, Carl had walked past the bathroom and caught his wife gripping the edge of the sink. She'd been gazing into the mirror, wearing this same perplexed and incredulous expression.

The vet shifted his feet. Carl recognized the sign: They were supposed to pick up their blind cocker spaniel and be on their way. But Hannah didn't move. After a polite thirty seconds or so, the vet cleared his throat and gave Neil a good-bye pat on the head.

"Hannah, darling," Carl said. "Other people are waiting."

She went on holding the table, her eyes closed, Neil stretched out in front of her. Just when Carl was wondering what to do next, the dog turned his blond head, yawned, and began licking Hannah's fingers. His wife came back to life then, reaching out and lifting Neil off the table. Holding him close, and without a word to either of them, Hannah marched out of the room.

"You know, if there were something I could do . . ." the vet said when she was gone.

"Thanks for your help," Carl said. "Hannah's just upset, that's all."

The vet smiled. "People get so attached to their animals," he remarked. "I see it every day, but I'm still touched."

"Here's the funny thing," Carl told him. "Neil is actually my dog."

The vet shrugged. "Once upon a time, maybe," he said, "but not anymore."

While Hannah wrote the check, thirty-five dollars for both of them to hear the obvious, Carl held his dog's leash. He wondered whether Hannah even remembered that Neil had been her gift to him. Like the red Blazer, Neil had been an impulse buy. The year had been 1982, the summer before they'd moved back to Austin from San Marcos, and Hannah was attending yet another baby shower. They were all getting pregnant back then, every teacher at the elementary school where Hannah worked—bang, bang, bang, up and down the hall—everyone except his wife, or so it had seemed. This particular shower had been held at a house out in the country; the hostess was a dog breeder with a litter of cocker spaniel puppies skittering around her kitchen floor. Five golden balls of fur. Hannah hadn't been able to resist the smallest one, and she'd carried him home and presented him to Carl as an early birthday present.

Now she turned and held out her hand for the leash, but Carl shook his head. "Let me take him," he said. "My birthday present, remember?"

Hannah gave him an arch look and headed straight for the door, that long braid swinging across her back, so inviting that Carl had to resist the urge to reach out and give it a swift tug. The dog pulled at his leash, anxious to follow her. Never mind the past; Neil was hers now, and all three of them knew it. But Carl couldn't help remembering. As they crossed the lot, he recalled the way his wife had thrust the puppy into his arms, her hands trembling slightly, though Neil wasn't the least bit heavy then. The puppy had come with a pale blue ribbon wrapped round his neck, undoubtedly a castoff from one of the baby gifts, and later on they'd laughed as he rolled about on the hardwood floor, wrestling it off. "I'll love him all the more because he's yours," Hannah had told Carl. At the time, he'd thought it an odd but romantic thing to say, touching proof of her love. Now he knew better. Turning the moment over in his head, holding it up in the light of a much later day, he saw that the gift was actually her way of taking Neil for herself. She loved best where she had the least to lose.

When Hannah climbed into the backseat for the ride home, Carl saw no point in protesting. Without a word, he placed Neil in her arms and closed the door, climbing into the driver's seat and starting the car. This time, he would try a different route across town, longer but hopefully quicker since it was mostly expressway. Turned out, the Blazer was lighter and faster on the highway than his small Mazda. The sensation of being higher off the ground was pleasing, and it thrilled him to pass the slower cars in a hot blast of wind. Hannah sat silent in the backseat, and for a few moments, Carl managed to forget his passengers. Pressing his foot to the pedal, he pushed the speedometer to seventy-five, then to eighty, until Hannah called out to him: "Slow down!"

Halfway home, she began to wonder aloud about sheltering Neil. How could they keep him safe? Should they close him in a smaller room at bedtime, the laundry room, say, or the bathroom? "And what about during the day?" Carl asked, speeding up again to whiz past a Honda Accord. At the right moment he could glimpse the other driver down below, in a slower, slightly subterranean world. I could get used to this, he thought.

"That's right," Hannah said slowly. "What am I thinking? He's blind during the day as well." She lapsed into another silence.

Up ahead, Carl spied a police car and, reluctantly, let off the gas, until the needle pointed to sixty. It felt like they were crawling. "You know," he told Hannah, "I see blind people at the mall all the time. Tapping those white canes up and down the concourse. They do fine. Ask them if they want some help, they'll tell you no, hell no."

"They have canes and dogs to help them. They have Braille and sunglasses."

Sunglasses? Carl thought. He glanced in the rearview mirror. "So let's get Neil a Seeing Eye dog and maybe a pair of glasses."

She rolled her eyes. "I hate when you do this."

"What?"

"Make jokes about something awful."

"Who says I'm joking?" He was still gaining on the police car, so he slowed to fifty-five. "Another animal in the house would be good for him," he told Hannah. "Something to smell, something to follow."

Hannah thought about it a minute. "Maybe," she said. Then: "Can you pull over?" All of a sudden, she sounded a little strangled.

"What's wrong?" He craned his head to get a glimpse of Neil in the rearview mirror, his first thought being that something had happened to the dog.

"Carsick," she said. "Pull over now."

He waited by the side of the road while she knelt among weeds and tiny yellow wildflowers to heave up her breakfast, the sour odor of vomit rising up around them. When she was done, he helped her to her feet and wiped her face with his handkerchief. "Why don't you sit in the front seat?" he suggested, wrapping an arm around her waist. "I'll stop at the next exit and get you something to drink."

Hannah turned to Carl and, burying her face in his shirt, began to cry. "I'm sorry," she said in a muffled voice.

"For what?" he asked. "You have nothing at all to be sorry about."

ON SUNDAY morning, Carl got up before seven while Hannah slept in. He brewed his usual pot of coffee, let Neil out, then made his way down the hall to his studio. The studio was actually a converted second bedroom, situated across from the bathroom and just down the hall from where his wife still slept, and it served not only as home to his easel and paints but also as a breeding ground for flamingos. Years ago, Carl had remarked to Hannah that he admired the gaudy birds, the sheer improbability of their coloring, the way they stand so gracefully on one leg, the other tucked up neatly inside their feathers. Since then, Hannah had given him a whole series of flamingo gifts, each of which he was required to make a fuss over and then install in the studio. By now, the room was crowded with them. A curling zoo poster was taped to the door, and a wooden flamingo hung from the ceiling; with the tug of a string, the brightly painted bird flapped its heavy wings. Hannah was most proud of the desk-lamp flamingo, more fluorescent pink neck than anything else, but Carl was a traditionalist. He preferred the plastic lawn flamingo propped in the corner.

Nearly every morning, he worked in his studio, and had for most of the years of his marriage. In fact, if it weren't for his art, he'd never have met his wife in the first place. Hannah had gone to the Methodist Student Center at the University of Texas only once, on a Sunday afternoon in late November of 1973, tagging along with a friend. At the time, Carl was practically living there, in the midst of his first and last mural project, a Nativity scene on butcher paper. The mural was divided into three sections, each of which was taped to a rec-room wall. Two other artists were supposedly participating, but neither had shown up for days. In the meantime, Carl had finished his own section—the approach of the three Wise Men—and begun encroaching on the next one, blocking out the manger scene, Joseph, Mary, and Baby Jesus.

This was, of course, the part of the mural Carl had coveted. The student it had been assigned to was technically more proficient, but he lacked Carl's passion and perseverance, or perhaps he was simply applying them elsewhere, to his girlfriend, say. On the day Hannah walked into the rec room, Carl was furtively sketching in the figure of Mary, but he couldn't help noticing the beautiful stranger. In a rash moment, certainly one of his finest, he asked if she would consider sitting for him. "You have such a lovely face," he told her, "perfect for the Madonna."

Less than a week later, he realized he was in love. It was one of those rare moments he would always remember. He'd been in the midst of his morning shave—leaning close to the mirror, lifting his chin—but instead of seeing his stubble, he'd flashed to the down on Hannah's cheek, recalling her as she'd been the afternoon before. She'd sat in a wing chair by the window, ankles crossed, hands folded in her lap, a soft light wafting over her, so contained, so still, the perfect model, he'd thought. Then, just as he'd turned back to his sketch, she'd stuck out her tongue. One quick pink flick, so fast he might have imagined it. Razor in hand, Carl had chuckled, alive in the moment, peering past the water spots on the mirror, past his face, and into Hannah's solemn eyes. He'd been head over heels ever since.

Carl wasn't much of a student, but with Hannah's urging, he'd managed to graduate with a degree in fine art. Not that he ever tried to make a living from his work. The prospect of so much rejection depressed him, and he wasn't competitive enough to make money as a commercial artist. Instead, he'd fallen into the bookstore trade and contented himself with dabbling in his spare time, experimenting with forms and mediums rather than perfecting his technique. All summer, he'd been working with watercolor and still life, painting and repainting a disparate group of objects—a cow skull, a withering pineapple, a stepladder, dried sunflowers—from slightly different angles. Most of his efforts ended up in the trash. Then, one day last week, he'd simply tired of still life altogether and dismantled the dusty display. Now he was planning an acrylic landscape, something recognizably Texan but without the requisite bluebonnets, armadillos, and longhorn steers. His inspiration was a photograph of Big Bend country from a travel magazine. So many shapes and colors! The sky was a brilliant blue; the jagged cliffs, a rusty red; and in the foreground, sprawling prickly pear cactus in varying shades of blotchy green.

Early Sunday morning he spent on preparatory sketches, stopping around ten o'clock to shower. Hannah was just getting up, and he was surprised when she pulled aside the shower curtain and stepped into the tub with him. He couldn't recall the last time they'd bathed together.

"Morning!" he greeted her, then moved aside and turned the warm spray on his wife's narrow back. She leaned the length of her body against the tiles while he trained the water up and down her spine. "How are you feeling?" he asked. When she shrugged, he let go of the shower head to knead her shoulders. Her skin was tantalizingly smooth, but the muscles underneath were tight. "Relax," he whispered. He wished they had time to make love, preferably right here in the tub, but he was due to work at eleven and had to make do with kissing her neck and fondling her breasts. "I love you," he whispered.

"You too," she replied.

Sundays were often slow at Barton Creek Mall, but Carl didn't mind. After he'd opened the store and his assistant had clocked in, he took his usual stroll down the concourse. Not far from Walton's Bookstore, lush plants flourished around a large fountain. Usually, the benches surrounding it were occupied by a group of old men, most of whom Carl knew by sight and a few by name, but on Sundays even the seniors stayed home. Today, Carl headed for the Nut House. The walk took three minutes, and by the time Lydia weighed the mix, rang it up, and updated Carl on the sad saga of her life, another five minutes had ticked away. Lydia was a fixture at the Nut House. She seemed to live behind the counter.

"How's the book business?" she asked. She always asked.

"Sold a few," Carl replied.

His wife had a standing joke: "Carl sells magazines and comic books and audio tapes and itty-bitty reading lamps and the occasional Stephen King novel." She neglected to mention videotapes, lap desks, bookmarkers, stuffed versions of Sendak's Wild Things, and calendars, but then she hadn't set foot in the store for at least a year. Hannah ordered her books from Quality Paperback Book Club or the Daedalus catalog of remainders. She took pride in reading what others didn't, turning up her nose at the *New York Times* Best Seller List. Carl accused her of being a snob, but he had to admit that she read more than he did, finishing at least one book a month, usually a novel, in the snatched moments before she dropped off to sleep each night.

Lydia was Hannah's polar opposite, and Carl enjoyed her company for precisely that reason. Fifty-five years old and seventy pounds overweight, Lydia spent her days nibbling nuts and driving away customers. Most people didn't want to hear her sad tales, but Carl found them endearing, even reassuring. Set next to Lydia's, his own life looked pretty good. In the last month or so, she'd been bemoaning the fate of her eldest daughter, Trish, who was serving time for some unspecified crime. A son in prison was bad enough, but a daughter? Only someone with truly lousy luck could raise a daughter to be a criminal.

"Trish says she wants a sweater for her birthday." Lydia peered up at him, blinking repeatedly, as though she couldn't quite bring him into focus. Her face was a pale moon, round and bland, marked by a number of small craters scattered across her cheeks. Apparently, a difficult adolescence had given way to a bleak adulthood, which didn't seem at all fair. Lydia's saving grace was her mouth, a pair of plump red lips and straight white teeth. She had a lovely smile. Long ago, some man must have coaxed her to smile, maybe Trish's father, though Lydia had never mentioned him.

She handed Carl his nut mix. Mostly raisins, he thought, as he rummaged in the tiny bag. He considered complaining but realized that it was Lydia's job to shortchange people. "Says it's cold in that penitentiary." Lydia never called it a "jail" or a "prison," only the "penitentiary," as though length and formality added an air of sophistication to her daughter's predicament. "Lavender. A moody color, don't you think?"

Carl nodded and handed her two dollar bills. Sometimes she asked questions, but he knew she neither expected nor appreciated a response.

"Come to think of it," she said, "that Trish has always been a moody girl, so maybe it all works out in the end." Carl blinked, trying to erase the image of a girl wearing a lavender sweater in a jail cell.

Lydia slapped the two quarters and the penny onto his palm. The coins were damp and warm. Carl dropped them into his pocket, wiped his palm on the back of his trousers, and said good-bye.

"Off to see the bird?" she called. He nodded again. "Tell Noah I say hi!"

Noah's Ark was a small pet store at the far end of the mall, well off the beaten path. A sign in the window claimed it was A FAMILY-OWNED ESTABLISHMENT, even though Noah Osgood didn't have a family, not unless you counted his three cats and his current lover, Juan. Noah would have counted the cats—they'd been around for years—but Juan was another matter, one much more fleeting. Carl had known Noah for years. One day, shortly after he'd started as a clerk at the bookstore, Noah had ambled in, holding his middle finger, in search of a chocolate cookbook and a Band-Aid. "I met someone marvelous with a weakness for chocolate," he'd explained. But Carl had been curious about the finger. "Oh, that," Noah had answered. "Gerbil." Customers who bought the little rodents insisted on knowing the sex, he'd said, rolling his eyes. "You have to turn them upside down and hold their tails back. The sensitive ones get pissed."

Today, Noah wasn't at the helm of the Ark. Likely he was out playing golf or still away on a long weekend trip to Padre Island. He'd left the store to a high-school girl he'd hired last summer. Most kids quit when school started, but this one had stayed on, working weekends during the school year. She knew a good job when she saw one: The phone was close by, and the long counter was the perfect surface for polishing her nails. "Is Noah gone to Padre?" Carl called out as he negotiated the far aisle, headed for the back of the store. The girl, whose name was Jill or maybe Janice, didn't answer. Carl could hear her chirping away on the phone behind the counter, completely oblivious to her surroundings. She might as well be at home, he thought, painting her toenails on her canopied bed.

The store was as crowded as an old person's garage, piled high with things Noah just couldn't let go of, and so disorganized that a boa constrictor spent every day staring steadily at a group of panicky hamsters. Noah didn't much believe in clearance sales either. When new merchandise arrived, he shoved over the old; when one set of shelves was piled high, he erected a new shelf.

At Carl's approach, E.T. squawked loudly and flapped his clipped wings. The bird occupied the place of honor at the back of the room.

No cage for E.T., just a long pipe for a perch and, underneath, a rectangular box for catching droppings and food. "Hungry, fellow?" Carl asked.

The parrot screeched in reply. He was both elegant and beautiful, his body a rich gray that set off his bright red tail feathers. To Carl's mind, his eyes were not like an ordinary bird's. They were curious and intelligent, like the real E.T.'s.

"No food till you talk," Carl told him, edging closer to the perch as E.T. backed up. This was their dance, refined over time into a satisfying ritual. Carl never walked up directly on E.T.; rather, he slipped around behind him, allowing the bird to back onto his shoulder, one claw at a time. If children were around, they enjoyed this act, which was punctuated by the bird's loud chatter. "E.T. phone home!" he screeched. Once, a big-eyed child had tugged on Carl's belt and asked, "Did you used to be a little boy named Elliot?"

"Yes," Carl had replied without thinking, "I did."

Today, E.T. found his footing easily and soon had his beak in Carl's shirt pocket, searching out his favorite morsels—pumpkin seeds. Carl was smiling when he turned and spotted the banner hanging on the side wall nearest E.T.'s perch. Obviously, it had been taped up hurriedly; one end drooped over a cage of lovebirds. It read: OWN THE BIRD WHO THINKS HE'S AN EXTRATERRESTRIAL! NO UNREASONABLE OFFER REFUSED!!! The words had been scrawled in purple marker, something of the writer's distress captured in the angular slant of the letters. Carl recognized Noah's handwriting.

"What the hell's going on?" Carl cried. E.T. belonged to Noah, always had. His residence in the pet store was purely a matter of convenience, a way to draw in a few customers. Whenever business was bad, Noah would move E.T.'s perch to the front of the store and put up a sign: TALK TO THE BIRD FROM OUTER SPACE. It worked wonders.

Hurrying down the aisle, Carl felt the tightening grip of E.T.'s claws on his shoulder. In his rush, he forgot to put his hands into his pockets and, instead, let them swing. Every second or third step, he knocked something else from the shelves: fish food, plastic spider boxes, bells molded from birdseed. The boxes made a real racket. Janice or Jill looked up, alarmed, and hung up the phone without saying good-bye.

"Can I help you?" she chirped, as though Carl were a stranger.

"Don't you remember me?" he asked.

She shook her head. "Sorry," she answered, her eyes straying to the mess in the aisles. "Lots of people come in here." She was a little pudgy and reminded Carl of a cheerleader he'd had a crush on in high school. The last time he'd been home to Terrell, he'd spotted the cheerleader in the grocery store checkout line. She'd gone to fat, of course, her hair pulled up in a no-fuss ponytail, a little girl riding on one large hip. When the cheerleader had glanced in his direction, he'd smiled at her, overcome again by the yearning he'd felt at sixteen. He wanted her now, he'd realized, for different reasons, not for her beauty but for the way she'd shrugged it off, and not for what he had seen then as her charmed life but for her embrace of the ordinary. Just as she went out the door, Carl had opened his mouth to call hello to her, then closed it again, realizing he no longer knew her name.

"Yes, Janice, you can help me," he said pointedly. This cheerleader wore a name tag. "Since when is E.T. for sale?"

"Since he bit Noah on the nose." She turned to a box of doggie treats, half-unpacked, but the prospect of the task seemed to daunt her. She looked back at Carl. "I remember you now." She cocked her head and studied him. "With E.T., right?"

"Right," Carl replied, resisting the urge to roll his eyes.

The bird flapped his wings and brushed the side of Carl's head. The gesture felt oddly affectionate. "Right," E.T. echoed.

"Hey," Janice said. "I never heard him say that before."

"He has quite a vocabulary. A little nip on the nose? I don't get it."

"More than a nip." Janice reached in the box for a bag of treats and dropped them on the counter. If Noah was lucky, she'd get those Doggie Delights put away by the end of the day. Carl's employees were no different; on an eight-hour shift they worked maybe four, which was why he had taken to hiring part-timers. "Noah had to give a speech at some banquet with a gauze pad taped to his nose," Janice went on. "I don't know whether you've noticed, but Noah puts a lot of store in his looks."

"He'll change his mind," he said, reaching up to stroke the bird's tail feathers. "He can't just sell E.T.; this bird is family."

"If I were you, I'd keep my nose out of reach," Janice cautioned. "Otherwise, you may end up with your own nose job. You should have

heard Noah scream. . . . No, I don't think he'll change his mind."
She smiled smugly, making Carl think again of his own cheerleader.
She'd had the same tight way of turning up the corners of her mouth,
lips pressed together, as though dirt might fly in.

"Do you have any idea what Noah wants for him?"

She shrugged and glanced toward the back of the store, where the
banner hung. "No unreasonable offer refused." His bird—Carl did
think of him that way—might be gone by the end of the day.

"Twenty-five dollars?" he asked. He was thinking of Neil now and
the companionship that E.T. would offer him. At least, that's the way
he'd broach it to Hannah. And didn't he deserve his own impulse buy
every once in a while?

"Sold," Janice replied, "to the highest bidder."

Chapter 3

ON MONDAY MORNING, Hannah found herself in Walgreen's drugstore again, stymied in the feminine-hygiene aisle. She'd never have believed herself capable of this sort of behavior—an adolescent, maybe, or a deranged woman, but certainly not her. It was positively self-indulgent. She paced up and down, scanning the rows of cheerful pink and blue boxes, trying to make a decision. They weren't cheap, these tests. No, this was turning into an expensive habit. She'd splurged the first time around, spent $13.99 on the Cadillac version, with a see-through stick to watch the test in progress. Positive showed two blue lines, ninety-nine percent accurate and foolproof, the results in less than a minute. She'd gotten just what was promised on the back of the box, two lines, ironically the same shade of blue as the skirt hiked up around her hips. She'd sat in shock, staring first at the stick in her hand and then at the stall door. For a few hours afterward, she'd been convinced of the result, long enough to call her sister, Helen, and tell her the news. Helen, herself the mother of three, knew to be measured in her response. "Well, that's wonderful," she'd said. "Isn't it?" To which Hannah had replied, "It might be, but let's just keep it to ourselves for right now, okay? The test might be wrong." Helen had snorted, then tried to disguise it with a little cough. "You coming down with something?" Hannah had asked.

She'd completed the first two tests in the women's rest room of the teacher's lounge. It was convenient; it was safe. She could simply drop the test and wrappings in the trash without worrying that Carl might come across them. Who cared what the janitor thought? With all the women going in and out, any one of them capable of peeing over a stick, Hannah felt safe enough. The first time, she'd used Clear Blue Easy, but for the second test, a week later, she tried Fact Plus, which showed a plus sign for pregnancy. Once again, she called her sister, a little breathless this time. "I'm still pregnant," she blurted out, hearing the amazement in her voice. Here she was, nearly forty, and it had never happened before. Surely she was allowed a little disbelief, an extra test or two.

Helen had laughed. "What did you expect?"

A good question, but Hannah didn't have an answer for it. She'd never given pregnancy much thought. She'd never had to. Until six months ago, when her gynecologist had pronounced her too old to keep taking it, the pill had been as much a part of her daily routine as brushing her teeth. She'd been popping that tiny bundle of hormones for over twenty years, every day of her adult life. Periodically, Carl had raised the subject of children, and she'd joined in, no harm in considering it, but the discussion was always speculative and hypothetical, like the trip to Europe they batted about year after year. This was Sunday morning breakfast talk, and as everyone knew, it didn't cost a dime. Babies and trips to Europe, those required preparation and money in the bank. And commitment. Later, she'd always thought. Not until this past Saturday, standing over Neil, hearing the verdict—old and blind— had she suddenly realized that the vet was speaking of her as well.

Vomiting by the side of the road had been more convincing than any two pregnancy tests. She'd even considered confessing her condition to Carl. But on Sunday she'd felt fine again, not a hint of nausea, and by the end of the day, she'd begun to hope. Now here she was, studying boxes and looking for the one that wouldn't fail her. She was running out of time; her doctor's appointment and counseling session were scheduled for this afternoon. Hannah picked up a box called Confirm. The results showed in a cutout heart, and the kit included a keepsake card to display in a baby book. Good grief, she thought. As Helen had told her, it was time to face facts. Why not one called Face Facts, she wondered, the pregnancy test for skeptics? Instead, Hannah grabbed up the Walgreen's brand and headed for the front register. She'd have to wait until lunch to take this last test. She and the principal had their usual Monday morning "state of the school" meeting to get through. If she didn't hurry, she'd be late.

Mr. Pilsner spent their hour together rubbing the smooth round surface of a glass paperweight, turning it over in his long, pale fingers, feeling its heft. His wife was undergoing chemotherapy for breast cancer, and Hannah knew he hadn't been sleeping well; she could see the weariness in his shoulders, the bruised-looking skin under his eyes. She considered getting up and throwing her arms around him; with anyone else, she would have, but it wouldn't do for Mr. Pilsner. He was carrying on with business, pretending a calm he didn't feel, and he expected her to do the same.

For the most part, they discussed problems with the band teacher, who strutted around campus in tight black jeans, arrogance etched into his features and whose unconditional reaction to every disciplinary problem was to kick the offender out of the program. The marching band continually shrank. When Mr. Boswell had taken over, Travis High boasted a healthy band of nearly one hundred and thirty. Now, five years later, they'd been reduced to a paltry fifty-four players and three pudgy flag girls. Hannah was itching to get rid of him, but Mr. Pilsner said no. Mr. Boswell was the type to sue, so unless they could pawn him off on another school, they were stuck with him. More supervision, Mr. Pilsner insisted. He suggested that Hannah stop by the band room at least three times a week. "Be sure he sees you're there. Look sharp," he said, one of his favorite sayings. While Hannah was making a note on her legal pad, a wave of nausea rolled over her, but she chalked it up to the breakfast burrito she'd grabbed after leaving Walgreen's.

At lunchtime, she stowed the pregnancy test in a bag with her tuna sandwich and headed for the teacher's lounge. She would eat first, then slip into the bathroom for one last test. Deep down, she knew that it was futile. Her last period had been eight weeks ago, around July 13, as best she could remember. She'd never kept track before, had never needed to. After Dr. Kemp had fitted her with the diaphragm, he'd warned her to take note on the calendar, but she hadn't paid much attention; she was too busy fuming. *I'm not old*, she'd thought. *How dare he? He's the old one.* Take a look at those bristly white hairs in your nostrils, she'd wanted to say. Why doesn't your wife hand you a pair of tweezers? Consequently, she'd gone home with a diaphragm in her purse that she hadn't the slightest idea how to use. It might as well have been a child's toy. She'd squeezed the rim and sent it flying across the room.

Hannah had just finished her sandwich and was taking a last sip of Diet Coke when her pager beeped to let her know a troublemaker was waiting in her office. As senior assistant principal of William Barret Travis High School, she was responsible for the truancy and delinquency problems of students whose names began with *A–F*. Not that her duties stopped there; in fact, that was precisely where they seemed to begin, stretching outward to the offices of the other assistant principals she supervised and upward, to the classrooms of teachers all over school. Hannah was, in effect, a troubleshooter, though if anyone referred to her as such she was sure to set him straight. "I'm an administrator," she'd say, staring the offender square in the eye, knowing that her go-to-hell look was the envy of everyone in the building.

Though her job was rife with them, Hannah hated surprises. She called out a quick good-bye to the others in the lounge, folded the brown bag around the box inside, and rushed back down two flights of stairs, straightening her navy skirt and jacket as she went. The sandwich had gone down just fine, not a bit of nausea. If only she'd had time to take the pregnancy test. It might have turned out negative; it was possible. Hurrying through one dark hallway after another, she maintained her cool by listening to the click of her heels on the scarred linoleum. The closer she got to her office, the harder she stepped. Turning the corner, Hannah spotted her "guest," Erica Faber. The girl sat cross-legged outside the office door, dressed completely in black; everything except her pale face and blond hair receded into the gloom. When Hannah got close enough, she noted that Erica's eyes were closed, but her posture was excellent—her spine straight, her shoulders back, hands resting, palms up, on her knees.

"So, it's you again," Hannah remarked briskly.

When Erica didn't respond, Hannah turned and unlocked the private door to her office. Light from the one narrow window poured into the hallway. She intended to duck inside and close the door—let Erica camp in the hall until she came to her senses—but suddenly, Hannah felt so dizzy she had to grab for the door frame to keep from falling. The bag fell from her hand; the pregnancy test slid out and hit the floor. Shit, she thought, bending over to scoop it up. Another wave of nausea rolled over her as she stuffed the box back into the bag.

"You okay?" Erica asked, gazing up from her spot on the floor, hands still resting on her knees.

Hannah flushed. "Fine," she replied, determined to keep her legs from wobbling. "So, are you practicing yoga?"

"Meditation."

The girl stared back at her openly, a slight smile on her wide lips. If she'd seen the pregnancy test, she certainly wouldn't let on, at least not in any way she could be called to task for. Erica had an extraordinary face, Hannah thought, not pretty in the conventional sense, not Most Beautiful material, but the sort of face an artist is drawn to, all angles and lines. A wide forehead, a strong chin, and a nose that drew a straight line between them. If Carl were to see her, he'd rush for his sketchbook. At this stage of life, Erica looked older than her age, but later on she'd look younger. That is, if she survived this period of rebellion.

Some didn't. Back in March, a former student had committed suicide. Didn't even bother with a note. Hannah remembered him clearly. William Fox. He'd been to her office several times in his years at Travis High School, both alone and in the company of his parents. In the newspaper article, his mother and father claimed they had no idea why their son had put a gun to his head and pulled the trigger. Always such a happy child, they told the reporter. But Hannah remembered him differently. She could still see the boy leaping out of a chair and shouting at his parents, his thin face blotchy with emotion. The whole time the father had stared out Hannah's window, preferring the view of a parking lot to his son's tearstained cheeks. Why didn't he leave us a note? the parents had wailed. Why indeed?

"So you feel the need to meditate outside my door?" Hannah asked, pretending a calm she didn't feel. For William Fox's sake, she vowed to do better with this one.

"Mr. Walters was yelling at me again. Bad vibes. I'm trying to attain a higher consciousness."

Bad vibes, Hannah thought. This one has been digging in a box of sixties slang. "Yes, well," she said, feeling more herself again. "Just so you don't *lose* consciousness, my dear." She moved the short distance to her desk, the clicks of her heels more tentative now. "Come in. My feet hurt. I need to 'attain' my chair." Glancing back across the space of her tiny office, Hannah noted that Erica rose effortlessly and that she closed the door without being asked, two marks in her favor.

Behind her desk at last, Hannah kicked off her shoes and slipped the bag into her purse. "Have a seat, Erica," she said.

Erica cast a dubious look at the visitor's chair. "I'd rather sit on the floor."

"Naturally," Hannah answered. "If other people sit in chairs, you'd rather not. But I'd like to contemplate your lovely face."

Erica smirked. "Lovely face." She snorted. "My nose is too big."

"No," Hannah said. "It's just right. Later, when you're an old woman, it *will* be too big." She cocked her head and considered the nose again. "Much too big."

"What do you mean?" Forgetting herself, Erica edged over to the chair and sat down.

"Ears and noses grow as long as we live."

"No way!"

"Would I lie? Ask Mr. Walters." Mr. Walters was a chemistry teacher and, evidently, the person responsible for this visit. He was a small man given to complaining about his salary, and Hannah didn't like him. She thought he sent students to her office far too often, preferring to hand over the distasteful part of his job. Already, Hannah felt a certain kinship with the girl: they both had the good sense to recognize a jerk. "So, you and Mr. Walters had a little disagreement?" Her tone was only slightly sarcastic, but Erica caught it. Her eyes lit up, and she leaned forward a little, as though to cement the alliance. But Hannah would have none of it. She kept her expression neutral and held out her hand for the note.

Erica hesitated, then slid a hand in her pocket and extracted something resembling a Christmas ornament, which she dropped in Hannah's palm. Hannah turned the origami over, admiring the crisp lines and careful folds. This was something new. No one had ever taken a teacher's note and turned it into art before. She glanced up at the girl, who looked a little smug, then back at what used to be a note from Mr. Walters. "If I had, um, what do they call it, X-ray vision, what might I read in this little gem?"

Erica spoke right up. "Even with X-ray vision you wouldn't be able to read it. Mr. Walters's hand was shaking when he wrote it. But I'll tell you what he's pissed about."

"Why don't you?"

"He caught me climbing out the window." Erica's hands were folded neatly in her lap, and she kept her eyes on Hannah's face. Was Catholic school in the girl's past? Hannah couldn't remember.

"Climbing out the window? Isn't Mr. Walters's room on the third floor?"

"Yes, but there's a ledge wide enough to stand on." Erica shrugged. "It's just around the corner to a fire escape. A few minutes of sheer terror"—here, she giggled—"and it's all over, which is more than I can say for Mr. Walters's class."

Hannah shuffled papers and did not look up until she was certain she could keep a straight face. But she hadn't fooled Erica. Even with that blond ponytail, the girl managed to look downright sassy.

"And where were you off to?" Hannah asked.

"Oh, I wasn't sure. My absolute first choice is the lake, but you can't get there on the bus. So my second choice, always, is the mall."

"Highland or Barton Creek?"

"Barton Creek is for dead people."

Hannah had to suppress a smirk. "My husband manages Walton's Books at Barton Creek," she offered quietly.

Erica didn't flinch. "I'm sure some awesome people work there, Dr. Solace, but it's still a funeral home."

Hannah smiled. Her sentiments exactly. She realized, then, how far afield they'd gotten. "You know, you could easily be suspended for this little stunt."

"I know. But who cares? My dad's not speaking to me anyway." Erica rose from the chair and wandered the few steps it took to reach the small painting on the wall across from Hannah's desk. It was a present from Carl in the early years of their marriage. Erica made a show of studying it. "Cool. I really like this. I'm into art, you know."

"Are you? It's my husband's work," Hannah responded, "from a long time ago." The painting was from Carl's Wyeth period, a girl and two boys traipsing up a country road, their backs to the viewer. Something about the children's postures, the way they walked three in a row, suggested a fierce alliance. Hannah had always wanted to be that girl, disappearing into the countryside with two boys who loved her and each other. Looking at the painting now, she yearned to be with them, so much so that she had to force herself to turn away. "What about your mother?" she asked. "Is she speaking to you?"

Erica waved at the painting. "Same guy that works at the mall?"

"I've only been married once."

Erica turned and appraised her coolly. "Really? Pretty old-fashioned, aren't you, Dr. Solace?"

This child would make a bang-up therapist. Hannah thought she'd have to be careful. "Your mother," she said again. "Is she speaking to you?"

Erica turned reluctantly from the painting. "I wasn't trying to be rude, but my mother's not a good subject."

Hannah tried to remember. Erica's parents had been divorced for several years; the mother lived in Colorado or California, one of those *C* states. Were there others? "Why don't you wait in the outer office while I call your father?" She couldn't help adding, "Suppose he'll speak to me?"

Erica glanced back at the painting before she drifted toward the door. She did seem genuinely interested. "If you weren't married," she tossed over her shoulder, "he'd ask you out." The door clicked shut behind her.

Hannah rested her head in her hands before looking up the number. She remembered Mr. Faber. He was a handsome and successful lawyer, the sort who carried a phone in his briefcase but didn't give out the number.

"McGinnis, Sturgeon, and Faber, Attorneys at Law." Hannah recognized the secretary's voice. This was the same woman she'd spoken to the last time Erica was in her office.

"Good afternoon. This is Dr. Solace at Travis High School. May I speak to Mr. Faber, please?"

"Mr. Faber is out of the office, *Ms.* Solace." Her tone was indifferent, verging on hostile.

Hannah bristled. The woman's slight was intentional, she felt sure. They had not gotten along on their first encounter either. Mr. Faber had been out of the office then as well, and this watchdog of a secretary had refused to contact him unless Hannah revealed the "nature of the problem," which she was not prepared to do.

"When do you expect him?" Hannah asked, speaking slowly, as though the woman on the other end were simpleminded.

"I'm not sure," said the secretary, slowing down herself. "I'll have him call you. Shall I tell him the nature of the problem?"

"No," Hannah said curtly. "You shall not." When she got Mr. Faber on the line this time, she would speak to him about his secretary as well as his daughter. Both had attitude problems. She hung up and rang Janet in the outer office.

"Tell Erica to return to class for the time being," she said, realizing that Erica's presence in Mr. Walters's classroom would be punishment for both of them. "In fact," she added, "tell Erica to sit quietly in the back of Mr. Walters's room—well away from the windows—during her study-hall period as well. Send Mr. Walters a note to that effect."

"Will do," answered Janet, who was an outstanding secretary, not the resentful, sulky sort they hired at McGinnis, Sturgeon, and Faber. "You'd better be leaving for your appointment, hadn't you?"

"Yes," said Hannah, letting another sigh slip out. "I'm on my way."

THE COUNSELOR'S office was every bit as cramped as Hannah's small space at Travis High, but this one lacked all personality as well: no original artwork, no artwork of any kind, not even a poster declaring the right to choose. The walls were a yellowish white, and the longer Hannah looked at them, the queasier she felt. The counselor, Maureen Fulcher, was busy behind her desk, studying the dog-eared calendar in front of her. It was already four o'clock, but she seemed in no particular hurry. Hannah's discomfort grew. In the first few minutes of the meeting, they'd established that Hannah was about seven weeks pregnant, that the doctor's examination confirmed this. They'd agreed on a number of other facts as well: that this was Hannah's first pregnancy, that she was married, about to turn forty, and nearing the end of her childbearing years. Ms. Fulcher had ticked these facts off one after another, reading from the notes in Hannah's file. Now they seemed out of things to talk about.

Being on the other side of the desk made Hannah anxious, and with nothing else to contemplate, she resorted to critiquing the clothes, manners, and social graces of the counselor. The fashion police would throw the book at her, Hannah thought. What need for paintings? Ms. Fulcher herself was the decoration. She wore a jacket that might have been cut from a discarded bedspread, printed with enormous pink and purple lilies, and quilted, of course. Her cheeks were splotched with blush, her lips turned up in a stubborn, unfriendly smile. An Avon lady, that's what she looked like, a ridiculous woman who would try to push her way into your house, regardless of how many times you told her no.

Hannah took a deep breath and, for a blessed few seconds, closed her eyes. When she opened them again, the counselor was studying her. "Just resting," Hannah explained. "Long day."

"What's on your mind, Dr. Solace?" Ms. Fulcher asked. She was no longer smiling.

Hannah faltered, then decided to get to the point. "Well, I've been sitting here for nearly fifteen minutes and we haven't accomplished much. I do a lot of counseling myself and—" She sounded childish; she knew she did. "I'm sorry," she said, rushing ahead: "I'm sorry for my tone, I'm sorry for my attitude, but most of all, I'm sorry to be here."

"You and most everyone else who walks through the door," Ms. Fulcher replied. She closed the calendar and folded her hands on top of it. "Good," she said evenly. "That gives us someplace to begin. Is it fair to say, then, that you're sorry to be pregnant?"

Hannah uncrossed her legs and put both feet squarely on the ground. "Yes," she said. "Yes, it is. I don't want to be sorry, but I am."

"How sorry are you? Sorry enough to end the pregnancy?"

Hannah thought carefully before nodding. "I think so," she said.

Ms. Fulcher sighed. "I often talk to women about their options, but you know your options, don't you?"

"Yes," Hannah said, "but I don't much care for them. None of them seems the sort of thing *I* would do. My sister is the mothering type, but I'm not. On the other hand, I'm not the sort to dispose of my problems or to turn them over to others. There, listen to me. I'm talking about this pregnancy as a *problem*, something to solve. I think that's indicative, don't you?" She paused to take a breath, then went gingerly on. "I guess I was hoping you'd tell me something to make me feel different."

Ms. Fulcher offered a new smile, lips pressed together and turned up, patient, long-suffering. "I don't know what it would be. If you were a young girl, maybe, but you've been around the block a few times already, Dr. Solace. It's not likely that I'll tell you anything new."

Carl had said this same thing last week about the vet: "He's not going to tell you anything new, Hannah." And that had been true in a way. The vet hadn't said anything new, but he'd forced Hannah to hear something she hadn't heard before. Maybe that's what she wanted now, for Ms. Fulcher to redirect her attention, force her to focus. But the counselor was right. It didn't seem likely to happen.

"We rarely see first pregnancies in a woman your age," Ms. Fulcher continued. "You must have been very surprised."

"I was," Hannah said. *Surprised* did not really cover it. She couldn't think of a word that began to describe the barrage of emotions—anger, fear, sadness, and behind all that, a peculiar and piercing joy that caught Hannah completely off-guard. If there was one thing she knew by now, it was the arbitrary and mysterious nature of emotions. She could not imagine making a decision based on them. Emotions were like vapors rising over a marsh. You breathed them in, you breathed them out, allowing them to pass over and through you. "My sister thinks it's fate," Hannah told Ms. Fulcher. So far as Hannah could tell, Helen made all her decisions on the basis of emotions.

"And what do you think?"

"I don't believe in fate," she said, though that wasn't entirely true. She didn't believe in fate when it hurt, when it took someone away from her, when it forced her into a corner. Like anyone else, she was ready enough to believe in fate when it seemed to bring her happiness.

Ms. Fulcher consulted the notes on her desk. "And your husband," she went on, "does he believe in fate?"

Hannah had underestimated Ms. Fulcher. "Carl? Well, I suppose he does." She hesitated, her eyes on the blank wall. "But he doesn't know about the pregnancy. I haven't told him."

"But you're going to tell him?" A little prod. "You had to make sure it was real first, right?" Hannah glanced up at her, startled. Had she told this woman about all the tests, that she had one in her purse right now? If only she'd had time to consult it, she might not be here. Ms. Fulcher's pink and purple lilies swam before Hannah's eyes. She could hardly see. Old, blind, and pregnant. "Listen to me, Hannah." The kind voice came from a great distance, but it reached her. "It's real," Maureen Fulcher said. "Nearly two months real."

Instead of going home to tell Carl, Hannah headed in the opposite direction, across town to her sister's house on Mount Bonnell. Whenever she wanted comfort or advice, Hannah always went to Helen, or at least she always had before. As she negotiated the last of the rush-hour traffic, Hannah decided it had been a mistake to turn to a stranger. "Get it off your chest and out in the open," the counselor had suggested. "You'll be surprised at how much clearer things will be." Clearer? Hannah thought. Ms. Fulcher didn't know Carl. Hannah had been looking for objectivity when she visited the counselor, but maybe that wasn't what she needed. Maybe what she needed was someone who knew Carl, someone who knew her. In other words, Helen.

Before Austin had gotten so big, her sister's house had been on the outskirts of town, a gray-walled structure surrounded by mesquite trees and yucca plants, the only thing to recommend it a spectacular view of the Colorado River. The breakfast area had a huge window opening onto the craggy hillside and, if you stood with your nose pressed to the glass, you could see all the way down to a ribbon of green water. Now the house and land were worth a small fortune. Helen was lucky that way. She wanted the same things everyone else wanted, but she had the good sense to want them sooner.

In one way, though, she wanted what no one else seemed to these days. Helen was practically an endangered species, a homemaker; she even referred to herself that way. She'd quit nursing in order to devote herself to three children, two boys and a girl, and an expensive house

full of repainted, refinished, reupholstered furniture. Hannah was always pestering her to open a shop on West Sixth—"you could make a
killing!"—but Helen was content with her husband, her children, her
crafts, and her good causes. Just recently, she'd been talking of taking in
a foster child. This obsession with creating warmth and welcome was
anachronistic, even a little ridiculous in Hannah's eyes, but it was also
endearing.

Pulling into the gravel drive, Hannah was relieved not to see Helen's
husband's truck parked beside the house. Of course, it might be in the
garage, but she doubted it. Jimmy was probably still at the site of his
latest spec house or else golfing or playing tennis. He was a big man
prone to throwing his weight around, and he liked nothing better than
to find out whose personality could dominate in any given situation.
"So, you're pregnant," she could hear him say. "Do they make maternity power suits?"

As usual, the sun was a little hotter on Mount Bonnell, but the
breeze coming off the water felt cool and moist on Hannah's skin. She
slipped out of her red Blazer and took a few deep breaths. The watery
blue sky served as backdrop for the limestone cliffs, dotted with mesquite trees and scrubby firs. Down below, the green river curled, thin
and secretive as a snake. She loved this view. Something about staring
off into the distance put her life in perspective. She supposed she was
not alone in this, that people paid good money for a view precisely
because they enjoyed the sensation of feeling larger than life, bigger
than rivers, immense enough to survey hills, even mountains.

Helen was in the kitchen, feeding an early dinner to her older son,
Grayson, and a friend of his, a scruffy-looking boy with red ears.
Helen's three-year-old daughter, Cassandra, perched on a booster seat
strapped to a dining-room chair. Intent on a bowl of ice cream, Cassie
busied herself with pushing melting blobs around the bowl. Her red
hair bobbed on top of her head in a ponytail that reminded Hannah of
Pebbles Flintstone. As little girls, Helen and Hannah had loved the
Flintstones. Every day, they'd rush home from school, drop their books
and jackets on the living-room floor, and settle down in front of the
television. Their mother wasn't the sort to push homework before fun.
Once, she'd admitted that she didn't much believe in homework.

"Children were put on this earth to have a good time," she'd said. Helen probably didn't remember that, Hannah thought. She didn't remember much about their mother.

"Hi!" Helen called. She was ripping lettuce leaves and dropping them into a wooden bowl. Though she'd been dieting since Shane's birth four months before, that extra twenty-five pounds just wouldn't budge. "Finished with the counselor?" she asked, looking up and waiting for Hannah's nod. Helen was draped in a chambray shirt several sizes too large for her, so big in the shoulders and sleeves that it must have belonged to Jimmy. The jeans were probably Jimmy's too; only the red tips of Helen's toenails were visible. Either she didn't fit into her own clothes or else they were so tight she wouldn't be caught dead in them.

"I'm finished with her all right," Hannah sighed, "and ready for a glass of wine. You've got some, don't you?"

"There's white in the refrigerator."

Crossing the kitchen, Hannah passed baby Shane, strapped into his seat at the bar and waving a set of red rings. The bell in the center jingled, its sound muffled by Shane's tiny fist. Hannah started to smile at him, then remembered what she'd read, that human beings can't help responding favorably to round faces. The entire species is wired to smile at babies. She forced a frown. "You want a glass?" she asked Helen.

"A little one, maybe. How about some salad?" Helen was busily hacking a tomato into tiny squares.

"Carl's fixing dinner," Hannah told her, feeling a little guilty even as she said his name. "I can't stay long."

Hannah reached into the cabinet set aside for stemware, three shelves lined with mismatched glasses, most of which Helen had picked up in secondhand shops in Tyler and other tiny towns between Austin and east Texas. Junking expeditions, she called them. Hannah chose a tiny wineglass for Helen and a large one for herself. Then, thinking better of it, she traded large for medium. Much as she felt like drowning her sorrows, she knew better than to allow herself the pleasure. She'd been dizzy off and on all day, and in a little while, she'd be back in her Blazer, finding her way down the side of this mountain.

"Don't give me that Barbie glass," Helen said.

She must have eyes in the back of her head, Hannah thought, returning both glasses and taking up two large ones. Might as well drown your sorrows, she thought. Once Carl finds out, you won't get another drop. Now that Hannah thought of it, she was surprised she hadn't received a scolding from Helen. "No wine for the little mother," or something like that. Maybe her sister was determined to be reasonable after all.

While Hannah poured the wine, Helen directed the boys to take their plates into the den and told Cassandra to stop playing with her ice cream, which had turned to soup. "Pick it up, please," Helen said calmly, "and carry it to the sink." Just once, to assert herself, Cassie spun her spoon in the bowl and raised a fine spray of melted ice cream. Then she got up and carried the dish across the room in her two small hands, keeping her eye on it as she walked. The boys left without a word. It always surprised Hannah how easily Helen kept her children in line. No bad behavior in this household—no pretty girls mincing along ledges, no boys with guns in their pockets. So many parents made such a mess of things; Hannah saw it all the time. But not Helen, who had a knack for doing the right thing at the right time—now a gentle touch, later a firm one. Where had she learned all that? Hannah wondered.

Helen was making her way to the table with the salad when Shane began to fuss. First, he let out a little hiccup, followed abruptly by a shriek that made Hannah slosh wine on the floor. "What's wrong?" she cried.

"You've never heard him do that?" Helen sank into a chair. "It means he wants his pacifier. Would you get it? It's somewhere on my bedroom floor."

To reach the bedroom, it was necessary to take the trip down memory lane, Hannah's name for the long, windowless hallway Helen had turned into a family gallery. Framed and matted photos hung on both walls, grouped tastefully, as though for an art exhibit. The frames were various and interesting in themselves, scoured from junking expeditions. Just as each person got a different glass at Helen's parties, every photo got a distinctive frame, some gilded and ornate, others plain. Hannah enjoyed visiting memory lane now and again, but if she were Helen, forced to trudge up and back many times a day, she was sure the trip would become something to suffer, a sort of penance.

Nearest the kitchen were the framed photos of Helen and Hannah's childhood, a few in black and white, some in color. Generally, the girls were posed together, Helen sitting on a stool or in an armchair, Hannah standing just behind her, a hand on Helen's shoulder or draped over the back of the chair. In all these pictures, Hannah looked painfully thin, even anorexic, stick arms jutting out of loose sleeves, but those were the days before anorexia, during the heyday of Twiggy, when knobby knees and sharp elbows served as a fashion statement rather than as evidence of a psychological disorder. She didn't know now why she'd gotten so skinny, just that for a period of years, everything she put in her mouth tasted the same.

Photographs are the province of the young, Hannah thought. Once a person reached a certain age—say, high-school graduation—she was rarely singled out for them. Pictures became scattershot, a matter of accident rather than intention. When Hannah came across pictures of herself these days, she was usually one face among many—at a wedding, a Christmas celebration, or a school board meeting. She looked a little worn in these photographs, she thought, a little off-center. Helen had long since refused to be part of any photo. No documentation, she said, until she lost some weight. This had been going on for years now, so that her behavior was established. She arranged her children for the shot, then hurried out of the way, like a lab technician escaping X-ray exposure.

At the end of the hall nearest the bedroom, Helen had hung a tinted studio shot of their mother, specially matted to fit an antique oval frame. In the picture, Naomi was still very young, maybe fifteen or so. She was perched in a porch swing, a full skirt spread out around her, cradling a small bouquet of daisies in her lap. Clearly, it was a picture from another time. The backdrop was regrettable, someone's idea of an oak tree and grass, but the studio floor was wooden, like a real porch. Her mother was smiling for the camera, head thrown back, a pair of slender bare feet in the air, all that beautiful hair draped over the back of the swing. She might have been modeling for a shampoo ad, trying out, say, to be a Breck girl.

Helen's bedroom door was closed, as usual, to discourage the roaming curiosity of children, so Hannah thought nothing of pushing it open and walking in.

"Hi there, Hannah," Jimmy called.

Her brother-in-law was standing in the middle of the room, naked. His tennis clothes lay on the bed in front of him, but he made no move to put them on. His body was big and fleshy, the wide chest dark with curly hair. But none of that was surprising. Hannah had seen him in a swimsuit often enough. The part of him she hadn't known about—the part that shocked her—was his penis, which emerged from a nest of dark hair and hung between his legs like a snout. It was longer than Carl's and unlike any other she'd ever seen. For an instant, she wondered if Jimmy was deformed—why hadn't Helen ever said anything?—then it dawned on her: He was uncircumcised. Here she was, nearly forty, and Jimmy's was the first unaltered prick she'd ever laid eyes on. By the time her gaze returned to his face, Jimmy was grinning, his wide mouth stretching from one side of his face to the other. He was a big man, Hannah thought, big all over. Her face flushed, and he grinned wider.

She stepped back into the doorway. "Excuse me, Jimmy," she said. "Helen sent me to find the pacifier."

"Oh." He glanced about, then spotted it on the other side of the bed. As he turned and bent to retrieve it, Hannah averted her eyes. She would not look at his butt. She would save herself that much dignity. For a moment, she thought she'd recovered the situation—that is, until he moved toward her, carrying the pacifier in his outstretched hand, that big dick of his swaying hypnotically. Hannah was desperate to look elsewhere, but what else was there to see? She stared; he caught her staring, and, finally, it became easier to look at his cock than to meet his eyes.

Jimmy reached for her hand, and pressing the pacifier into her palm, he closed her fist around it. The soft rubber poked at the inside of her fingers as Jimmy's big hand squeezed. "Have a nice evening, Hannah," he said softly. He smelled spicy and musty, and for a second, she was afraid she might pass out. Only the shame of such a scene kept her upright: No matter what she told him later, no matter the pregnancy and the dizzy spells, he would believe it was his naked body that had sent her into a swoon—and for all she knew he'd be right.

Hannah stumbled out of the room. Turning, her eyes passed once more over the photograph of Naomi. Her mother's mouth was open, a dark slice between even teeth. She was laughing, Hannah realized. All the times she'd looked at this photograph, it had never occurred to her that her mother's apparent happiness was not for the camera. It was real—something was funny, and her mother was laughing.

As Hannah started back up the hall, Helen called to her from the living room. "I'm nursing Shane. Bring your wine and join me.

"It never fails," Helen complained. She sat at one end of a long beige sofa. "Every time I sit down to eat, Shane decides he's hungry." Helen glanced up and smiled apologetically. All the while the baby nursed, his head butted against the soft white pillow of her breast and, periodically, he reached out with one tiny hand to stroke his mother's skin. The gesture of a lover, Hannah realized, her heart melting a bit. Maybe I can do this, she thought.

She dropped onto the sofa next to her sister. "Here it is," she said, letting the pacifier roll from her hand onto the coffee table. "Don't any of you wear clothes in this house?"

"My bare breast offends you?"

"No. It's just that Jimmy was in there—"

Helen let loose with a little chirp of a laugh. "Oh, sorry. No big deal, is it?"

Hannah hesitated. "Actually, it's a bigger deal than I'd realized."

They both laughed then—guilty, childish little twitters—and Helen pushed aside a wisp of her sister's golden red hair. Both were redheads, but Helen's hair was a darker auburn. As teenagers, they'd argued over which of them had inherited their mother's hair color, taking the dispute first to their father, who refused to settle it, then to their grandmother, who'd reluctantly crowned Hannah victorious. At the time, it had seemed important, a small but significant claim of kinship, and poor Helen had been inconsolable, refusing to speak to any of them for days. Finally, Hannah made a concession of sorts, digging up the very tinted studio shot that now hung in the hallway. She'd carried it into Helen's tiny bedroom and shoved it into her hands. "See there," she'd hissed, pointing at Naomi's head. "Your color, just like yours." But in her heart, Hannah had conceded nothing, telling herself even as she soothed her little sister that the photograph was a paint job, not the real thing at all.

"So tell me about your appointment at the clinic," Helen said.

Hannah shrugged. "Not much to tell, really. I'm seven weeks along. Everything seems to be proceeding normally. They recommend amniocentesis, given my age. . . ." There it was, her age again. Why did pregnancy make her feel so old? Shouldn't it make her feel young again?

"Bye, honey!" Jimmy called from the front door. Then, "Bye, Hannah."

The sisters yelled good-bye in unison and, when the door slammed, lapsed into silence. Helen turned to the bay window, draped now against the setting sun. Hannah knew what she thinking: These past few months, she'd convinced herself that Jimmy was having an affair, and why? Because she'd found a moth on his dresser. A luna moth. This was her proof of his infidelity. "Dead or alive?" Hannah had wanted to know, but Helen hadn't laughed. Of course it was dead, she'd replied archly. She'd gone on to point out that Jimmy had never shown the slightest interest in the insect world, until one morning when she'd awakened to find him cradling a large green moth in the palm of his hand, stroking the wings with one finger. She'd watched him from the bed, her eyes narrowed to slits so he'd think she was sleeping. "All summer, he's gone night and day," Helen had continued. "And when he does come home, he behaves peculiarly." Helen behaved peculiarly too, Hannah thought. She spent too much time cooped up with her children. It made her prone to fantasies.

"Should I say congratulations, then?" Helen asked, shifting until she could look directly into her sister's face. As she moved about, Shane hung on with his lips until he stretched the skin of Helen's breast. It looked painful.

"What does that feel like?"

"Nursing?"

Hannah nodded.

"Intense. That's the only word for it. The first few days, it hurts like hell, but that goes away. Then it's just this intense experience, the baby's sucking, the milk letting down, the bond it builds between the two of you. So close, Hannah. You'll see. You've never been this close to anyone, not even Carl."

"I know," Hannah said quietly. "That's the problem. I'm not sure I want to be that close."

"You won't know until you're there."

Hannah responded with a derisive little snort. "Come on, Helen," Hannah pushed. "It'll be too late. This isn't a wait-and-see sort of thing."

"No," Helen replied. "It's not."

Shane released the nipple and turned his head, signaling that he was ready to change breasts. Hannah waited while her sister shifted the baby from one side to the other. So far, Shane didn't resemble his mother's side of the family. At four months, he had a full head of fine brown hair. Unlike most babies, he'd never lost his infant fuzz; his hair had simply lengthened and thickened until it grew down around his ears and the back of his neck. A tiny child with so much hair looked odd, as though someone had plopped a wig on his head. Shane was pudgy, with delicate hands and feet, and his eyes were a clear and brilliant blue, like Lake Travis seen from a distance. They reminded Hannah of Carl's eyes, she realized, looking away.

Had Helen orchestrated this little moment of motherly bliss? she wondered. No, that wasn't fair. Now that Hannah thought about it, she'd witnessed Helen's breast-feeding dozens of times before, only she'd never paid much attention. Now she wondered why she'd never been the least bit curious. "I'm not sure I'm cut out for this," Hannah finally said, waving her arm to include Helen and the baby, the whole scene, the entire house. She heard the edge of fear in her own voice.

"It's natural to be scared."

"No it's not."

"Is too."

Hannah shook her head firmly.

"Look," Helen finally said, "I'm not going to try and talk you into this, Hannah. If that's what you think, then you're wrong. Let me ask you something: Did you like being my mother?"

Hannah was surprised. She thought for a minute while Helen buttoned up and arranged Shane on a quilt their grandmother had made, stationing toys at each corner. The two of them watched Shane inch toward a beach ball. "I was a child myself," Hannah finally said. "It was hard, but I liked some things."

"Did you like being close to me?" Helen had settled herself in the middle of the living-room floor, halfway between Hannah and Shane.

"Physically close?"

Helen nodded.

"Yes," she lied. They'd slept together after their mother died, Hannah crowded onto Helen's narrow bed, pressed up against her sister, so close she could feel Helen's heart beating. Each time she'd tried to slip away and return to her own bed, Helen had awakened and cried out. And so Hannah had lain awake, for what seemed the entire night, for what seemed an entire season of nights, staring at a small patch of wallpaper illuminated by the night-light.

"What else did you like?"

Hannah was suspicious of the turn this conversation had taken. She wasn't sure she wanted to enter this territory. Memory lane. Helen couldn't seem to get enough of it. "I can't remember, Helen. It was so long ago, and anyway, what does it have to do with today?"

"Everything," Helen said simply. "So, have you told Carl?"

"No, not yet," Hannah admitted. "The counselor said it was up to me whether I told Carl." This wasn't true. Not at all. Hannah felt her own heart beating strongly. It scared her that she would lie this way. She wasn't a liar. She wasn't any of the things she'd been these last few days.

Suddenly, Helen was angry. "Up to you? I don't care what that counselor says." Her voice was shrill. "She's there to make you feel better, Hannah." Helen raked her fingers through the thick beige carpet, and Hannah noted that her sister's nails were painfully short again. The habit went way back, one of those things Helen declared victory over periodically, only to admit to defeat a few months later. "Don't forget, she's an employee, and the abortion clinic is a business," Helen said. "There's a bottom line to consider—"

Hannah broke in. "Your nails look like hell."

For a second or two, Helen studied her nails. "They've been worse, much worse," she said. "Anyway, you're trying to change the subject. You came to hear what I think, didn't you? Well, I think there are still a few 'shoulds' left in this world, and telling your husband you're pregnant is one of them!" She curled her stubby fingers into fists and pounded the carpet for emphasis. "I hate all these secrets! All this sneaking around!" Startled, little Shane abandoned the beach ball and began inching in his mother's direction.

Hannah knew her sister was talking about Jimmy, so she took a sip of wine and waited. There was no use discussing that damn moth again.

"If it's as simple as you say it is," Helen went on, "if it's all your decision, why come to me? Why tell me about it? If there's no moral dilemma, then just get on with it—like you would a permanent or a dye job. It's your hair; it's your womb; whatever."

"I hate that term, womb. You know I hate it."

"Womb. What's wrong with it?"

Shane was about to reach the edge of the quilt. Drool dripped off his chin and onto a bright red square of material. Hannah remembered that scrap and a long-ago afternoon when she'd studied the squares one by one. Tiny bluebirds whirled around a red background. Likely the square had been cut from a little girl's dress, one of theirs or maybe one of Naomi's. "I don't think you should be using that quilt for the baby to drool on," Hannah said.

Helen ignored her. "You're afraid to tell him because you know he'll want the baby. You're afraid he'll convince you. To lose control for a single minute. It just scares the hell out of you."

"Helen—would you let go of this righteous motherhood shit? Is that possible?"

"No. It's not. It's not possible, actually. That's me. A righteous mother who cleans up shit."

Hannah rose to go, but the dizziness surged over her as she stood. She had to squeeze at the thick carpet with her toes to stay upright. "You should have told me you don't approve of abortion," she said. Her tone was stern, the sort she used with students and sometimes with Carl, but hardly ever with Helen.

"Nobody *approves* of abortion," Helen replied. "It's a necessary evil. We both know that."

Hannah stalked out to the kitchen to collect her shoes, ignoring the waves of dizziness as best she could. "Where are you going, Hannah?" Helen called. As if she didn't know, Hannah thought. It had always been this way. Hannah hated arguments—people losing control, the ugly stretching of their mouths, tears streaming down their cheeks. Arguments were so much recycled garbage, big bags of ancient crap people held on to year after year. She had her own, certainly, but she'd try not to dump it out in front of Helen.

Helen was back on the sofa with Shane when Hannah crossed the living room, headed for the front door. In one hand, she carried her high heels, and on impulse, she reached down with the other and grabbed up the quilt as she passed. "You're not taking care of this," she said sternly.

Helen remained silent until Hannah reached the front door. "You have to tell him, you hear me?" Helen paused, then called a little louder. "Hear me, Hannah? If you don't tell him—I will." In reply, Hannah slammed the door behind her. She hesitated there on the porch, burying her face in the quilt for consolation. The material was soft and lumpy against her lips. It smelled of talcum powder and mold.

Maneuvering the Blazer back down Mount Bonnell, Hannah recalled something else about being Helen's mother, something she hadn't thought of in years. She and her sister had been in the throes of adolescence at the time, or at least Hannah had been, sweet sixteen and given to sour faces and bitter invectives. Hannah had just begun to date and to buy daring dresses and to take long afternoon baths, but at eleven, Helen was still mostly a little girl. One afternoon, Helen had barged into the bathroom—"I can't wait to pee!" she'd crowed—only to discover Hannah soaking in the tub, her large breasts floating on the surface of the water. Little Helen had stopped in her tracks, staring openmouthed. "What's wrong with you?" Hannah had cried, covering her breasts with one arm and waving her sister away.

After that, Helen began speaking to her sister in a baby's voice, pleading with Hannah to do things she could do for herself. "Make me a sandwich, Mannah," she'd begged. Yes, Hannah had forgotten that part. Helen had taken to calling her sister Mannah. At first, Hannah was accommodating, but that only encouraged the fixation. Helen wanted Hannah, wanted her in the most desperate and pervasive way, wanted her to go to the movies, to help with her homework, to starch her blouses and drive her to the swimming pool. It was suffocating. Finally, Hannah had lost patience and yelled at her sister or slammed the door in her face or called her names. The more pitiful Helen looked, the more determined Hannah was to drive her away.

"Why are you so mean?" their father had asked one night. Fresh on the heels of yet another rejection from Hannah, Helen was sobbing in her room. They could both hear the breathless little hiccuping sounds she made. But Hannah had hardened her heart against the noise. She wouldn't hear it; she didn't feel it. By way of answer, she'd simply turned and walked away.

At the intersection of 2222, Hannah stopped at the light and took a deep breath before turning right toward town. "Come to think of it, Helen, I didn't like being your mother," she said aloud to the empty car. "I didn't like it at all."

Chapter 4

PENELOPE'S BALLOONS AND BOUQUETS was located on West Sixth Street, at the edge of downtown Austin. Penny's first memories of this area were of a residential neighborhood, working-class, with stay-at-home mothers and children playing on the porches of small white frame houses. When she was still a girl, she'd sometimes accompanied her grandmother on visits to an elderly cousin, a woman who'd lived on West Lynn, only a few streets away. Mattie had been protective; she wouldn't allow Penny to play with strangers, so while the women sat on the living-room couch, their voices droning in the air above her head, Penny occupied herself by playing jacks. Mostly, this had amounted to chasing a red rubber ball under end tables and down a dusty hallway.

Today, driving to work, it occurred to her that Mattie's cousin was long gone now, as were most of the residents—dead and gone or filed away in nursing homes—but the houses were still here, renovated and reclaimed as boutiques, restaurants, and expensive hairstyling salons. The white frame fronts had been sprayed over with sky blue, lavender, even a southwestern shade of orange. Lawn maintenance crews sprayed for weeds and rotated hanging baskets outside shops with names like Out of Africa and Buttons and Bows. Women wearing Birkenstock sandals and fake fingernails roamed the sidewalks, pushing strollers as complicated as small cars. It was too chic for Penny, but she knew a good business address when she saw one.

Her shop was squeezed into the top floor of an old Victorian house, split up to accommodate five small businesses. Baby Books, Feats of Clay, and Jack's Candlesticks—owned not by a man named Jack but by a sour woman named Eileen—occupied the first floor. Penny shared the smaller upstairs space with an Americana shop called Knickknack Paddywack. The owner seldom showed up for work and paid her help so poorly that they came and went almost as quickly as the customers. Penny no longer bothered to learn their names but simply called out a blanket hello as she passed the door.

Not that she was in that much herself. Most of her orders came over the phone, and she spent afternoons making deliveries and running errands. For the first year she'd been in business, she'd simply locked the doors and left, but after things picked up, she'd hired Juanita, a friend from church, to work half days. Juanita had no interest in the flower part of the business and almost always carted along her baby. Fortunately, Juanita enjoyed helping out with the balloons. These days, she did almost everything with the balloons except deliver them. The flowers Penny kept for herself.

For her flower arrangements, Penny preferred natural containers. Baskets were her favorites, but she also created displays in driftwood, coconut shells, large gourds, copper pitchers, goldfish bowls, and even old bean pots. In the summertime, she used seashells to hold small, delicate posies. This past summer, she'd developed a following for these "Flowers from the Sea." Wealthy women in West Lake Hills ordered them for engagement parties and wedding showers.

Her first task today was to create a posy for a large conch shell. To begin, she cradled the shell in her palm and admired the bright pink outer lip, which would serve as a background for the smaller flowers. She felt inside the deep crevice, where she would hide the anchoring material. The shell would hold more flowers than most. Moving from the cooler to the worktable and back again, Penny began assembling the arrangement. She decided to use peach roses, cream freesias, pink bachelor's buttons, and a bit of asparagus fern, which reminded her of seaweed, then to finish it off with just the smallest spray of baby's breath, for that misty look. As she stripped the lower leaves off the stems of the roses, she watched her hands at work—slender, pale things with lives of their own. She ran an index finger across a thorn, pressing hard enough to feel the sharp edge against her flesh, then cupped the largest of the roses in her palm and traced the soft, velvety skin.

"We keep our hands away from beautiful things," Mattie had instructed her as a child, grabbing her wrists before she could fondle the satin of a wedding dress or finger the icing of a cake. By force of habit, Penny's hands had become tentative, reaching out only to draw back. But in the last few years, she'd learned to touch again. In her first job in a florist's shop, and later in her six-month design class, she'd been urged to stroke and caress. "Flowers don't break," her instructor had told her. "God made them to be explored by bees and bent by the wind. A little touching only encourages their beauty."

Her instincts for design were good, and she'd learned not to second-guess herself, but this morning her fingers quivered as she pressed the flowers into place, and after the posy was complete, she stepped back and puzzled over it. Was it balanced, she wondered? Was it complete? She was carrying it over to the window for a closer look when Juanita called out a boisterous "hello there!" from the doorway. The tone was familiar—Juanita used it when she was good and late, as though an attitude of cheery disregard might somehow excuse her. Of course, it didn't work that way. "About time you got here," Penny replied.

Juanita shrugged—"I get here when the bus driver lets me off!"— and started across the room. She was all motion and commotion: long black hair flying loose around her shoulders, baby Buck bouncing off one hip. The plastic flip-flops on her small feet slapped at the wooden floor. When she reached Penny's side, Juanita took the posy and held it out to admire. "Mag-nee-fi-cent!" she crowed. Enthusiasm for Penny's work was one of Juanita's chief virtues. "Don't you love it?" she asked. Penny looked skeptical, so Juanita pushed on with her compliments. "It's one of your best, I think." After she'd convinced Penny of the posy's perfection, Juanita carried it back to the worktable, then stood and watched her friend fashion a sea-green bow. "You're so good with those bows!" she exclaimed. Juanita kept silent while Penny wired the bow to a tiny stake, which she inserted into the anchoring material. Then she spoke again. "I have a surprise for you," she said, and shifted the baby from one hip to the other.

The shifting was necessary, she'd explained, to keep from getting lopsided. The child was as dense as potting soil, and Juanita was small, smaller even than Penny. Juanita's mother had carried seven babies on her left hip; Juanita's grandmother, thirteen. Now they both stood off-center, one hip higher than the other so that their skirts hung unevenly and had to be specially altered. Juanita was determined not to suffer the same fate. But this time the shifting was about something else. She fished in her pocket and, grinning broadly, flipped a driver's license onto the worktable. "See what I got!" she cried.

Penny gazed down at the license, issued to one Juanita Gonzalez. In the small photograph, Juanita looked washed out but exultant, her hair jerked back in a ponytail, exposing earrings that dangled to her shoulders. Penny glanced up. Sure enough, Juanita was wearing the same earrings now. They resembled tiny chandeliers. "I didn't know you had a car," Penny said.

Juanita snorted. "Shoot! If I had a car, I'd have me a job delivering pizzas. There's some good money in that. I've got a cousin in San Antonio, she puts her baby in the car and—zoom!" She made a cutting motion with her hand, as though the cousin were a race-car driver. "So, what do you think?" she asked, slipping the license back into her pocket. "Can I drive sometimes?"

Penny sighed and opened the cooler, storing the posy on a shelf, and shifting the plastic barrels around the cooler floor so she could reach, first, a handful of Peruvian lilies, then Gerbera daisies the color of fruit punch, and, finally, more baby's breath. "Let me think about it," Penny muttered.

"Sure," Juanita replied. She lugged Buck to the playpen in the corner and heaved him over the side. The playpen floor was littered with plastic chewies Penny had picked up at Wal-Mart: a hamburger, an airplane, a transparent ring filled with colored water and multicolored stars. These Buck sat on or hurled at passersby—he had a strong arm for a baby. The only thing he teethed on was an old tennis shoe; he'd gnaw on the rubber toe until saliva leaked down his chin. Today Buck ignored the shoe and struggled to his feet, grasping the railing for support. He didn't begin to cry, not yet anyway, but his round face was the picture of misery. As usual, he wore only a cloth diaper, which had slid down his round stomach and hung between his

legs. Little Buck was nearly as wide as he was tall; with his full head of
black hair and dangling diaper, he resembled a miniature sumo wres-
tler.

"How much is there to think about?" Juanita asked. She had her
hands on her hips.

"You want to drive *here* at the shop?" Penny asked quietly.

Juanita huffed. "Not *here* at the shop." She waved a hand around
the small space. "Here around town, silly. I can help you make deliveries. We can trade off."

"I don't know. . . ." Penny's voice died away. She didn't much
like the idea of Juanita driving the service van. It wasn't even close to
paid off, and the insurance was high. Plus, she'd just paid to paint the
name of the shop and her logo—a row of saw-toothed tulips—on both
sides. She was possessive of the van; it was one of the few things she
truly owned. But Juanita was determined. She wanted to demonstrate
her driving skills on the way to Seton Hospital, where they had several
deliveries to make. "What about the baby?" Penny asked.

"Easy," Juanita replied. "We'll put the playpen in the back of the
van."

"Absolutely not!"

Juanita shrugged. "Something else then. You need my help, Penny.
You have a date tonight, remember? Don't you want to get home
early?" Slyly, Juanita raised her eyebrows.

Penny bent her head to the flowers, breathing in their sharp scent.
She didn't want to think about the date, not now. She could count all
of her dates on the fingers of one hand. A dance in high school, one or
two trips to a restaurant, four dates altogether with a boy whose name
was Phillip. His last name escaped her, as did his physical presence. All
she recalled of him now was his face coming close to hers, his moist
breath, a quick kiss on her lips. A good-bye kiss, she'd thought later.
He'd never called again.

"Nervous, aren't you?" Juanita asked.

"A little," Penny admitted. She took up the florist's scissors and
began trimming the stems of the lilies.

"Is he taking you on his Harley?"

Penny was surprised at how much Juanita knew. "How do you
know about his motorcycle?"

"And why wouldn't I?" Juanita replied. "He talks about that Harley all the time. You think it's just you he talks to?"

"No," Penny began, "it's just that . . ." But Juanita wasn't listening. She was going on about love, about how it was all going to make sense soon. "You've been thinking I'm crazy, girl. But now it's your turn. You're going, and you're not coming back."

Love was Juanita's favorite subject. During the long hours they'd spent together in Penny's shop, she'd shared all she knew about it. Her education had started during her sophomore year in high school, when she'd fallen in love with a senior named Buck Thornton. When Buck graduated and left San Antonio for Austin in 1992, Juanita had taken it into her head to follow, waving good-bye to her high-school diploma and the approval of her large family. To make matters worse, she'd gotten pregnant shortly after arriving in Austin, and Buck, an economics major at the University and practical to the core, had insisted she get an abortion and return home. He was tired of her theatrics. "Don't make an ass of yourself," he'd told her. "Get an appointment at Planned Parenthood, and let's move on with our lives."

Raised Catholic, Juanita had turned up instead at the Pregnancy Crisis Center, where Mattie volunteered on Saturday mornings. Mattie had brought her home. For a time, Juanita had slept on the couch in the living room, then she'd moved into the garage apartment out back, the one Penny now called home. It had been Mattie and Penny who'd driven Juanita to the hospital when she'd gone into labor with little Buck; Mattie and Penny who'd been the first to see the baby and the only ones to bring flowers; and after she'd come home from the hospital, Mattie and Penny who'd provided her a place to stay. Juanita had lived out back for six months after Buck was born, until she'd collected enough money to put down a deposit on a studio apartment over by Town Lake. When she swore that Mattie and Penny were her adopted family, that she didn't know what she'd have done without them, Penny supposed it must be true.

Life hadn't been fair to Juanita, at least not so far as Penny could tell. While Buck Sr. attended classes, Juanita held down three jobs. Weekday mornings and some afternoons, she worked for Penny, inflating balloons and answering the phone; weekend evenings, she waitressed at Denny's; and whenever she could spare an hour or two, Juanita did the janitorial work at their church, Gospel Fellowship. All the while, she continued to adore a man who'd washed his hands of her. Maybe ten times now, Penny had consented to drive past Buck Sr.'s white brick apartment building, slowing down so her friend could point out the window. If a light was on, Juanita would hold up baby Buck. "Wave to your daddy, sweetie," she'd say.

"Where's Dr. Bill taking you?" Juanita asked now.

"To a restaurant at the lake," Penny replied. She pretended concentration on the flowers.

"How romantic!" Juanita cried. "I think he's in love with you!" She whirled across the small floor, waving her hands in the air. The mere mention of love was enough to send her spinning. Buck squealed in delight, and Penny looked up and smiled at the two of them. She had no idea what to say. Could it be true? she wondered. No one had ever been in love with her before.

DR. BILL was right on time. At exactly six, Penny heard the clomp of his cowboy boots on the wooden steps of the garage apartment, followed by a hard rap on the door.

"Come in!" she called, and watched him duck through the doorway. Most often, she'd seen Dr. Bill outdoors or in church, where the ceiling dwarfed even the largest of them, but here in her one-room apartment, he looked bigger than life. He was wearing the familiar black jeans and cowboy boots, but instead of a starched white dress shirt, he had on faded denim with pearl buttons. Penny couldn't help thinking of her mother, who was partial to all things western. As usual, Dr. Bill's hands were tucked in his pockets, and he rocked back and forth on his heels while he looked around the room. It was his first time inside her apartment.

"Wow," he said. "It's a mural, a sky mural."

Penny had painted each wall in the room a different color: deep blue, pale blue, tangerine, and winter rose. At the corners, where the colors met, she'd blended and streaked to create the effect of a sunrise, one shade melting into the next. She'd left the walls entirely bare, and early mornings she enjoyed lying in her bed against the back wall and watching the light play across the colors. A sky mural, she thought, turning the phrase over in her head. How lovely and graceful that sounded. "So you like it?" she asked, pleased and a little surprised.

"Love it," he exclaimed, crossing the room to press one large pale hand against the rose wall. He enjoyed touching too—painted walls, baby's cheeks, the parchment pages of his Bible—she'd noticed that about him. Whenever he reached a stopping point in the sermon, he'd stride back to the podium and run his fingers over the open Bible like a blind man.

"You're the only person to see it besides Juanita and Grandmother. . . ."

"I don't suppose Mattie admired it," he remarked, glancing back over his shoulder.

Penny smiled. "Not much," she admitted. Then: "Is it time to go?"

"No hurry. The Split Rail fills up around sunset, but we've got time. I am getting hungry, though. How about you?" He rubbed his hands together, loudly. "Barbecue. Doesn't that sound good?"

She nodded. She hadn't been to the lake all summer, and she loved barbecue. What Texan didn't?

"What's that?" Dr. Bill asked, nodding at the gift on the kitchen table. The orange metallic paper glinted in the warm light of early evening. All week, the present had stayed put, unopened. Now Penny wished she'd thought to put it away.

"A birthday present."

"But your birthday was weeks ago."

She nodded. He would know: He'd been a guest at the little party in the backyard one Saturday a few weeks back. Not knowing Mattie had invited him, Penny had been surprised to see him stride up the driveway, a little late, carrying a half dozen calla lilies wrapped in lavender paper. Those gathered round the picnic table—all members of their little church—had begun to nudge one another, stopping their chatter to watch Dr. Bill present the quivering white trumpet blossoms. When Penny bent her nose to the flowers, he kissed the crown of her head. She'd felt his breath, warm against her scalp. "Happy birthday," he'd whispered. She'd been so flustered then, and she felt a touch of it now. How to be herself with him? She wasn't quite sure she could manage it.

"Why haven't you opened your present?" he asked. Penny tried to keep her eyes on his face, the strong, square chin, the flat plane of cheekbone, and deep-set, dark eyes. A small knot of bone interrupted the straight line of his nose. Broken, definitely, but in a fight or an accident? She'd heard both. Could it have been broken twice?

"Busy week," she finally said.

"Too busy to open a present?" She could see that he didn't believe her. "So who's it from?" He picked up the package and gave it a quick shake.

"My mother." Delia's gifts typically arrived late, and Penny had fallen into the habit of opening them even later—days, even weeks after receiving them—after they'd ceased to matter, after she'd forgotten her expectations.

"Ahh." He nodded, as though it had all come clear; probably Mattie had told him about Delia, something anyway. Penny wished she knew what. "I'd like to meet your mother," he said.

Penny was cautious. "Maybe sometime," she replied. "Delia lives in Houston, and she doesn't get over this way very often."

He nodded thoughtfully, then carried the gift to her. "Indulge me," he said. "I like to watch people open presents."

Resigned, Penny took it and edged over to the red chair in the corner, sinking into the cushion and settling the box on her lap. Dr. Bill dropped to the floor beside her and remained silent while she ripped away the paper and struggled with the tape. Pulling back the tissue, she uncovered a dress, seafoam green, with a fitted satin bodice. As Penny lifted it from the box, Dr. Bill leaned over to finger the material. "Gorgeous," he said. "Don't you think so?" Penny nodded. She didn't have words for it. This was the most beautiful dress she'd ever seen. The long sleeves were sheer, the skirt fitted, satin with an overlay of chiffon. Penny held it out before her, a wonder of construction.

"My mother's a seamstress," she told him. Delia spent her days creating glittery costumes for tiny tap dancers and altering wedding dresses for dieting brides, but she hadn't made Penny a dress in years, not since the one Penny had cried over, a frilly blue dress that had been far too small. "I'm so sorry," Delia had said. "You're not a little girl anymore, are you? I lost track, sweetie. I just lost track."

"Your mother's very talented," Dr. Bill was saying. "Go try it on," he urged, tugging at the leg of her jeans. "Go on!"

Penny put it on in the bathroom and, turning to the mirror, was stunned at the transformation. Seconds before, she'd been a slip of a girl in baggy jeans and a T-shirt; now she was grown-up and elegant-looking, her neck long and graceful, her hair a sleek cap of brown. A simple change of clothes could do all that? Penny was amazed.

When she stepped out, Dr. Bill dropped the card he was holding and clapped his hands. "Wow! You look lovely, Penny!"

She smiled shyly, not sure how to reply. "Thanks," she finally said.

"There's a card here," Dr. Bill went on. "Hope you don't mind that I read it." He glanced up at her. "Seems your mother wants you to wear the dress in her wedding, as her maid of honor. What do you think?"

She shook her head, wondering how Delia had gotten it right this time. The dress fit her perfectly. "I don't know," she finally said.

In the driveway, Dr. Bill slipped a helmet over her head, then slapped the top of it with his palm, as though to wedge it in place. While he was adjusting the strap, Mattie wandered out the kitchen door and made her way across the back lawn. She walked slowly—a hand over her eyes, a puzzled look on her face—as though she didn't quite recognize this pair standing in her driveway.

"Not to worry, Mattie," Dr. Bill called out. "Never had an accident. Not a swerve, not a slide, not a skid." He threw his leg over the bike's sleek black body. "Got my first Harley in '88," he told them as he buckled the strap of his own helmet. "An old patched-together thing that wouldn't die; took me all the way from Idaho to South Carolina, with a few layovers for repairs. Got the Softail last year."

When Penny was settled behind him, he spoke to her over his shoulder. "It'll be fast. Put your arms around my waist and lace your fingers. When I lean, you lean. It's a dance—you, me, the motorcycle. Got it?"

He's showing off, Penny thought. "Got it," she said.

"Hold on tight," Mattie told her. "You two have fun."

Penny waved good-bye and wrapped her arms around Dr. Bill's waist, pressing her chest to the back of his sweet-smelling denim shirt.

"Bye, Mattie," he called as they rolled out of the driveway.

The traffic was heavy, but Dr. Bill zipped in and out, and within twenty minutes they were leaving the city, headed for Lake Travis. The sky hung huge over their heads, and the countryside flashed by—craggy cliffs dotted with scrub oaks. A few miles out, the road began to undulate, a series of ups and downs, so many hills Penny stopped holding her breath and simply relaxed into them. The evening felt soft and sweet around her, and she gave herself over to the sensation of flying.

By the time they arrived at the restaurant, afternoon had slipped into evening. Already the sun had begun to sink behind the trees; still, it was fully light and would be for another hour or so. From the outside, the Split Rail looked unremarkable, a small gray clapboard building fronted by a large gravel lot, already nearly full. While Dr. Bill maneuvered the bike between the rows, slowly taking them to the front door, Penny counted the trucks—ten, twenty, then twenty-five. She spotted Jeeps as well, and a few sport utilities. And right next to the door, a gleaming Mercedes parked next to a heap of junk. A little of everything, she thought. Dr. Bill found a place for his bike just to the left of the building, in the shade of an old cottonwood. "You've been here before?" she asked as she stepped off the bike. Her body hummed and she felt a little weak in the knees.

"Lots of times. So, did you like the ride?"

She nodded eagerly, wondering all the while if he'd been here on other dates; he didn't seem the sort to go places alone. When she pulled off her helmet, Dr. Bill looked downright amused. Evidently, what little hair she had left was plastered to her head. "Does it look awful?" she asked, rubbing the fingers of her free hand through the damp strands. "Grandmother cut it last week, and she never knows when to stop."

"Here. Hold still." He stepped in close and began fluffing it with his fingers. She closed her eyes and listened as a breeze brought strains of fiddle and steel guitar, then a burst of laughter from around back. "There," he said. "Looks great." She reached up, to check for herself, but he grabbed her hand in midair and firmly led her to the door.

Inside, it was dark, and the air was dense with mesquite smoke and something else, something sweet and tangy. "Best barbecue in four counties," he told her, leading her through a dark passageway and toward the back door, "and the best view too."

Most of the tables at the Split Rail were outside on three tiered, semicircular decks. The highest offered a panoramic view of the rippling blue-green lake, and the lowest jutted into a stand of scrub oak and mesquite. As soon as they pushed their way onto the upper deck, Penny and Dr. Bill were enveloped in a throng of laughing, drinking people. Most sat shoulder to shoulder around white plastic tables or bellied up to the railing, talking and waiting for the sunset. Country music poured from invisible speakers, wild guitar, then a woman's voice ringing out, "Whew, I go crazy!"

Dr. Bill sidled in close. "There's more people out here eating barbecue than we get in church on Easter Sunday," he said a little ruefully.

"It's true," Penny agreed.

He scratched his head, then ran a palm over his wavy brown hair. "Maybe I should minister to them," he suggested. "What do you think? I'd have to yell over this music, but it might be worth it." Penny studied his face. His bottom lip protruded in a thoughtful pout. She'd seen this same expression when he stood behind the pulpit. He looked serious, though she knew he must be teasing.

He leaned in closer. "We're way out in the country, you know. It would take the cops a while to make the drive; in the meantime, I might save a soul or two. As a group, drunks are rather suggestible."

She glanced up at him. "You're fooling, right?"

"We're talking souls here, Penny."

She cocked her head and gazed up at him. "You're off-duty." Amused, he let loose with an open laugh that slid into the noise of the place and made the two of them at home. He tightened his grip on Penny's hand and pulled her around the fringes of the crowd toward the stairs. They pushed past cowboys hunkered in groups of three and four, wearing stained straw hats and saluting one another with longnecks, and made their way around clusters of businessmen dressed in khakis and polo shirts. Penny was surprised to see couples embracing right there in the open, oblivious to the crowds, her open stare, the milky blue sky overhead, even the brilliant sheen of blue stretching out in front of them, lapping up to the very horizon.

The middle deck was less crowded, and although the view wasn't as grand, Penny preferred it: a bit of the lake, a few overhanging branches, and if she wanted sky, well, all she had to do was tilt her head to take in the whole of it. Dr. Bill found them an empty table on the edge of things and pulled out a white plastic chair. "How's this?" he asked, seating her and then sinking into the next chair.

"Perfect," she replied. It had been a hot day for late September, but now the edge was off, and the warmth felt good to her. Every once in a while the air stirred, and the beginnings of a cool breeze came off the lake. Dr. Bill stretched out his legs, and leaning back, laced his fingers behind his head. "That feels great. Now I need a beer. How about you?"

The truth was, she'd never tasted beer; Mattie didn't drink, so neither did Penny, at least not until now. "I'll try one," she declared, and swiped her damp hands across her thighs.

Moments later, a harried-looking, middle-aged woman in too tight jeans and a frilly red blouse stopped by their table. "What can I get ya?" she asked. Dr. Bill ordered two Tecates and a couple of cold mugs. As the waitress hurried away, he called after her: "And two plates of mixed meat. Sides of potato salad and beans." She nodded but didn't turn back. "Sound okay?" Dr. Bill asked.

"Sure," Penny replied.

Almost immediately, the waitress was back again with round pads, which she tossed onto the table with a practiced hand before plunking mugs down on top of them. The bottles of beer she set down alongside. "Be right back with your food," she promised.

Patiently, evenly, Dr. Bill poured his Tecate, raising the bottle higher as the mug filled, then slacking off before the foam rose over the edge. "Shall I do the honor?" he asked, gesturing toward her bottle. She handed it over. Obviously, he enjoyed the task; not a drop spilled, the foam rising slowly to just below the rim of the mug. "I used to drink a lot," he admitted when he pushed her mug in front of her. She blinked, surprised. He seemed to read her mind, to answer questions she hadn't yet gotten up the nerve to ask. She watched him take a long gulp and sigh. "Now I limit myself to two bottles a week," he said. "I can be a moderate man, but I don't enjoy it. My tendency is to overdo. Now it's the ministry, among other things." Penny knew he was referring to his ministry at the clinics, where he spent most Saturdays. More and more, he was urging his congregation to join him there. He smiled at her and took another long drink. "But I can go slow, Penny. Really I can."

She had her doubts, but she wouldn't voice them; instead, she took up her own mug and brought it to her lips. The smell was strong and bitter, and though she hoped the taste would be otherwise, she didn't expect it to be. Leaking a little past her teeth, she nearly choked. It was awful stuff, a foaming, sour mess in her mouth. If she'd been home, she would have spit it out. Instead, she forced herself to swallow before looking up to meet Dr. Bill's eyes.

"You don't drink beer, do you?" He was grinning.

She shoved the mug in his direction. "I guess not," she said, feeling silly, like a child trying on the bad habits of adults. She looked away from him, to what she could see of the lake, a boulder-strewn beach, the water streaking from blue to black as it lapped against the rocks. I know this view, she thought, and it hit her, an odd jolt of recognition that forced a small sound from her mouth.

"What is it?" Dr. Bill asked.

"I've been here before," she said slowly, "not the restaurant but this part of the lake. I just remembered."

"What?"

"My mother." She was still gazing off across the water.

"What about your mother?"

"I came here with her. A long time ago. I was maybe six."

The memory wasn't entirely clear, but she could see this much: herself perched on a warm rock, feet dangling in cool water that lapped over her ankles; Delia floating out a ways, sharing a raft with a man Penny didn't know; jealousy pinching at her as she watched them. It had been a dazzling afternoon, the reflection off the water so intense it had reduced her mother to a dark shape on the water. Occasionally, laughter had drifted back to Penny, and she'd felt the pinch a little harder. The lake, the sky, the day itself shrank to the size of a black dot on the horizon; then an inner tube drifted by and gently banged her heel. Meant for her, Penny had believed, a gift from God. The answer to her prayer, just as they'd promised in Sunday school.

"Were you swimming?" he asked.

She nodded. "Yes," she said, "I think so."

Finished with his own beer, Dr. Bill took up hers. Watching him lift the mug to his lips, Penny wondered whether he'd count this one as a bonus and not part of his two-a-week limit. He might be the sort to cheat on his promises, she thought, to haggle a bit with himself and with God and with her too, if she gave him the chance. Close enough, she could imagine him saying; let's don't nitpick. She watched him drink, still tasting the bitter froth of the beer. Finally, she asked if he'd order her a Coke.

"Next time the waitress comes by," he promised. "Go on. What else do you remember?"

She shrugged. "Not much." Part of her resented his gentle urging—the minister never really goes away, she thought—but another part of her wanted to tell him.

The waitress appeared then, laying down two steaming plates piled high with ribs, brisket, a length of coiled sausage, and heaps of sliced turkey. She hurried off and returned with bowls of potato salad and beans, enough food for four people. When she asked what else she could get them, Dr. Bill ordered Penny a Coke. "No more beer," he added before the waitress could ask. After she was gone, he picked up a rib, dripping sauce on the scarred plastic table. "What say we get started?" By the time the waitress dropped off an enormous plastic glass of Coke, the two of them were bent over their plates, devouring the rich, stringy meat.

Both were quiet while they ate, and Penny thought again of that inner tube floating on the lake. She'd reached for it, but it had drifted a little beyond her. Leaning out over the water, she'd stretched her arms, and before she knew what was happening, her body had slipped into the cool depths of the lake. Immediately she'd started swallowing, gulping, taking in mouthfuls of water. Sinking. I nearly drowned, she thought, and heard herself repeat the words out loud: "I nearly drowned."

Dr. Bill pushed away his plate and wiped his face with a napkin. "What'd you say?" he asked, leaning toward her.

"I nearly drowned in this lake. I'd forgotten all about it."

"Tell me."

She realized she wanted to. "If it hadn't been for my mother's friend," she began, "I wouldn't be here now. He swam back to shore and pulled me off the bottom. I was wearing a red suit, and he said he could see me floating under the surface of the water. That he plucked me out 'like a flower.' That's what he said later. I heard him telling the story, to my mother, I guess."

"What else?" Dr. Bill asked.

Penny stared off in the distance, out toward the lake, darkening now as the sun sank, another day come and gone. "He held me upside down and banged my back, and finally I started to cough and choke up water. I remember his feet," she said. She could see them now, wrinkled white toes splayed against the rock. In the space of an instant, she'd gone from staring at the smooth brown stones on the bottom of the lake to contemplating a strange man's hairy feet. It had happened just that quickly.

"Is that all?" he asked.

She shrugged. "That's all I remember." So remote it seemed; she might have been talking of someone else's life, relating someone else's small store of memories. One long evening, she thought, and he'd know all there was to know of her. "Why don't you tell me about a childhood memory?" she suggested.

He began by revealing that he'd been born in Shreveport and raised by his grandmother. "Sort of like you were," he said. But when Penny inquired further, Dr. Bill admitted that his grandmother had died in a house fire when he was seven. His expression was pained—clearly, she'd pushed past the point of comfort. Penny told him she was sorry and reached out briefly to touch his sleeve. It was true; she was sorry, but she was also convinced that his childhood had not been like hers, not at all. She'd gone to live with her grandmother when she was six, and she hardly remembered her life before. A few scattershot memories like the one she'd just related were all she had left.

Penny let him talk, sipping her watery Coke and enjoying the breeze coming off the water. He'd been intent on his ministry, he told her, determined to win over his first congregation. "They weren't all sold on me, you know." Penny pretended not to. "Then one day I was in the midst of a sermon, and I happened to look down and see the top of your head." He whipped his hand through the air, suddenly agitated. "Your hair was all I could see of you. No matter how I raised my voice, no matter how I gestured and invoked the scripture, I couldn't get your attention. You wouldn't look up at me."

"I was listening!" Penny protested. She didn't remember, really, but she was sure she must have been. "I like to study the program or the Bible passage," she explained. "I think better that way. Looking down."

Dr. Bill didn't seem convinced. "Every Sunday, same thing," he went on. "Penny and Mattie, third row, center aisle. From time to time, your grandmother would glance up from her knitting, but not you. No eye contact at all. You were a hard case, Penny. I kept wondering: Does she care what I'm saying, or has she already seen through me, to my imperfect core?"

He's dramatic, Penny thought. They were all of them imperfect, but that wasn't the point, now, was it? What she recalled was how much he'd wanted to convince them. He'd been new to the ministry but not a young man, and coming late to God had made him all the more intense. She'd been suspicious of the theatrics he employed, the pacing, the pounding, the yelling and imploring. For all of that effort, he hadn't seemed quite convinced himself. From her spot in the third row, she'd heard it in his voice, a faltering, and each time this had happened, he'd returned to the pulpit, running his fingers over the scripture, taking a deep breath followed by a ragged exhalation. He's afraid, she'd realized. He believes in his message but not in himself.

He was still talking, saying something about how he'd invested her, Penelope Reed, with the power of acceptance. "If I could just get your attention," he exclaimed, "if I could get it and keep it, then I knew I'd have the rest of them." The waitress interrupted his train of thought, stopping by to clear their plates. Dr. Bill paid the bill, then suggested they return to the top deck and find a spot at the railing. "If we hurry, we can still see the last of the sunset."

On the way up, he put an arm around her, guiding her through the crowd. Once they'd claimed a spot and admired the pink-streaked sky, he resumed. "One Sunday morning, you simply turned your face up as I walked past, and I was stunned. I literally lost my place and came to a complete standstill. Do you remember?" Penny shook her head. "Well, of course you don't, but I do. That was the day I noticed how beautiful you are." He's practiced these words, she thought. This was a little sermon meant just for her. He tightened his grip on her shoulder, turning her toward him, and she knew that he intended to kiss her. She didn't want that, not here in the open with all these people around. She didn't want to be one of those embracing couples, not yet, anyway.

"Slow," she said. "You promised you'd go slow." Not wanting to sound ungrateful, she hastened to add: "Don't get me wrong. That's one of the nicest things anybody has ever said to me."

Reluctantly, he returned his attention to the sky. The sun had disappeared, the last of its light streaking the gathering darkness. "Slow," he repeated. "All right. I'm just asking this one thing. Will you try to call me Bill, not *Dr.* Bill?"

Penny smiled. "I'll try."

"And one more thing?"

"What?"

"Will you come to the clinic for the next few Saturdays? We need you. *I* need you." Mattie had already told her the gist of what he went on to say: They were staging an "interference," as Dr. Bill liked to call them. In the last year, the congregation at Gospel Fellowship had pledged to do all they could to end abortion. This was a war, Dr. Bill had told them, a long hard war, and with his urging, they'd dedicated themselves to the fight. The struggle over the right to life was the crux of his ministry, something he'd carried with him and thrust into their arms, a great gift and a heavy responsibility. "Never simple," he told them, "never easy."

Penny sighed and looked out over the lake, a shining black surface that had already begun to reflect the first light of the stars. "I work on Saturdays," she said, "but Juanita has her license now. Maybe we can trade off."

He nodded eagerly and squeezed her shoulder again. "That's a great idea!" he said.

The drive back to town was exhilarating, a wild carnival ride through the darkness. She closed her eyes and held on tight, leaning when he leaned. Already it felt natural, as though she'd been doing it all her life. He dropped her off before midnight, kissing her forehead as they stood by the stairs. "Did you have fun?" he asked.

"Oh, yes," she replied, looking up into what she could see of his face, the strong nose and dark eyes. "I had a wonderful time." Her voice sounded clear and loud in the night air.

"Let's do it again, then."

Turning away, Dr. Bill brushed the tips of his fingers across her cheek, exactly the way she'd stroked the petals of the rose earlier in the day. Dazed, Penny climbed the stairs to her apartment. Once she was inside, once the door was closed behind her, she leaned against it and raised a hand to her cheek, touching where he'd touched, feeling what he'd felt, the smooth warm skin beneath her fingers.

Chapter 5

ON TUESDAY MORNING, Noah invited Carl down to the pet store and made him a bet. "The terms are simple," Noah explained. "Fifty dollars says you can't convince that wife of yours to bring E.T. into the Solace family." Although Noah's nose was still covered in white gauze, he'd seen fit over the weekend to pardon the parrot, who, after all, couldn't be expected to know better. Noah had a quick temper, but he was nothing if not forgiving. Now he paced back and forth in front of the aquariums, his energetic walk sending blond hair sifting into his eyes. "Spring the bird on her over dinner; talk her into it by morning." He paused in his speech long enough to sweep the wayward hair back into place. "Tonight or never. Let's keep it clean. What do you say, buddy?"

Carl shrugged. What was there to say? If he prevailed, he'd get E.T.—already his, he reminded Noah, and he had the cash register receipt to prove it—and fifty bucks. If he lost, as Noah predicted, then Noah would get his bird back and a fifty-dollar bonus. A friendly wager between friends, that's all it was. In the past, they'd bet on Cowboys games and on University of Texas basketball games; they'd even wagered on when the mall manager would get the ax, but never on anything *this* close to home. "You act like Hannah's my mother," Carl complained, "like I've got to have her permission."

Noah pursed his lips. "Call it what you like," he said.

They were standing near the back of the store, and while they bickered good-naturedly, the object of their bet maintained a dignified silence, no screeching, squawking, or shrieking. He seemed to understand the gravity of the situation. "If I want to," Carl went on, "I can carry the bird in the house and set him up in my studio. Fait accompli." This last was something Noah would say, something Noah often *did* say, as a matter of fact, which made Carl sigh. Not only was he lying through his teeth, he hadn't even summoned up his own words to do it.

Noah simply raised a bushy, blond eyebrow and wandered over to the last aisle, where he set to work unpacking yet another box of cat toys. Carl thought to follow him but didn't; instead, his attention was drawn to a collection of neons in an aquarium nearby. The way they swam together, one large flash of silver and red, it was mesmerizing to watch. No need to say it, he thought, his eyes following the endless progression of the fish. They were both wimps when it came to love. If anything, Noah was worse than Carl. He fell often and hard and, once he turned dreamy-eyed, lost all sense of self-preservation. "The guy's after your money," Carl always warned him. "Isn't that perfectly obvious?" Not that Noah had any money, really, but he did enjoy the role of successful entrepreneur—"pet store magnate," as he liked to call himself. He drove a five-year-old yellow Mercedes and took frequent trips to Mexico in the company of one or another of his boyfriends. He lived in a good neighborhood on Exposition Boulevard, in a red brick bungalow with a white front door accented by a gleaming gold knocker. The house was Noah's inheritance from his mother and one of the few possessions he could point to that was actually paid for. Once or twice in the past, Carl had happened upon credit-card statements in the passenger seat of his friend's car. The balances were downright frightening.

Noah and Hannah had never hit it off, not since the first time Carl had invited his friend to the house for a game of cards, nearly four years ago. It had been a lucky night for Noah; all evening he'd trounced people and gloated, cackling and clapping his hands until an indignant Hannah had refused to play with him again. She was a poor loser, and Noah was a poor winner—a bad combination, Carl realized later. And Hannah disapproved of the way Noah ran his business as well. "The Ark is adrift," she'd observed after her first visit to the pet store. "No one at the helm." They'd been ambling down the concourse, making their slow way back to the bookstore through the Saturday afternoon crowd. Bristling at this remark, Carl had halted in his path, forcing a sea of others to divert around him, even as Hannah had continued without him. "What's wrong with a little drifting now and then?" he'd called after her. "Does it always have to be full speed ahead?" At this, she'd turned, shot him a cool look, then strolled back to stand directly in front of him. "Drift for too long," she'd replied, "and you're no longer drifting. You're just plain lost."

From Noah's perspective, Hannah was "a tough bitch," though he was sure she had her reasons. "You don't get that way without someone punching you in the gut a few times," he'd pointed out. Grudging respect is what he gave her, though he was forever saying that Carl deserved a more attentive, more supportive wife. "I'd like Hannah better," he'd admitted, "if she were married to someone else." Ironic, Carl thought now, that the very things Noah disliked about Hannah— her tendency to be controlling, for instance—might be the very things that would win him this bet.

"Hey you?" Noah called. To get Carl's attention, he slung a cat toy at the front of the aquarium. "So, do we have a bet?" he asked.

"Sure." Carl bent to retrieve the odd feathery thing, which looked like a headdress for pygmies. "Do people really buy this crap?" he asked.

Noah gazed up at his friend under a fringe of blond bangs. "They're for cat lovers," he said. "You wouldn't understand." The tension had lifted a little, but Noah wasn't through. "Even if you win E.T., you lose—money, I mean. You're gonna have to build an aviary. This is a sensitive bird we're talking about. He requires space."

Carl rolled his eyes. Noah's Ark was so crowded the walls seemed to lean inward. "And what's he got here? All of Rhode Island to stretch his wings in?"

Noah ignored him. "African grays need stimulation," he said.

"Mark my words: You keep him in a cage, and he'll pluck himself bald in a matter of weeks."

That night, Carl stood in front of the kitchen counter, slicing broccoli into bite-size florets. Despite a bad headache, he was making good progress on the beef stir-fry, one of Hannah's favorites. Neil lay on the floor alongside, so close that the dog's stubby little tail tickled Carl's bare foot. "Scoot over, boy," Carl said, nudging Neil aside, but the dog didn't budge. These days, the cocker found his way around by smell and, consequently, stayed right on Carl's heels, especially when cooking was under way. When it came time to cut the carrots, which were draining on a paper towel at the other end of the counter, he tried again: "Move, Neil." No response. The dog was a passive and unmoving lump of flesh. Awkwardly lurching for them, Carl lost his balance and stomped Neil's leg so hard the dog howled in pain, then scuttled away.

Knife in hand, Carl whirled about and glimpsed Neil's fat behind beating a swift retreat into the living room. "Sorry, fella!" he yelled, and returned to the task. At least, his hands returned. His eyes stayed with Neil just long enough to make sure the dog wasn't limping, a second too long for his index finger. The knife in his hand slipped and sliced into his skin, a quick, clean cut that went straight toward the bone. For a moment, Carl simply stood, head pounding, and watched his blood seep onto the cutting board. It began flowing immediately and, in thirty seconds or so, formed a small crimson puddle in the midst of the vegetables. The sight fascinated him. Now, that's some still life, he thought, before heading off to the bathroom for a Band-Aid. Back in the kitchen, he mollified Neil with a bit of beef and set to work rinsing the vegetables. The finger throbbed as the cold water poured over it, and by the time he heard the front door open, Carl was wondering whether he might need to get the damn thing stitched up. He dumped the vegetables in the wok and turned on the burner.

Hannah never entered the kitchen immediately. Instead, he'd hear her heels click across the hardwood floor as she crossed the living room to the dining-room table. Every day, Carl carried in the small bundle of mail from the box and left it on the table for his wife's inspection. He rarely opened any of it, not even those few pieces addressed exclusively to him. Hannah took care of it all, ripping a side off each envelope with the sharp end of a nail and fishing out the contents with the tips of her fingers. If there was news for him, she'd perch on the kitchen stool and read it aloud while he finished the dinner preparations and served the plates.

Apparently, the mail was a bust today, nothing but bills and pleas for donations, because Hannah came into the kitchen with only those expensive high heels in her hands.

"Ready to eat, hon?" he asked. He smiled, but when she didn't smile back, Carl's smile faded. Perhaps it wasn't true of every marriage, but in theirs at least, the negative was more infectious than the positive. Good moods, it seemed, were fragile and in need of constant sustenance—like cut flowers—while a bad mood was a highly contagious cold. A simple sneeze in the other's direction, and they were both under the weather for a week. "There's a bottle of chardonnay in the fridge," he tried. "Want some?" His plan was to ply her with a little wine, then spring the parrot.

"Oh, I guess," she answered, lingering in the kitchen doorway while he retrieved the bottle, unscrewed the cork, and poured.

As he handed her the glass, he noted that she hadn't moved a muscle since coming in the room. It wasn't like Hannah to stand still. He took the shoes out of her hand and pressed the glass into it. "Tired?" Carl asked. "You're working late these days." Her waist-length red hair had begun unwinding from a soft bun, spilling strands around her face and neck.

"Last week I was consulting on a grant. Yesterday I was at Helen's." Her voice drifted away.

"You didn't tell me. Everything all right at Helen's?"

She shrugged. "The usual. I mean, I guess it's all right, but the motherhood shit gets old, you know? She can't give it a break and have a simple conversation, grown-up to grown-up. She treats me like one of the kids."

Where Carl was concerned, Helen could do no wrong—she was simply the sweetest, kindest, warmest woman he'd ever known—but he wasn't about to come to her rescue right now. "Well, it makes sense," he said. "She's home every day taking care of kids. Hard to turn that off, I imagine. Not like your job or mine."

"I don't know about that," Hannah replied irritably before taking a sip of her wine. "One good thing," she went on. "I finagled one of Grandma Bowman's quilts." A smile came over her face. "Actually, I stole it. Want to see?"

"Sure," he said.

She was back a minute later, shaking out the quilt and holding it up above her chin. The pattern was intricate, a series of interconnected boxes in shades of red and blue. "What do you think?" Her voice was muffled, recalling for him a little girl from his childhood who'd put on plays just this way, raising a quilt over her head for a curtain, then dropping it to step forward, surprising all of them with some elaborate costume. Another drama queen. Evidently, he had a genetic weakness for them.

"What do you think?" Hannah repeated.

Carl stepped back to get a better look at it. "Beautiful," he replied, careful to sound interested. "What's it called?" He knew Hannah: If she detected any lack of enthusiasm, she'd remind him that quilts were a legitimate art form, maybe even accuse him of sexism. He'd heard it all before.

"You mean the pattern?" she asked.

"Yes."

"Log cabin, I think. Here, hold it up for me, will you?" The quilt moved forward, and Carl thought again of the little girl. In her plays, she was always wearing hats with feathers, her narrow little neck weighted down with bangles and beads, her feet wobbling in her momma's high heels.

"Better not," he said. "I might bleed on it."

She let the quilt drop until she could peer over it. "What'd you do?" she asked.

He held up his finger. Blood had seeped around the edges of the bandage; the little pad was dark and spongy with it. "Oh, you know me. I get all worked up chopping vegetables. Don't worry. I rinsed them thoroughly."

"Maybe you should get that looked at," she suggested.

He shrugged. "Maybe. Or maybe you could kiss it and make it better."

She didn't smile, just bundled the quilt in her arms and walked away. He returned to the stove and discovered the bottom layer of vegetables had begun to burn. He could smell them. "Shit," he muttered.

In a minute, she was back, standing behind him. "Carl," she said, "we need to talk." He didn't like the distance in her voice. Her mood had changed.

"More wine?" he asked, reaching for the bottle, then pointing it at the glass in her hand.

"Okay," she agreed.

As he poured, wine sloshed out of the glass and onto the floor, but he pretended not to notice, simply turned back to the wok. "I want to talk to you too," he said, wielding the spatula. "But dinner's ready. Can we take it up at the table?"

They shoved aside the flotsam and jetsam of the last week's mail, mostly catalogs and entreaties for money, and Hannah set their places, taking cloth napkins from the large china hutch she'd inherited from her mother, her most prized possession.

"So what do you want to talk about?" he asked. Their plates were heaped with rice, thin strips of beef, steaming vegetables. Hannah speared a piece of broccoli, her face luminous in the last light of the evening.

"You first," she said, waving with her fork.

"No, you."

"You, Carl," she insisted, popping a bite in her mouth and turning her lips up in an imitation smile. This wasn't an auspicious beginning; nevertheless, he forged on.

"Well," he said. "It's occurred to me that Neil might be happier if he had company during the day. Being here all by himself in the dark, it can't be pleasant." Hannah sat quietly, her eyes on her plate. "You okay?" he asked. She nodded vigorously and brought another large bite to her mouth, but he knew she wasn't telling the truth. "Anyway," Carl continued in what he hoped was an earnest-sounding voice, "I was thinking about bringing E.T. home. You remember E.T., the African gray parrot from Noah's?" He paused and waited for another nod, which was slow in coming. "So, don't you think he'd be great to have around? Someone to talk to Neil while we're away." Hannah shook her head. His heart sank, but he pressed on. "Listen, Hannah. The bird can say things, lots of things. He's a feathered genius. And I can teach him more. I was thinking about 'hey there, Neil' and 'good boy.' He'll pick them right up. A week or two, tops."

At the sound of his name, Neil came trundling across the living room, sliding to a stop before the table. Clearly, the dog was hoping for a little morsel of this or that, but the vet had been adamant: no table scraps. Carl tried to ignore his plaintive, begging face. Despite his bulk, Neil could look truly hungry when he put his mind to it. Now he stood at attention, waiting to see if he could melt his master's heart. "Really, Hannah," Carl finished. "E.T. would be a great little addition to our family."

Better stop there, he decided, and after loading up his fork, Carl filled his mouth with food. This was his first real bite, and he almost gagged. The broccoli was burned and acrid-tasting, the carrots soggy. Lousy, seriously lousy, but Hannah hadn't complained. Not one word of protest. She'd gone right on, dutifully eating. He watched her now, negotiating a bite of rice. It looked sticky.

"We can't afford a parrot," she finally said, then brought her napkin to her lips and scrubbed, as though to wipe the taste away.

Carl hadn't considered finances. After all, he already owned the bird, but he couldn't let Hannah in on that little secret. "I can get a really good price," he ventured.

"A really good price would be in the hundreds of dollars." She was right, of course, but he was surprised to hear her say so. Since when did she know the price of exotic birds? "It's completely out of the question, don't you think?" She covered her mouth, as though indigestion were already setting in. "Given our finances, I mean." Although her words were muffled, the meaning was clear. "I'm thinking about your job, Carl."

"What about my job?"

"It's not taking us anywhere."

"Where's it supposed to take us?"

"Into the future." She reached for her wineglass and took a quick sip. "We're stalling, right here in the present. We've been stalled for years."

"Hannah, what's going on?" Had she met someone else, then? This was always his first thought when they disagreed. With a woman as

beautiful as Hannah, he couldn't help worrying. Half of him was surprised it hadn't happened before now. She's in love with someone else,
he thought, and dropped his fork with a clatter. His wife jumped in her
seat; her expression was pained. Under the table, Neil nudged Carl's
feet apart and settled down between them. Just like Neil to find a way
to offer Carl warmth when he most needed it.

"I need to say this," Hannah insisted.

"So go on." He looked out the window at the backyard, the grass so
tall now it threatened to hide the birdbath. No self-respecting husband
would let a yard go to pot this way, he thought. No wonder she was
leaving him.

"When I was driving home, I was thinking that if you'd painted
cacti and lizards instead of my face, we'd never have gotten married."
She spoke in a rush, as though she'd been practicing the words.

Carl turned back to her. The evening light shone on her features,
lending them the smooth definition of carved marble. "What's your
point?"

"I thought you were an artist, Carl," Hannah said, grabbing the
edge of the table. "A real artist, not a dabbler, not a hobbyist."

He struggled to maintain his calm. "Let me get this straight," Carl
said quietly. "A: I'm not making enough money for you. Okay, I hear
that. B: I'm not the artist you thought I was, not serious enough, not
committed enough. Do I have this right?"

She nodded.

"You can't have it both ways. Artists don't make money, at least
most don't. Look at Van Gogh—"

"Look at Picasso," she put in forcefully.

Carl took a deep breath. "Let's just stay with Van Gogh for the
minute, okay? Picasso was a lucky exception and a bastard to boot.
Believe me, you'd have hated living with Picasso. Money isn't everything." Hannah made a face. *Money isn't everything.* He'd said it quite
often over the years—in fact, every time this subject came up. Only this
time it made him sick. What a bullshit argument, he thought. "What
do you want, Hannah?" he asked.

"I don't know what I want!" she cried, all anger and anguish. "Here
we are, nearly forty years old and still living from paycheck to paycheck. We can't afford anything extra. Nothing extra, Carl."

"What? What is it?"

"I'm pregnant," she said.

My God, he thought, my God. It's finally happened. He'd waited so long for this moment, years and years. Truth be told, he'd almost given up. Now he was dumbstruck, so much so that it hardly registered when his wife got up and ran from the room.

"She's pregnant," he whispered, and held out the wineglass in a solitary toast. "I'm going to be a father!" he announced to the empty room, and, after raising the glass to his lips, took a long, anxious gulp.

Minutes later, he found Hannah stretched out across the bed, both Neil and the quilt wrapped in her arms. "Are you all right?" he asked.

She sighed and sat up. "I've been better. Let's say I've had moments of clarity here and there, but mostly I'm a mess." She rolled over and faced him. "What do you think?"

He took a step into the room. "I think it's fantastic." He heard it in his voice, the happiness.

"I knew you'd say that, those very words."

Carl took another step. "It is. It's wonderful."

"What's wonderful about it? We don't have money, we don't have time, we don't have room. We can't afford a parrot, much less a child."

He flinched. "Those things can be sorted out, Hannah. Other people have less money, less time, less room."

It was the wrong thing to say. She rolled her eyes. "Other people live on the street. Let's don't compare ourselves to the unfortunate, Carl. It doesn't help matters."

He folded his arms across his chest and struggled to think of the right thing. He'd wanted a child all his life. Should he tell her that? Should he pour out his love for her and this child? Did he love this child already? Was that possible? Or did he just love the idea—*some* child, *his* child.

"I blame Dr. Kemp," she finally said. "I'd still be on the pill if it wasn't for him."

He moved a few steps in her direction. Not too close, he told himself. Go slow. Be calm. "Hannah, you know that's not fair," he said, keeping his voice steady. "He told you it wasn't a good idea at your age. He was doing what any good doctor should do."

"My age," she complained, gathering up her quilt and burying her face in it. "Everyone keeps bringing it up." Her hair spilled out across the white backing, and the vision of a red-haired baby came unbidden to Carl.

"The baby will have your hair." He inched forward, taking a seat beside her.

"No, Carl." She put out a hand. "Don't."

"Don't what?" He was suddenly aware of the pain he was feeling: His head pounded, his finger throbbed, but the rhythms were off, out of sync, so that he felt dizzy, even nauseous.

"Don't talk that way," Hannah moaned. "It's not a baby."

"It will be a baby." He stroked her head. "In just a matter of months. It happens so quickly. Really, it's a miracle, don't you think?"

She responded in a little girl voice: "No, I think it's an accident, something that wasn't meant to happen."

"You can do this, Hannah."

"I'm not sure I can," she said, shaking her head. "Lots of people aren't cut out to be parents. I see it every day, children whose misfortune it was to be born to the wrong woman. We aren't all cut out for motherhood, you know." She took a deep breath and looked him in the eye. "I have to be honest. I'm not sure I can love someone the way children need to be loved."

"I know you can, Hannah."

"Do you, Carl?" She gazed up at him, red-eyed, ready to be convinced.

"Yes." It wasn't the complete and total truth, but it was the only truth he could afford to tell. "And what about me?" he asked. "Where do I come into the equation?"

"Do you mean where the child is concerned or where the decision is concerned?" Hannah spoke slowly and carefully, taking on the distant voice of an interviewer. She had all sorts of voices.

"Either one," Carl replied, swallowing his fear. If he couldn't get her to agree to a parrot, how could he get her to agree to a child? Where was his control in this relationship? "Shouldn't I have *some* control?"

She was petting Neil now, her face turned away. "Where the child is concerned or where the decision is concerned?" she asked.

"Either one." He sighed. "We're going in circles, Hannah."

"Of course you're important, Carl," she said, but it was her inter-viewer voice. She was reassuring a stranger.

The anger came out of nowhere. "Goddamn it, Hannah! This is my child too." He slapped the mattress with the flat of his hand, amazed he could care so much and so quickly. "Mine as much as yours! Do you hear me?"

She didn't move. He felt desperate, a little crazy even. He wanted to wrestle with her, shake some sense into her, drag her into the closet if necessary. Lock her up. But he was a sensible man. "You always said we'd have a child in time. In time, you said." He knew he was plead-ing. Hannah was silent, like some statue you say prayers to. He didn't know if he could stand it.

Finally, she spoke. "Things haven't worked out the way I thought they would." Her last word was followed by a short snort, and they both looked down to find that Neil had gone off to sleep.

He took a deep breath. "You're talking about me, aren't you?" he said. "*I* haven't worked out the way you thought I would. Is that it?" She didn't answer. Instead, she pulled Neil into her lap. The dog opened his eyes and stared up at her.

"That child is mine too, Hannah," Carl said. "Mine!" He sounded childish, even to himself.

"Oh God, I'm so sorry," Hannah moaned. She put out her arms to him, but Carl knew she was only offering consolation. Was there noth-ing he could say? After all these years, was pity the only concession he would get? The pain in his head intensified. He got up and lurched out of the room.

"Carl," she called after him, "are you all right? I'm sorry. I said everything the wrong way."

"No," he shouted. It hurt his head to shout, but he did it anyway. "I'm not all right, Hannah. I'm not." He stopped in the hall and waited for an answer, but none came. That was Hannah for you—silence was always her last word.

Cleaning up the mess in the kitchen, Carl recalled a Friday evening some months back. They'd come home from a restaurant and Hannah had gone straight in to run her bath. It was one of her rituals, the Friday-night bath. She kept a small black-and-white TV on the long counter, and while she soaked, she watched old movies starring actresses like Barbara Stanwyck or Susan Hayward or Bette Davis, the more histrionic the better. From the living room, he'd hear wavery music interrupted now and then by the sound of Hannah running more warm water.

That night, he'd gone in around eleven and found her dozing, Neil curled up asleep beside the tub. The sight of them had touched him. He'd gone to get his sketchbook, then, sitting on the toilet, made a few drawings while she slept. Hannah's hair had come down around her face; wet strands drifted on the surface of the water like seaweed. She was completely submerged except for her head and the tips of her breasts. Usually, her breasts were heavy, but in the water they rose to the surface, the nipples dark, like twin fish. Hannah's breasts had always embarrassed her. They'd developed early, right after her mother died, but she'd been too embarrassed to ask her father for a bra. Hannah told Carl she'd kept her hair long to obscure them and learned to walk softly so they wouldn't jiggle inside her blouse. "Despised them," she said vehemently, as though the hate was still there, shuddering inside her. He'd always loved them.

Seeing her stretched out in the tub, he'd wondered what she'd look like in pregnancy, going so far as to try a few sketches of a pregnant Hannah. He'd imagined her stomach pushing up until it broke the surface of the water, an emerging island, something insistent and miraculous, nature forcing itself on her. The thought had been so strong; if he could have had his way, he would have made her so right then, utterly pregnant.

As he carried out the trash, it occurred to Carl that he might have willed this pregnancy, that the sketches and his longing might have worked some miracle. It was a crazy thought, but for an instant, he was filled with something approaching joy. Let Noah have his bird. What need had he for a parrot when he was going to have a baby?

"HAVE you given up coffee?" Carl asked the next morning. As usual, he'd made a pot when he'd gotten up. Weekdays, Hannah rose about an hour after he did and started on coffee first thing, drinking at least three cups before she left for work. This morning, though, the pot was still full, and Hannah sat fully dressed at the kitchen table, chewing a piece of dry toast. She looked miserable, her jaw tight, her eyes puffy. Any anger he'd been holding on to drained away.

"It's given up on me," she said. "My stomach won't tolerate it." She smiled grimly. "You'd be surprised how fast it begins. Hormones taking me for a ride." She gestured with the hand that held the toast, made the bread into a rocket headed for space.

"Give it a little time," Carl suggested. He wanted a cup himself, but he wouldn't pour it, not now. If Hannah couldn't stomach coffee, he'd pretend he couldn't stomach it either. It was the least he could do. Later, after she left for work, he'd drink a big cup. Now he recalled Hannah hunched over in the weeds, heaving her guts out. Why hadn't pregnancy occurred to him? He'd registered carsickness and never given it another thought. Only now did he remember her tears and the odd apology that had followed. "I wish you'd told me sooner," he said. "If I'd known—"

"You'd what?" Hannah interrupted. She tossed what was left of her breakfast toward the trash can. It missed, skidded on the red tile, and hit the wall. Neil lumbered after it, nose to the floor, tracking toast. "I considered not telling you at all," she said, so quietly Carl almost missed it.

Who was this woman? he asked himself. Did he know her at all? Maybe Noah knew her better than he did. Tough bitch, he thought, wanting to lash out, but too much was at stake. Instead, he took a deep breath and stepped to her side, cupping his hand to her cheek. "Give it a chance, Hannah. Give *us* a chance." By *us*, he might have meant the two of them, the three of them, him and the baby, all possible combinations. And Neil, and the parrot too, by God. Even if Hannah had asked, he couldn't have sorted it out. Their little family. Where did it start and stop?

She nodded and leaned her head into his hand, resting against him. She counted on him, he thought; she always had. He didn't really believe in himself, but he'd always believed in her. He wished he could tell her that: I've been here for you, Hannah, he might say. All these years, I've been here for you, baby. Marriage is settling for one set of strengths, another set of weaknesses. What can you live with; what can't you live without? He wanted to spill his guts, all of this and more, but instead he stood and held her head in his hands for as long as she'd let him. She looked tired and pale and more than a little fragile. But just as he was gathering himself to speak, she pushed back from the table and got up, stepping away from him and into her heels. "Gotta go," she said. "I'll be late for work."

That evening, neither of them mentioned babies or pregnancy. Give it a break, Carl thought. Hannah went to bed early, and after she was asleep, Carl lay awake beside her and went over the possibilities. Like a man in love, he closed his eyes and focused his whole being on the face taking shape in his mind. If not a whole face, then the eyes, a nose, even the line of a cheek. He'd known few babies in his life—a youngest child, a childless husband—so this exercise of imagination was very nearly an act of will. For hours he tossed and turned, but if Hannah heard anything, she didn't let it show. All night, she lay quietly, a long graceful curve in the darkness.

He remembered, too, the last time they'd made love, over a week ago now. They'd come home from a movie and, weary, Hannah had dropped facedown onto the bed. He remembered the way he'd undressed her, slowly and gently, then roamed over her body with his tongue and finally entered her when she wasn't expecting it, from behind, all in one swift thrust. As he'd listened to her moans, his hands had kneaded her smooth buttocks. He liked the sounds she made almost as much as he liked the rest of it. She'd had an orgasm that night; he was sure of it. To make Hannah come, you had to sneak up on her and surprise her into losing control. It had been so good that night, but they hadn't made love since. That was the way she was—the better the sex, the less she seemed to want it afterward. It made him crazy, really, because he was just the opposite: a little of something wonderful only made him greedy for more.

Near morning, exhausted with imagining and remembering, Carl allowed himself to cry. He held back as long as possible, until it hurt to cry, until his throat swelled shut and his eyelids felt bruised. And when the tears finally trickled down the sides of his cheeks and onto the pillowcase, he forgot about the baby and thought instead about how women deny themselves all sorts of pleasure while men deny themselves all sorts of pain.

A few hours later, he opened his eyes to find Neil waiting on his haunches by the bed.

"Morning, buddy," Carl said in his raspy morning voice. He lay motionless and watched as the dog began pacing in a labored waddle. He wanted to go back to sleep, but Neil was whining now. It was nearly seven-thirty, time to go out.

"Bladder about to bust, boy?" he asked.

Usually, he let Neil into the backyard, but this morning the dog rushed out the front door as Carl leaned out to check for Hannah's Blazer in the driveway. His wife was gone, long gone. Halfway down the steep front steps, Neil stumbled and rolled, landing on the sidewalk, legs waving in the air like an upended bug. "All right, boy?" Carl asked, coming out on the porch to check. Neil was fine. Once he found the grass and relieved himself, the cocker wandered off to explore, his face blissful. The front yard was new territory, and smelling one of his few remaining pleasures. Carl didn't have the heart to deny him. He went in for his sketchbook and came back out, settling on the steps to draw. There was plenty of time. Thursdays, he generally worked twelve to nine. When the phone rang a few minutes later, he groaned, sure it was one of his employees-of-the-month, so-called because they seldom lasted longer than thirty days.

He was pleasantly surprised to hear Helen's whispery voice on the other end of the line. Carl had always attributed her quiet tone to a background in nursing, which she gave up after her first child. Helen must have been the ideal nurse, he thought, soothing and unobtrusive, and he was certain she was the ideal mother too. Loving and supportive but firm—clean sheets, and dinner at six. A kiss at bedtime. Over the years, Hannah had frequently complained that Carl romanticized Helen, overlooking her less-than-desirable characteristics, but it wasn't true. He simply didn't see them.

"Hannah's already left for work," Carl told her, moving from the kitchen to the living room, pulling the cord as far as it would go. Craning his neck, he peered out the front window. Nothing. Green grass in need of mowing but no golden cocker. No big deal, he thought. How far can a blind dog go?

"I called to talk to you," Helen replied.

Carl was puzzled. Much as he admired his sister-in-law, they rarely had a real conversation. The last time Helen had called for him was to plan a surprise party for Hannah. That had been, what, last year? Carl waited for an explanation, but none came. It was like being on the phone with his mother, listening to her breathe while he racked his brains for something to say. Finally, Carl got it. Helen wasn't out of things to say. She was waiting.

He sighed deeply.

"So, she told you?" Helen asked.

"Yes." Carl turned from the window and trod back to the kitchen, sinking down on a barstool by the phone.

"Oh, Carl, I'm so sorry." Helen spoke as though his child were already gone.

"It's not over," he said quietly. "She hasn't made up her mind."

"Maybe not," Helen acceded, "but she isn't the least bit happy about it. When I talked to her, she was leaning toward—"

"Don't even say it," Carl said sternly, abruptly fearful. This baby was so new to him, but the desire to bring it into being had swept over him with all the fury of the unattainable.

While Helen went on speaking, her voice soft and soothing, Carl stared down at the red tile floor, rubbing his bare feet across the cool surface, pressing a toe into the grout. Last night, he'd had an idea, and it was coming back to him now. Once upon a time, all those many years ago, he'd seduced his wife with his hands, drawing his way into her heart. Perhaps he could do it again. She wanted an artist; well, he'd give her one. When Helen ran out of comforting things to say, Carl asked if she'd be home a while. "Can I stop by on my way to work?" he asked.

An hour later, Carl stepped onto Helen's front porch, sketchbook under his arm. On the first knock, she opened the door, ushered him into the foyer, then pulled him in for a close hug. Carl stiffened—this felt like condolence, and he didn't want that, not from Helen or anyone else—but she wouldn't let go, and eventually he relaxed and leaned his head into her shoulder. Helen was a couple of inches shorter than Hannah, her figure rounder and softer, but she had the same pale skin and lemony scent.

"So what can I do?" she asked.

"Pictures. Of Hannah when she was a little girl."

Helen pursed her lips and looked thoughtful. "Make yourself comfortable," she said. "I'll be right back."

Hearing the chatter of children in the kitchen, Carl wandered in with his sketchbook to have a look. The chairs had been lined against the wall, and the breakfast table was draped with several cloths—green and white and red—that hung down tentlike on three sides. When Carl bent to have a look, he discovered Cassie and a little blond-haired friend sitting underneath with their dolls and dishes. They were in the midst of a tea party, and for a minute or two, Carl watched them go about their pretend business, pouring and sipping—that is, until they discovered his face in the doorway. Then, tiny china cups poised in the air, the girls froze, big-eyed and silent.

"Hello, Cassie," Carl said.

"It's Uncle Carl," she whispered to her friend. The cups came down, and the girls relaxed. Both murmured hello. "Want some tea?" Cassie asked.

"Love some," he said. The fit was snug, but he managed to crawl inside and to crouch, bent-necked and hunched, beside them. "Thanks for inviting me." His niece smiled in the charming, openmouthed way of children and handed him a cup so small he could close it inside his fist. "Mind if I draw?" he asked. When the girls shook their heads, he balanced the cup on his knee and flipped open the sketchbook.

By the time Helen discovered him, he was halfway through a sketch of the two girls at tea, his pencil lead scratching across the paper, dark lines accumulating quickly. "Want to come out and play with the big kids?" she asked, pulling up the tablecloth. "I've got the picture album."

"So I have to go back to being a grown-up?"

He was asking Helen, but it was Cassie who offered a sad little nod. "Momma says so."

Carl crawled out and, after getting to his feet, followed his sister-in-law back to the living room. "Give me a minute?" he asked, dropping to the sofa. "I want to finish this up."

Helen settled herself on the coffee table across from him, so close that their knees touched, hers in baggy jeans, his in khaki Dockers, and, hugging the album to her chest, waited while he drew. When he lifted the pencil and sat back, she smiled and held out her hand for the sketchbook. Reluctantly, he gave it to her. Seeing the face upside down, he realized Cassie's chin was too narrow and had to fight the impulse to snatch the book back and correct the defect.

"This looks just like her!" she exclaimed, running an index finger around the edges of her daughter's face. "Can I have it?"

"Of course," he told her. After she'd torn out the page, Helen flipped through the sketches he'd done earlier in the week, then earlier in the month, coming eventually to the nudes of Hannah in the tub, the pregnant one first.

"Oh, Carl," she breathed. He wished he'd taken it back while he'd had the chance. People rarely looked at his sketchbook. It was easy to forget how much of himself he revealed there.

"Funny thing," he said. "I did those studies over a month ago. Hannah was taking one of her Friday-night baths. I went in to check on her, and she was asleep. It just came to me, Helen. This vision of how she might be."

Helen's wide mouth twisted. "But you didn't know, did you?" Her tone was slightly incredulous, as though he had managed some sleight of hand and she wanted him to reveal the trick.

He shook his head. "No. No one knew, not even Hannah."

"Amazing!" She returned to studying the sketch, bending her head closer to the page until the ends of her dark red hair brushed the rounded dome of Hannah's belly. "This is exactly the way a pregnant woman looks, Carl. You've even got the dark line down the center of the belly." She traced it there with her finger, rubbing it so that the pencil line smudged. "How did you know all this?"

How did he know? He'd never paid much attention to pregnant women, other than to notice the things everyone else noticed: the way they rested their hands on the roofs of their bellies; the way they tottered when they walked, Humpty-Dumpty-like; the way they gazed dreamily into the distance even as they complained of indigestion. As the younger child, Carl had never experienced his mother pregnant. Unless you counted Demi Moore on the cover of *Vanity Fair*, he'd never seen a naked pregnant woman. But he supposed some things were knowable through the sheer force of imagination, and his wife pregnant was one of these.

Carl picked up the photo album and began turning the pages.

"I could only find a few pictures," Helen told him. "Dad must have some, or Hannah. Doesn't Hannah have pictures?"

He shrugged. "Not that I know of. She says you're the keeper of the family history."

"Hannah likes to give other people tasks. Have you noticed that?"

"I have indeed," he replied, turning to a photo of a little girl sitting cross-legged in the grass. The picture was black and white—the kind with a white border, crimped along the outer edge—and it captured a polite little southern belle, hands clasped in her lap, the flounce of her dress pulled down over the tops of her dimpled knees. Hannah smiled sweetly in the photo, but her eyes shone with defiance. Apparently, she'd resisted posing but for her mother had given in. Yes, Carl thought. It had been Naomi who'd coaxed the picture. Hannah stared straight into the camera, her smile all love in spite of the defiance. He'd never seen this expression on his wife's face. Angry as he was with her, he couldn't help hurting for her too. She'd never gotten over the loss of her mother; her sister had managed, but Hannah had not.

"This one," he said. "Can I take it out of the album?"

"Sure," Helen answered. She was flipping through some sketches of Neil. "Your drawings have such feeling, Carl. Even the ones of Neil. I get the sense—"

"Neil!" he cried. His knees banged Helen's as he leapt to his feet.

"What is it?" she asked, gazing up at him, bewildered and concerned.

"Neil. I forgot him." Carl tucked the photo in his pocket and rushed for the door. He'd been gone over an hour. By now, there was no telling where his blind dog might be.

He held his breath as he pulled into the drive, hoping against hope that Neil was still in the yard, but of course the dog was gone. Carl wandered the neighborhood, but no one had seen a golden cocker spaniel. Driving to the mall, an hour late to work, he pondered how he would ever explain this to Hannah. He had no idea.

Around six, she called the bookstore. It had been a slow afternoon, giving Carl plenty of time to work up dread. He'd hoped her call would come while he was out to dinner, but no such luck. As soon as he said, "Good evening, Walton's Books," Hannah began a rush of words that didn't require or admit a response. She was saying something about the suits she'd picked up from the cleaners, then something else about sitting on the porch to read a letter. "A short letter," she added, "very short."

"I don't understand," he finally told her.

Hannah sighed and started over. "It took me two trips to the car to bring in the stuff from the cleaners. I left the door open while I carried things in. That's what I always do, right?"

"Yes," he replied, nothing new about that.

"Then I decided to check the mail."

"You never check the mail." He wondered if she was expecting something.

"It was only a few minutes, Carl—I swear to you! I didn't even see him go out." Hannah was crying. His wife wasn't a crier, but here she was shedding tears for the second time this week. "He's gone!" she sobbed. "I can't find him anywhere!"

He was about to confess, he would have confessed, but he couldn't quite think of what to say. The truth wouldn't do: "I let Neil into the front yard, then ran off to your sister's house to sort through your baby pictures. I have this idea, you see. . . ." There was a greater good to consider here, so Carl took a deep breath. "Did you check in the neighbors' yards?" he asked. Blood pulsed just under the surface of his skin; he felt it brightening his cheeks.

"Yes," she said, her voice quavering. "Oh God, Carl, I'll never forgive myself if something happens to him."

So easy, this deception. He told her he'd leave work early. "We'll look for him together," he promised. Something was sinking in him while something else emerged, a small, twanging hope. Losing things drove his wife to distraction. A few years back she'd lost her wedding ring, and rather than go to work without it, Hannah had called in sick and spent the whole day in her bathrobe, combing the house. Another time they'd taken in a stray cat, a ginger-colored bag of bones. Carl had been the one to buy cat food and fill the water dish. Until the animal disappeared, Hannah had hardly noticed it, but after it was gone, she couldn't stop thinking about it. She'd even gone to the trouble of tacking flyers to telephone poles, all for a cat they hadn't bothered naming.

"It'll be dark by the time you get home," Hannah told him. "I'm going out now. He's my dog, Carl. I've got to find him." Those words echoed in his ears. You're a lucky bastard, he thought as he hung up the phone.

Carl prayed she wouldn't find Neil, actually closed his eyes at the cash register and said a few words. He didn't believe in God, but that didn't stop him from praying. Suddenly, he was certain that as long as their dog was lost, their baby would be safe. He'd have to work quickly, but he had a chance. His wife wouldn't stop looking until she found Neil. The fates, he thought, were cooperating.

He dialed his sister-in-law's number and listened while it rang, once, twice, three times. Be home, Helen, he thought. Outside the store, the mall was dead. Not a soul passed on the concourse.

"Hello?" Helen's whispery voice again.

"Helen? I have a favor to ask," Carl said slowly. "A secret—I need you to keep a secret."

During his dinner break, Carl carried his sketchbook into the mall and sat down on one of the benches by the fountain. This late in the day, the benches were usually empty, but tonight one man was still there, and when Carl got close enough, he saw why—the old guy was sound asleep. Carl considered rousing him but didn't; instead, he sat down on the bench that afforded the best view of passersby, and flipped open his sketch pad. The photo of Hannah slid forward, but he pushed it to the back. He would not look at it now. He felt terrible about Hannah, out there searching for Neil as darkness descended, her heart heavy with guilt and worry. By all rights it was his guilt, but for now, he'd have to let her carry it. At least for this little while. Part of him felt awful, but another part couldn't help wondering how she could care so much for a dog and so little for him and this child they might have.

The mall was nearly deserted; most self-respecting babies were busy painting themselves with their supper. The few Carl spotted were captives in hot-rod strollers, propelled by speed-walking mothers in stretch pants and Reeboks. Carl got little more than a quick glance, but it was enough. After half an hour, he had sketched a pair of clenched fists, several broad feet, one waggling big toe, the beginnings of an arm.

"Body parts. A little gruesome, don't you think?" It was Noah leaning over Carl's shoulder. "You're good, you know it?"

Carl didn't answer. He was busy forcing little swirls into a chubby, dimpled elbow.

"Reminds me of that old Beatles album." Noah came around and plopped down beside Carl. The bench shook, settled, then shook again. Carl sighed, holding the pencil away from the page, waiting for Noah to get comfortable. He was wearing Birkenstock sandals that slid off and on as he jiggled his bare foot. "Remember?" he went on. "The cover where John, Paul, George, and Ringo were dressed as butchers, brandishing dolls' arms, legs, torsos?"

Carl did remember, vaguely. Late sixties. The cover had been con-sidered so tasteless it had been banned in the U.S. The first shipment into the country had been pasted over with an innocuous photo of the Fab Four, something wholesome enough for consumption by innocent American teens. Who promptly went on a binge of steaming and peel-ing, hell-bent on seeing for themselves what adults sought to deny them. It all seemed so silly now. These days, no one would have blinked twice.

"I used to have a copy," Noah went on, folding tanned arms over his favorite red T-shirt. "I remember, some friends and I steamed off the outer cover and then hung the Beatle butchers on the wall. My mother had a cow." He cocked his head in a way that reminded Carl of E.T. "Isn't it funny how when you talk about the past, you resurrect the slang, fall right back into it?" Noah asked. " 'Having a cow.' I like that image."

"You would," Carl muttered. Noah bounced his foot so hard that he sent a Birkenstock sailing. It plunked down near the fountain. "That was a close one," Carl remarked.

Noah didn't bother to retrieve it. He went on sitting there, waving his foot in the air. "If I stay in the sixties another few minutes," he said with a little snicker, "I may let go with a great big 'groovy, man.' "

"Then come back to the present, by all means." Carl was studying the bits and pieces on the page. All at once he was thinking of something he'd seen on television. He couldn't recall the source anymore, must have been some documentary, but the images had stayed with him: doctors performing second-trimester abortions, pulling off tiny arms and legs in their efforts to extract the fetus. The vision was like a car wreck, something horrible but real that compels the eyes to look long and hard. It stayed with him, this vision, hooking itself into his consciousness, a bloody little sore of a thing. Carl shuddered and closed his sketchbook.

"Cranky, aren't we?" Noah observed. "So, Hannah said it was out of the question?"

Carl went perfectly still. How the hell did Noah know? No one knew, no one but Helen. He couldn't speak for a moment, and when he did, his voice was quiet. Noah leaned in to hear it. "She's undecided," Carl said. "I'd say she's still undecided."

Noah stared at him a minute. "It's all right, buddy. I knew she wouldn't go for it."

"How'd you know?"

Noah shrugged. "I explained that, didn't I? But just for the record, you were a real asshole the other day. There, that's a nineties' word, isn't it? Asshole. But it was an eighties' word too, and a seventies' word now that I think of it. . . . But don't worry about the fifty bucks. Just give me back my bird, and we'll call it even." Noah raised himself and limped off to retrieve his other shoe.

"Oh, E.T.!" Carl exclaimed. It came back to him. The wisecracking bird and the bookstore manager with seeds in his pockets—this was the man he'd been days before. Now he was someone else, someone who felt sorry for a man who'd make do with a talking bird.

"So what do you say?" Noah asked as he slid the sandal onto his foot. "Can I have my bird back?" Carl noted that the bandage was gone and that a long red streak curved across the bridge of Noah's tanned nose.

"Hannah's pregnant," Carl said quietly.

"Whoa!" Noah cried. The old man across from them sat up and rubbed his eyes, then gazed about, trying to decide what had awakened him. "So congratulations are in order?"

Carl shook his head. "Not yet. I have to convince her to keep it."

Noah shuffled forward to give Carl a tight hug. He gestured toward the drawings. "Better get back to work," he whispered.

ON FRIDAY morning, Hannah slept in and, a little before seven, appeared in the doorway of Carl's studio, just as he was clipping paper to the easel. He'd heard her in the bathroom a few minutes earlier, flushing the toilet, then washing at the sink. While the water ran, Carl had turned the easel to obscure her view. She would think nothing of his working—he painted every morning—but she might wonder about the clips and paper. It had been years since he'd done anything in pastels.

"Good morning," he said, trying a little smile.

"I have this feeling he's gone for good," she announced quietly.

"You don't know that."

She didn't answer, just glided into the room, making her way around the easel to the window. The blinds were up; the sun poured over her, melting into her golden red hair and illuminating the slender body beneath the gown. It hurt to look at her—that's how beautiful she was. She turned to him, and Carl slid the photograph beneath a flamingo coaster.

"I keep thinking he's on someone else's porch, wondering why we won't let him in."

Carl shrugged. He had no idea where Neil was, but the image was unmistakable, their blind cocker waiting patiently in the morning sunlight. He pushed it away, pushed toward something else. "Could we talk about the baby?"

"No!" Her voice was vehement. "I can't think about that right now. I have to find Neil first. Do you hear me?" Carl did hear. He heard exactly what he'd hoped to hear.

"You work twelve to nine today, don't you?" she asked.

He nodded.

"Would you go by the pound on your way to work? Do you have time? I guess there's not much point—he was wearing tags, after all. Still, it's something we should do."

Carl sagged with this new burden. Neil *wasn't* wearing tags. He could picture the collar and tags on the back steps, right next to a bottle of flea shampoo. A couple of days earlier he'd given the dog a bath in the backyard. And forgotten to replace his collar.

"Be glad to," he told her. As soon as she left for work, he'd rush to the back steps and get it.

"It's awful to think of him out there all alone," Hannah said. "Wandering, not able to see a goddamn thing."

"Oedipus, the dog," Carl muttered. He sounded heartless, even to himself. Fortunately, Hannah didn't hear him. She was staring out the window, all of her attention focused on the empty street.

The Humane Society was in a long, low building surrounded by an enormous parking lot, a floating dock on a calm black sea. When he pulled in front of the building, only one other car was there, an old, yellow Chevrolet with two open doors and man in a wrinkled suit rummaging in the backseat. Carl parked next to him, then turned off the ignition and waited while the man set a large box on the roof of his car and closed the doors.

Carl trailed up the sidewalk behind him. "Here, let me get it," he called, hurrying to grab the door. The fellow jabbed Carl's stomach with one corner of the box as he shouldered past, not a word of thanks. The box was full of kittens. Carl glimpsed pink mouths and wet fur on a background of soggy newspaper. Newborn. Their eyes weren't even open yet.

Inside, the room was a large open space, entirely empty except for three or four plastic chairs and a long stretch of counter, where the man dropped the box with a thud. The kittens let out a startled mewing, but he didn't bother to check on them; he simply pivoted on his rundown heel and started back the way he'd come. Shouldn't he fill out a form? Carl wondered. Make a donation? He was considering chasing the guy down, forcing some gesture of decency out of him, when a middle-aged black woman appeared at the counter. She eyed the box. "What's in there?" she asked.

"Kittens," he answered.

She sidled over and peered inside. "They too young to be away from their mother," she said matter-of-factly. "What fool left them?" She gave him a sharp look.

Carl waved toward the door. "Guy put down the box and stalked out," he told her, stepping up and peering over the lid. Five tiny ginger-colored kittens curled together. Those he'd seen as the man shouldered past. But he hadn't noticed the white one. Someone had tied a red ribbon around its neck, and the dye had turned the damp newspaper and the kitten's neck a sickly shade of pink.

"This is a damn shame," the woman said. Her name tag read Donita.

She slid the box off the counter and motioned for Carl to follow her down the hall and into a large room lined with cages nearly to the ceiling. The top rows were well above their heads. Carl assumed they had to be accessed by ladders, but he didn't see any.

"We're out of space," Donita told him. "The only thing left is to put up some freestanders in the middle of the floor." Carl couldn't believe it. The room was quiet, but everywhere he looked, a pair of cat eyes gazed back at him. He could feel their interest, all those animal hopes trained on him. Hopeless, he thought. At Noah's, he didn't give the felines a second glance, but that was a pet store, and this was the Humane Society. Here, he couldn't help hurting for them.

"How long can they stay?" Carl asked.

"Depends on the animal, but no more than three weeks." Donita slid the box onto a long examining table and began scooping kittens onto the scale. "Too small," she kept muttering.

"Are the dogs through this door?" he asked, pointing to the opening on the other side of the room.

"Yep." She swung her head in the general direction. "That'd be the dogs over there."

They began to bark as soon as he entered the long corridor, cage #1 alerting cage #2, and so on down the line until the whole room pulsed with sound. When Carl passed, they hurled themselves against their chain-link doors. Some leapt into the air while others twirled on hind legs or rolled over and over on their small cement floors, trying every trick they knew to get his attention. Carl's steps slowed, then stopped altogether. He blinked his eyes and gazed about, befuddled by the noise and the combined will of so many frenzied creatures. No wonder people stayed away, he thought. This was painful.

The cages held dogs of every age and description: puppies, gangly adolescents, and sickly dogs with graying muzzles. German shepherds, sheepdogs, collies, black Labs by the score, beagles, and squat dachshunds, dozens of dogs who could have passed for pedigrees. And then there were the mutts: barrel-chested pooches with squat little legs; pointy-headed dogs with long sweeping tails. Yippy little pests and huge brooding monsters. It took Carl several minutes to walk the length of the long center aisle, and he was just turning back when he spotted Neil in a cramped little cage against the wall. From such a distance, Carl could only have been a dark shape to his dog, but even as he drew nearer, the cocker seemed not to notice, not to see. What about smell? Carl thought. If Hannah had been this close, that lemony essence seeping from her pores, Neil would have taken notice. Instead, he lay curled in the cage, head on his paws, one big ear draped over his face. A single milky eye was visible, and it stared blankly in another direction. The other dogs in the area were doing their best tricks, barking, jumping, running in circles. But Neil was in his own little world, oblivious to them and to Carl.

"That poor fella's blind as a bat." Donita had moved up next to Carl, and she wiped her wet hands on her jeans as she talked. "He don't know coming or going. And *old*, that dog is older than my TV." She said the word *old* as though it were an obscenity. It occurred to Carl that in a place like this, a place where puppies and kittens were put down every day, being old was a crime. "If you don't find your dog," Donita said, "you come on back, and I'll fix you up." He wondered how she knew he was looking for a dog. Had he told her that? He didn't think so. "I got a dog up front that's smart as a whip," she told him. "Knows lots of tricks. Honey, that dog can fix your supper."

"Okay," Carl said. At the sound of that one word, even in the midst of mayhem, Neil's head jerked up, and his blind eyes turned to Carl's face. Oh God, Carl thought. He knows I'm here, and I can't take him home. I can't take you home, Neil. Not today. He beamed that thought through the chaos of the room to the animal that used to be his. It hadn't occurred to him that he would have to make this choice. I have to finish the portrait, he thought. I have to try to change Hannah's mind.

In the midst of his misery, he couldn't help noting the irony. Minutes before, he'd felt superior to the man who'd left the kittens. Now it was Carl's turn to walk away, to do what was expedient. What assholes we both are, he thought. He steeled himself to keep walking, to push right through the barking, whining, yelping dogs until he reached the front door. He couldn't hear; he couldn't see. He didn't even say good-bye to Donita.

Outside, the sun was baking the earth, not a cloud in the sky. Across the street, runners made laps beside the wide, green river. Carl opened the car door and dropped into his stifling little car. The parking lot stretched out around him, entirely empty, not a customer in sight. He sat for a minute, clutching the steering wheel while a tear or two ran down his cheek. This hurt, he thought. This hurt like hell.

Chapter 6

On Monday evening, Hannah settled on the porch steps and watched the sky turn a purple so dense and pure that it drew the eyes in and held them. As the last light receded and the world around her went dark, she was there, alive in the moment. She saw night fall, but she couldn't have said exactly when it had happened. She'd witnessed it, and yet she hadn't. Some changes were like that, she thought, impossible to fix in time or pin down because they accreted so slowly, like stalagmites on the floors of caverns. Others were as abrupt and instantaneous as a car wreck. As it turned out, pregnancy was both—instantaneous and slow—or at least it seemed that way to Hannah. One day she wasn't pregnant and the next she was, a cosmic shift she should have felt inside her cells and under her feet, the ground moving, the world groaning in anticipation of yet another mouth to feed. But her awareness of it increased ever so slowly. Even now, there were moments when she didn't quite believe in it.

Once it was fully dark, Hannah rose from the porch and crossed the yard to the sidewalk. The neighborhood she and Carl lived in was about thirty years old and solidly middle class—brick houses set back in expansive front yards, trees grown tall and stately—an established and comfortable place to live. The streetlights glowed, illuminating asphalt and sidewalks but not much more. The yards fell away into darkness. The search for Neil had been going on for four days now, long enough for it to be ritualized, a walk at dusk that became, day by day, less about finding a dog and more about remembering one. That's why she'd taken to waiting for nightfall, when she could conjure him out of a tree stump or a bag of garbage, and for an instant, until reason kicked in, feel happy.

Hannah rarely spoke to her neighbors, but she assumed most were retired. Sunday afternoons, children appeared for a few hours, then disappeared for another week. Parties were a rarity, a few couples over for backyard barbecues but nothing more ambitious than that. This time of evening, only a few older men were out, moving water sprinklers. Hannah called to one of them from the sidewalk, inquiring as to whether he'd seen a cocker spaniel. He raised himself and hobbled over, listening carefully as Hannah explained that Neil was blind. In the dimness of the street lamp, she watched him ponder her question. "Can't say as I've seen him," he finally answered, shaking his large head slowly. "But *my* eyesight's not what it used to be either." He spoke to Hannah as though they'd traveled some distance together, but she couldn't remember ever seeing him before.

It occurred to her that this man wasn't much older than her father, who might be out in the twilight of his own yard, moving the sprinkler while his wife, Harriet, washed the dinner dishes. Some neighbor woman might be inquiring about another lost dog. Sad stories, stories much sadder than her own, were unfolding all over Texas. Even so, she hoped her father's shoulders were straighter, that his breathing wasn't quite so ragged. She seldom thought about her dad, and as she stood before this old man, a wave of regret passed through her. She wanted to take this stranger in her arms and hold him for a minute, and she went so far as to reach out and touch his sleeve. If it hadn't been dark, he would have seen the tears in her eyes. Why are you crying, he might have asked; she couldn't have said, not really.

For a while, she called Neil's name, but the sound of her own voice, so small and plaintive in the quiet of the evening, made her unaccountably sad. So far, the hardest part about being pregnant wasn't the nausea or the vomiting but the thoughts and feelings that came over her with the urgency of an illness. All that she was forced to consider and reconsider: her childhood, her marriage, her sense of herself as someone too tight, too emotionally controlled for motherhood. In her heart, she knew she wasn't like them, never would be. Hannah wasn't a "mother-woman," her name for those females who are drawn to children, their own or anybody else's, with a strange instinctual ardor. To coax a smile, kiss a cheek, sing a lullaby, or brush away a tear—these were a mother-woman's great joys. Helen was such a woman; Hannah was not. Even as a child, Hannah had shown no interest in babies and very little in dolls. The only one she remembered asking for was Chatty Cathy, a doll that had created the same sort of fervor as Cabbage Patch Kids would years later. What a disappointment! Chatty Cathy's voice had grated, and her words were empty. She did say "I love you," but she said it so often that it meant nothing. Even as a nine-year-old, Hannah had realized that the doll would declare her love to anyone who pulled her string.

This, finally, was Hannah's objection to mother-women. They were indiscriminate when it came to the objects of their affection. Any round face, any wet chin or grasping little hand would do. Hannah understood why this had to be. Mother-women lived in the present, never thinking past babyhood. When it came to infants, you had no other choice. Babies were not like Chatty Cathy dolls, all cast from the same mold, all dressed alike and mouthing the same empty phrases. No. While babies might have superficial similarities, bald heads and dimpled knees, there were all sorts of profound differences. Some were colicky; some were peevish. Some grew up to be sniveling cheats, wife beaters, even—God forbid—serial murderers. They broke their mothers' hearts. Let's face it, Hannah thought, giving up her search for another day and turning back the way she'd come. Every piece of shit on the face of this earth began life with a round face and a silly grin. When it came to babies, mother-women were hopelessly naive.

Thoughts like these made her want to cry. One shot of hormones and she was all over the place—laughing, crying, laughing and crying at the same time. And if she was this bad at eight weeks, who knew what she'd be like in a few months? Maybe you're just tired, she told herself. The day *had* been trying. Around two o'clock, she'd stuck her head in the door of one of the girls' bathrooms—just a simple air-quality check to discourage the smokers—and discovered Erica Faber passed out drunk on the floor of the first stall. When Hannah had looked in, a sophomore and a junior were standing in front of the mirror smearing on lipstick. Both turned to meet her gaze at precisely the same instant, their mouths pursed in bright red circles, like targets at a carnival. Erica wasn't visible from the door, and if it hadn't been for the sophomore, whose eyes strayed, Hannah might simply have gone on. But she was suspicious, and, stepping inside, immediately spotted the black spandex-clad legs poking out from under the door of the first stall.

"Way to go," Hannah had heard the junior whisper.

To reach the other toilets, it had been necessary to step over Erica's legs, and evidently any number of girls had been doing just that. Erica's stall door was locked, which meant Hannah had to grab the girl's feet and drag her into view. Once she'd established that the body was still breathing, she turned to the bystanders.

"What's going on?" she asked.

The two shrugged in unison. "She was like that when we came in," the junior offered.

"And it didn't bother you?" Hannah asked. "How'd you know she wasn't dead?"

"Dead drunk, maybe. Let's just say it's not her first time, Dr. Solace." The junior was remarkably self-possessed. She turned up her red lips in a little sneer, then fished in her bag for a well-used bit of Kleenex to blot them with, something Hannah hadn't seen in a good while. Probably the junior had picked up lip-blotting from her mother, who'd seen fit to teach her smart-alecky daughter makeup tips but nothing at all about common human decency.

"Go get the nurse," Hannah had ordered the girl. "Then sit outside my office and wait."

In response, the girl had twisted her red lips and wailed, "What'd *I* do?" so loudly that Erica had actually stirred and moaned.

Hannah had pointed at the door. "It's what you *didn't* do," she'd said. And what your mother didn't do, she'd thought, as the junior flounced away, her little friend slinking after her.

But what about Erica Faber's mother? Hannah thought, trudging up the sidewalk toward home. Blaming mothers for the sins of this world was wrongheaded and destructive, but she couldn't help indulging in it now and again. Her own mother had died before Hannah reached the age of fault-finding, so what memories she had of her were comforting but suspect, consisting, as they did, of rosy scenes of domestic bliss. For instance, Hannah could have sworn that her mother had awakened her early every school morning to wet-comb and plait her hair into one long braid. She could still feel the heavy silence of the house and the tickling sensation of her mother's fingers on her neck. Yet she had never found even one photograph to corroborate this memory, her hair having been too short in all of them for even the stumpiest braid. It troubled her, sometimes, that she'd lost not only her mother but her memories, the reality having been pasted over with several layers of Hallmark sentimentality. All Hannah had left now was a papier-mâché model of a mother, something homemade and of all the wrong proportions. Had her own mother lived into Hannah's adolescence, the world and all the mothers in it might have appeared quite different to her; as it was, she held them to very strict account.

Hannah had hoped that Carl would beat her home, but she found the driveway empty, the house dark. For a moment or two, she hesitated on the sidewalk and contemplated the white front door. She'd forgotten to turn on the porch light. Alone, some women were afraid to venture out after dark, but Hannah was afraid to go indoors; she'd been this way since adolescence. Before going inside, she had to talk to herself, force her feet up the driveway then up the steps, another challenge met. I did it, she thought, as she fumbled with her keys, unlocked the front door, and stepped over the threshold. The house was silent— no dog, no husband—just Hannah to do battle with whoever or whatever might be waiting. Perhaps she'd seen too many horror movies as a teenager, but her impulse was to flip on light switches and throw open doors, cast out the bogeymen. Which was why she noticed the closed door to Carl's studio. How odd, she thought. Her husband was the sort to leave everything open: lids on jars, shower curtains, closet doors. So she had to check, she just had to.

With the flat of her hand, she pushed open the door and flipped on the light, revealing the cluttered, dusty studio, splotched here and there with bright pink flamingos. She was about to go on, but something told her to have a look around. Sometimes Hannah acted on instinct, like this afternoon when she'd discovered Erica Faber. Only this time it wasn't a girl passed out on the floor. It was a girl-child on Carl's easel, or the outlines of one. The figure had been boxed in with just the faintest outline of the background.

Hannah knew immediately that Carl must be working from a photograph, and it took her only a minute to find it, tucked under the flamingo coaster on the desk. She didn't recall the picture, nor did she recognize herself immediately. It was the house in the background that spoke to her first. Her house, she realized, the house she'd grown up in. On the day the picture had been taken, the sun had been shining brilliantly, and little Hannah had sat, squinting and cross-legged, in the summer grass. Whoever had taken the picture had stood directly in front of her, casting a shadow over her legs, one side of her face, and a stretch of grass behind her. With a start, Hannah recognized Naomi's outline. The picture said it all: a little girl situated smack in the middle of her mother's shadow, smiling up into a familiar face, a face the adult Hannah could no longer bring to mind.

"Mother," Hannah whispered. It was the shadow, the shadow that broke her heart.

Twenty-eight years had passed since that January afternoon, but the memories never blurred or diminished. It had been Helen in the car with their mother, the two of them on their way to the grocery store for bread or milk or something else their mother thought they couldn't live without. Helen had never tired of these excursions to the A&P, but they'd made twelve-year-old Hannah groan. "Bor-ing," she'd liked to say. Looking back, it seemed Naomi had always been on her way out the door to the grocery store, two, even three times a day. "Holy moly!" she'd cried, smacking her forehead with the palm of her hand, "I forgot the eggs," or the coffee or the Cheez Whiz. Hannah remembered Cheez Whiz as a staple in their household. Cheez Whiz and Tang—the food of the astronauts. That last generation of homemakers had wholeheartedly approved of anything carried in a spaceship, anything that came in a jar.

Although Helen seldom talked about the accident, although she claimed not to remember any of it, even so, Hannah knew how it must have happened. She'd been a passenger on these trips many dozens of times and knew their mother as a creature of habit. Day after day, Naomi had driven the blue Chevrolet along the same route, pulled in at the same intersection, parked in the side lot beside the red brick building, in the same spot if that was possible. The year was 1965, and everybody listened to the radio when they rode in the car. Naomi was probably humming along with the Everly Brothers or the Supremes while Helen swung her legs against the seat and chewed Juicy Fruit. The newspaper account had spelled out the rest: They'd been waiting to turn into the grocery-store parking lot when a white pickup came roaring down the street. As it reached the Chevrolet, the truck crossed the center lane and plowed straight into Naomi and Helen. Just as though the driver had intended it, according to bystanders. Of course, he hadn't. Who would intend such a thing? The truck was traveling 45 in a 25-mile-an-hour zone, but that didn't explain its careening out of control in broad daylight on a city street. The driver wasn't drunk; he wasn't tired; he wasn't in the midst of any particular turmoil. Just late, he said. And that's the only answer he could ever give. Instead of living without milk for a day, they'd had to live without their mother forever.

Hannah stared at the photograph until it blurred before her eyes, then she replaced it, backed out of the cluttered studio, and closed the squeaking door. When Carl arrived home a few minutes later, she was leaning against the kitchen counter, sipping a glass of water with trembling hands. She waited for him to say something, ask what was wrong, but he only glanced in her direction before opening the refrigerator. He looked tired and a little rumpled, she thought. And hadn't he been wearing that same plaid shirt all week? While she drank her water, he browsed through the leftovers in the refrigerator, then moved on to the contents of the pantry.

"Hungry?" Hannah asked.

"I skipped dinner," he told her. "Went to the food court but ended up sketching instead of eating."

"A real live starving artist."

He looked at her over his shoulder, grinning at her wisecrack. "Yeah, guess you could say that."

She felt bloated now and a little nauseous. "I just got back from looking for Neil," she offered.

"So late?"

"Well, he's out there somewhere. It doesn't matter what time I look, does it? Day or night, it's all the same to him."

Carl took a can of soup from the shelf. "To him," he said, "but not to you. You can't see at night. How do you expect to find him?"

"I don't expect to find him." She thought she might cry again, but she didn't. She felt numb.

Carl slid the can back onto the shelf and, without looking at her, strode from the room.

"Where you going?" she called after him.

"The studio," he said. "Got some work to finish up." She heard the creak of the door open, then close. Right about now, he'd be examining his work in progress. She could see it in her mind's eye, a little girl sitting cross-legged on the grass. It broke her heart, just as he'd hoped it would, but for all the wrong reasons. It won't work, Carl, she thought. Not this time.

HANNAH left for work early the next morning, pulled out of the driveway shortly before seven. She had a phone call to make, and she was determined to do it first thing, before the office got busy or she had a chance to change her mind.

But Erica Faber's father had a head start on her. She arrived at seven-thirty to find him sitting in a straight-back chair outside her office, an open briefcase in his lap. Already, Gabe Faber was at work, making every minute count, and for a few seconds Hannah stood in the doorway and watched. They'd never met, but she recognized the familiar chiseled features. Now she understood why Erica was handsome rather than beautiful. The girl had inherited her father's strong nose and square chin; they even had the same deep-set eyes. Where had the mother's genes gone? The only physical difference Hannah could discern was their hair color. Erica was a blonde, but Gabe Faber had brown hair, fine and thinning, carefully cut and combed.

Her first impulse was to avoid him, to simply wheel around and go back the way she'd come. Only where? Where else would she go to make such a private call? Her second impulse was to reach out and scatter his papers, knock them all to kingdom come. It was practically physical, this need to create mischief. Suddenly, she had new insight into juvenile delinquents and new empathy for them as well. All those hormones seething through their systems—no wonder they behaved like maniacs. Pregnant women and teenagers. They just can't help themselves, she thought. He looked up and smiled, holding out his hand. "Dr. Solace, I presume?"

She swung open her door. "Come in, Mr. Faber," she said, waving him into her office. As she settled herself behind the desk, he went on standing in her doorway, a short, stocky man wearing an expensive gray suit and a flashy silk tie, obviously dressed to impress or intimidate. Your clothes may mesmerize judges and juries, she thought, but they won't work with me. She offered him a seat.

"I understand that Erica has been suspended," he said.

Hannah was surprised. Most people needed to ease into the situation with preliminary chitchat about the weather or the state of public education, especially upper-middle-class parents who expected better of their children and of themselves. Generally, such parents were overly polite, prone to thanking her profusely, whereas those of longtime troublemakers tended to be hostile, deny the problem, then blame her for it. Frequently, they slammed the door as they went out. But Gabe Faber was too sophisticated, too civilized for any of those tactics. She did note, however, that he didn't look her in the eye. Instead, he studied the spot on the wall over her right shoulder, often the focal point for parents in pain. "I'm sorry we have to meet under these circumstances," she said.

He nodded and allowed a short sigh that spoke volumes: They should have been introduced at a scholastics awards ceremony or at an orchestra concert—that is, if they ever had the occasion to meet at all. The daughter of Gabe Faber's dreams would have no need of an assistant principal; she'd be too busy playing violin, modeling for the local department store, volunteering to shut-ins. Sweet, smart, and sophisticated, such a girl wouldn't have been caught dead on the floor of the high-school bathroom.

"Is there any way she can return to school tomorrow?" Mr. Faber asked now. "I think she's learned her lesson, don't you?"

Hannah shook her head and folded her hands in front of her. "Three-day automatic suspension for attending classes under the influence."

"But she wasn't in class when you found her—"

Hannah interrupted. "Mr. Faber, please. You're not in court here."

He blinked and ran a hand over the top of his head. "Sorry," he said, looking a little rueful, a little roguish, and, Hannah suddenly realized, very handsome. "I'm not trying to squeeze out on a technicality. Let me start again." He took a deep breath and forced a grin. In spite of her misgivings about his parenting skills and his bulldog of a secretary, Hannah's heart went out to him. "You may not believe this," he said, "but Erica's fine at home. A little belligerent sometimes, a little sullen, but nothing you can't live with. Most of the time she's playful, even girlish. Still keeps a legion of stuffed animals on her bed. Wears earphones and dances up and down the halls." His eyes shone; Hannah could see that he loved his daughter very much. "Sunday mornings, she fixes breakfast for the two of us." He sighed again. "You say you found her passed out on the floor of the bathroom, people stepping over her on the way to the toilet?"

Hannah nodded.

He shook his head and turned his eyes to the floor. "I can't believe that, Dr. Solace; I just can't imagine such a thing."

"I saw it with my own eyes."

He put up a hand. "I believe you. I believe you. It's just . . . that's the sign of a really unhappy girl." He paused. "I hadn't realized that Erica fell into that category."

"She's troubled. Certainly, she's troubled."

"Do you think I should get her some counseling?"

"I do."

Another sigh. "Probably should have done it a long time ago, after her mother left. Erica was six when Angela ducked out. Ten years ago. You'd think it'd be behind us now."

"Has Erica seen much of her mother in the meantime?" Hannah realized she was wringing her folded hands. Relax, she told herself. This isn't about you.

"Not at first. Angela ran off to California to"—he raised his fingers and made imaginary quotation marks in the air—" 'find herself.' Such a stupid idea, as though her real self were elsewhere, growing grapes in Sonoma or painting pictures in Sausalito." Still bitter, Hannah thought. Ten years. You'd think it would be behind *him*. Hannah wondered how much of this anger Erica was privy to. A lot, she imagined. "Just like in the movies," he added.

Hannah nodded.

"At first, I was shocked shitless." He clapped a hand to his mouth and pretended remorse. "Sorry. I've got two personas, the in-control lawyer and the out-of-control ex-husband. No, that's not true. I can be a loving father. I *am* a loving father."

"I don't doubt it," Hannah said, and she didn't.

"But I'm all out of ideas."

Hannah didn't doubt this either. "Where is Erica now?" she asked.

"Sleeping," Gabe Faber replied.

"Go wake her up," Hannah told him. "Make her clean house, paint the living room, pull weeds. Take away the car keys. Whatever you do, keep her busy and bored out of her mind for the next two days." Hannah hesitated and then plunged ahead. "This isn't a vacation. It's a suspension. Make sure she knows the difference."

He stood up, clutching the briefcase with one hand, saluting Hannah with the other. "Got it. Good-bye, Dr. Solace."

"Good-bye, Mr. Faber."

As soon as he was gone, Hannah looked up the number of the clinic and dialed it, quickly, before she could waver. While the receptionist checked the schedule, Hannah mused on Erica's mother, who'd "ducked out" for California. Although she wouldn't have told Gabe Faber, Hannah couldn't help pitying the woman, who must regret her choices, all of them—marrying the handsome lawyer, having his lovely little daughter, then being forced to leave the two of them behind. She could see how it had happened, how it might have happened to her if she'd gotten pregnant when she was younger, before she knew herself, before she really knew Carl. Before Roe vs. Wade. While Hannah might blame mothers for the sins of this world, she felt sorry for them as well. Such a heavy burden, she thought, the life of another person, yours to carry across days and weeks and years. Yours to make or break. Only the truly naive, only the mother-woman, could imagine she was up to such a task. When the receptionist came back on the line, she said, "You're in luck! A Saturday-morning appointment has just canceled." Hannah noted the time on a pad of paper. Eight-thirty. "Thank you," she said. "I'll be there."

After hanging up, Hannah sat for a few minutes, remembering her mother's shadow. It hadn't been blocked into Carl's picture, she realized. The shadow in the photograph was the flaw he'd decided to leave out.

HERS was the first appointment of the day, and Hannah arrived early, a little before eight. The receptionist was still having coffee, the smell of which turned Hannah's stomach. She took a seat on the other side of the large, empty waiting room and, a rarity in her life, spent several moments doing nothing at all. Finally, the care counselor, Maureen, appeared in the doorway and signaled for Hannah to follow her back. Today she sported a shimmery tunic of gold, green, and orange—jungle colors. "How are you?" the counselor asked when they were closed inside the examining room.

"Resigned," Hannah replied.

Maureen nodded and, after a brief hesitation, handed over a hospital shift. "One size fits none," she quipped before leaving the room. It was a standard line, obviously, her lame way of apologizing for the awful printed thing she pressed into women's hands. Putting it on, Hannah was mystified by the snaps, some at the shoulders, some in the back, none of which seemed to match up, no matter how she put the damn thing on. Finally, she gave up and slung the largest piece of cloth over her chest, sliding her arms into one hole or another, knowing, of course, that it should be open in back, to afford the maximum exposure of her rear end.

Eventually, she got her feet up in the stirrups, legs spread-eagle. Just looking at her knees wobbling above her head gave Hannah a small, sick feeling. Perversely, the air-conditioner vent was trained so that it blew cold air directly between her legs. When Maureen returned, Hannah thought to point this out, correct the problem for future sufferers, but she was afraid the counselor might feel obliged to take action right now. Above all, Hannah wanted to avoid any sort of fuss.

"Good thing you got here early," Maureen offered.

"Why's that?" Hannah asked. Turning her head, the paper sheet crinkled against her ear.

"That goddamn Dr. Bill is back."

"That preacher?" Hannah asked. She remembered hearing something on the news. "I must have just missed him. Three cars pulled up right behind me."

Maureen nodded. "Lucky you," she said in an angry voice. "Self-righteous bastard." Then, seeming to regret her vehemence, she lapsed into silence.

Hannah shifted her face to the opposite wall, which was decorated with an odd series of paintings featuring tan and white owls. At least these were someone's idea of owls, each one shaped like an inverted triangle, scrawny-looking creatures, barely able to cling to the bare branches that intersected the bottom of every picture.

"Awful, huh?" Maureen commented.

"Terrible. Who did these?"

"The doctor's mother," Maureen replied. "She gives them as Christmas presents and for birthdays." Hannah thought of Carl. He'd get a kick out of her description of the little examining-room gallery. He enjoyed other people's artwork—even in paintings as abysmal as these he could find something to admire. Then, remembering where she was and why she would never tell him, Hannah felt an odd twisting pain in her chest; her breathing turned quick and shallow.

"Maureen," she whispered, and the care counselor, clearly trained to detect subtle shifts in mood, stepped forward and took Hannah's hand.

The doctor was an older, shuffling man who smelled soapy and had a big veiny nose. Hannah wondered briefly whether he might be an alcoholic, then told herself to stop worrying. Even an alcoholic could manage this simple procedure. A tiny nurse scooted in behind him and set to work opening drawers and arranging equipment, a faint smile at the edges of her lips. Hannah marveled at her happy competence; the nurse, she realized, was thinking of something else entirely, a date this evening or a funny joke she'd heard on the way to work, utterly at home in this sterile little owl gallery. The rest of them were awkward and a little claustrophobic—shuffling, gripping, flinching—ready to play out their roles and be done with it.

The doctor introduced himself, but Hannah took no notice of his name or of the name he called her. In fact, she thought it might have been preferable to avoid names altogether. Not that she was ashamed of what she was doing, just that it was a relief to be anonymous now and then. She did hear the doctor say he would be performing an aspiration abortion, that it would take no more than five to ten minutes, that she'd be uncomfortable, and that she should expect cramps and bleeding afterward, all things she knew. He gave his little speech from the end of the examining table, then edged around and stood over her.

"Do you have any questions?" he asked.

"I've asked them all."

He smiled and patted her shoulder. They would get along, his expression said.

Hannah heard the squeak of his stool below her, and feeling his rubber-sheathed fingers brush against the outside of her vagina, she turned her head away. Besides the odd little owls, there was little to distract her. Casting her eyes about, she found nothing but the print on Maureen's long, flowing tunic, abstract palm trees that twisted across the counselor's lumpy torso. Hannah blinked and tried to bring them into focus.

When the cramping began, when her uterus tightened into a fist and forced the pain in long streaks down her thighs, Hannah clamped her mouth shut and gripped Maureen's hand.

"It's all right, now, darlin'," Maureen murmured. "Just a few minutes more. You're doin' fine, just fine." The woman was a professional consoler, Hannah thought. She went to work and held people's hands. Consolation was an industry all in itself.

"Just hold on," the doctor called to Hannah. He seemed very far away now. All that was close was the pain, which was centered in her belly but radiated down into her legs and up into her chest until she trembled with its power.

"Are you all right?" Maureen asked, bending so close that Hannah could see the fuzz on her upper lip. She nodded, then cried out a little, not from the pain, but from the frustration of being herself, of being locked away in this very body. It felt good to let go, so she tried it once more, a low wail that seemed to leave her body and hover in the room with its own small presence.

"Not much longer," Maureen murmured, reaching with her other hand to stroke Hannah's hair. "What lovely hair you have."

"It's my mother's hair." Hannah forced the words between clenched teeth, aware that every muscle in her body was tensed against the pain. Relax, she told herself, willing limpness into her feet and legs. Here it was, a realization more visceral than intellectual: She, Hannah, was really two separate beings—body and mind—one hopelessly harnessed to the other. Not that she hadn't known this all along, but it had never struck her with such certainty and clarity. There were consequences, she realized, to having a mind and a body at odds with one another. Her body might want to stay in bed, might want to eat another serving, might yearn to have a child. But her mind said no. Was it so surprising that she was overcome with dizziness or that she woke up at night with her teeth clenched tight? Hannah cried out again, a piercing scream that shamed her.

"I'm almost finished," the doctor offered.

When it was over, Maureen helped her up and into the recovery room next door. The doctor patted her shoulder as she went out, and Hannah noted that his eyes were a bewildering shade of blue. His face was tan and a little craggy; it registered concern and something else, maybe boredom or fatigue.

She wanted to address him. "Is your mother still painting the owls?" she asked.

"More every year, I'm afraid." He looked truly sad. There was more to this story, Hannah thought.

"I'm sorry," she said.

"Me too," he replied, and shuffled out.

The recovery room was larger than the exam room, big enough, in fact, for three single beds. Someone had taken trouble with the decor: Framed prints of flowers hung above each bed, and small quilts, color-coordinated to match the prints, covered the bottom half of each mattress. The room had a chaste, feminine quality that brought to mind a dormitory in a girls' school.

Sighing, she lowered her body onto the nearest bed. All she wanted was to rest her head on the plump pillow, to close her eyes. Would it be possible to sleep here, she wondered, to fall into dark, muggy dreams and wake up tomorrow on the other side of all this? But she knew that shortly, Maureen would wake and gently usher her out the door. They had their own lives, these people at the clinic, their own difficulties to go home to. The room was chilly, and it was a relief when Maureen lifted Hannah's legs and drew the sheet and quilt over her. She could not remember the last time a woman had taken such pains with her.

"There now," Maureen said. "How's that?"

Hannah rubbed a hand over the quilt. "Better." She recognized this pattern as wedding ring, one circle entwined with another.

"An anonymous gift," Maureen said, fingering the fabric. Hannah noticed Maureen wore a wedding ring, or what might have been mistaken for one. In fact, the fingers of her left hand were crowded with rings, one on each finger— gold and silver, turquoise and diamonds— but she wore no rings at all on her right hand.

"Why do you wear all your rings on one hand?" Hannah asked.

Maureen smiled. "This other one's my squeezing hand," she explained. She reached for Hannah's hand and gripped it tightly. "You close your eyes and rest for a few minutes." Maureen patted the quilt down around her, and Hannah felt as though she were shrinking, returning to girlhood. Any minute Maureen might lean down and kiss her cheek, wish her sweet dreams. "In a minute, I'll bring you some orange juice, and some Tylenol 3 for the pain. Is someone out there to drive you home?"

Hannah opened her eyes. She'd asked Helen to accompany her and been stung by her sister's refusal. "I thought you said it wasn't necessary," she replied.

"It's not." Maureen smiled and let her fingers stray to Hannah's hair, smoothing back the strands that had loosed themselves from a long French braid. Hannah sighed and closed her eyes again, so soothed by this strange woman's touch she thought she might cry.

She dozed off and waking again, had no sense at all of where she was. Except for the faint glow of a night-light, the room was dark and unfamiliar. She recalled this feeling from childhood, this faith in the night and the power of dreams. When she was five or six, it had seemed possible to do anything, even to travel in her sleep and wake up someplace entirely new. Now she wanted to slip back into slumber, but the pain was tugging at her; a small animal biting at her insides, it kept bringing her back. Someone's footsteps sounded in the clinic hallway, followed by a whiny, fearful voice: "Sir! Sir! Come back—you hear me?"

"Where is she?" The voice was familiar; the voice was Carl's.

But she hadn't told him where she was going. In fact, she'd slipped past the closed door of his studio and left without a word. So how could he be here? It felt as though he'd pursued her into a dream. Perhaps it was a dream, she told herself, just her mind playing tricks on her. To be sure, she rolled out of the narrow bed and lurched across the room. The smooth, cold floor smacked against her feet, and she wrapped her arms against the chill coming through the hospital shift. Pressing her ear to the door, she heard the voices again, murmuring now.

Hannah cracked open the door, just enough to see a clot of people blocking the hallway. At first, she couldn't tell how many there were. The receptionist stood with her back to the recovery room, hands on her hips, her long red nails pointing at each other from across her back. The doctor—a tall man, much bigger than Hannah had realized— stood wedged between the receptionist and the wall. As the receptionist continued to talk, the doctor shook his head mournfully.

Only after he'd moved aside did Hannah glimpse Carl's head. The rest of his body, and his progress toward Hannah, had been blocked by Maureen. She was a wall of orange, gold, and green, a solid presence, as hard now as she had once been soft. She seemed to have grown to fit this job, going from consoler to bouncer in the blink of an eye. "Go on back to the waiting room, sir," Maureen instructed.

Hannah went weak with gratitude. How seductive it was, this being cared for. No wonder women succumbed to it. While she stood, trying to decide whether to close the door against him or to go out and meet him head-on, blood began running between her legs, a steady stream that instantly turned both her pad and her underwear sticky and wet. The blood was warm, but chill bumps rose on her bare arms. She shivered, the dizziness returning, so that she wavered a moment too long.

"Hannah?" Carl called. He was looking right at her. Squinting, she tried to gauge his expression.

"Oh, Carl," she moaned. "Why in the world did you come?"

"It's too late. It's too late, isn't it?" Carl asked. His voice sounded choked and labored, as though he'd run all this distance. He'd been a track star in high school; she could imagine how he must have looked then, pushing toward the finish, his arms pumping, that lean body all one curved, yearning line.

She nodded. "I'm sorry." It was true, absolutely true. She was horribly sorry, though not for being here. The abortion had been a necessity, though it had obviously turned out all wrong. Nothing could be worse than having her husband out in the hallway, staring at her with this stricken expression, not a thing in this world she could do to comfort him. Some things have to be, Hannah thought; some things simply *are*.

"That was my child, my child too, Hannah!" he cried out. "You had no *right!*" Here, he broke off in a strange strangling sound. He was trying not to cry, Hannah realized, trying and failing. The sound of his pain served as a cue for the counselor. Instantly, her hands came down off the walls, the big sleeves fluttering like wings as her arms swooped around Carl's shoulders. Astonished, Hannah stood in the doorway and watched her husband sob in this strange woman's arms.

Chapter 7

ALTHOUGH FOUR CLINICS in Austin provided abortions, Gospel Fellowship had targeted only one. "The strategy," Dr. Bill had explained, "is to not spread ourselves too thin." If the protesters made appearances at all four, they could be an occasional nuisance but nothing more. By concentrating their efforts on one, by picketing every weekend and sometimes weekday mornings as well, they had a chance of shutting it down for good. "Then, on to the next death factory!" was his battle cry. About a year before, Dr. Bill had made an announcement at Sunday service: He'd had a message from the Lord to begin with the clinic on 40th Street. The congregation had sat in awed silence. Penny remembered shifting on her hard wooden pew, vaguely troubled by the notion of God mentioning street names. It was almost unbelievable, but she couldn't imagine anyone lying about such a thing. Who would be brave enough to put words in God's mouth? Certainly, she thought, not Dr. Bill.

Where the clinic was concerned, she supposed location made it particularly loathsome to the Lord. Certainly, 40th Street was an unlikely spot for a business of any sort, especially one that specialized in abortion on demand. The small concrete building squatted in the midst of a residential section not unlike old West Sixth: rows of rundown white frame houses with overgrown, weedy yards, on the very edge of respectability. Children tore up and down the sidewalks on tricycles and bicycles, shouting out hellos to passersby—friendly children, full of fun and mischief. The building had two floors; the upper one housed an ophthalmologist's office and eye clinic, its plate-glass front wall jutting out over the parking lot. Chairs ranged along this wall, and the people waiting in them were as visible as fish in an aquarium. They squirmed and hunched until their names were called, then leapt to attention and hurried out of sight. On the other extreme, the building's bottom floor was constructed like a bomb shelter, all concrete, no windows whatsoever. Women going in that door disappeared entirely.

When nothing else was happening, the protesters watched the patients in the eye clinic read magazines and try on glasses. Most of the eye patients ignored the ruckus beneath them, but occasionally the younger ones would stand with their hands pressed against the glass, peering down at the scene below. Penny often waved, but they seldom returned her greetings. She supposed she didn't seem real to them, or else they'd been warned against her by their mothers. "It's okay," she wanted to shout. "I'm on your side." When Gospel Fellowship had begun its siege against the clinic, the protesters had made mistakes and yelled slurs at young women going for routine eye checks or a new pair of glasses. "I've got bad vision," one woman yelled back, "not bad morals." That put them all to shame. Afterward, to be on the safe side, Dr. Bill had instructed them to ignore the young women wearing glasses. "But they have abortions too," Esther had complained. She couldn't bear to think that anyone might slip through. Mattie brought up contact lenses and women being fitted for glasses for the first time. "It's not a perfect system," Dr. Bill had conceded. "We do what we can."

Last Saturday, he'd been unexpectedly absent, which was too bad because they'd had a good turnout. As it happened, he'd left late on Thursday evening for an emergency trip to Shreveport and hadn't returned until very early on Sunday morning, just in time to deliver his sermon and drag himself home to bed. From her place in the third pew, Penny had made a point of looking up at him, taking note of his bloodshot eyes and the gray tint of his skin. Evidently, he'd driven straight through. His father was in the hospital, he'd told them from the podium, and he'd be grateful for their prayers. No one knew for sure what was wrong, but Mattie claimed that the man was a heavy smoker, had been all his life. "Bad habits will catch up to you sooner or later," she'd said.

Today, the protesters numbered twenty, though later in the day they might grow to twenty-five. More would have been better, but the numbers were respectable. Dr. Bill didn't think so, Penny knew. He needed at least twice that many "to make a showing," as he called it. When it came to his mission, he was as idealistic as a child and every bit as prone to disappointment. If he had his way, they'd all be single-minded in their devotion to the cause. As it was, Penny supposed only Mattie fit this description.

His most devoted followers were a group of middle-aged women who marched up and down the asphalt like an out-of-shape drill team. Today, two men had joined the ranks: Esther's husband, a huge, gloomy man who worked for the post office, and his friend, a short, quiet bachelor who wore his cowboy hat a size too small. Right now, the street was empty, not a soul in sight. The protesters didn't bother with their chant but raised their placards aloft each time a car passed: THE UNBORN SHOULDN'T GO UNHEARD. CHOOSE LIFE. DON'T DESTROY A MIRACLE. Penny had done most of the work on these signs. "Now, why did God give you all the talent?" Esther had teased her. "So I could do all the work," Penny had replied, wielding her markers and paintbrush. They'd offered to help, but she knew better than to accept. They couldn't letter, and, furthermore, they couldn't spell. One Sunday morning, Penny had ducked into the ladies' room at church and on the mirror she'd found this message smeared in red lipstick: DON'T BE AFRAD TO MEAT YOUR MAKER! Wobbly letters, unshakable devotion. God was always on their minds, even while they were sitting on the toilet.

The morning had been long and hot— the calendar said October 1, but the weather insisted on July. Driving to the clinic, Penny and Mattie had passed a bank sign flashing the temperature: seventy-eight degrees. That had been just after eight o'clock. Last Saturday, an ambitious little girl had set up a lemonade stand directly across the street from the clinic. Penny had bought three Dixie cups for herself and one for Mattie. Today, the little girl was nowhere to be seen. From time to time, Penny glanced across the street, hoping to spot a freckle-faced child hauling a card table down her driveway, but it was too hot and sticky for such an enterprise. Most of the children who lived on this street were holed up indoors, probably watching cartoons in front of a fan. Penny yearned to join them.

By ten-thirty it was sweltering. All morning, Mattie had looked wilted and confused, as though she'd been plucked from her green backyard and planted here in this asphalt desert. Business at the clinic was slow, and without her knitting, Mattie didn't know what to do with herself. Finally, she'd offered to spell Penny with Buck. Pushing the baby stroller had given her purpose and momentum; for the last half hour, she'd looked almost happy. Dr. Bill had spent most of his time leaning against the side of the building, studying the small spiral notebook in the palm of his hand. In it, he recorded the license numbers of all the women who went into the clinic, the "baby killers," as he called them.

He was dressed in his usual fashion: black cowboy boots, tight jeans, a white dress shirt, and red tie. And the Houston Astros ball cap. Too neat for a roper, too casual for a businessman. So who did he look like? Penny wondered. Like himself, was all she could think. Surely no one driving by would take him for a minister. He wore his thick brown hair longish, and on humid days like this, the ends curled around the edges of his ball cap. So calm he was, so contained. The back of his shirt stuck to his skin, but she knew he'd never complain of the heat. The heat *was*, the heat could not be changed. What would be the point in remarking on it? Now he ventured out to chat with Penny, pulling her away from the others and reminding her of their date this evening.

"What do you think?" he asked.

"I think it's too hot," she replied. "I think I need an umbrella or a garden hose."

He took a handkerchief from his back pocket and gently wiped her forehead. "No, I mean about the wedding," he said. "What did you decide?" More than once, he'd advised her to accept the dress and all that went with it, the maid-of-honor role in her mother's wedding. "Who knows?" he'd asked. "This could be the beginning of a whole new relationship for you." Privately, Penny doubted it, but his optimism had given her the courage to make the call.

"I decided to go," Penny told him. "I called Delia yesterday."

He grinned widely and slapped her on the shoulder. "See there!" he crowed. "And I'll bet she was pleased, wasn't she?"

"She said she'd been keeping her fingers crossed," Penny replied, eyeing the protesters clustered near the street. Mattie had parked the stroller and was busy waving her placard over little Buck and several others standing nearby. All had turned their faces to her, grateful for the breeze. Mattie was talking to Esther while she fanned, and the two seemed absorbed in their conversation. Still, Penny felt compelled to lower her voice. "Delia wanted to know if Grandmother will come." Dr. Bill leaned in closer, till the bill of his cap grazed the side of her head. "I told her I didn't know. The thing is, I do." She shook her head. "I know it would take a telegram from God Himself to get her there."

Dr. Bill put an arm around her shoulder and drew her to him. "That's between the two of them," he said. "Let *them* sort it out." He hesitated, then went on to share a bit of his own history. "You know, my father was a stranger for most of my childhood," he began. "Wouldn't have recognized the man on the street." A little anger had crept into his voice. "To tell you the truth, I hated his guts for not caring enough to look me up once in a while. My mother, she hated him even more than I did."

Confused, Penny drew back and looked up at him, searching his face for the truth. "But wasn't that him in the hospital? Didn't you just go see him?"

He nodded knowingly. "That I did. It's a long story, but let's just say that I was wrong too. We can all be wrong. *The Lord maketh poor, and maketh rich: He bringeth low, and lifteth up.*" About then, Buck began to cry, his wail sailing over the black asphalt. "Someone's calling you," Dr. Bill said, reaching out to pat her shoulder before retreating to his spot against the clinic wall.

Already, Mattie was rolling the broken-down stroller in Penny's direction. It took real effort. One wheel stuck, and the handles were too short for comfort. She arrived at Penny's side red-faced and panting. "I'm worn out," she called over Buck's screams, "and this baby's wet." She wrinkled her nose. "Smell him?" Mattie shoved the stroller in front of Penny. "Your turn, Ninny-Penny. Why don't you find someplace to change him?" She pointed to a shady patch of grass in the front yard of a small frame house facing the clinic. "Doesn't look like anyone's at home over there."

Buck was batting at her knees with his sneaker. "It's all right," she told him. She didn't blame him for being angry; he was overheated, poor darling, and so was she. Straightening, she looked off across the street. The shade beckoned. "Fine," she agreed, giving the stroller a shove. "I think I'll let him crawl in the grass, cool off a bit."

Eyes on her destination, Penny didn't see the rust-colored Mazda until the last moment, when it screeched up to the curb in front of her. The driver was in a horrible hurry; he lurched out of the car and left his door hanging open. A tall, lithe man in gray sweatpants and a white T-shirt, he rushed past her and toward the protesters, waving his hands, as though to shoo them out of the way. Penny turned back and saw Dr. Bill step out of the shadow of the building and raise his arms skyward, a cue for the others to take up their chant: "Freedom of choice is freedom to kill. We won't stop until you will." They edged together and held hands, a long line stretching across the lot and blocking the man's path. She couldn't see his face, only the back of his curly head as he stood directly in front of them, stomping his foot and shouting something she couldn't hear.

Dr. Bill raised the bullhorn and roared into it: "We're not the enemy, they are!" The line of protesters jumped at the volume—God Himself seemed to be speaking—but the man held his ground. Dr. Bill lowered his bullhorn but went on yelling. "You're here to save your baby, right?"

The man nodded.

"Then get to it!" Dr. Bill boomed.

The line of protesters opened, allowing the distraught father to run through. When he'd disappeared into the concrete bunker, Dr. Bill suggested a silent prayer for this man and his unborn child. They all lowered their heads. Penny clutched the handles of the stroller and asked God to show her his plan. Give me a role to play, dear God, she prayed.

Sighing, she opened her eyes on Buck's gleaming black hair. Sweet little Buck. Now he was busy sucking his shoe. Mess or no mess, who couldn't love such a child? Who wouldn't want him? But she knew Buck's father wasn't the least bit interested. He'd visited his child just once, at the hospital shortly after the birth. Penny had been there; she'd seen him skulk in, a stocky blond man who hadn't even bothered to bring flowers. He'd spent maybe fifteen minutes with Juanita and glimpsed his son through the glass on his way out. Clearly, he couldn't have cared less, and nothing Juanita had done since then had made the least impression on Buck Sr. And here was this frantic man, desperate to save a child, only this time the *mother* didn't want it. How could that be? Penny didn't begin to understand it, not any of it, but her heart hurt for all of them.

After the prayer, Dr. Bill found his way to Penny's side, and together they stared at the Mazda parked at the curb, its door still hanging open. "Poor bastard," he said, shaking his head and tugging on the bill of his baseball cap. "I've been there; I feel for him."

"I wish there were something we could do," Penny said. "Shouldn't we at least close the door?"

Dr. Bill strode away to take care of it and Penny pushed on with the stroller, heading for the grass. On her way, she glanced through the car window and spied a sketchbook on the backseat and a dog collar curled on the floorboard, evidence of a life lived. Probably a very nice man, she thought, an artist, a dog lover. It wasn't until she'd settled in the grass and lifted Buck out of the stroller that Dr. Bill's remark sunk in: "I've been there," he'd said. "I feel for him." Did that mean what she thought? Had he really lost something so precious?

She lay Buck in the grass and dug in the diaper bag for supplies. She hadn't changed many diapers, but Buck made it easy, obliging her by raising his feet into the air and spreading his dimpled thighs, then clamping his eyes shut, as though to spare her any further embarrassment. Underneath the soaked diaper, she discovered an angry-looking rash that wrapped around his genitals and spread down across his bottom. It looked painful, and when Penny touched his skin with a wet wipe, Buck whimpered pitifully. Tears leaked from the slits of his closed eyes, and Penny scooped him up, bare-bottomed, to kiss his face. "It's all right," she murmured. "We'll leave this old thing off for a while. Let your little bottom get some air."

She was still cuddling him when a burgundy Volvo station wagon lumbered into the lot across the street. Penny watched its progress, fascinated and a little frightened. The car was as wide as a tank and just as effective in scattering the protesters—the woman driver maneuvered right through the crowd and pulled into the spot closest to the clinic door. Maybe she thought the size of her car would intimidate the protesters, but if so, she was wrong. As soon as she and her young daughter had ventured from the car, Dr. Bill raised the bullhorn, and his voice rang through the heavy air.

"Ladies and gentlemen, let's say a prayer for this child and for this child's child."

Hearing their cue, the faithful rushed into position. "Now I lay me down to sleep," they intoned. Even from across the street, Penny could hear them clearly. Their voices were solemn, and several fell to their knees in the attitude of praying children. It was theater, really, and the mother and daughter, a pair of blondes in shorts and T-shirts, were the captive audience. They stood and stared, mouths open. From this distance, Penny couldn't gauge their ages, but without the car surrounding her, the mother looked nearly as small and helpless as her daughter. "I pray the Lord my soul to keep. If I should die before I wake—" Silence. "I pray the Lord my soul to take."

They'd practiced at church, over and over, Dr. Bill shouting at them to hold on to those silent seconds. Penny had practiced with them, but now she was part of the audience, and like the other two, rapt and appalled. She bit her lip and clutched at Buck, who squirmed to get his shoe, half-hidden in the high grass. Penny leaned forward to grab it, and by the time she returned her attention to the scene across the street, the mother and daughter were struggling. The girl strained to get away—from her mother, the clinic, and the protesters—but the older woman wouldn't let go. She gripped her daughter's arm, legs braced as though for a game of tug-of-war. Dr. Bill stood off to the side, hands on his hips, like a referee.

"Let her go! Let her go!" shouted the protesters.

A storm of emotion crossed the older woman's face—grief, frustration, rage. What was she to do? Her daughter was still a child, after all, dressed in a pink T-shirt and white sneakers, cheeks rosy with exertion, tears running down her face. The mother's grip said, I know what's best for you, as she literally dragged her child toward the clinic door.

Dr. Bill shouted through the bullhorn for the whole block to hear: "Will you force her to lie down on that table as well? Will you hold her while they wrest the life from her body? Your grandchild! That life is your grandchild!"

It took only seconds for his words to sink in. Penny witnessed the mother's response, watched it unfold, as though in slow motion. Later, it occurred to her that all important moments are perceived slowly, each anguished or ecstatic second pulled and stretched to fit over a wider, longer space. Time is unpredictable that way. Years pass in minutes, minutes in years. The mother turned to Dr. Bill and abruptly let go of her child. The daughter staggered backward and fell to the asphalt with a cry, but the mother paid her no mind. Only Dr. Bill was in her field of vision now. She walked numbly in his direction. His face shone with sweat and victory as he lowered the bullhorn and put out a hand. Penny could see it: him so pleased, her so full of grief, which is why what happened next didn't surprise her. The mother's fist swung out and smashed into Dr. Bill's jaw with all the force she had left. It was enough. Penny heard him groan, saw him wobble then drop to the ground. The protesters rushed to him, but Penny stayed put. She felt in this moment that she didn't know him, that she didn't know any of them, really. The world around her loomed immense. The blue sky over her head, once a benign bowl, became a vast empty space even God could get lost in.

Now the mother was spent. She trudged to her car, fell into it, and, bending over the steering wheel, managed to start the ignition. She didn't seem to notice that her daughter had disappeared. Penny expected her to drive away and leave her child. But as the station wagon pulled into the street, the girl appeared in the next yard, stepped out from behind a tree, and waited. The mother braked and, once the daughter was safely inside the car, leaned across the seat to lock the door. Penny watched as they held each other tightly, both of them crying, the station wagon stalled in the street.

Chapter 8

Outside the goddamn birds were singing—twittering, twerping, chirping their little lungs out. How dare they be happy? Carl thought. How dare the sun shine? But it did shine, gloriously, bowing its head over him as he slumped against the back wall of the clinic and stared across the chain-link fence to a slope studded with the bright yellow heads of dandelions. Where was the Dumpster? he wondered. There had to be one. This was what they did with the garbage, wasn't it? Shoved it out the back door?

The large, soft woman in the hallway had allowed him to finish his crying—she'd sensed when it was over, even before he did—and chosen just the right moment to lead him away from his wife, and away from the waiting room too, he'd realized too late. She'd been all warmth and solicitude until they reached the back of the building. Then the comforting arm around his shoulder had tensed, and he'd been pushed out an open service door and into the alley.

The midday light was blinding, but the shock wasn't just to his eyes; no, this was a shock to the psyche as well. Carl had just turned forty and should have been used to it by now, this tendency for one absolute to give way to its opposite. Dark to light. Happiness to despair. Life to death. The world was full of such shifts, but he still hadn't managed to believe in them. He'd whirled about and beaten the door with his fist before throwing himself against it for good measure. Nothing. It was locked tight. "Hannah, you selfish bitch," he screamed. "I could kill you, do you hear me?" And then again, louder, the loudest he could ever remember screaming. "YOU HEAR ME?" But he knew she didn't. Hannah wasn't on the other side of this door; she was down the hall and behind another one. The walls were concrete, the door reinforced metal—strong enough, he supposed, to withstand artillery, even a goddamn grenade. Carl's feeble pounding would make no impression whatsoever.

As he sank down beside the door, something feathery brushed the side of his face and he waved his hand to chase it away. A mosquito, a moth, a horsefly, a ghost? Who knew? If anyplace in the world was haunted, surely it would be this one. He'd never believed in ghosts as a child, but now he felt sure of their presence. They swirled above and about him, barely conceived beings. Carl imagined the large woman in the hallway, shooing the little nuisances out the service door as her last duty of the day. "Go back where you belong," she told them. Only where did they belong? Now his child was among them, a faceless, bodiless something. It was so damn sad. Didn't Hannah realize how sad this was?

To keep from crying, he kicked at a small pile of cigarette butts, sending them rolling in a dozen directions. Evidently, someone slipped out here periodically to smoke and ponder her place in the universe, probably the receptionist with the long red fingernails, who looked permanently peeved. In any case, the smoker had to be a *she*. The only *he* in the building was the doctor, that shifty-eyed bastard who'd met him in the hall. The man was nervous, sure, why not? Outside the clinic, they'd as soon shoot him as look at him—abortion doctors were good for target practice these days. Inside, he wasn't much better off. He was in alien territory: the Rape Crisis, Abortion, Death-To-All-Men Clinic. If the sisterhood tolerated his presence, it was only because they needed him.

Carl, well, him they had no use for. Carl they tossed out the back door with a swift kick to the butt. No, he told himself, don't indulge yourself, no wallowing in self-pity. You were not kicked. You were pushed, your intelligence insulted. That's all. "Your car's around front," the lady bouncer had said, as though, left to his own devices, he might have wandered the neighborhood for weeks. Better get up, Carl, he told himself. Better get a grip.

Something was going on out front. The closer he got to the parking lot, the more noise he heard: shouting, the screech of tires, the sound of someone sobbing. Carl edged along the wall until he had a vantage point. The protesters had formed a tight circle in the center of the parking lot, all of them clustered around something or someone. Through a gap, he glimpsed someone on the ground, a length of leg and a black boot. Of course, the preacher, Dr. What's-His-Name. His picture had been in the paper a few weeks back. He'd even been interviewed on television. Sanctimonious bastard, Carl thought. Likely someone had decked him. Plenty of people had good reason. Hell, given the chance, Carl would hit the guy too. Dr. Bob, was that his name? Whatever. Carl resented the way the preacher had cheered him on as he'd run into the clinic. Making all kinds of assumptions about whose side was whose. Angry as Carl was with Hannah, he found no comfort in this ragtag little band of fundamentalists. They weren't his comrades. They didn't know a thing about his pain.

While he watched, a television van equipped with a satellite dish pulled up behind his Mazda, inching forward until the two vehicles were bumper to bumper. The doors slid open, the crew leapt out, two at time, tense-faced, shoulders laden with equipment, like Marines landing on an enemy beach. Seeing them, the protesters opened their ranks and broke out in song: "Yesterday, all my troubles seemed so far away." Even with the sun beating down on him, Carl felt an instant chill. Something of the pitch and tenor of the voices disturbed him, but they were halfway through the song before he understood.

The lyrics were the same, but they were no longer those of a lover left behind; now an unborn child wailed a lament. "Why she had to go, I don't know, she wouldn't say. I said something wrong, now I long for yesterday." Carl couldn't believe it. Everywhere he went, the music he'd loved as a teenager was being subverted and twisted, used for every sort of selling, from tennis shoes to automobiles. And now this. Surely, John Lennon was spinning in his grave. The singers raised placards depicting a fetus in the womb, a photograph enlarged hundreds of times, one fishy eye staring out into nothingness, the tiny arms pressed against a distended belly. Everything was distorted and exposed, the fetus, the song, the scene before him.

Given the distraction, Carl thought he might skirt the edge of the parking lot and make his way back to the car. If he was careful, he could maneuver his car around the van and be off the street before anyone noticed. He was making good progress, had just reached the corner of the building, when a police car slid around the corner and coasted up in front of the Mazda, sandwiching his car. "Shit," he muttered. When a second patrol car screeched to a stop beside the first, Carl shrank back against the building. All at once, he realized that the cops might be there for reasons other than Dr. Bob. Wasn't it possible that someone in the clinic had heard his threats and called the police? "I could kill you, Hannah!" he'd screamed. He hadn't meant it, but that wouldn't matter now. A threat was a threat. The doors to the patrol cars swung open, and the whine of a police radio filled the air.

Pressing himself to the clinic wall, Carl retreated, moving back one step at a time, until he was standing in the alley, a long, straight stretch of concrete that led down the hill and into a residential neighborhood. He didn't really think about it, just took off running and kept it up—two blocks, then three—until he reached a shady sidewalk and a row of white frame houses. Winded, he slowed to a walk, turning toward 38th Street. He hoped the police would be gone by the time he reached the corner, that he'd be able to retrieve his car, go home, and change clothes. He guessed he was already late to work, maybe an hour or more. After Helen's call, he'd dashed out of the house in sneakers and sweats, without shaving, showering, or combing his hair. And now that he thought of it, without his wallet or a handful of change. If his car was still blocked in, he couldn't even call for a cab.

He was a house or two away from 38th Street when another cop car sped past, no siren but quite a bit of speed. That told him all he needed to know: The cops weren't leaving anytime soon. Rather than head back toward the clinic, he crossed at the corner, and when the first vehicle came by, a white service van, stuck out his thumb. It was a gesture of futility, really. God knows, he didn't expect anything to come of it. To his surprise, though, the van stopped, and when he stepped up to the passenger-side door, a lovely young woman leaned over and rolled down the window. Maybe it was her old-fashioned white blouse, her narrow face and wispy hair, maybe it was her dark somber eyes, but she appeared kind. Just looking at her made him feel better.

"Can I give you a ride?" she asked in a clear voice.

He told her yes, and when she asked where, he didn't even think about it. "The Humane Society," he answered. If he couldn't save one thing, maybe he could save the other. It surprised him the way she responded, all business, like a taxi driver. "Get in," she said, and in less than a minute, they were on their way.

On the drive over, they were mostly silent. He told her his name and she told him hers. "Penny Reed," she said. When she mentioned her business, delivering flowers and balloons, Carl assumed she was on the job. She remarked on the heat. He agreed that it was unseasonably hot and, leaning back in the seat, closed his eyes. Talking was such an effort. His jaw was rigid, his tongue swollen. Slowly but surely, he thought, I'm turning to stone. The van sped up as Penny Reed swung onto the highway. It felt good to let her drive, to relinquish responsibility. He kept his eyes shut and tried not to imagine what he'd find—or not find—at the Humane Society. Why hadn't he asked Donita how many days Neil had left? Better yet, why hadn't he taken his dog home when he'd had the chance? How could he have been so trusting? So cruel?

When he opened his eyes, Penny was turning the van into the parking lot of the pound. "Here we are," she said quietly. After turning off the ignition, she leaned over the seat and grabbed her canvas bag. She was getting out, Carl realized. "You're going in?" he asked. It had been a long time since he'd hitchhiked, but he was pretty sure this wasn't standard procedure. The driver was supposed to drop off the passenger and be on her busy way.

"Is that okay?" she asked.

"Don't you have other things to do?"

"Yes," she said. "But this isn't going to take all day, is it?"

"I hope not." Then: "No, of course it isn't. Sure, come on in. Free country."

Penny Reed swung open her door and sprang from her seat onto the sidewalk. She was full of energy, but Carl couldn't move. He was afraid, he realized, afraid of losing something else. Afraid he might go all to pieces. In the meantime, the young woman was patient; she stood on the sidewalk in front of the building and gazed out over the sparkling river. Carl stared at her through the windshield and saw that she'd buttoned her blouse wrong; it hung unevenly over her jeans, the collar higher on one side than on the other. So, she'd been in a hurry this morning as well.

If the man behind the counter had been elsewhere, back feeding the dogs or scooping poop as his job description called for, things might have turned out differently. But he was a gawker—Carl knew the type, the sort of employee who hangs out at the counter and stares at customers until they're so uncomfortable they rush for the door. He'd hired his share of them, and they were hell to get rid of.

"Can I help you?" the young man asked in a supercilious voice.

"Yeah," Carl said. "I'm here to look for my cocker spaniel." He glanced around for Donita and was relieved not to see her. He had no idea how he would explain leaving his dog, the old, blind animal she had such contempt for.

"Adopt or reclaim?" the guy asked. He put down the pamphlet he was reading and reached for a form in a basket on the counter.

"Reclaim," Carl said. "Neil wandered off a little over a week ago, and someone told me he's here." Penny was standing just behind him, listening. Her presence calmed him; he began to feel a bit hopeful.

"Someone called from our office?"

"No," Carl replied irritably, "not someone from your office, just a friend who happened to be here."

The gawker looked around the empty room. "Not many people *happen* to be here."

"What difference does it make? I have reason to believe my dog is here. I'd like to check."

"Okay." The guy had a pen in his hand, and he raised it to his mouth and bit down so hard the plastic cracked and broke. "You'll need to fill out this form," he said, shoving a piece of paper across the counter and holding out the pen.

"Thanks for your help," Carl replied, and stalked away to a corner chair, wiping the end of the pen on his pants leg. He got busy scrawling answers in tight little boxes; not until he was halfway through the form did he think to check on Penny. When he looked up, he saw that she was studying a poster of a mother cat surrounded by kittens. HOW MANY KITTENS CAN ONE CAT PRODUCE IN TWO YEARS? The answer, he read, was 72,000. By the time he finished the form, she'd wandered off.

At the counter, the young man skimmed Carl's answers. "Okay," he said. "I need to see some I.D."

"Excuse me," Carl said slowly, pretending a patience he didn't feel. "Why do I have to show I.D.?"

The young man sighed. "So I can be sure you are who you say you are, that you weren't in here last week reclaiming some other dog." He paused and gave Carl a close look. "That you're here for legitimate purposes."

Carl was tempted to say something smart, but he answered politely: "Can't you just take my word for it? I left this morning without my wallet. I'm a regular guy having a bad day. I know my dog is here, and I want to take him home." The cold weight of guilt settled in his gut, metallic and heavy.

"Look," the employee said, his tone jacked up to the level of argument. "We've got rules and regulations and reasons behind them. You gotta show I.D. before going back to reclaim. If your dog's there, you'll pay a twenty-five-dollar fee to take him home."

"I don't have twenty-five dollars. Not with me, anyway."

"Then you'll have to come back when you do."

"You're kidding me, right?"

The young man shook his head. "Afraid not."

Carl left the counter to pace the room a couple of times, pausing at the entrance to the cat room. All he could see were the cages, floor to ceiling. The third time around, he spotted an elderly couple coming through the front door. The man was carrying a leash, the woman a handful of wadded tissues. Just the distraction he needed. Carl ducked inside and discovered Penny behind a row of freestanding cages, in the midst of lifting out a long-haired tabby, an immense cat so overgrown she couldn't pull him out of the cage.

"What are you doing?" he asked.

"Give me a hand?"

"What?"

"This cat is stuck."

Shit, Carl thought. He'd just hatched a plan and this cat wasn't any part of it.

"Here. Let me," he said. Penny moved aside, watching as he grasped the cat under its front legs and yanked. The tabby meowed, a ragged, pitiful sound, then slipped free. Carl thrust the animal into her arms. She was slight and small; he'd seen bigger ten-year-olds. Pressed to her narrow chest, the cat looked enormous.

"I need your help," he told her. "I'm going to get my dog, and then we're gonna have to leave in a hurry." She listened carefully. "I'm talking a bank-robbery situation here—only it's my dog I'm stealing. Do you understand?"

She nodded, her expression earnest. Was there nothing he could say to surprise her?

"You're the getaway driver," Carl told her, "so could you jam that cat back in his cage?" It was then that he noticed the other cats milling at her feet.

Her eyes followed his. "Sorry," she said softly. Tails waved in the air like dancing question marks. One cat stretched dramatically, lengthening its body along the cement floor. A kitten with mottled fur turned the corner and padded toward them. So she'd taken it upon herself to free the felines, Carl thought. Part of him was enchanted, but he couldn't stay to watch. The counter employee would come looking for him any second now, and he still had to find Neil.

He literally ran down the corridor between the dog cages and reached Neil's cage in only a few seconds. Neil was still in it, still alive. "Neil," he panted. "Here I am, buddy." The animal raised his head and moaned, conveying his feelings so clearly that Carl's throat clutched. "I'm sorry; I'm sorry," he said.

He was pulling Neil out of the cage when the employee cried out: "Put that dog back!" The guy was hurrying in Carl's direction, arms pumping, the slick soles of his shoes sliding on the concrete floor. He was bigger than he'd looked behind the counter, dangerously large really, but he moved awkwardly.

Carl's hands were full. Neil was maybe forty or fifty pounds and unwieldy. He'd never liked being held, and he didn't make it easy.

"Hold still," Carl muttered, then, over his shoulder, he spoke to the man coming up from behind. "This is my dog. I filled out the form, and I'm taking him home."

"How do I know he's yours?"

"Easy," Carl answered. He turned so the guy could get a good look at Neil's gray muzzle and milky eyes. "This dog is thirteen years old and blind. Why would I want him if he wasn't already mine?"

The logic was inescapable. The guy shrugged. "So take him. Only I've got to have the fee. Twenty-five dollars to reclaim."

"I told you. I don't have twenty-five dollars." Carl's voice was shaking, but he forged on. "This is my dog. His name is Neil. First thing tomorrow, I'll send you a check for twenty-five dollars . . . on my word."

"Your word doesn't mean a thing to me," the guy replied, but the sneer was gone. His expression was sober now, perhaps even vaguely friendly. There was something a little doglike about his face, the nose long, like a collie's, Carl thought. But he wasn't going to prove he was a human being. No way would he give in.

Penny Reed had come up behind them. "I've got twenty-five dollars," she said.

Carl thanked her all the way out the door. "You saved us; you saved us both."

She didn't turn back to look at him, so he had to content himself with talking to the back of her neck, a lovely slender length of skin that disappeared into the white collar of her blouse. "I'll get the money back to you, don't you worry."

"I'm not worried," she finally told him. She seemed embarrassed, though he had no idea why.

Back in the van, they were silent until Penny was about to get on Mopac. Carl held Neil in his lap, arms wrapped tightly around him.

"Where to now?" the young woman asked. "Should I take you back to the clinic?"

The clinic? Carl was too stunned to speak. He turned to her. Was the woman a psychic or what? He knew he hadn't mentioned the clinic. Her eyes were on the road; she seemed to be concentrating on driving, but Carl noted that she kept one hand on the canvas bag in her lap. He blinked and looked closely. Was he crazy or did the bag seem to be moving?

Penny repeated her question. "Your car's at the clinic. Should I take you back now?"

"How do you know that?" Neil was struggling, trying to nose his way toward Penny's lap. "Stop that," Carl told him.

"I was there," Penny was saying. "I saw you go in."

"You did? Did you know my wife had an abortion this morning?" Hearing the words hurt like hell. He had to close his eyes and concentrate to keep from crying, send the tears back where they came from. And that's when he saw her in his mind's eye, the slight young woman dragging a stroller away from the crowd. I've been picked up by a pro-lifer, he thought, a beautiful zealot. But he couldn't follow the thought because his dog was determined to scramble out of his lap and into hers. "Neil!" Carl grabbed his back legs and pulled. And then he spied the mottled kitten peering out of the canvas sack.

"It's all right, kitty," Penny said softly as she reached down to caress the tiny head. "I know it's a sin to steal," she told Carl, "but I couldn't just go off and leave him." She smiled to herself, as though pleased with the decision, but she kept her eyes on the road.

Part

II

Chapter 9

HANNAH DROVE HOME SLOWLY, rumbling above the street in her Blazer, both hands on the wheel. It felt strange to be on her own again, negotiating intersections, blinking away the sunshine. The buildings on either side of the street looked strangely unfamiliar in the bright afternoon light: pawnshops, hardware stores, governmental agencies. Her eyes had passed over them hundreds of times, but she didn't recognize them now. They looked like movie sets to her, the people going in and out suspiciously like extras. This wasn't real life, she thought, but something approximating it. Only a few hours had passed in the clinic, but she'd gotten used to the quiet and the dark, to Maureen hovering about, her very own guardian angel. Funny how reassuring the lumpy woman's presence was. Leaving the dark little dormitory room had made Hannah teary-eyed and clingy. "Are you sure I have to go?" she wanted to ask. Fortunately, her sense of dignity had rescued her. Bad enough to have a husband who made scenes in front of perfect strangers. Hannah was determined not to make matters worse. She'd listened quietly to Maureen's instructions. Bed rest, fluids, pain relievers when necessary. And no heavy lifting for the next few weeks. Expect light to moderate bleeding, the counselor had said, and watch for signs of complications: fever, vomiting, fainting. "We'll expect to see you for a follow-up in three weeks. Go ahead and make your appointment on the way out."

Before leaving, Hannah had tried to apologize for Carl, but Maureen had shushed her. "Not your fault," she'd said, though that wasn't entirely true and they both knew it. In a family situation, no one person is ever to blame. Counseling 101. Hannah had recognized the glancing pat on the shoulder and Maureen's forced little grimace of a smile, having used them herself on stunned and suspicious parents. "Not your fault," she'd whisper, aware of her lie and of the absolute necessity for it. Perfect strangers couldn't go around blaming each other, not if they wanted to get anything accomplished.

Halfway home, Hannah was beset by craving. The cramping had abated, and for the time being, she felt like her old self again, only hungrier. Suddenly, she was ravenous for a cheeseburger and a strawberry shake. Maureen had told her to drive straight home, but their cupboard was bare; a bowl of soup or a peanut butter sandwich was the best she'd do there. Hannah had in mind thick slabs of tomato, curly lettuce, melted cheese, and tender charbroiled beef. Maybe, she thought, I can find a good burger at Holiday House or the Nighthawk, two local restaurants. She thought she'd seen a Holiday House on Airport Boulevard, not far from Highland Mall, so she headed in that direction. She was in no hurry to get home. The house would be empty. Carl would be at work by now, or at least she hoped he would be.

Here was the odd thing: Leaving the clinic, she'd spotted his Mazda parked out front, one wheel bumped up over the curb. Before she sent Hannah on her way, Maureen had hugged her tight and whispered, "Be careful out there." Having braced herself for a swarm of protesters, Hannah was relieved by the peace and quiet that greeted her. Nothing and nobody about. Almost eerie. Then she'd seen Carl's car and gone cold inside. Her husband, then? She had to be careful of him? But he hadn't sprung out at her as she crossed the lot, popped up out of the backseat, or jumped from behind a tree as she pulled away. In fact, it seemed he'd disappeared altogether. Just to be sure, she'd driven past the Mazda and, from the high perch of the Blazer's driver's seat, glanced inside. Carl's car, no doubt about it. She'd spotted his sketchbook on the backseat and, if her eyes hadn't deceived her, Neil's red collar curled on the floorboard. What was that all about? Just now she was too disheartened to figure it out.

The Holiday House was right where she remembered it and still very much in business. Lunch rush was on, the parking lot respectably full. Hannah squeezed the Blazer into the nearest empty space and slipped gingerly out of the driver's seat, feeling unaccountably fragile. For a second or two, she simply stood and took stock of herself, all there and relatively steady on her feet. The smells of grilling meat wafted through the air of the parking lot, and Hannah's mouth watered as she walked up to the door.

Inside, the decor was a cross between a hunting lodge and a diner— wooden beams and fake chandeliers presided over orange Naugahyde booths and shiny linoleum floors. Some of this, a little of that. Holiday House had the menu of a restaurant and the service of a fast-food establishment. Customers stood in one of several lines to order and then took a table to wait for hamburgers delivered on plastic trays. This time of day, more people were waiting than eating, but the burgers looked juicy, the buns plump and liberally dusted with sesame seeds. After deciding on a Hickory Burger, home fries, and a strawberry malt, Hannah got in line to place her order. Her hunger had been appeased somewhat by the smell of grilling beef, and she was content to wait, at least until the cramping resumed or the bleeding got out of hand. The pad they'd sent her into the world with was thick and chunky, like a chalkboard eraser shoved between her legs. Hannah couldn't help worrying that it could be detected through her jeans. If she were to stand in front of a mirror, she was certain *she* could see it. Not that anyone else would look so closely. She knew better. She was older than most of the people milling around her, and one of the only singles.

In the line next to hers, a teenage couple were talking. "So, do you want a number five or a number eleven?" the boy asked his girlfriend, a distracted-looking girl in a skintight sundress. Wrong size and season, Hannah thought, then chided herself for being judgmental.

"A number five with cheese," the girl replied, "and a large Coke." She was staring off toward the pair of glass doors, as though her real boyfriend might arrive any minute. In the meantime, the stand-in boyfriend plucked at the hem of her dress, either to straighten it or to get her attention. The girl paid him no mind. Her stomach protruded from the flocked material, and her breasts spilled out over the neckline. Was she pregnant, then? Hannah wondered. No telling. Every week, virgins sat in her office looking six months pregnant, while other girls well on their way to motherhood zipped up size-six jeans.

To her left, an angry-looking man cleared his throat. He seemed to want to get something off his chest. Hannah turned slightly to study his slumped shoulders and graying, flyaway hair. He might have been an English professor or an accountant or an appliance salesman at Sears. Unhappily employed, no doubt. Then she noticed a little boy, dashing about below eye level and tromping the man's foot with a chunky red and blue shoe, too small to cause real pain but irritating nonetheless. Oh dear, she thought. The angry man's a father, and an indifferent one at that.

The child was maybe three and clearly agitated. While she watched, he disappeared into the weave of legs ahead of them, then doubled back to stomp his father's toes again. Either he's hungry, Hannah thought, or else he has attention deficit disorder. Or maybe both. Hannah wished she could tap the man on the shoulder and make a polite observation: "Your child is running amok here." Surely she'd be doing the rest of the world a favor. But, glancing about, she realized no one else was paying the child any mind. These days, people were inured to bad behavior. When the child rushed back by, the angry-looking man bent down and scooped the little body into his arms. Hannah expected irritation, maybe even threats. Instead, the father broke into a positively beatific smile and kissed the child's cheek. At which point the little cherub puckered his lips to the man's leathery face and gave him a smacking kiss.

"I like french fries, Daddy," the boy said.

"I know you do," his father replied.

"I like lemonade, Daddy."

"I know you do."

"My stomach hurts."

"You're hungry. We'll be to the front of the line in a minute."

Hannah took deep cleansing breaths, breaths so ragged the boy glanced over his father's shoulder and caught her eye. She managed a smile, and, in return, he raised his little hand in a jaunty wave. I can't see into these people's lives, Hannah realized, and they can't see into mine. This should have been comforting, but it wasn't, not at all. The realization left her more alone than ever. When her turn came, Hannah ordered her food to go. She'd take it home and retreat to her bed. You'll feel better tomorrow, she told herself. This aching regret, it'll be gone before you know it.

The bleeding resumed as she walked up the sidewalk to her front door, a gush of warmth followed by a spreading wetness. She decided to shower before she ate. Just to feel better, more like herself. Lifting a leg into the tub, she noticed blood running in rivulets down both thighs. A surprising amount of blood. When would it stop? She trained the spray to wash it away, gone, she thought, all gone. The water was warm and soothing, and Hannah took her time, soaping herself all over. The cramping crept back, but it was intermittent and not as sharp as before. When the water turned tepid—which happened rather too quickly—Hannah stepped out and dried carefully, then shrugged a new white gown over her head. In defiance of the doctor's orders, she inserted a tampon. Helen would have had a fit. Why take such a chance? And why wear white at a time like this? What an indulgence! Even though entirely alone, Hannah was compelled to answer aloud: "Because it makes me feel better."

At least she was honest with herself. All over the world women were grunting children into being, and for what? To please some man they couldn't live without? To provide them with a reason for living? To leave something behind when they were dead? What could be more self-indulgent? And after the first flush of new parenthood, what then? Some lost interest altogether, allowing their children to run wild through their schools and neighborhoods, to pull every damn stunt they could think of to get attention, to wind up on the floor of a bathroom stall, dead drunk, or worse.

Even good parents were suspect. Here in Austin, Hannah knew a gay couple, two charming and well-to-do men who wanted domesticity more than anything else. They'd designed and built a house, furnished it scrupulously, dug flower beds and a pool, and installed an extra-large dishwasher. Then they'd set about having dinner parties, which received rave reviews, but after all was said and done, the couple felt let down. Obviously, it was time to have children. Some twenty thousand dollars and twenty thousand miles of red tape later, they were flying to

Peru to adopt a small dark boy who would dump bowls of colored cereal on their white carpet. And they were happy, no doubt about it, because children are an endless task, and that's exactly the sort of thing they were looking for. Their friends were always marveling at what good people these men were—how unselfish—but if truth be told, they'd spent a lot of money to fulfill their desires. Since when was that unselfish?

She ate her lunch in bed, devouring all of the fries but only half of the burger. The rest she left on the floor beside the bed and quickly dropped off into an exhausted sleep. Dreams rose and faded like ether; she passed through one after another of them, a series of wavery doors, each more mysterious than the last. She might have slept through the afternoon and on into the night, except for the rustling of the paper followed by a clicking noise that struck her as both familiar and strange. Opening her eyes, Hannah lay still, waiting for the sounds to recur. The clicking was gone, but something more subtle had taken its place, a soft panting. Could it be? She lifted her head from the pillow, and there he was, nosing his way across the rug, pushing the Holiday House bag in front of him, every morsel of food gone.

"Neil!" At the sound of her voice, the dog made an odd woofing noise and lumbered back to the bed. He looked a little the worse for wear from his travels—his fur matted in places, lumpy in others—but satisfied to be home. "Where have you been, Neil?" she cried.

Leaning over to pet him, Hannah got a good whiff of his coat, musty smelling and a little rank, so real that it didn't allow for a moment's doubt. This was no dream; this was real life, waking life; her dog had come back home. As she stroked his neck, her fingers grazed the collar, and she sat up in bed. What was this? With effort—and considerable complaint from Neil—she hoisted the cocker into her lap to examine the red collar and tags. Yes, she thought, this was the same collar she'd spotted on Carl's floorboard only hours before. She pushed Neil aside and sprang out of bed, then ran down the hall as though pursuing a thief. Carl was gone, the driveway entirely empty. For the second time today, her husband had simply disappeared. Hannah stood at the front door with Neil nosing about her feet, trying to think what to do. She registered mild cramping but pushed the pain aside, too mad to hurt. She considered tracking her husband down at work, demanding answers in a loud voice. After that scene at the clinic, he deserved as much. Only she wasn't sure she could summon the energy to dress, much less to drive to the mall and yell in front of perfect strangers. Instead, she returned to bed, this time with Neil, who stank and snored but was worth all manner of trouble in terms of simple reassurance. Life could go back to normal now. Or if not now, at least very soon.

Shortly after midnight, Hannah woke again. The anger she'd carried to bed with her—bulky and sharp-edged—had dissipated into a lingering sadness, shapeless and melting. Sadness made the limbs heavy and the days long, but it was familiar; she could master it. She had only to acknowledge its presence and then to endure; at bottom, sadness had to be outlived. With effort, Hannah raised herself and looked around the darkened room. Light from the studio streamed down the hallway, illuminating the edges of things—the high dresser, a rocking chair heaped with dirty clothes, the filmy curtains at the windows. The world held still while Hannah heaved her legs over the side of the bed. It took time to get used to this feeling. Hold on, she thought. Ask yourself why you're sad. But the answer had preceded the question. Loss. She was sad about loss, all that she'd already lost and all that might yet slip through her fingers. Not the baby, but all the baby represented, her ability to take hold of life and wrest some happiness from it. Some people were experts at holding on, but she was the mistress of letting go. Carl kept a grip on what he loved, which explained how they'd stayed married all these years. If he'd let her, she realized, she'd have drifted away.

Neil was gone from the bed, but the musty smell of him lingered on the sheets. He was somewhere in the house, probably in the studio with Carl. Hannah sighed and headed for the bathroom. Perhaps, she thought, I can slip in and out, get back into bed without attracting his attention. Wait until the morning to talk. It was a coward's way out, but she'd take it. The truth was this: She was afraid. In the abortion clinic, when she'd discovered Carl in the hallway, for a second or two she hadn't recognized him. Yes, that was it. She hadn't known him. Now she was struck by this fact, that without the familiar surroundings of their house, she could take the man she'd lived with all these years for a stranger. Even if it was only for an instant, how could that be? He'd looked older to her—gray streaking his curly brown hair, his shoulders stooped from years of leaning to the easel—but the physical changes were the least of it. Those were things she'd known about. What surprised her was the way his vulnerability could be twisted into rage. She hadn't known Carl was an angry man, capable of angry acts. Her sadness, she thought now, was no match for his anger.

The door to the studio stood open, and Hannah forgot her fear. As she crossed the threshold into his presence, Carl took no notice of her. He was standing before the easel, staring at his work. The pastel was more complete now; the child had taken on a presence, plump and ruddy. He'd managed something wonderful with the eyes, captured that glint of restlessness Hannah sometimes still saw reflected in the mirror. The child's face—her own face—drew her in and held her. For the first time, she recognized something he'd known all along, that his work aroused a yearning in her, a hankering toward wholeness. Much as she wanted to resist it, the picture drew her in.

She'd been standing there for at least a minute when he turned and saw her in the doorway. He didn't appear displeased, only gave her a long look before stepping away from the easel. In his open palm he held a number of chalks—reds, purples, and blacks, colors he seldom used. Offering her a grim little smile, he closed his fingers around them and squeezed, forcing chalk dust from his fist.

"What are you doing?" she asked.

He took a step toward her, arm outstretched, and shook his fist. "I'm inspired, Hannah!" he cried. Then he returned to the pastel, studying it dispassionately before opening his hand and contemplating the ruined chalks. His palm was dark as a wound. Hannah's heart pitched. "Don't do it," she said softly.

Briefly, he looked back at her. "No?" He clasped his hand again and pressed what was left of the chalks between them. "This, I believe, belongs to me, Hannah," he said. "Is mine to do with as I wish." He hesitated and let out a little sigh before reaching to the girl on the easel, pressing his fingers to the paper and smearing darkness across her face and down her body, rubbing his fingertips over her contours until they ceased to exist.

Hannah held her breath, horrified and fascinated. His intention was to destroy, but even in this, he had something of the artist's touch. He was careful: His strong, blunt fingers caressed the paper, easing the streaks of black, red, and purple over and around. He bent to the easel, his expression curious and soft, absolutely intent on the mix of colors, on the swirls descending into darkness.

When he'd finished, he stepped back briefly to survey the results before turning to her. His face registered regret and resentment. Her fault, his expression said. Hannah felt tears run down her cheeks, and she reached up to swipe at them.

"It's a mess, isn't it, Hannah?" he said softly. "A big, fucking mess."

Those were the last words he spoke to her all weekend. On Sunday, he left early for work and stayed gone all day and into the evening. Very early Monday morning, she found him curled on the sofa, his eyes squeezed tightly shut. She wanted to touch him, to run her fingertips over the lines in his forehead, but she was afraid to wake him. Even in sleep he looked angry, positively furious, and for the first time it occurred to Hannah that they might not recover from this.

She was relieved to return to the confines of the school building and be swept up in the Monday morning routine of Travis High—several meetings in the morning followed by two afternoon assemblies on AIDS. The auditorium wasn't large enough to hold the entire school body, so the freshmen attended with the seniors, the sophomores with the juniors. Hannah's presence was required at both presentations; part of her job was policing, though she didn't call it that. She patrolled the aisles, guarded the exits, and scanned the crowd for troublemakers, all of this in three-inch heels. As Mr. Pilsner had noted, she'd have made a bang-up recruit for the Secret Service.

The subject matter of the assembly wasn't entirely new, but it wasn't old hat yet either. AIDS was a subject the administration addressed in various ways throughout the school year, but despite her knowledge and experience, Hannah was still shocked by what she heard. Those kids who skulked about the building, bitching loudly to each other about the sorry state of their lives, were right: Being a teenager in the nineties "sucked big time." By comparison, her own coming of age had been a piece of cake and a reefer to make it taste good. In the late sixties, they'd had drugs to deal with, Vietnam, and the reverberations of three assassinations, but these kids had gang wars, and designer drugs, and the specter of AIDS, all of it perched on their front doorstep, waiting for them to venture outdoors. And for many of them, not a parent in sight.

The presentation was certainly poignant. One at a time, two young men and a young woman introduced themselves in the manner of AA members. The young woman's voice was whispery, like Helen's, and she bent to the microphone, as though confessing a secret: "I'm Clarissa Wheaton, and I'm HIV positive." Next, she stepped to the side of the podium and, for several seconds, stood stock-still before revolving slowly, allowing the students to study her. She wanted them to take a good long look—at the blond hair tumbling to her shoulders, at the blue jeans and Birkenstocks with white socks, at the grace of her pivot. It was clear that she'd had the obligatory ballet lessons and that this was the use she'd put them to. Clarissa was thin enough to be a dancer, but not too thin, not yet.

She spoke right up, and though her voice trembled at first, she was frank in relating her own brief history: "I wasn't supposed to get AIDS," she said, "and when it happened, no one believed it, least of all me. I mean, really. I wasn't a male homosexual in San Francisco. I never shot crack in the alleys in New York. For God's sake, I was a high-school girl in Houston, Texas." This last with a trace of defiance. She raised her hands, palms out, as though to prove she had nothing up her sleeves. "I'm not a slut," she told them. "I can count my boyfriends on the fingers of one hand. None of them caught it from me. I guess I was lucky. . . ." Here she coughed and sniffled. "*They* were lucky."

One of the other speakers, a young man in a suit, stepped forward to touch her elbow. Clarissa turned back and smiled, then moved even closer to the microphone, close enough to kiss it with her pink lips. "This is my first time center stage, ya know?" she said. "And it feels really weird, being up here and not out there. I wish, I *really* wish, I could trade places." She was crying now, tears streaming down her lovely cheeks. Hannah could feel the audience hold its collective breath, all of them caught up in the moment. This girl might save a life, Hannah thought. Maybe more than one. "I'd give anything to be out there, cracking gum, a little bored but happy to be missing French class. Being up here sucks big time. Sex isn't that great, not if you have to pay for it with your life."

Stationed at the back of the auditorium, Hannah released a long, heartfelt sigh. Later, making the rounds of the auditorium, she scanned the faces and said a small prayer for these children, some pockmarked, some brooding, a few—even now—stoned past knowing or caring. Not that Hannah expected anything from God. Although she still believed in Him, she didn't hold out hope that He would intercede on her behalf or anyone else's. Hannah's mother, Naomi, had loved God and worked to pass on her devotion. Every night, she'd knelt beside the beds of her two young daughters and coached them in their prayers. After their mother died, Helen had wanted to go on praying, but Hannah had refused. Why pray to a deity so selfish and uncaring? What had their mother ever done to God? What had Hannah or Helen ever done? And Clarissa. What had she done?

By the end of the second assembly, Hannah's feet were swelling and the cramping had resumed. You've overdone it, she thought as she limped back to her office, determined to write one last letter, to make a couple of phone calls to parents, and to get the hell out. The only problem was, she had nowhere to go but home, and home wasn't where she wanted to be, not now, not with Carl in his present state of mind. Retreating to Helen's was out of the question as well. Her sister wasn't speaking to her, or rather she was speaking, but in a loud, vindictive tone of voice.

Hannah had called on Sunday afternoon and quickly confirmed her suspicions: Helen had betrayed her confidence and was therefore responsible for the scene at the clinic. She'd sent Carl; it had actually been her idea that he go. "Damn right it was," she'd hissed into the receiver, adding that she had only one regret. "If I'd called him in time," she sighed, "things might have been different. I'll never forgive myself for oversleeping. I should have set the alarm." In the past, they'd always been on the same side, always. Now they weren't. Angrily, Hannah had assured Helen that Carl couldn't have made a difference, no matter what time he'd barged in the door, but in her heart of hearts, she wasn't so sure.

To add insult to injury, Helen had gone on to suggest that Jimmy's affair—assuming he was having one—was all Hannah's fault. As if ruining her own marriage weren't enough for Hannah, now she had to go and ruin Helen's as well. "Isn't that science teacher's name Cecile?" she'd asked Hannah.

"Are you talking about Cecile Barbone?" Four months ago, Hannah had hosted an end-of-school party, and the new biology teacher had attended, along with Jimmy and Helen and at least thirty other people. Hannah vaguely remembered the willowy teacher huddled with Jimmy in the kitchen, the two of them erupting into simultaneous laughter, but what of that? Jimmy took notice of every attractive woman in a five-mile radius. Everyone knew the man had enough testosterone for any two normal males.

"The other day," Helen told Hannah, "Jimmy was sitting in his truck in the driveway talking on the cellular. I saw him from the window and sent Cassie out to spy on him."

"My God!" Hannah exclaimed. "Have you no shame, Helen?"

Evidently not. "Cassie told me he was talking to somebody named *Cecile*. Now, how many Cecile's are there, Hannah?"

More than one, Hannah thought, and she said so. "Are you crazy?" she'd cried. "What are you doing bringing your children into this?"

Until today, she'd written off Helen's suspicions as lunacy, but now something was troubling her. This afternoon in the auditorium, Cecile had obviously been avoiding her. Both were walking the aisles at the second assembly; now, what were the chances they would never turn a corner together? Never pass each other? It didn't happen, which was a bit strange, as though Cecile was intentionally avoiding her. And once, when Hannah happened to catch the science teacher's eye from across the aisle, she'd looked away, pretended not to see her. Hannah had to admit that the woman *was* uncommonly tall and beautiful, though she was also low key about her beauty: she wore very little makeup, and her dress wasn't the least bit flashy or seductive.

"Maybe there's a real-estate agent named Cecile," Hannah had suggested.

"Nope," Helen replied. "I checked the Yellow Pages."

You've got too much spare time, Hannah had wanted to say, but she knew better. Mad as she was, she'd managed to keep her thoughts to herself. One of these days, she and her sister would be friends again, and Hannah wanted it to be sooner rather than later.

By the time she was ready to leave her office at around five, almost everyone else was gone. Nothing new about that; she and the evening janitor had become downright friendly. She would have been relieved to speak to him, about anything, anything at all, but this evening he was at the other end of the building, lights going on and off in the tenth-grade classrooms as he emptied trash and washed the blackboards. And she couldn't bring herself to hunt him down. She wasn't that desperate, surely. She decided to pick up a couple of burgers on the way home, one for her and another for Neil. To hell with his diet, to hell with hers.

On her way out the door, she felt a gush of blood soak the pad between her legs, which sent her scurrying back to the nearest bathroom. She'd never make it home without ruining her beige skirt. What an idiot she'd been to wear it in the first place. Maureen had warned her she'd bleed for days. As Hannah closed the stall door, the cramps stirred deep inside her, willing her to pay attention, to remember what she'd done. It had been two days, but the pain wasn't finished with her. She grimaced as it bit down. Her surroundings—stall doors splashed with graffiti and God-knows-what-else, broken locks, white streamers of toilet paper heaped about her feet—made her recall that adolescent-girl pain and fear, the horror of being exposed to the world for what she was, a woman bleeding.

She dug in her purse for a fresh pad. There had to be one in here somewhere. Surely she hadn't used them all. Her purse was stuffed with all kinds of junk: a bag of cosmetics, a tin box of Band-Aids for her blistered heels, a notebook for doodling during boring meetings. But no sanitary pads, no tampons, not even a wadded Kleenex to stanch the flow. Hannah had just sat back on the toilet and was taking deep, calming breaths and reading the scrawled messages—STEPHANIE LOVES KENNY, KENNY LOVES CLARISSA—when she realized she wasn't alone. Someone stirred in one of the stalls at the other end of the bathroom. Instantly, she imagined a man peering over the top of the wall, but the idea seemed more laughable than lascivious. "You can't be too careful," the female teachers were always reminding one another.

"Dr. Solace, is that you?" It was a girl's voice, choked by tears.

"Yes," Hannah replied.

"I recognized your shoes," the voice said, an edge of sarcasm beneath the sniffling. "No one else wears shoes like those. Where do you buy them, Dr. Solace?"

"Erica?" Hannah guessed.

The girl sighed deeply. "Good guess, but no. It's Cassandra Nelson."

Yeah, right, Hannah thought. Cassandra Nelson was head cheerleader and a smug little brainchild to boot. Her parents were so proud of her they'd been known to wear plastic buttons sporting her picture. And Cassandra didn't even seem to mind. Of course they adore me. What's not to adore? Hannah bent double and peered down the length of the stalls. Sure enough. She spied a pair of black Reeboks, the soles edged with mud.

"Cassandra wouldn't be caught dead in those shoes," Hannah called. The cramps were easing a bit. Maybe if she stayed bent double, she'd live till tomorrow. She dropped her purse to the floor and searched again without luck. Here she was, assistant principal, stuck on the toilet in the girl's bathroom. "Erica, listen, this is a little embarrassing, but I need your help." She waited for the smart-alecky response, but it didn't come.

"What do you need?"

"Do you have a quarter?"

Hannah directed the girl to purchase a pad from the machine and hand it to her under the stall door. Erica did so quietly and quickly, and when Hannah emerged from the stall, the girl was waiting, dressed in black, as usual, and leaning on the sink. A little smirk came and went on that lovely mouth of hers. "So you bleed," Erica observed, "just like the rest of us."

"Very funny." Hannah smoothed her skirt and peered over Erica's shoulder at her reflection in the mirror. Presentable but barely so. Her bun was loose; several strands of hair had escaped down over her shoulder. She looked pale, her features strained with pain. But Erica was worse off, her eyes red and puffy, her makeup long gone. Hannah managed a small smile. "And you cry like the rest of us," she replied.

"Touché, Dr. S. We're women. See us bleed *and* cry." Erica held her jaw rigid, and she didn't so much as smile at her own joke.

"I'm surprised you know that song."

"My mother sang it to me in my cradle." Erica hesitated. "She's a woman. See her leave." So angry, this girl was, so bitter. Hannah understood entirely.

"You helped me," she said. "Maybe I can help you?"

Erica whirled around to the mirror and addressed Hannah through the glass. "Not *bloody* likely. By the way, Cassandra Nelson refers to you as Dr. Prissy." The bathroom went silent. Hannah knew better than to respond; she waited. "I need an AIDS test," Erica finally said. "Got one of those in that big purse of yours?"

For a few seconds, Hannah was at a loss. Please God, she prayed, not my lovely Erica. Then she hoisted the bag to her shoulder and turned toward the door. "My purse is full of junk, but there's a phone in my office. Let's go make a call?"

As they trailed down the hall, it occurred to Hannah that she had her evening cut out for her. If possible, she'd take Erica for her test right then and there. No time like the present. Some of the clinics had evening hours, and, after all, she had hours to kill. "Will you tell your father?" she asked when they reached her office.

Erica gave a grim little shake of the head. "Not unless I have to."

"Your mother then?"

Another little shake.

"Oh, Erica," Hannah moaned. "You're putting me in a difficult position here."

Erica's hands were jammed into the pockets of her baggy black jeans. She turned her face to Hannah's for the split second it took to shoot her a withering look. "I tell you what," she said. "Let's change places. I'll be big-shot assistant principal and you be the scared-shitless teenager. What do you say?"

"Sorry," Hannah answered quickly. "You know I'll do what I can."

The only clinic with evening hours was over by the University, housed in a squat one-story building on 24th, one block off Guadalupe. Years ago—a whole lifetime, it seemed to Hannah—this same building had been home to Inner Sanctum Records, a hippie hangout in the late sixties and into the mid seventies. Back then, the front of the brick building had been one big pulsing mural dominated by enormous psychedelic letters—INNER SANCTUM RECORDS. And what else? Hannah couldn't remember the details, but she imagined a battalion of armadillos bursting out in every direction. In those years, armadillos were omnipresent in Austin, the symbol of the counterculture. The artist Jim Franklin had made his career on the back of the lowly mammal, penning them on posters and painting them on murals. Armadillos were everywhere you looked, realistic renditions giving way to fanciful cartoon creatures sporting cowboy hats and boots, playing guitar and dancing the cotton-eyed Joe. A concert hall and beer garden had been named for them: Armadillo World Headquarters. She'd heard the Grateful Dead there and Bruce Springsteen and B. B. King. Whatever had become of Jim Franklin? Hannah wondered. Surely, he missed those days. She missed them too.

"I used to come here to buy records," she told Erica as they climbed the concrete steps and stepped through the threshold into the dark hallway. In the early seventies, the hardwood floors had been so worn they were depressed in places. Now they were even worse. Her heel caught in a rough spot and she pitched forward before catching herself. "Watch your step," she warned Erica, who was grinning quizzically.

"What are records?" the girl asked.

"Ha, ha," Hannah replied. "I suppose you've never heard of eight-tracks either."

"Eight-tracks? Dinosaur tracks?"

"Those were the days, my friend," Hannah sang, half serious.

"So my father says," Erica replied. "The man has made nostalgia into an art form."

Hannah wanted to hear more, but the dreariness of the clinic waiting room silenced them both. Worn hardwood gave way to yellowed linoleum, rows of molded plastic chairs, curling Health Department posters, all lit by buzzing fluorescent lights. Near the back of the room, two young women dressed in identical jeans and T-shirts sat close enough to spread a magazine across two sets of knees. Their brown heads bent to the page, they were engrossed in their reading and paid the newcomers no mind. Otherwise, the room was empty.

If she wasn't mistaken, this very room had been part of the record store, which meant every square inch of these walls had once been splashed with color, lots of red, purple, yellow, and black. Hannah imagined caricatured rock stars: Jimi Hendrix, Janis Joplin, Jerry Garcia, Jerry Jeff Walker. Had their pictures really been here then? If so, they were gone now, covered over with several coats of institutional white. Gone, too, the long-haired, tie-dyed salesclerks who lounged behind the counter. Instead, they were greeted by a middle-aged woman dressed entirely in green scrubs. "Can I help you?" she asked. She was a plump pincushion of a woman, gray-haired, no nonsense, the sort who had little use for Hannah and the gumption to let her know it. Some women were intimidated by Hannah's manner, while others were jealous or downright oblivious. This sort—the feminist grand-mother—tended to be offended or disdainful. Hannah straightened her spine and strode to the counter. Either she'd win this woman over or else she'd piss her off. No point in delaying the inevitable.

"We're here for an AIDS test," she said. "Or rather, Erica is here for an AIDS test." Hannah glanced over her shoulder and spotted Erica hanging back by the entrance, pretending interest in a poster of a pregnant teenager smoking a cigarette. "Erica?" Hannah called. Now the girl pretended not to hear.

The woman pushed a clipboard across the counter. It held a badly Xeroxed form and a Bic pen. "Here. Have your daughter fill this out," the woman told Hannah.

"What?"

"Your daughter. She needs to fill this out."

Hannah opened her mouth, then closed it again. How could she explain, and why bother? If she were to tell the truth, the woman would probably send them on their way, tell Erica to come back with a parent in tow, someone who could give permission. Hannah picked up the clipboard and scanned the form before carrying it to Erica, who'd moved from the picture of the pregnant teen to a poster listing a litany of sexually transmitted diseases. Erica appeared engrossed, but like a well-behaved patron at an art museum, she moved aside for Hannah. The list was alphabetized and began with AIDS, then on to bacterial vaginosis, candidiasis, chlamydia, genital warts, gonorrhea, herpes . . . on and on, more diseases than Hannah had the heart to read. A CHECK-LIST OF STD's, it was called. It appeared that free love had given way to pay-with-your-life love. No, Hannah thought, she didn't envy this gen-eration of teenagers. It was all so serious now, so life and death.

"Erica?"

The girl turned; tears welled in the corners of her eyes. "Thank you for coming," she whispered before dropping into an orange plastic chair. She looked exhausted and overwhelmed. Gently, Hannah placed the clipboard in Erica's lap and watched as she hunched over it, the pen clasped tightly in her left hand. She's left-handed, Hannah thought with a start. Her mother had been left-handed as well. Hannah remembered the easy pleasure of riding in the car with Naomi, who steered with her left hand, leaving her right free to tickle whoever rode on the passenger's side. Each time they went out in the car, Hannah and Helen had fought over the privilege to sit in front. "My turn! My turn!" they'd cried. Suddenly, Hannah saw it in her mind's eye, what must have happened on that fateful day: Naomi waiting in the turn lane, leaning across the seat to tickle her youngest, stretching to reach Helen as she wiggled away. Even as the white truck careened toward them. She never saw it coming, Hannah thought with a start.

"You all right?" the woman in green called to her.

Hannah realized she was standing with her hand clasped over her mouth. She jerked it away, tried to smile. "Yes," she said. "Fine."

Erica was oblivious, so hunched in her seat that she appeared nearsighted. When Hannah noticed the shaking shoulders, she dropped down next to her and, after settling her purse in her lap, searched inside for a presentable tissue. She found one and nudged Erica, holding it out. "Here," she said.

Erica looked up, teary-eyed, and grabbed it. "I'm glad you have *something* useful in there," she quipped.

The test was over in only a few minutes, and afterward, Hannah took Erica out to eat at a nearby Schlotzsky's. The results wouldn't be back for two weeks; even so, Erica was obviously relieved. In less than half an hour she devoured an entire vegetarian sandwich and two servings of potato salad, then drained a large Dr Pepper. They didn't talk much, but in the middle of the meal, Erica suddenly looked up from her food. "You're pretty cool, Dr. Solace."

Hannah smiled and shrugged.

"I mean, you didn't ask questions. Just took me to the clinic and pretended to be my mom." Erica cocked her head and smirked across the table.

"I didn't pretend to be your mom." Hannah heard the defensiveness in her tone, and so did Erica, who raised a hand, as though to ward off the imaginary blow.

"Whatever. It's just you're really and truly nice, Dr. Prissy, and it makes me want to tell you something. Something truly stupid from last summer."

Hannah braced herself. When teenagers said "truly stupid," they generally weren't exaggerating. "Yes?" She opened her mouth, took a large bite of her sandwich, and chewed slowly, so she wouldn't be tempted to respond. That's where lots of parents went wrong, she thought. They felt forced to respond to everything, even when they had no idea what to say. Sometimes it was best just to listen.

"Last summer I was with my mom in California. You know my mom lives in California?"

Hannah nodded.

"Anyway, I had a crappy time. Spent every day in July taking care of my baby brother, Stephen. My *half* brother, Stephen. Soon as I got there, my mom and her new husband dumped the baby in my lap. 'Look, sweetie, our live-in baby-sitter has arrived from Texas.' And that's the last I saw of them." She sighed. "Not really. They didn't actually disappear. They just assumed I had come all that way to change poopy diapers."

Hannah wrinkled her nose and took a sip of iced tea, remaining quiet. Erica was trying to tell her something.

"So one Saturday, I get just fed up to here." She made a slicing motion at her neck and looked across the table for confirmation. Hannah nodded and took another bite. "So I ask my mom if we can go to the beach, I mean, get out and do something fun. She said no, maybe next week. But that wasn't good enough. All of a sudden, I'm crazy to see the ocean, to smell the salt air, to take off my shoes and walk on the sand." Erica sighed. "I just couldn't stand it, her saying no to me.

"So when Mom and Hubby go to the grocery store, I take off. Leave Stephen in his crib. . . ." Here, Erica looked away, out the window to the street, and Hannah followed her gaze. It was dark out. A homeless man stood under the streetlight on the corner, shifting from one foot to the other, his hands raised skyward, as if he were singing. Erica went on. "The rest is embarrassingly simple. I hitched a ride—a guy, of course. Bleached blond hair and skin so brown—the color of my bedroom furniture. A surfer. I mean, it's embarrassing to be seduced by a surfer, some sixties thing. The Beach Boys probably wrote a song about it, but why lie? When the sun went down, we fucked on the beach." Inside, Hannah flinched, but she didn't let on. "And the whole time," Erica said, "I'm worrying about leaving Stephen in his crib. I didn't think to worry about AIDS." Her voice died away.

"Oh, Erica," Hannah sighed. She was reminded of her first time, some senior boy she hardly knew. She no longer remembered his name, but if she allowed herself, she could still feel a little sick at the thought of his grunt of satisfaction and the stale smoke smell that permeated the seat cushions.

Across the table Erica was smiling and motioning toward the window. "He's pretty good," she said. The homeless man *was* dancing now, dancing his heart out, spinning about the streetlight in a jerky rendition of "Singin' in the Rain." Only it wasn't raining. There wasn't a cloud in the sky.

Chapter 10

"I GUARANTEE YOU that bitch will get her comeuppance," Mattie said, pounding the steering wheel with the flat of her hand. She glared at the line of cars in front of them and at the red light swinging above the intersection, as though all of it, everything that moved, was further evidence of corruption and sin. All morning she'd been slamming about, banging cabinet doors, closet doors, and finally the trunk of the car. She couldn't get enough noise to suit her. Now they were late to Sunday services, which gave her something else to be upset about. For the last two weeks, Mattie's share of patience had been meager, her good humor absent altogether.

Penny took a deep breath. "What 'bitch' do you mean?" she asked. The word was easier to say than she'd thought.

Mattie didn't react. "You know perfectly well who I'm talking about," she said.

"I don't. I'm lost, Grandmother. I thought we were discussing pets."

Moments before, they'd been talking about Penny's cat, Flash. Mattie had insisted that Penny get rid of it, which she had no intention of doing. Until today, she'd managed to keep her pet a secret from Mattie, who had no use for animals. Unfortunately, Penny's secret had bolted out the screen door this morning, running right over the top of Mattie's house shoes. Her grandmother had gasped, then glowered.

"I'm talking about . . . Margaret Stecker."

Of course, Penny thought. "Dr. Bill says she's part of God's plan." She invoked Dr. Bill's name because it generally calmed Mattie. The man walked on water as far as she was concerned. "Nothing to be angry about, he says. In fact, he's happy with the publicity. If it weren't for Margaret Stecker, we wouldn't be fighting a crowd in church this morning."

"That's true," Mattie conceded.

Dr. Bill's broken jaw had made the evening news in Austin, and after the local paper ran a story, newspapers in Dallas and Houston had picked it up as well. In the photograph, Dr. Bill sat with his back to the clinic wall, his face so swollen Penny hardly recognized him. The *Austin American Statesman* headline read ANGRY MOTHER SOCKS PRO-LIFE PREACHER, which some of the congregation at Gospel Fellowship found insulting, the paper taking its own swipe at Dr. Bill, but Penny thought otherwise—the journalist was simply stating facts. The newspaper article had identified the woman as Margaret Stecker, a divorced mother of three and a buyer for Foley's department store. In an accompanying photograph, Mrs. Stecker held up her bandaged hand like a trophy. She'd broken two fingers when she'd smashed Dr. Bill's jaw. "And I'd do it again," she told the reporter. Dr. Bill's followers were outraged, none more than Mattie. At their urging, he pressed assault charges. Oddly, the papers didn't mention Mrs. Stecker's daughter—you'd have thought the mother was the one getting the abortion—but Penny had been there. Several times, she'd wondered how the girl felt now, whether she regretted leaving the clinic, whether she'd return when everything died down. Maybe she'd already returned. Maybe the abortion was over and done with.

This would be Dr. Bill's first sermon since suffering his broken jaw, and the newspapers were covering the service. The headline of the Saturday story had read WIRING MY JAW SHUT WON'T SHUT ME UP. And it hadn't, though he still looked awful, a little mangled even. The bruise across his jaw had faded to a greenish yellow, and the swelling was gone, but all that wire was impossible to ignore. Dr. Bill had managed to adapt, eating through a straw and talking from behind his teeth. "It's not so bad," he told Penny, his tone guttural and mono-tone. "I get as many chocolate shakes as I want, and people listen to me. They lean in close and give me their undivided attention." He made jokes about it, seemed downright cheerful.

"I hope we don't have to stand through this service," Mattie said when the light finally turned green. "You know the crowd will be out the doors."

"Which will thrill Dr. Bill," Penny replied.

By the time they made it across town, the small gravel lot behind Gospel Fellowship was completely full, and cars, trucks, and vans lined the curbs for blocks in every direction. Penny marveled at the crush of people making their way up the sidewalk: families and couples interspersed with a surprising number of single women, all blinking in the early-morning sunshine. Most were newcomers who looked happy to be out and about, some attired in their best, others dressed a good deal more casually, as though they'd leapt out of bed and pulled on whatever was closest at hand.

As they circled another block, Penny wondered whether so many could squeeze into the modest chapel. What a turnout! If she were Dr. Bill, she'd have been struck dumb at these numbers; of course, she'd never have made a public speaker. All her life, people had chided her for her shyness, but she wasn't shy, just quiet. Most people confused the two, but not Dr. Bill. Which reminded her: These people were coming to see the same man who'd called her just yesterday to talk, the same man who'd asked her out for the coming Saturday night. "If it weren't for all this wire, I'd give you a kiss," he'd said the last time they met. This same man wanted to kiss *her*, Penny Reed. "I can't believe this," she said out loud.

But Mattie was too busy avoiding jaywalkers to pay her any mind. "I can't believe this," she echoed, braking to let a family cross the street. Then: "Praise the Lord."

The next time they passed the church, Penny suggested that she take over the wheel. "Go on in and find a seat," she urged Mattie. "I'll park and join you." They were idling in front just then, watching the crowd advance slowly up the concrete steps. Penny didn't have to offer twice. Mattie threw the station wagon into park and climbed out, rushing off without the black trash bag that had made them late to begin with.

"Wait!" Penny cried, but her grandmother was gone, swept up in the throng.

After breakfast, they'd spent a good half hour digging in various grocery bags, pulled by Mattie from every closet in the house. Penny had never seen so much yarn. Slowly, the two of them had assembled a selection of skeins in various pastel shades: pale blue, yellow, mint green, pink, and peach. Next, Mattie had brandished her big black scissors and cut long lengths of each color, directing Penny to stuff them into small plastic sandwich bags. Snipping and stuffing, snipping and stuffing, punctuated by Mattie's breathless little directive: "Hurry up." It was all very mysterious, made even more so by her grandmother's secrecy. Throughout, she hadn't volunteered a single word of explanation. Now she'd gone off and forgotten it.

One of the last through the doors, Penny stood at the back of the chapel, clutching the plastic bag and scanning the crowd. Mattie was nowhere and everywhere; at least a dozen white-headed women in navy blue were scattered through the pews. Those with hunched shoulders Penny could quickly eliminate—Mattie was adamant about posture—but that still left at least eight white heads to choose from, all of them facing the podium in anticipation of Dr. Bill's entrance. The press of people prevented Penny from moving up the aisle to search out her grandmother. Even on the way inside, she'd been buffeted about. With some effort, she sidled her way to the back wall and lowered the bag of yarn to the floor. The draft from the open doors was chilly, and she wished for a jacket and the comfort of her tennis shoes. Her black pumps had already begun to pinch—not surprising, since they were a half size too small, one of those bargains Mattie hadn't been able to pass up. "They'll stretch," her grandmother had promised, but they'd done no such thing.

The chapel was a long, narrow room, barely wide enough for two short rows of pews and three aisles. Everything had been done modestly and with an eye to practicality by some former congregation—Baptists, if Penny remembered correctly. All except for the circular stained-glass window built into the wall over the front doors. Just now Penny stood directly under it. The design was reminiscent of a kaleidoscope Delia had given her when she was six or so. One evening, her mother had whisked in for a surprise visit, carrying a shoe box full of treasures under her arm. The kaleidoscope had been the first thing out of the box, and pressing the tube to her eye, Penny had cried out in disbelief. At the time, she'd been perched on Delia's lap, and her mother had helped her twist the end, shifting the bits of colored cellophane so that Penny had gasped. Now the rose window gave her much the same feeling. Often, she'd gazed up at the huge wheel of color and blessed the artisan who'd created it.

When Dr. Bill strode to the pulpit—long black robe swishing between his legs, revealing the frayed hem of his jeans and those polished black boots—the crowd roared. Within seconds, they were all on their feet, clapping and stomping. For a few seconds, Penny lost sight of him, but standing on her toes, she managed to glimpse that grin and a blinding flash of metal. Arms raised over his head, he swayed, as though literally moved by the noise. Would he dance next or maybe grab the microphone and belt out a tune, something rollicking and rebellious? Nothing would have surprised her just then. Do I know this man? she asked herself, and was struck by the conviction that she did not. Not really.

Slowly, ever so slowly, he lowered his arms, spreading his fingers to indicate a call for quiet. The sound came down, diminishing as the seconds passed, until at last his hands were at his sides, and the room was utterly still, not a baby crying, not an old man coughing, not a car rumbling by on the street outside. Sweet silence. He nodded his head in appreciation, then leaned to the microphone and uttered his first words: "Let us pray." Enunciated perfectly. Simultaneously, all two hundred or so heads bowed. Penny felt the air around her go thick with so many private prayers ascending slowly to heaven. Finishing her own a few seconds early, she was able to look over the bowed heads to the altar arrangement, a large crystal vase of long-stemmed red roses and white carnations, donated by Penelope's Balloons and Bouquets. Penny sighed in relief. Juanita had begged to make the delivery, and, reluctantly, Penny had agreed. Her friend had been so distracted lately, rushing to answer the phone every time it rang, oblivious to Buck's wailing from the playpen. Yesterday morning, she'd popped three balloons in quick succession, sending the baby into a frenzy of tears. He hated loud noise, except when he made it himself. "I just can't seem to get the hang of it today," Juanita had admitted. It had taken her all morning to fill the orders and all afternoon to make a few simple deliveries. Penny had been left to clean up and entertain Buck until he went off to sleep in the bottom of the playpen. When Juanita finally returned after six, looking a little shamefaced, Penny's irritation had gotten the better of her. She'd said a few things she regretted.

As the choir began to sing, Penny scanned the ranks for her friend. Unfortunately, more people were milling in front of her now. Standing tiptoed, she could just make out the top two rows, but Juanita always stood near the bottom. Penny could hear, though. The choir was sing-ing "On a Hill Far Away," and on the chorus—"So I'll cher-ish the old rugged cross"—the sopranos sounded patchy. Juanita's voice was miss-ing. How could that be? Her friend loved to sing, and she'd been blessed with a sweet, high voice. Today of all days, Penny had expected to hear that familiar soprano sailing over the room, bright and trilling. Was Juanita sick, then? Now that Penny thought of it, Juanita *had* seemed feverish last evening. And little Buck had been coughing and sniffling all week.

When a tall thin man stepped directly in front of Penny, completely blocking her view, she decided to stop shifting about like a stranger. This was her church, after all. Even in this crush, surely she could find *someplace* to sit. Holding the bag to her chest, she edged forward, slipping around the man and a dozen or so others before reaching the aisle, and immediately spotting her destination, hurried toward it. She had just settled onto the bottom step leading to the stage when the choir launched into another hymn, something new she didn't recog-nize. Now she was so close she could practically see the music, a wave of sound traveling over the heads of the congregants and washing against the far wall. From her new vantage point, Penny turned and surveyed the crowd, row after row of faces, most focused on the choir off to the left. But not all. Out in front, a woman in a vivid crimson dress caught Penny's eye and waggled her fingers in a small wave.

Juanita! Penny hardly recognized her. She had on red lipstick this morning, and her abundant black hair was twisted into a bun. Next to her sat a pudgy blond man with skin that seemed stretched a little too tight, the sort who was always pulling at his collar. For heaven's sake, Penny thought. This was none other than Buck Sr. She was sure of it, though they'd met only once before, in Juanita's hospital room, the day after the baby was born. Most of his visit he'd spent backed into a corner, looking downright dejected. "He's not a talker," Juanita had explained. At the time, Penny had felt for him, not being a talker herself, but her sympathies had been misplaced. As it turned out, he wasn't a talker or a father or a provider or even a presence in his son's life. After that one visit, he'd disappeared entirely, only to reappear now, right here in the house of the Lord. How dare he? Penny glared at him from her spot on the steps and shook her head sadly at Juanita's broad smile.

Dr. Bill cleared his throat and gave the scripture from Chapter One of the Gospel According to St. John, John the Baptist's witness to Jesus. He read slowly and loudly, his voice a bit flatter and deeper perhaps, but still full of feeling. Those who hadn't heard him before might not have realized the difference: *"In the beginning was the Word, and the Word was with God, and the Word was God. The same was in the beginning with God. All things were made by Him; and without Him was not any thing made."* Here, he stopped and looked up, scanning the faces of his swelled congregation. His face was still but his eyes burned. Penny wondered briefly whether he might be looking for her, whether he needed the reassurance of her face. So many had come to hear him; surely, he felt the burden of all this need. How to touch their lives? How to move them to touch the lives of others? For a second or two, she considered standing up and stepping into the aisle where he would certainly see her. Quickly, though, she came to her senses. He looked completely at ease.

"All things were made by Him," he repeated, *"and without Him was not any thing made. The scripture goes on to say, In Him was life; and the life was the light of men."* He gazed out over the crowd, smiling as best he could. "No doubt, all of you have heard about my broken jaw and the woman who slugged me—one tough lady." The church erupted into laughter, and he raised his voice to be heard over it. "Let's be honest: You're here to witness the spectacle of the preacher they can't shut up." More laughter and a scattering of applause.

When the noise died down, he continued, "But I want to tell you something you haven't heard, something only those present that day at the clinic would know." Here, he paused and searched the faces in the crowd until he found a few familiar ones. Grandmother, Penny thought; he's spotted her there in the middle row. Sure enough. Penny recognized Mattie's white head and straight shoulders. Dr. Bill went on: "Something happened before Margaret Stecker arrived on the scene with her iron fist." The crowd snickered and hissed at the sound of her name, but Dr. Bill raised a silencing hand. "Something much more worth our time," he added.

Penny felt a tightening in her chest, a sudden recognition of what was coming. He was going to tell them about Carl Solace, the man who lost his child. And he proceeded to do just that. He described the screeching of the brakes, the man bolting out of his car and dashing across the parking lot. "He was there to save the life of his unborn child," Dr. Bill explained. "We prayed for him, of course we did, even as we hurried him on his way." Was that true, Penny wondered? Had they hurried him on his way or held him up? Over the past two weeks, she'd been tempted to mention Carl Solace to Mattie or even to Dr. Bill, to describe the impulse that had led her to pick up a stranger. "God just put my foot on the brake," she'd considered saying, but that wasn't true, was it? The decision had been hers, not God's. Her two hands had steered the van to the curb; her arm had reached across the passenger seat and rolled down the window. Her voice had asked where he was going, told him to climb in and she'd take him there. She, Penny Reed, had been in control from start to finish. How to explain? How to make them understand what she didn't quite understand herself?

But she had lost track of the sermon. "I've never quite figured it out," Dr. Bill was saying. He'd come out from behind the pulpit and was standing in front of it, so close to the edge of the stage that the tip of one black boot hung off. "Some of us are just born with a reverence for life while others have to learn it the hard way. And some of us"— here, he shook his head sadly—"some of us never learn it at all.

"You might not believe it, but I was a hard sell." Dr. Bill seldom talked about himself, so a hush fell over the room. "I was ten years old," he began. "We'd just moved to Salina, Kansas. My stepfather was in the Air Force. In three and a half years we went from Shreveport, Louisiana; to Alamogordo, New Mexico; to Salina, Kansas. Not to make excuses for what I'm about to tell you, but I was one unhappy little boy. My stepfather gave me a BB gun for Christmas, and that was all I thought about. I'd sit in class, and while the teacher wrote on the blackboard, I'd dream about that gun. Evenings, I'd bolt down my dinners just to get back outside. First, it was paper targets that I shredded with a pop, pop, pop of my gun." Very deliberately, he closed the Bible on the podium, then made an odd little grimace with his mouth. "When that got boring," he continued, "I switched to birds, shooting at whatever moved in the big trees in my backyard. Got to where I hardly looked at 'em after they fell, but I kept count. Then, one morning I woke up and found the gun gone.

"You won't be surprised to hear that my mother had taken it in the night. Seems she'd gone out to the clothesline and found the small crumpled body of a mourning dove. Said she couldn't abide it anymore." He sighed and surveyed the faces in the room. "My adolescence was nothing to write home about either. I came of age in the late sixties, one of those 'disaffected youth.' Back then we called them hippies. You know the uniform—tie-dye and frayed denim." He grinned and stepped out from behind the pulpit, lifting his robes so everyone could get a good look at his jeans. "Some things never change," he said with a shake of his head. The crowd loved it. Every face gazed up at him, rapt.

"And you know what's synonymous with hippies—drugs." Penny noticed some of the women shift in their seats, while the men sitting next to them cleared their throats. They weren't so sure they wanted to hear such things about their minister. But Dr. Bill forged ahead. "At eighteen, I was living in a communal house in Kansas City. Must have been ten or twelve of us holed up on one floor. Got me a job mopping floors at a hospital. Good and boring. One day, I dropped acid before I went. LSD." He opened the big Bible again, stroked the pages as though for solace. "Tripping, we called it. Oh, the sights I saw that day—tearful relatives, people in pain, the dying and the newly dead. The big D, and I'm not talking about Dallas here, friends. I'm talking *death.*" He curled his hands into fists and pounded the parchment pages.

"Once I got a good look at it—and believe me, a hallucinogen will open eyes you never knew you had—well, I just"—he lifted his fingers and made quotation marks in the air—" 'freaked out.' Spent all afternoon trembling in the alley behind the hospital. Never touched drugs again." He ran his fingers over the pages, smoothing them. "I could have been saved that day. Could have spared myself lots of future grief, but I was a tough nut to crack."

Penny took a breath. She had a feeling she knew what was coming next. "Years passed, years and years. I was thirty." He grimaced and checked himself. "Tell the truth, Bill. . . . Okay, then. I was thirty-*four* years old, and would you believe I found myself in a similar situation to that man in the parking lot?" She nodded. It seemed he was talking directly to her. She'd known this was coming, a confession of sorts. "Only I wasn't there, you see. I didn't go, didn't do the right thing, though I knew in my heart what it was." Here, he unclenched his fists and pressed both hands to his chest. "I ran away from that *problem*; I ran away from that woman." His voice rose until he was practically shouting. "I ran away from God Himself. I was tough, don't you know?" One last smile. "I'm still tough, but I've been cracked, cracked wide open."

"Praise the Lord!" a few voices called, and "Hallelujah!" He'd brought them round again, but they were somber and restrained.

He waited for the room to go entirely still before speaking again: "Those of us without a reverence for life, well, I'm convinced that we just don't know the first thing about death. Not really. I nearly killed myself with drugs because death wasn't real to me. Jesus said, *I am the resurrection and the life: he that believeth in me, though he were dead, yet shall he live.* That man running through the parking lot, he has reverence for life. Maybe his momma beat it into him or maybe he was born with it, one of those gentle souls you run into from time to time. You can see it in their eyes, their humanity, their innate goodness. Too bad his wife didn't believe in life or in life after death. . . . Let us pray." Penny closed her eyes and Carl's face swam up before her, just as it had been that day, a pair of pained blue eyes meeting hers. It's true, she thought. He's a gentle soul; everyone can see that. Lots of people would have come to his rescue, but God saw fit for me to do it. I was drawn to his goodness; it's as simple as that. Relieved, she said a short prayer of thanks.

Next, Dr. Bill led the congregation through a series of prayers. The first was for the unborn and the innocents. Next, he asked for their prayers for Paul Hill, who'd been convicted the week before in the shooting deaths of an abortion doctor and his escort in Pensacola, Florida. Most assumed he'd be sentenced to death when the jury made its recommendation in November; after all, he'd been convicted of two counts of first-degree murder. Penny prayed along with the rest of them because she didn't believe in the death penalty, and she wasn't about to stand in judgment of Mr. Hill or anyone else. On the other hand, she couldn't fathom how someone who claimed to believe in the precepts of Jesus could gun down another human being, no matter the cause. When it came down to it, the unborn were like the rest of humanity; their fate rested in God's hands. She wondered what Dr. Bill thought of Paul Hill, and those others who'd taken up guns, Michael Griffin and Rachelle Shannon.

Rachelle Shannon was the hardest for Penny to understand. An Oregon housewife with two children at home, she claimed to have been called by God to drive up and down the west coast bombing abortion clinics. In August of 1993, she had climbed in her car and driven from her home in Grants Pass, Oregon, to a clinic in Wichita, Kansas, where she pulled out a .25 caliber pistol and shot a doctor four or five times, hitting him in both hands. Luckily, the man lived, or at least Penny called it lucky. She wasn't sure anymore what Mattie and Dr. Bill would say on that subject. No doubt, Rachelle Shannon would be convicted as well. It turned out, she'd kept a detailed journal recounting each and every act and even distributed a manual to instruct others: "Join the Army, or How to Destroy a Killing Center if You're Just an Old Grandma Who Can't Even Get the Fire Started in Her Fireplace." Mattie claimed to have a copy of the manual, though she'd never shown it to Penny.

When the service was over, Dr. Bill strode offstage in Penny's direction and, catching sight of her, grinned. Flustered, she leapt up and, grabbing the bag, scrambled down the steps. She was embarrassed to be there—it seemed an informality, maybe even a transgression—but within seconds, she realized he'd misread her presence. He'd assumed she was waiting for him, and just before she'd backed into the aisle, he'd raised his arms to enfold her in that big black robe of his. His expression had gone from jubilant to distressed before he disappeared through the side door without a word. It felt like a slap, that look of disappointment. Hurt on both sides. This is what comes of caring for people you don't really know, she thought. It had been the same with her mother. One way or the other, they'd managed to disappoint each other. Sometimes, it had been Delia who'd gone away crying. Other times, Penny had been the one in tears.

After the side door slammed, Penny turned away, cheeks smarting. The church was still half full, people getting to their feet and gathering their things, filing out the double doors. Mattie slipped out of her pew and rushed up the aisle. "Where have you been?" she cried, reaching for the bag.

Penny clung briefly to the handles before letting it go. "What are you doing with the yarn?"

Mattie pretended not to hear. "I'm in a hurry," she said.

"You're always in a hurry," Penny complained. Then: "Wait! Did you see who was sitting next to Juanita?"

Mattie stopped and turned back, exasperation written all over her face. "If you're asking about Buck Sr.," Mattie said slowly and pointedly, "if you're asking whether I saw him sitting with Juanita, the answer is yes. I saw and I said a prayer."

"You don't seem surprised."

"I'm not. She's been seeing him off and on for over a month."

Penny shook her head in disbelief. "Why didn't she tell me?" She could hear the pain in her voice, and her grandmother heard it as well. Penny could see it in her eyes.

Mattie sighed. "If you must know," she said, "she's been using your van to pay him visits. You better talk to her. Now, I've got to go." She hurried back up the center aisle, heels clattering on the hardwood, calling out to Esther and Janeen as she went. They were nowhere in sight.

Penny trudged back to her place on the bottom step. She didn't want to venture outside, not now. Moments before, she'd been among family, but suddenly these people felt like strangers. She sank down and, head in her hands, looked around for consolation—at the white walls, the dark pews, the shining hardwood floors. This is your church, she told herself, raising her eyes to the rose window. But after a few seconds, the stained-glass wheel appeared to spin, an enormous kaleido-scope that threatened to pull her into its dizzying swirl. She had to shut her eyes against it, pull her knees to her chest, take a few deep breaths. By the time she opened them again, the church was empty, and she was alone.

"HE'S not right for you," Penny told Juanita at the shop the next day. She wanted to say that Buck Sr. wasn't good enough for Juanita either, that he looked like a sausage, the kind that hang from the ceilings of delicatessens. Discolored, overstuffed, full of chemicals and preserva-tives, everything bad for you. Who needed him? Certainly not Juanita. She was a quick little sprite, always ready to dance and laugh, whereas Buck Sr. was sluggish and dense. It surprised Penny that he was able to hold his own at the University. He seemed too thick to read difficult textbooks. "You can do better, Nita," she added.

As though voicing his agreement, Buck shrieked from his outpost in the front room. Ordinarily, he would have been in the thick of things, in the big middle of the workroom, but today was no ordinary day, and they all knew it. Like an unhappy couple intent on sparing the child, Juanita and Penny had hauled Buck's playpen to the front and filled the bottom with toys. "He'll be fine out here," Juanita had muttered as she heaved him over the side. And he had been, for the most part. After wailing for several minutes, Buck had quieted and begun flinging his toys onto the floor, a satisfying physical task that he'd evidently com-pleted.

"My love life is nobody's business," Juanita repeated. She sounded injured and indignant, but she looked lovely, all rosy cheeks and raven hair, like a fairy-tale heroine. Anger did good things for her. All morn-ing, she'd been upset, and yet she'd worked quickly and efficiently, doing her usual tasks in half the time. Now she was stationed at the helium tank, filling the last of a dozen Mylar balloons for a six-year-old's party. The other eleven squeaked and jostled above her head, their gold and silver curling ribbons trailing over her shoulders and past her face.

"Did you hear me?" Juanita asked, brushing the ribbons aside. Several caught and tangled in her hair; where the sunlight touched them, they looked like streaks of angel's dust.

"I hear you. I've heard you already." She was clipping the stems of pale pink fuchsia, lovely, languid flowers. While Juanita talked, Penny cupped a bell-shaped blossom in her palm and studied the soft pointed petals and frilly center.

"Penny, are you listening?" Juanita asked. "If you'd just listen for a minute!"

"I'm listening!"

So Juanita started up again, telling Penny how much she loved Buck Sr., how important it was that she see him. "Buck Jr. needs a family!" she exclaimed. Penny couldn't argue with that, though she sometimes thought that *she* was Buck's family, she and Mattie and Dr. Bill and Esther.

"So why didn't you tell me?" Penny interrupted. "Why didn't you ask to use my van? Why sneak out during work hours?"

"I knew you wouldn't like it. I knew you'd try to talk me out of it. You disliked Buck from the first time you met him."

"I've only met him once. That's part of the problem." She remembered the way he'd skulked in a corner of the hospital room. She didn't like him. That was true. "How can I like him? He's not a father to Buck, and I know what it's like not to have a father."

Juanita steamrolled ahead, overlooking the pain in Penny's voice, ignoring her admission. "It's not all his fault he hasn't come around," she insisted. "He doesn't feel comfortable with you." Juanita jerked a knot, tying the last ribbon to the last balloon and letting it rise up to join the others bobbing on the low ceiling. "Is it so hard to believe?" she asked. "Nobody's good enough for you, Penny. No man anyway. Not even Dr. Bill."

"What are you talking about?"

"Mattie sees it. I see it. Dr. Bill may be blind, but the rest of us aren't. It's so ungrateful, not to love someone like that."

It was Penny's turn to say nobody's business, but she bit her tongue. "I don't know what you're talking about," she said, although she did know, now that it had been pointed out to her. She could see it: Penny backing up, Penny holding off, Penny driving away. She didn't want to be close to him, not really, and maybe it wasn't just him, Dr. Bill, but all men. Was that true?

"Mattie is *so* disappointed," Juanita was saying. "Your one chance at happiness, she says. Your one chance and you're so cold with him."

"I'm *not* cold with him," Penny said. "We barely know each other." Her one chance? What did that mean?

"Oh yeah? What about at the clinic, after he got hit? You didn't stay to hold his hand or to go to the hospital with him. Mattie did all that. *You* got in the van and left."

Penny couldn't deny it. How could she possibly argue? In her fist, she clutched a stem of fuchsia; the pendulous flowers swayed in the air. Juanita took a breath to say something else. There was more? More she'd done wrong? But in the interval of silence they heard a man's voice coming from the front room, a gentle sweet voice talking to the baby. Juanita looked curious, then quickly concerned. She hurried out front. "Can I help you?"

"Is this Penelope's Balloons and Bouquets?" he asked. "Is Penny here?"

His voice drew her through the doorway. Carl Solace, she thought.

Sure enough. He was sitting cross-legged in front of the playpen, gazing through the mesh at little Buck, who'd taken up the identical position and was staring right back. While Penny and Juanita stood behind the counter and watched, Carl tossed a teether into the air. It spun lightly above the playpen and fell just out of Buck's reach. Grinning wildly, the baby lurched for it, pulled himself to his feet, and fired the teether directly at his opponent's face, hitting him on the bridge of his nose. "Ouch!" Carl cried in mock pain. Buck clapped his hands and crowed. The baby looked happier than Penny had seen him in months, positively gleeful. He needs a father, Penny thought. It wasn't the first time she'd made this observation, but seeing Carl with Buck made the abstract concept of fatherhood—something Penny knew little about—painfully concrete. Maybe Juanita was right to try and bring Buck Sr. back into their lives. Maybe a halfhearted father was better than no father at all. Wasn't it a shame for both of them that Carl couldn't be Buck's father? Why did God see fit to give Buck Jr. a stuffed sausage for a father and to give this sweet man no child at all?

"Hello, Carl," Penny greeted him.

Smiling, he turned. "Hello there, Penny. How are you?" He had a slow, deep drawl that pulled her closer. She leaned over the counter.

"Fine," she heard herself say. Juanita stirred beside her. Penny knew her friend was curious, but she decided then and there: Carl was her secret, and he'd go on being her secret. Juanita could wonder all she wanted about the identity of the stoop-shouldered man in khaki pants and a wrinkled plaid shirt. "He has curly brown hair shot through with gray," Penny could imagine Juanita saying, "and the most amazing blue-gray eyes. Do you know him, Mattie?" Her grandmother would shake her head. "Never seen him." Oh, but you have, Grandmother, Penny thought.

Carl was getting to his feet, brushing off the back of his pants, moving toward her, squinting a bit as he came, as though the room were too bright for his eyes. Actually, the corners of the room were shadowy, and the shop itself—with its narrow windows and dark hardwood floor—was a little gloomier than Penny would have liked. Carl must be nearsighted, Penny decided. She hoped it was true, that he couldn't see her clearly just now. She was dressed in her oldest and baggiest pair of jeans, and she wasn't sure she'd combed her hair this morning.

"It's good to see you," he said, and put out his hand. His fingers were long and well-formed but stained under and around the nails with something dark and purplish. His eyes followed hers to his hand, and before she could react, he withdrew it and examined his nails a little ruefully. "Sorry," he said. "It's not dirt, it's chalk. I was working on a pastel this morning, and all of a sudden, it hit me. I owe Penny twenty-five dollars." He smacked himself in the forehead and grinned sheepishly. "Forgive me for taking so long."

"It doesn't matter." She was still clutching the stem of fuchsia, and she held it out to him now, as though the apology had been hers. He took it from her and examined the drooping bell-shaped flowers in the palm of his hand. When he looked up, he had a question. She could see it on his face.

"Fuchsia," she said, and he nodded, clearly pleased.

"Fuchsia," he repeated. "Like the color?"

She nodded. "Not this one, of course. It's one of the pale pink varieties." She turned back toward the workroom. "I don't have any of the bright shades right now. We tend to get those in the summer."

"I like this color better," he said, touching one of the flowers tenderly before returning it to her.

From time to time, Penny met men like him. They opened doors to her when she made deliveries, looking a little mussed, a little absent-minded, wiping the hair from their eyes or tucking in their shirts, bending down to tie a shoelace, as though they weren't quite ready to meet the world and were slightly embarrassed because of it. Gentle souls, she thought to herself. Wasn't that the phrase Dr. Bill had used just yesterday? And hadn't he been describing Carl?

"Why don't we go outside for a few minutes?" she suggested. "Take Buck next door for a cookie."

Juanita was clearing her throat, on the verge of introducing herself. If Penny didn't know her manners, Juanita would teach them to her. And knowing Juanita, she wouldn't stop with the introduction. She'd ask a few questions as well. "So how did you and Penny meet?" And Carl would tell her. The cat would be out of the bag. Penny smiled to herself, thinking of Flash. This is nobody else's business, she told herself, and, turning, handed Juanita the stem of fuchsia. "Put this in water with the rest of them. Don't worry about arranging. Just put them in the vase. Then you can start loading the van." Her tone was brisk and no-nonsense, an imitation of her grandmother that sounded surprisingly like the real thing. "I'll be back."

"Well, I guess I knew that," Juanita replied, and spinning on her heel, she disappeared into the back room.

Carl watched closely until she was gone. "I hope I'm not getting in the way here," he said.

She shook her head. "Not at all. I need a break." And after lifting Buck from the playpen, she led the way out the door.

"Beautiful baby," Carl offered as he followed her down the stairs.

"Yes, he's a sweetheart."

"At first I thought he was yours."

Penny stopped stock-still on the landing. Buck leaned back over her shoulder, anxious not to lose sight of his new best friend. "Are you serious?" She didn't know why this should startle her so. She *could* be a mother. Certainly she could be. Carl wouldn't have any way of knowing that she was still a virgin, that she'd never even been properly kissed.

"Why, yes," he said. "Wasn't that you pushing him at the clinic? Later, when I thought back, I realized I'd seen you there."

"How could you remember?" She shifted Buck to her hip, and, immediately, the baby began to squirm. "You were so upset."

"We remember what we want to remember. Don't you think so?"

Penny didn't reply. She made her way down the last flight of stairs and carried Buck onto the porch and out into the sunshine. She'd heard a prediction for rain on the radio this morning, but for now it was glorious outside, a big blue sky scattered with cotton-ball clouds. A summer sky, really. Carl emerged from the darkness of the doorway to stand beside her. She turned to look at him, thinking of what he'd been saying. "If that's true," she said, "I must not want to remember much. I've always told myself I have a bad memory."

He shrugged. "Maybe. What do you think?"

She shook her head, recalling the night at the lake with Dr. Bill. How out of the blue she'd remembered flailing in the water, being pulled out and held by her feet. How she'd blurted something about nearly drowning, a revelation, or so it had seemed. Now she wondered whether it had been the lake that elicited the memory—as she'd assumed—or whether it was something else, some yearning deep inside her?

"What's the very first thing you remember?" Carl asked. She turned to him in surprise, gazed up into his face. No one had ever asked such a thing, but she could see that he was serious; he wanted to know. Carl was a tall man, over six feet, and he stood with his hands thrust in his pants pockets the way Dr. Bill always did, but there the similarities ended. Dr. Bill was forever moving, peering off into the distance, making plans. Carl, on the other hand, seemed in no particular hurry. He walked slowly; he talked slowly. Now he waited patiently for Penny to sort through her memories, to find the one with yellowed edges, a black-and-white remembrance. "Hey there, baby," he said, making a funny face.

"His name is Buck," Penny told him. "I'm going to have to think about this. How about if we get our cookie?"

He shrugged. "Sounds good."

They walked next door to Sweetish Hill Bakery and peered through the glass cases at napoleons, croissants, Danishes, and other delicacies Penny had no names for. Whenever she stopped by the bakery, once or twice a week, she ordered the same thing: a large, flat chocolate-chip cookie. No chitchat, no questions. Standing here with Carl, this no-nonsense approach seemed unfriendly, but it was the way she'd been raised, polite but distant.

He was perfectly at home here. "How's the baklava?" he asked the young woman behind the counter. Today, she wore her long blond hair in pigtails that bounced when she walked.

She shrugged her shoulders. "Too sweet for me," she said. "But lots of people swear by it."

"Got any day-old muffins?"

"Bran, blueberry, carrot." She clipped them off. Already, she'd reached inside the case for Penny's cookie. She didn't bother to ask, simply handed it over. She knows me, Penny thought. But I don't know her.

"Give me a half dozen of the blueberry." He turned to Penny. "I'll take them home for breakfast," he explained. "I guess you like chocolate-chip cookies. What's Buck's favorite?"

At the sound of his name, the baby squealed loudly. "He likes everything," Penny called over the noise. "But he can't eat everything. He crams his mouth full and then he chokes."

"What about a cruller?"

"What's that?"

He pointed at a long twisted doughnut coated with cinnamon and sugar. "Easy to hold, unlikely to crumble."

"Perfect," she replied.

He ordered himself a bear claw along with the muffins and insisted on paying for all of it. When Penny tried to protest, he gently put a hand on hers. "You know better than that," he said slowly. "You came to my rescue, remember? The least I can do is buy you a cookie."

While he had his wallet out, Carl pressed several bills into her hand, the twenty-five dollars, she assumed. She didn't really check, just slipped the money into her pocket and followed him to the grassy slope in front of her building. As soon as she put him down, Buck squashed the cruller in his fist and scurried off, circling the scrub oak once, then again. Most of the time he crawled, but occasionally he would labor to his feet and toddle a few steps. He knew how to walk now but still preferred all fours.

"I thought babies gave up crawling once they learned to walk," Carl said. Although the man might talk slowly and walk slowly, he certainly didn't eat slowly. Already, he'd wolfed down half the bear claw.

"Buck is the first baby I've ever known," she told him. "I wasn't around kids much when I was little. I think you're right, though. Most babies prefer to walk. The thing is, Buck is really good at crawling. He started early and got to where he could crawl someplace lickety-split. Walking is tough for him. Even now, he's as liable to fall as he is to move forward."

Penny watched as Buck barreled away again on all fours.

"He reminds me of a little train," Carl said, "all engine and no cars. Chugging along. Wish I had my sketchbook."

"You're an artist, then?"

He turned and smiled at her. "Sort of." Penny looked into his face a little longer than she should have, took note of the cleft above his full lips and his gray-blue eyes. He's sad, she thought, and having Buck here must cut him to the quick.

"I'm so sorry," she said in a quiet voice. She was breaking her cookie into tiny pieces when Carl's hand came down and rested on hers.

"You don't have a thing to be sorry about, not on my account, anyway." He took a piece from her hand and popped it into his mouth. "Too crunchy," he said, but his voice was tight, controlled.

"It's not fair," she went on. "You seem like such a nice man. . . ." She was working up to telling him that he'd been in her prayers.

"Buck, Buck, get back here, buddy!" he called.

The baby had reached the edge of the sidewalk, and showed no signs of stopping. Penny leapt up to retrieve him, dashing down the slope and grabbing him up just as one pudgy hand touched the curb. "Good grief, Buck," she cried. Part of her wanted to shake him, but instead she lifted him against her chest and squeezed him tight.

Her heart was pounding when she started back up the slope to Carl, who'd already gotten to his feet and was gathering their trash. "I better let you get back to work," he said. "And I've got to be getting to work myself."

"Hold on a minute." She reached out to touch his sleeve. "Let me take him upstairs. I'll be right back."

He was waiting on the bottom step when she returned, his long legs stretched out in front of him, eyes closed, face to the sky. When she sat down beside him, he straightened and turned to her.

"So, you never answered my question. What's your first memory?"

"I'm not sure," she said, caught off-guard. "There's something else I want to tell you." She took a deep breath, worried about what he might think. "Our church is praying for you," she blurted. "Dr. Bill mentioned you in last week's sermon. He asked the congregation to say a prayer for you . . . and your baby."

Carl looked out at the traffic on the street where the cars whipped by with such regularity that they didn't seem quite real. For the longest time, he didn't speak. Penny wrapped her hands around her knees and waited.

"I don't want to hurt your feelings," he finally said. "But I wish you wouldn't pray for me. It doesn't make sense to pray for someone who's not a believer. You see, Penny, I don't believe in God."

She hesitated, but she had to say it. "Then you need my prayers even more than I thought." It hurt her heart, this talk, but she wasn't sure why. She knew there were lots of unbelievers in this world, that you couldn't save all of them. Her mother, for instance. She'd given up on Delia a long time ago.

"Look at me, Penny." His lips were tightly pressed, and his eyes had gone almost entirely gray. "I don't agree with my wife," he said in a slow deliberate voice. "I hate what she did. But that doesn't mean that I agree with you. I *don't* agree with you. What happened two weeks ago, that was between my wife and me. You and that minister and all those other people, you had no right to get in the middle of it that way."

Penny heard herself say the words. "It was nobody else's business."

"That's right." Carl reached over and slipped one of her hands between both of his. "But I'm glad that you were there. I don't know what I would have done without you that day. And I wanted to come and tell you how much your kindness meant to me." He squeezed her hand, then dropped it in her lap. "You know," he said, standing and brushing the back of his pants, "I've made at least a dozen sketches of your face, and I just now realize that I've gotten your mouth wrong." He gazed down at her. "Will you do something? Will you smile for me?"

Penny twisted her lips into what she hoped was a smile. "There," he said, backing away, his hands held up, as though he were taking her picture. "That's it. Now I've got it." He waved and started down the slope toward the rust-colored Mazda, which she spotted now, parked on the side street.

"Bye, Carl!" she called. That's the memory, she thought. It came to her in a flash. Her earliest memory was of standing at the window and waving good-bye. Holding the curtain in her fist, waving and crying. "Bye-bye, bye-bye," she'd shouted. She could feel it now, the heartbreak of that departure, though she had no idea who was leaving or why. Delia, she thought. It must have been Delia.

Nearly to his car, Carl turned back. "If you're ever over at Barton Creek," he called, "stop by Walton's Books and say hi."

She nodded and said a brief thanks to God; this wasn't another good-bye.

THAT evening, Penny curled up in the red chair and watched Flash slowly advance on her food. A pink flick of the tongue reassured the cat of the contents, and she settled on her haunches, front feet folded under her. Eating was a delicate and deliberate affair, no matter that the food was consumed directly from the can. Penny wished she'd thought to tell Carl how happy she was with her cat. How could she have forgotten that? "You did me a favor," she might have said. And why hadn't she asked about his dog? What must he think of her? When the phone rang, she hoped it was him, though she knew it wouldn't and couldn't be. Frightened by the sound, Flash dashed under the bed, and as Penny reached for the receiver, she glimpsed the cat's green eyes, glowing in the darkness. "Scaredy-cat!" she chided.

"Penny?" A man's voice but not Carl's.

"Hello, Dr. Bill," she said.

"Bill," he corrected. "You said you were going to call me Bill. Am I disturbing you?"

"No, Bill." She expected him to laugh, but her joke didn't register.

"Do you have company?" he asked.

"Just my cat. I was talking to my cat."

"Your cat? I didn't know you had one." He was silent for a moment, as though sorting something out. She supposed it might be his jaw that made him sound so awkward, but she also wondered whether Juanita might have talked to him, told him about their visitor. For whatever reason, they seemed to be going backward, getting more formal rather than less. She wished they could be easy with each other. This afternoon, she'd forgotten herself and taken pleasure in a man's company, and now she craved more of it.

"I've had her for about two weeks," she explained. "But my landlord's upset. Grandmother's not an animal lover." Flash was edging out from under the bed one leg at a time; then she scooted on her belly across the floor, quickly making her way back to the can. The pink tongue began flicking away.

"After the sermon, you must think I'm not an animal lover either."

It hadn't occurred to her, but she understood that he was talking about the birds and the BB gun. Instantly, she had a vivid picture in her head of a young Dr. Bill, clutching a gun with piles of bird carcasses about his feet. "That was a long time ago," she said. "And you were just a child."

"An angry child," he admitted. "But you must have been angry too, Penny. And I'll bet you didn't take it out on innocent birds."

No, she told him. She hadn't killed so much as a caterpillar, not on purpose anyway, but there were all sorts of ways to be angry, weren't there? She knew what anger felt like. She wondered to herself, though: Had she been angry as a child or only sad? The answer was obvious: Of course she'd been angry. She had no difficulty recalling the day her mother brought her a tricycle with streamers spouting out of the handlebars, red and white and so new that tears had leaked out of Penny's eyes. Three years earlier, it would have been the perfect gift, exactly what she wanted, but this was her seventh birthday. No matter how small she was for her age, she was certainly not small enough for a tricycle. Her mother had blubbered and made excuses even as Mattie pushed her out the back door and down the steps. "I was so angry, sometimes," Penny said slowly, "angry enough to call my mother names."

"Oh, Penny," Dr. Bill sighed. "That's hard to imagine."

"Why?"

"You're such a gentle soul."

Like Carl? Penny wondered. Was she like Carl, then? Is that why she liked him so much? She glanced down at the hand in her lap, the one Carl had cupped in his own this morning. She wanted it back, that feeling, and closing her eyes, she sighed.

Dr. Bill heard it. "What's wrong?"

"Nothing," she replied. She picked her words carefully. "I was thinking of the man at the clinic. Remember? You said he was a gentle soul too."

"Did I?"

"Yes," Penny insisted, surprised by his doubt. "In the sermon yesterday. You described how he ran into the clinic, how he had a reverence for life."

"So I did," Dr. Bill said. "But it wasn't the important part of the sermon. I'm surprised that's what you remember."

What was he saying? "Of course it was the important part!" she blurted out, her voice raised so that Flash looked up from the nearly empty can. Penny's heart beat faster. "Everything led up to that," she insisted. "The stories you told, the passages from John. It was all about Carl. Don't you remember what you said to me at the clinic? 'Poor bastard. I know how he feels.' " She took a breath and waited for his response. Silence on the other end, a long, deep silence, and in the midst of it she realized she'd given it away, said his name. Fool, she thought, you silly fool. "Dr. Bill, are you there? Did you hear what I said?"

"I heard you. How do you know his name?"

"I don't," she replied. "I saw something in the paper." It was a bad lie, completely transparent. She was no good at lying, especially to her minister. I can't keep secrets from him, she thought. He can read my mind; I just know he can. Part of her wanted to get it over with, confess it, all of it: picking up Carl and taking him to the Humane Society;

stealing the cat; visiting with Carl this morning; his soft, slow voice and full pink lips. All the way home this evening, she'd thought of him, imagined him at his store, ringing up customers, answering the phone. Speaking kindly to everyone who crossed his path. No wonder she'd said his name; no wonder she'd let it slip. "I have to go," she said. "I think someone's at the door."

The receiver clicked on the other end. Dr. Bill was gone without so much as a good-bye.

Chapter 11

FOR THE FIRST MONTH after the abortion, Carl believed that habit would sustain him. He was sad and angry too, but he expected his heartache to pass. To keep his mind occupied, he rose even earlier every morning to work in his studio, but he didn't clean up the mess he'd made destroying the pastels. Bits and pieces of chalk still littered the studio floor, and Carl stepped over them, or around them, or sometimes, when he was feeling dark himself, he deliberately ground the chalk into the wooden floor with the sole of his foot. Each morning, after finishing work, he tracked pastel dust down the hall to the kitchen, dark smudges of red, black, and purple, marks of where he went and where he no longer chose to go.

Hannah was every bit as stubborn as he was, refusing even to remark on his behavior. In fact, she and Carl spoke very little. He gave up cooking for the two of them, and they ate separately, furtively—bolting toast on the way out the door, warming frozen dinners in the microwave and consuming them standing at the counter. After a couple of weeks, the dining-room table was heaped with unopened mail. Once and only once, Hannah worried aloud that the hardwood floor in the studio would be permanently darkened by the chalk dust. Carl nodded, as though he'd known this all along, as though it had been part of his intention to make an indelible record, something they would have to explain when buyers came to see the house. He didn't say this last part out loud, but even to think it was to acknowledge that this period of their lives was more than time passing, that this, too, was change, some movement toward the inevitable.

Although tempted, Carl did not throw away the mess he'd made of the beautiful pastel. Instead, he sprayed the surface with fixative and hung it on the wall with strips of masking tape, placing it where Hannah would have to see it each time she passed down the hall. Sometimes, before going to bed, Carl would stand and study the pastel. Much as he wanted to think of it as ruined, the artist in him was fascinated. He'd intended to destroy his work, but in fact he'd simply transformed it, made of it something even he could not have imagined. The girl in the pastel wasn't gone, just gone into hiding. In places, the swirls of dark chalk hadn't done their job. The toe of the girl's tennis shoe was still visible, and so was the crown of her head.

On a night in mid-October, Carl woke with thoughts of making up. What's done is done, he told himself, a truism that often came to mind. His mother used to say it—about broken glasses and failed tests—and now he said it too, as a consolation and a way of coming to terms with life's ironies. What's done is done. He did not want to undo his marriage. Seventeen years and one stunning betrayal later, Carl still loved his wife. Coming to that decision, he slowly and cautiously rolled toward her. Hannah was awake too; he was sure of it. Her breathing was irregular, and she stirred as he approached. He was hoping to make love, even if they had to pretend the next morning that it hadn't happened. He was willing if she was.

It had been a long time, over a month now, he realized. They'd never gone this long before. Never. He still remembered their first time, on the twin bed in his studio apartment. How wonderful it had been. Afterward, Hannah had stretched her legs, edging Carl over with her knees and marveling on the happenstance of their meeting at the Methodist Center. She'd called it fortune, whereas he'd insisted on fate. Their first disagreement—it had seemed a small thing, but now he understood how large it actually was, how this difference in world view set them at cross-purposes. From Hannah's perspective, pregnancy, too, was an accident, a misfortune, something she needed to correct. She'd said so, hadn't she? And for him? For him, it had been kismet.

Now he reached out and ran his fingers down her narrow back and along her haunches, but she didn't move, not a muscle. Her body was hard to the touch. "I can't do this, Carl," she finally said. Her voice was cold.

"Why not?" he asked. He was close enough to whisper.

"We go weeks without talking and suddenly you want to fuck? Don't you see how wrong that is?"

He didn't, really. It made good sense to him. Sex was a way of talking, wasn't it? Often it was better than talking: hard to argue when you're making love. Sex was where they'd started, and if they were good to each other, it was where they'd end up.

"Are we ever going to make up?" he asked.

"I don't know."

"Don't you want to?"

She turned over to face him and spoke in a rush. "Maybe we've fooled ourselves all these years. Don't you ever wonder what other couples have? Don't you ever wish you could trade places for a few hours, try on someone else's marriage? Then you might know whether yours was good enough, worth all the heartache?"

"I don't have to wonder, Hannah. I know."

And he did. He knew how much he loved her, that loving her had always been worth the considerable heartache. About the marriage itself he was less certain. For better or for worse. From his earliest memories, his parents had been bitterly unhappy. Discord, disappointment, despair, these he knew by heart. *Better* was harder to gauge, and the relationships around him were no help. No one knew the inside of a marriage except the two people involved, and sometimes they didn't have a clue either. "Do you still love me?" he asked.

"Yes," she whispered, "but it's not just a matter of loving, is it?"

Here, he had to concede: "I guess not."

They both went silent, and after a while Carl heard her drift off to sleep. Her breathing evened and deepened, but he lay awake until four o'clock, when he gave up on sleep and padded down the hallway to the living room. Deliberately leaving off the lights, he felt around in the dark, finding his sketch pad on the floor by the sofa and a sharpened pencil on the kitchen counter by the phone. Briefly, he considered working at the dining-room table, which was partially lit by the neighbor's porch light, but decided against it. Instead, he returned to the deep darkness of the living room, edging around the coffee table and flopping down on the sofa. For a minute or two, he sat and looked around, his eyes wide open and searching for form and shape in the furnishings of the room.

As his eyes adjusted, he made out the boxy shape of the television and the long lines of the bookshelves. On any other night, he wouldn't have questioned what he saw, but now he began to wonder. Did his eyes see the furniture, or was it a matter of his mind creating the familiar from the sawdust of memory? He flipped open the sketchbook and had just put pencil to paper when Neil joined him, clicking across the hardwood floor. The dog's cool wet nose nuzzled his bare calf, and Carl reached down to rub his soft fur, each hair distinct beneath his fingertips. Once Neil settled against him, Carl began to draw in earnest, the loudest sound in the room the scratching of pencil on heavy paper.

Early the next morning, as honeyed light pooled on the dining-room floor, Carl stirred, then opened his eyes. He was slumped on the couch, disoriented and stiff, and it took a minute to recall the sketchbook. In the night, it had slid to the floor. When Carl bent to pick it up, his head was still too fuzzy to remember what he'd done. He was surprised, then, to find Penny, her long, lovely neck, the curling tendrils of hair. But the most interesting part wasn't his choice of subject, but this: In the darkness, he hadn't turned to a blank sheet of paper.

The sketch had been done right over the top of work he'd finished weeks ago. Penny's slender neck intersected a baby's ear, and barely visible beneath the penciled strokes of hair, an infant's eye shone, almond-shaped and staring. Carl thought of little Buck, how he'd bent to lift the baby from the grass and, raising the small body to his chest, felt the child's breath on his cheek. Suddenly, he was filled with a sense of hope so keen it struck him as painful. Where it had come from or what it meant he didn't know, but he trusted it all the same. Pressing the sketchbook to his chest, Carl raised himself from the sofa and slowly, deliberately, walked down the hall to the studio.

ON THE Saturday before Halloween, Noah stopped by the bookstore. It was closing time, and Carl was bushed. Business had been nonstop all day. Already, the conscientious had begun Christmas shopping. Carl had even overheard a few of them bragging about being finished. So much energy and initiative made him ache. He'd just rung up the last sale, waved good-bye to the part-timers, and was in the midst of lowering the metal gate when Noah scooted under it, bending backward in an awkward-looking limbo. Anything for a dramatic entrance or exit. "You rang?" Noah asked through gritted teeth. Earlier in the evening, Carl had called the Ark and been told that Noah had just stepped out for a bite.

"You got my message?"

"Of course. You think my employees are total flunkies, don't you?"

"Don't you?" Carl countered. Noah didn't rise to the bait. He was busy rubbing at the small of his back. "You all right?"

"I'll be all right in a minute," Noah said irritably.

"You're too old for stunts like that," Carl scolded. "Hold on a minute, and I'll help you to your car. Do you think you can drive?"

"Don't be ridiculous. I'm not going home. I'm stopping by my bar. Great jazz piano on Saturday nights. Wanna come?"

"So it's *your* bar now?"

Noah shrugged. "Well, all right. I'm a part owner." He stood rigidly, one hand still pressed to his back. With the other one, he held out two fingers to show the small space in between. "A wee little part. What do you say?" He was dressed up this evening, in gray slacks and a shimmering green silk shirt.

"I don't think so," Carl replied, though he was tempted. It would be a relief to have something to do on a Saturday night, some reason not to go home to Hannah, who would give him yet another dose of the silent treatment. Who knew? Maybe if he was gone long enough, she'd find she missed him. He missed her, but recently he'd begun to wonder if it were *this* Hannah he missed or an earlier version, a younger, lighthearted Hannah, the one who slept in on weekends and brought a puppy home from a baby shower. The Hannah who surprised him now and again, in a good way.

"Come on," Noah urged. "Do you good. Cheer you right up." He edged closer, until he could pinch Carl's cheek, tugging on it the way an old aunt would do. "Let Hannah worry a little. Do *her* good."

"Ouch!" Carl slapped at his friend's hand. He doubted that going to Twitters would cheer him. He'd been once before. It had been his first time at a gay bar, and he'd expected something similar to the sports bars Jimmy frequented: crowds of loud and rowdy men, guzzling beer and acting like asses. The reality had been entirely different—murmuring voices, oriental carpets, and dark green walls. Later, it had occurred to him that the men at the sports bar were taking a break from women, thus the raunchy, rude atmosphere. But at Twitters, women weren't part of the equation. As Noah had told Carl early in their friendship, "We like women, we just don't *like* them." And Carl had quipped, "We *like* women, we just don't like them." Not true, but not entirely untrue either. "You know me," he added now. "I like men, I just don't *like* them."

Noah was in the process of recovering his mobility. He paced back and forth in front of the gate, stopping now and then to stretch tentatively from side to side. "Well, if you won't have any fun," Noah complained, "at least tell me why you called so I can be on my way."

"I wanted to borrow E.T. for Monday evening. Is that possible?"

"Borrow my bird?" Noah paused to consider. "Dressing up as a pirate, then?"

Carl had waited until the last minute to plan his costume. Too busy being depressed. Every year he was at pains to outdo himself, to surprise Helen and her kids. This year's disguise wouldn't be much, but he figured the bird would give it flair. "How'd you know?" he asked.

Noah frowned in mock irritation. "Please," he said. "What other costume needs a bird to complete it?" He shook the gate with one hand. "Are you going to keep me locked in here?"

"Until you give me my answer."

"Yes, by all means, yes! But if he shits on you, don't come to me with your cleaning bill."

"It's a deal." Carl raised the gate and watched his friend hobble off down the empty concourse. "Take care of your heart!" he called after him. Noah was in love again, this time with his business partner, Harry. Carl had a bad feeling about it.

Noah didn't turn back, but he waved over his shoulder. "To hell with my heart!" he shouted. "It's my back I'm worried about."

THE trick-or-treaters would begin ringing the doorbell any minute. Carl stood before the bathroom mirror and weighed the merits of his costume. Swashbuckling or lewd? The black stretch pants were . . . well, revealing, but when he cinched the scarf at his waist, the ends hung down far enough to hide the bulge of his crotch. The frilly white shirt was too snug as well, so tight across the chest and upper arms that he had to open the top three buttons, exposing his nearly hairless chest. He had no idea what he looked like from behind and no intention of checking. Best not to know. Overall, the effect was far from perfect. Maybe he should have kept looking, but he'd been browsing at Goodwill for nearly half an hour before he'd discovered a white ruffled shirt with long puffy sleeves. The price was right, $3.50. He hadn't tried anything on, just held it up in front of him. So far as he knew, people didn't try on clothes at Goodwill, especially men who were trespassing in the women's section.

"This shirt is perfect," he'd told the girl who rang it up. She was a gum-popping teenager, not at all the sort of help he'd have expected at Goodwill. Shouldn't you be in school? he wanted to ask. Instead, he told her that he was dressing as a pirate for Halloween.

"Just so you know," she snapped. "This is a blouse, not a shirt. Shirts are for men; blouses are for women."

Carl tried to set her straight. As far as he was concerned, it didn't matter which side the buttons were on. "Once I leave this store," he said, "it's a shirt."

"Whatever," she'd replied.

Now that he was wearing it, he could see that she was right; clearly, it was a blouse, meant for a woman with smaller shoulders than his and preferably some kind of breasts. Now that he looked closely, he noted that the damn thing had darts at the chest. He tightened the scarf around his waist and hoped for the best. If Grayson spotted the darts, he'd never let Carl live it down. Grayson was at the age where he was just itching to belittle someone, especially an adult too polite and civilized to pound him to a pulp. Uncle Carl fit the bill. He shrugged at himself in the mirror. "To hell with it," he said. If he was lucky, all eyes, including his nephew's, would be on E.T.

Just before it was time for Helen's family to arrive, Carl clipped on a gold hoop earring and slipped a tarnished silver chain over his head. A huge cross studded with simulated turquoise dangled near his breastbone, the perfect touch and yet another Goodwill find. The eye patch he saved for last. He'd cut it from an old black T-shirt and right away discovered that the material was too thin. The slightest gust of air would flip the patch against his brow, revealing a perfectly serviceable blue eye. Even so . . . "Not bad," he said to the mirror. He wished Hannah were home. She never dressed up herself but was generally appreciative of *his* efforts. Sometimes she even came to his aid. The year he'd dressed up as a woman she'd put on his makeup and chosen his jewelry.

The Halloween tradition had been established years ago, back when Grayson was a toddler. Helen and Jimmy had just moved into the house on Mount Bonnell, and the area was so remote their only neighbors were deer and armadillos. That was fine, mostly, except on Halloween, when Grayson had nowhere to trick-or-treat. Back then, Hannah had been in grad school at the University of Texas, and Carl was halfheartedly taking a class or two as well. The two of them had lived in a dumpy apartment building, one that turned out to be ideal for the needs of a toddling trick-or-treater: numerous doors close together, with occupants who were delighted to be interrupted on an otherwise boring evening.

By the time Carl and Hannah moved to their present house, Grayson was ready to roam more widely, and his sister, Cassie, had joined the family. The staid neighborhood was perfect for them, off the beaten path and not many other children to compete for the loot. Retirees were certain to burn porch lights, and, excepting widows with a fondness for lemon balls, they gave good candy. On a typical Halloween, Helen and Jimmy came to dinner and afterward sat in folding chairs in the front yard, passing out Snickers to the grandchildren of a few neighbors but mostly watching Grayson and Cassie make the rounds. Costumes were optional for the adults, but Carl always made the effort.

When the doorbell rang, he rushed down the hall, stopping off at his studio to retrieve E.T. from the small traveling cage. The bird was in a bad mood and only grudgingly edged up Carl's sleeve. Riding caged in the car had irritated him to no end. Aside from an occasional high-pitched squawk, the bird had been entirely silent. Not a good sign. Noah had warned Carl that E.T. might misbehave, that riding on Carl's shoulder for most of the evening would test the relationship. "It's a dominance thing," Noah explained. "If his head is level with your head, he starts to think he's as big as you are. All of a sudden you're a rival, and he bites the hell out of your nose. I know whereof I speak. Every now and again, walk him down your arm to remind him who's boss."

Throwing open the door, Carl yelled out: "Yo-ho-ho, and a bottle of rum!"

Clustered under the porch lamp were Helen, Jimmy, Cassie, and Grayson, in varying degrees of disguise. Jimmy was Frankenstein's monster in a polo shirt; Helen, the fairy godmother in jeans. Cassie was dressed as a hula girl in a lei and grass skirt. Across her small flat chest, she wore a bikini top fashioned from two halves of a coconut strung together with purple grosgrain ribbon. For modesty's sake, she wore a skin-colored leotard underneath. Helen was known for her puritan streak, but not Jimmy. There was something raw about Jimmy, something greedy and lascivious. When the four of them ate together, Carl always expected to look up and catch Jimmy licking his fingers.

"Is that your bird, Uncle Carl?" Cassie asked when they were inside. She couldn't take her eyes off the parrot.

"My friend's bird. Just visiting this evening." Carl turned his face to E.T., on the off chance that the bird might relent and speak. "Polly want a cracker?" he coaxed. E.T. stared straight ahead, no more lifelike than the pink flamingos in the studio.

"Is that thing alive?" Grayson sounded incredulous. He was on Rollerblades. In one hand, he clutched a hockey stick, in the other, a pillowcase for treats. Not much of a costume, Carl thought. Then he noticed the cap. Grayson sported a ball cap, worn backward of course, to which he'd glued half a hockey puck. To the casual observer, it appeared that half the puck had just entered his skull. Fake blood dribbled down his forehead and over one ear.

"Nicely done, Grayson." Carl nodded his approval. "And yes, the bird's alive. His name's E.T. like the extraterrestrial."

"E.T.?" Helen echoed. "Funny name." She looked lovely this evening. She'd piled her auburn hair on top of her head and sprinkled it with glitter. Over her eyes, she wore a blue velvet half mask, and in one hand she brandished a wand. There, however, her efforts stopped. Below the shoulders, she was the same old Helen in an oversize chambray shirt, baggy jeans, and white tennis shoes.

"Is the fairy godmother on vacation?" Carl asked.

"She likes to be comfortable," Helen replied.

"You look fetching," Carl told her, and was pleased to see the bright smile his compliment drew. She did look lovely, but she also looked tired, or worried, or maybe ill. As though to confirm his thoughts, she slipped over to the couch and took a seat, a small sigh escaping from her lips as she leaned back into the cushions.

"Hot for the end of October," Jimmy put in. His voice was muffled by a rubber Frankenstein mask. Otherwise, he was dressed as himself, a burly, middle-aged real-estate developer in Dockers slacks and a golf shirt going dark under the arms. All you had to do was mention heat and Jimmy sweated like a damn pig.

Carl offered his brother-in-law a Shiner, Helen a glass of wine, and the kids a Coke. Helen and the children refused politely, but Jimmy followed Carl into the kitchen for a beer, pulling off the mask as he went. "So much for Halloween." He gestured toward the bird. "That thing well-behaved?"

"The bird?"

"Of course, the bird."

Carl shrugged, causing E.T. to rise on his shoulder and then descend, the clipped wing feathers brushing against his ears. "We'll see," he said. "He's always been a gentleman in the store. Usually talks up a storm, but he's giving me the silent treatment right now—like someone else I know." This last had slipped out.

"Hannah?"

Carl nodded.

"She mad at you?"

Another nod. Carl reached into the fridge for Jimmy's beer, passed it to him, and grabbed one for himself as well. Turning back, Carl caught Jimmy twisting off the cap and making a small grimace that was probably just for show. He was strong as an ox, this guy. "God she's got a lot of nerve," Jimmy said.

Carl froze. Just what did that mean? Now Jimmy's face wore a variation of a grimace; maybe this expression spoke concern. Carl hoped not. "What do you mean?"

"Helen told me about the abortion." He shook his head. "It's a goddamn shame, Carl."

Carl's little stab at intimacy had gotten completely out of hand. This was real intimacy, with his brother-in-law of all people. Now Jimmy was glancing around the kitchen, as though sizing up its resale value. "So where is Hannah?" he asked.

"At school. Halloween dance. Assistant principals trade off going. It was Hannah's turn."

Jimmy took a swig of beer. "Yeah? Teachers go to those dances?"

Carl shrugged again and felt E.T. shift his perch and ruffle his feathers. He made a mental note not to move his shoulders. The bird clearly didn't like it. "Some of them," Carl replied. "They always need chaperons."

"You don't say?" Jimmy wandered to the doorway and peered around the corner. Carl was suddenly aware of the mess. The chalk dust had made its way out of the hall and into the living room, a strange dark track, the sort of thing strangers were sure to notice and comment on. But Jimmy wasn't interested in the floors. "Think I could watch the Cowboys and pass out the occasional candy bar while you and Helen make the rounds? I figure you want to get some use out of that costume. No use hiding in here."

Carl had forgotten it was Monday-night football season. He wasn't much of a fan. His resentment of high-school athletics still hung over the sport, tainting it for him. Every football player he saw looked disagreeable, an older version of one of those rude seniors who liked to slam the artistic boys into the lockers. Even the fact that he'd run track hadn't exempted him. True to form for a beefy real-estate developer, Jimmy loved football—every yard, every inning, every grunt and groan.

"Fine with me," Carl said.

"Dad!" Grayson called from the next room. When Carl and Jimmy reentered the living room, the boy was stationed next to the front door, his sister beside him. "It's dark. Can we go, already?" Grayson whacked the hockey stick at the baseboard, just hard enough to make a satisfying smacking sound.

"Where's your mother?" Jimmy asked.

"Gone to the bathroom," Cassie piped up.

Carl sighed. The place was such a mess. Hannah usually insisted on cleaning up a little before her sister's visits. Helen was an immaculate housekeeper. Just now Carl wouldn't have been surprised to discover her in the bathroom, scrubbing out the tub. When she called to him from the hallway, he half expected to find his sister-in-law with a can of Comet in her hand.

Instead, she was stationed in the doorway of the studio, surveying the room. The worst of the mess was here, right in front of his easel. Carl waited for the question: What the hell's going on? But Helen wasn't looking at the floor. Instead, she pointed to the ruined pastel, hanging on the wall. "What happened?" she asked.

Without thinking, Carl shrugged, and E.T. let go with a screech of protest. Helen jumped back against the doorjamb. "Good grief!" she cried. "That bird seemed stuffed until now."

"He's real." Carl followed her gaze to the pastel and then to the floor. "It's all real. Guess I had a little temper tantrum."

Helen shook her head in that motherly disappointed way he'd seen her use with Grayson and Cassie.

"I wish you hadn't made a mess of it, Carl," Helen said. "It didn't hurt *her*; it hurt you."

"Actually, I kind of like it this way."

"Serious?"

He nodded.

"But you can't see the little girl anymore." She squinted at the pastel. "At least I can't see her."

"Not much," Carl admitted. "But if you look closely . . ."

Helen stepped into the room and stood with her hands on her hips, studying it. After a minute, she returned to his side. "It's a damn shame." She echoed her husband, but, coming from Helen's lips, the sentiment sounded sincere and heartfelt. She wasn't talking about the pastel anymore. "A baby would have been so good for her," she said sadly.

Carl sighed and folded his arms across his chest. What could he say? "Hannah worried that she wouldn't be a good mother," he told her.

Helen let out a little snort of disbelief. "You're so forgiving, Carl. I'll tell you what she was worried about." She ticked them off on her fingers. "Her figure, first of all. Getting up in the middle of the night. Cleaning spit-up off the shoulder of her favorite suit. And this—here's the big one—she was worried she'd finally have to pack up and move out of her comfy little tower. You can't be a mother and a princess both."

Carl was taken aback. "Don't you think you're being too hard on her?" he asked. This wasn't his sweet Helen talking. The woman in the mask sounded bitter, maybe even a little jealous.

She cocked her head and tapped his forehead with the wand. "Wake up, sweet prince," she said. "You're the real royalty in this family. Only she's got you convinced you're a peasant."

Carl didn't know what to say. "I thought you two were close."

Helen shook her head and laughed. "We *are* close," she told him, "as close as you can be to Hannah. No one loves her more than I do. But I'm not blind."

Just then Grayson shouted down the hallway: "Mom, Uncle Carl!"

"Be right there, sweetie," she called back. As Carl turned away, she grabbed his sleeve. "Listen to me. I'm telling you the truth here. Where Hannah is concerned, we're all just standing under the tower shouting up at her." She nodded her head at the pastel. "Why do you think you like it better this way?" She searched his face. "You know, don't you? It's more like real life. You can't quite see her. She's hidden."

Abruptly, the television blared, but the noise was no match for Jimmy, who bellowed over it. "Hey, you two! Time's a wasting."

Quickly, Helen pulled Carl's face to hers and pecked his cheek. "I'm sorry if I upset you," she whispered. "It's just you deserve more than that." He followed her up the hall. She wasn't talking to him anymore, but he heard her nonetheless. "We both do," she said.

Chapter 12

A HALF HOUR BEFORE the dance began, Mr. Pilsner pulled Hannah aside and he told her his wife was being admitted to the hospital for more tests. They were in the hallway outside the gym, alone for the moment. "Her lungs," he said with a little gasp. "She's having trouble breathing." Hannah reached out to touch his arm. Did he want the reassurance of a hug? she wondered. Or should she go on pretending everything would be okay?

"I'm so sorry," she said, which covered everything and nothing. "Anything I can do?"

"Maybe," he replied. "There may be something."

"Let me know," she said. "Whatever you need."

"I might leave a little early this evening. And I may take off a couple of weeks. Which would make you acting principal."

Hannah nodded. "Maybe you should leave now," she suggested.

He shook his head. "Not yet," he said, "but early."

"Take it easy. Let me run interference." He loved sports metaphors, and Hannah was pleased to see a slight smile and a nod. But he wasn't really with her. His eyes were vacant and fixed on something in the distance. "Is someone with her now?" she asked.

"Her sister's there." He smiled and shrugged, and she saw the way it was, the family gathering round the bedside.

Hannah had always wanted to be principal, but not this way, never this way. Give him a hug, something told her, and so she pulled him in close. She expected an awkward retreat; instead, Mr. Pilsner settled against her, head on her shoulder. They were about the same height, a couple arrested in the midst of a slow dance, only the roles were reversed. She was leading now. For a minute, Hannah expected him to weep. Then she expected *she'd* weep. The man's anguish was nearly palpable. It was horrible and so unfair. What had Dorothy Pilsner ever done to deserve this? Or Mr. Pilsner, for that matter? Over the last two years, Hannah had been privy to the progress of the illness: the initial diagnosis and subsequent mastectomy, the grueling months of chemotherapy followed by the euphoria of a brief remission, and now the despair of metastasis. Once in a while, she stood in the bathroom and held tight to her own breasts. Don't turn on me, she told them. Please don't.

Hannah's first official act of the evening was to toss out a boy dressed as a tampon. The boy timed his entrance well, slipping in the gym doors as Mr. Pilsner announced the rules for the costume contest and pointed out the foil-covered box where students could drop off nominations. Hannah was one of the first to spot his entrance through a side door. Giggles broke out, heads turned, first a few and then the whole crowd.

The boy—what girl would dress as a feminine-hygiene product?—wore a long white tube suspended from his shoulders, the way rodeo clowns wear barrels. His neck and head were painted white, and to the top of his skull—shaved for this little ruse—he'd glued a large puff of cotton. Hannah's first impulse was to laugh out loud but she stifled it, particularly when Mr. Pilsner leaned into the microphone. "Dr. Solace, are you out there?" he asked, clearing his throat. They'd developed a series of signals—or rather, the principal had developed signals—and Hannah had learned to anticipate and interpret them. Clearing his throat meant Hannah should rid him of a problem, and, in this case, that meant the tampon had to go.

While Hannah watched, the tampon minced its way toward the stage, rather like a bride approaching the front altar. When the audience began clapping and cheering, the tampon grinned ear to ear, and Hannah guessed he would have waved, if his arms hadn't been trapped inside the tube. By the time she reached him, the sharper students had begun to protest. Evidently, she wasn't the only one who understood the import of a frog in Mr. Pilsner's throat. Ignoring the boos, Hannah wrapped one arm around the tampon and twirled it about-face.

"Let's go," she hissed. The costume was complete with a long length of string trailing from the end of the tube, and Hannah had to watch her step to keep from tromping on it.

"It's not in bad taste," the tampon complained. He'd probably begun this argument with his mother or father before leaving the house and thought to continue it with Hannah.

"Did I say it was in bad taste?" Her mind was on Erica and their little encounter in the bathroom last month. "Was this your idea?" she asked the boy. His greasepaint was smearing a bit, and she noticed he'd forgotten to cover one ear. Against all that white, the skin of his earlobe looked pink and vulnerable.

"My idea?" he huffed. She leaned in close to hear him. The crowd was raising a ruckus, booing and cheering all at once. "Of course, it was my idea!"

Hannah recognized his voice now, slightly nasal and arrogant-sounding. He was one of the art gang, one of Clendon James's protégés. She glanced about for the art teacher, or rather, for his wildly gesturing arms; the man was constitutionally incapable of holding still. His declared life goal was to encourage the artistic spirit. Let him help me out with this, she thought. But although she saw several other teachers in the crowd—Donald Reeves, Barbara Avery, Cecile Barbone—Clendon was nowhere in sight. Cecile, Hannah noticed, was dressed as a katydid, complete with flowing green dress and antennae. (Last year, for her first Halloween party, she'd come as a spider, complete with slinky black tights. And what would she be next year? Hannah wondered. A roach? A beetle? Ah, yes, a butterfly.) Hannah was certain that several ardent boys would nominate their science teacher for best costume, while everyone else in the room would stuff the ballot box with votes for the world's biggest tampon.

After the boy in the tube had shuffled out to the parking lot—she felt a little sorry for him, to tell the truth—Hannah made the rounds of the room and decided everything was under control. Mr. Pilsner finished his announcements, then slipped away, waving good-bye from the door. The disc jockey took over. Usually, the chaperons for these affairs could count on one disruption per evening; to get it over with early was all to the good. Hannah mingled, ate a few too many chips, and had a good laugh with Erica, who sidled over and whispered to Hannah, "Bet you thought I put him up to it, didn't you?"

Hannah replied that she'd thought nothing of the sort, but a small smile gave her away.

"I wish I had," Erica admitted. She was a cat for the evening—a black cat, naturally—and the costume seemed a good choice. According to legend, cats had nine lives, and Erica seemed to feel she'd been granted an extra one. Her first AIDS test had come back negative, and although the clinic recommended a repeat test in six months, Erica told Hannah that she thought she'd gotten lucky for once. "Sorry my dad's being such a jerk." She wrinkled her black nose. "I told him he ought to be grateful to you."

Hannah nodded. *Jerk* did not really cover it, but she knew better than to respond. Smart though she might be, Erica was still a child, and a child couldn't be expected to keep secrets, especially from her parents. Still, it was all regrettable. Erica had confided in her mother about the test, who immediately got on the phone with her ex-husband in Austin. When Gabe Faber called the school to complain, he asked to speak to the principal, but Mr. Pilsner was out. The call was redirected to Hannah herself, which seemed to further infuriate the attorney. He'd spent at least twenty minutes ranting about right to privacy, parent–child confidentiality, and a number of other issues that seemed entirely beside the point. And in the end, Gabe Faber had managed to do just what he'd intended to do, to scare and intimidate her. Who knew what grounds he could scrape up for a lawsuit? If a woman could file a suit because her coffee was too hot, anything was possible.

The party was about two hours old and beginning to thin out when the man in the Frankenstein mask arrived. At the time, Hannah was deep in conversation with Mrs. Redix, senior English, and so relaxed she might not have noticed him. But Mrs. Redix never missed a thing. "See that man in the monster mask?" she asked Hannah, pointing her plump, pink index finger at a husky man in a dark green golf shirt. He was standing in the doorway of the gym, easy to spot because he was half a head taller than most. "What do you suppose he's up to?"

The man was clearly having trouble seeing through the slits of his mask. He tried to adjust the rubber around his eyes; when that failed, he yanked the mask down at the neck, forcing the holes to stretch. Take it off, for God's sake, Hannah thought.

She shrugged. "Probably looking for his daughter." He had anxiety written all over him, in the set of his shoulders, in the jerky movements of his hands. "Some dads go bonkers when their little girls start to date," Hannah commented. It was true. She'd seen it many times, a profound and free-floating jealousy that completely robbed middle-aged men of their judgment.

"My father was just like that," Mrs. Redix said. Hannah blinked and tried to imagine matronly Mrs. Redix as a lovely young girl with a protective father. It wasn't so difficult, really. The English teacher still had wavy brown hair and a brightness to her smile that drew strangers her way. In fact, the man in the mask was looking in their direction now. When Hannah glanced over, they locked eyes. That did it. She didn't need to hear his voice or pull off the mask. She recognized the build of his body, the half-moon of sweat at his armpits, the way he appraised everyone and everything in his path. Bastard, she thought. Helen was right about you. All that crazy talk about luna moths was absolutely on the mark.

"Excuse me?" Hannah managed to say to Mrs. Redix.

"Certainly," she said briskly. "Go get him."

Jimmy tried to slip away, but Hannah was too fast for him. Before he could make it to the door, her hands grasped one massive elbow. She leaned in close, determined not to make a scene. "Are you out of your mind?" she hissed. "Either come with me right now, or I'm calling the police. I'll have you arrested for trespassing. I swear to God I will." After pinching his skin, digging in with her fingernails, Hannah let go, turned on her heel, and headed for the back doors and the parking lot. She didn't look back to see if he was following. He didn't have a choice.

She strode out into the darkness, around the corner of the gym to the dimly lit parking lot. Off to her right, she could make out two teenagers necking in the front seat of an old junk heap, completely oblivious to her and to the big man hulking behind her in the monster mask. If he wanted to, he could give them a good scare right now, she thought. She could hear him breathing, feel the dense presence of his body, like a boulder that had been rolled into her path.

"Are you drunk, Jimmy?" she called back, slowing her pace. She heard him plop down on the hood of a nearby car. The metal made an aching, resistant sound as it bent with his weight. She stopped but didn't turn back, not just yet.

"No," he replied. "I drank one beer at your house. I wish I were— drunk, I mean. This might be more fun. I wanted to see Cecile, that's all. Just to lay eyes on her. She won't let me come to her house, won't talk to me on the phone. I leave these long messages on her answering machine." Hannah couldn't believe he was telling her all this. Was he crazy, then? She gazed up at the stars, willing him to stop. But he went right on. "I know it's pathetic, Hannah. Are you going to tell Helen? Is that what you're going to do?"

Angry, Hannah whirled about to face him. He'd taken off the mask. It lay on the hood of the car, a lumpy mass of rubber. Jimmy wiped his sweaty face, then ran his fingers through his hair.

"I don't know, Jimmy," Hannah said. The funny thing was, she did know. For nearly thirty years, it had been her job in life to protect Helen, to shield her from whatever ugliness was bearing down on them at the time. She didn't even have to think about it. She would keep his secret. But that didn't mean *he* was off the hook. "You're a shit, you know that?"

"I know, Hannah." His tone was patient, long-suffering. "Grade B shit. Helen deserves far better. She's told me so time and again."

This response infuriated her. "Don't make fun of me, Jimmy. And don't you dare make fun of her."

He sighed deeply and kicked the side of the car with his foot, punctuating the noise with his denial: "I'm not, I'm not, I'm not." Then: "Goddamn it, Hannah! Much as I love Helen, I've considered divorcing her, just to give her a chance at somebody better."

"How noble of you," Hannah replied. It made her sick, this kind of talk. "I've got a simpler solution: Why not *be* someone better yourself?"

"Yeah, well, that would be great, if I could just manage it. Problem is, I've always been a jackass. I was a little boy jackass before I was a teenage jackass. Maybe I could cover up my jackass tendencies, disguise myself as something nobler, fool the world for a while. But I'm never going to fool my wife."

"All you have to do is be faithful to her."

"No." He shook his head mournfully. "There's a whole lot more to it than that." The headlights of the old junk heap switched on. They waited while the engine shuddered to a start and the two lovers pulled slowly away. "For what it's worth," Jimmy continued, "I advised her to stay out of yours and Carl's problems."

Hannah felt as though she'd been slapped. "She told *you?*" She must have sounded like a child, because Jimmy leaned forward and took her hand. It was a simple gesture, kindly meant. But it made her remember his naked body crossing the room, the way he'd taken her hand and pressed the pacifier into her palm. She'd felt as though she was going to faint then; she felt the same way now.

"Helen tells me everything." He stopped and thought about that for a minute, his thumb rubbing Hannah's palm. At last, he went on: "Or at least it seems she does. And that's fine, you know? I've always been glad to be that person for her. But here's the thing: If one person bares their soul, the other person is forced to keep secrets. That's just the way relationships work. There's a speaker and a listener. And the listener never gets around to revealing himself; he can't, really. It's not in the cards."

Hannah was surprised into silence. The evening was cool and breezy, and the stars blinked above them, dulled by the city lights but still visible. The high school was situated on the periphery of downtown, and if she turned her back on the skyline and looked out over the river, Hannah could almost believe in a smaller town, an earlier time. Was it true that the world was more complicated now, or did it just seem that way because people lived longer, had more time to tangle their lives into hopeless little knots? Obviously, she'd never given Jimmy his due. In her relationship with Helen, she, Hannah, was the speaker. It had always been that way. But did that mean Helen had been protecting *her* all these years? Had she completely misunderstood their relationship?

"Hannah," Jimmy whispered, leaning closer, holding tight to her hand. "Please. This crazy attraction to Cecile, it doesn't cancel out my love for Helen. I've always loved Helen, ever since she spoke three words in my direction. Give me a break here, Hannah. You know Helen. She's like Carl. It's hard to live up to people like that." What was he saying? What in the world was he saying?

He went on to tell her that Carl had dressed like a pirate tonight, complete with a live bird on his shoulder. "The fucking bird talks, Hannah. All that trouble, and no child to show off for." He stopped then, realizing what he'd said. "I'm sorry, but as long as we're having this little truthfest, I might as well tell you that Carl was tailor-made to be a father."

Hannah tried to wrench her hand out of his grip, but he wouldn't let her go, and, what's more, he took the opportunity to grab her other hand as well, forcing her to face him. She could feel his knee pressing against her hip. "The problem is, Jimmy," she said slowly and distinctly, "I'm not tailor-made to be a mother."

He snorted right in her ear. She wanted to hit him. If he'd let her go at that instant, she would have socked him. Maybe he knew that, because he held on tight. "You're *Helen's* mother, Hannah. Aww, shit, do I have to tell you this? This job you've got yourself here. It's professional parenting. Only thing is, you're stuck with the hard parts. You do the discipline and hope like hell that somebody else gets around to the love."

"Let go, Jimmy," she said. Her voice was shaking. She could hear it, and that meant he heard it too. But she couldn't worry about that. She had to get away. Jimmy dropped her hands in a gesture of defeat, and she stepped back. "I've had just about enough of this little 'truthfest,' " she told him. She wrapped her arms around her chest and shivered. It felt chilly, as though winter had suddenly slipped in. "I think you better go home."

He glanced back toward the open doorway of the gymnasium. Cecile was standing there, looking out at them. Hannah recognized the silhouette, the willowy frame and the silly antennae on top of her head. So, she'd seen him too. Now what? Now what were they going to do? "What were you thinking, Jimmy?"

"I wasn't thinking, Hannah. Isn't that perfectly obvious?" He jammed the mask back over his head, lifted himself from the hood, and stalked off into the darkness.

FOR Hannah, sex was always better in dreams than in real life, and the reason was simple: She was less inhibited in her dreams, more accepting and assertive. She didn't know whether this was true for everyone, but she suspected that no, it wasn't. Her dreams, not movies or talk shows, gave Hannah the sense that she was missing something in real life, that she was walking through her days as though down a long narrow hallway, white walls interrupted now and then by a door. Behind some of the doors, she could hear people making love: real love, physical love, unguarded, tender, and brutal. Hannah didn't think about sex very often, but occasionally something would happen to remind her, a dream maybe, or those accidents of real life that don't seem accidental at all.

On the Wednesday after Halloween, Hannah happened into the teacher's lounge late in the afternoon and discovered an aide sitting in the lap of a handsome young janitor. They were in the midst of a kiss so passionate, so all-consuming, that they didn't even hear her enter. He'd obviously been interrupted in the midst of mopping; the mop and the bucket on wheels waited nearby. Unnoticed, Hannah stood watching for several seconds before she turned and slipped out the door.

That night she had one of her sex dreams, and the worst and best part of this dream was its realism. It could have happened. It might happen. If only it hadn't been so real, she thought upon waking. If only Jimmy had been wearing someone else's head or body, or arrived in someone else's car. If only the sex had taken place in a house she'd never seen, in another town or century, she might have laughed it off. But it had happened in her house, in her bathroom, and Hannah, too, was absolutely herself, with her own hair, which came down around her shoulders as they began to move together. Those were her rounded breasts and thin thighs wrapped around Jimmy's hips. None other.

In the dream, Jimmy and Helen were over for dinner. Helen had brought a big salad, and they were drinking wine—Carl had opened the bottle, and he and Helen were sharing a joke. Hannah was busy cooking dinner, which was the only odd part of the dream. She seldom cooked. But that alone did not make it fantastic.

In the dream, she'd looked up from the stove and caught Jimmy leaning against the wall behind her, staring at her. He had on the exact clothes that had been laid out on the bed the day she'd caught him naked, white tennis shorts and yellow polo shirt. Perhaps he'd been out playing before they arrived; his face was flushed, and when he smiled, the lines around his eyes deepened. It was funny, she thought, that as you aged, you found yourself drawn to things that would never have attracted you in your youth. The lines around a mouth or eyes could be as handsome as a cleft chin or a strong nose. Human beings, she thought, were nothing if not adaptable.

As she turned back to the chicken browning in a skillet, Hannah felt Jimmy's gaze travel down her back to the curve of her buttocks, lingering there before it slid down her slender legs. She was wearing tight jeans shorts, and it occurred to Hannah that she'd put them on with him in mind. She shifted her body, reaching for the salt on the counter, so that he'd glimpse the rounded globe of her breast beneath the T-shirt. In the dream, she realized, she hadn't been wearing a bra. Helen and Carl were talking, but their voices were pure noise to her. All she could understand or hear was the crackling skin of the chicken and Jimmy's greedy ogling.

At last, she removed the skillet from the burner and carried it directly to the table, setting it down and immediately forgetting it. Deliberately, she walked through the living room and down the hall to the bathroom. Naturally, Jimmy followed. He opened the bathroom door without knocking, closing it again and locking it with a click. Neither of them said anything as they stood in the small space between the door and the bathroom sink, no invitations or apologies. This in itself was not unusual; Hannah's dreams were peculiarly silent places. Jimmy stood just inches away, staring at her. She waited for his touch; she yearned for it so that even in the dream she wasn't sure when it actually began, when his hand stopped being a wish and became real, a thing of substance. That was the odd thing, the way her life in dreams was so much more palpable than her waking life.

He unzipped her shorts and slid them off, then raised her off the floor. Jimmy could see them in the mirror, himself and her, the back of her anyway, her buttocks pressed to the counter. Later, Hannah realized that in the dream she'd been able to perceive the act from both perspectives—hers and his. At the time, this seemed only natural, the effect of commingling, to know at last what it is to be male, to be forever pushing and probing or yearning to do so.

He'd just begun pressing himself between her legs when someone knocked at the bathroom door. The knocks were polite at first, but as Jimmy began to thrust, the knocking grew more insistent, a pounding that was the only noise the dream could contain. Hannah arched her back and gave herself up to the pounding, a noise both inside and outside of her. This, she told herself, was what she'd been missing.

Maybe desire itself awakened her. Abruptly, she opened her eyes to real life, to the heavy darkness of the bedroom in the middle of the night. Without checking the clock, she guessed it to be about three-thirty in the morning. She had to pee, but Hannah was ready to ignore the demands of her bladder, ready to turn over and push herself back into Jimmy's embrace.

Unfortunately, she was awake now and feeling guilty. What business had she in the bathroom with Jimmy? It was a double betrayal—no, triple, she thought—because it betrayed herself as well. That was the worst part, to give herself to someone like Jimmy. She didn't really want him, not in her waking life. What she wanted was the wanting itself, and that she could have with Carl. She thought of his hands, the long blunt fingers, each one graced with a tuft of dark hair above the knuckles, tender careful hands, talented in every way. Hannah slipped her own hand across the sheet, in search of the smooth arc of her husband's back. He was such a gentle lover, Carl was, so patient and considerate. Occasionally, she wished he'd think more of himself, that he'd push himself on her. Damn the feminists. That was what she wanted sometimes, to be taken, the way Jimmy had taken her in the dream.

Carl wasn't in bed. The sheet was still warm to the touch, but the space was empty. Hannah slipped out of bed and padded down the hall. She expected to find him standing at the toilet. That was the way of things with the long-married; even their bladders were in sync. But the bathroom was vacant. She didn't need to turn on the light; she could feel the room was empty. Gathering her white gown around her hips, she sat down on the toilet and glanced about at the gleam of the faucet and the small hump of the black-and-white TV on the counter. A place of such passion in her dreams, the bathroom looked entirely ordinary now. And if she were to flip on the light and look at herself in the mirror, she supposed she'd appear ordinary as well, a forty-year-old woman who knew better than to have sex with her burly, bastard brother-in-law.

After checking in the studio and the kitchen, Hannah discovered Carl in the living room, hunched on the couch. In the vague light that drifted through the bay window, she could make out the roundness of his head, rising above the back of the couch, like a moon. Carl was staring straight ahead, but as she came closer, Hannah heard the scratch of pencil on paper. She stopped in her tracks and tried to look through the sludge of the night. Was he drawing in the dark? Was that possible?

"Hello, Hannah," he said. The scratching noise ceased.

What the hell? She felt her way to his side, and before he could reach out to stop her, she turned on the lamp. Carl looked up, his face yellowish in the lamplight. His eyes were ringed with dark circles, his beautiful curly hair matted from tossing and turning on the pillow. This was the real man in her life, and he didn't look particularly handsome; he looked sad and distrustful but, all the same, wonderfully familiar. Suddenly, Hannah was overcome by the need to hold him, to be held by him.

Then she glanced down at the sketchbook in his lap. He'd been drawing in the dark, after all. Cats, dozens of milling felines, their tails waving in the air like question marks. And right on top of the cats, he'd sketched a young woman's face. Feathery hair set off a pair of wide, deep-set eyes. The chin was narrow, the neck long and slender. Good God, Hannah thought. The young woman was beautiful.

"Who's that?" she asked, bending over the sketchbook. It was all she could do not to snatch it away.

"No one you know," he answered, and before she could look again, he reached over and flipped off the lamp.

Chapter 13

"If I'd known . . ." Penny began, her voice trailing away. Hard enough to say these things. She wanted to be sure her grandmother was listening.

Mattie moved distractedly about the kitchen, opening a cabinet and choosing a can of soup, reading the label and replacing it on the shelf, opening the refrigerator and peering inside. Nothing spoke to her, or maybe the shelves were empty. If Mattie had gone to the grocery store in the last two days, Penny didn't know about it. Certainly, she hadn't shopped over the weekend. Mattie had been in county jail. Booked on Friday, she'd had to wait the weekend before her bail was set on Monday. Dr. Bill had insisted on paying. "Not that I put her up to this," he'd hastened to add. "Not at all." Penny didn't know what to believe, but she was grateful nonetheless. He wanted to make up, and she saw no reason not to do so. So long as he kept his distance.

She knew now that she didn't love him, and she doubted she ever would love him—ironically, it was Juanita who'd convinced her of this; sooner or later she'd have to tell him so. But not now, not yet. Just yesterday, he'd tucked a note inside her screen door. *I wouldn't counsel your grandmother to break the law,* he'd scrawled across the page. *That decision is between her and GOD.* This last was all capitals and so much larger than the rest of the message that it left no room for anything else. And that's the way Penny felt about God, that He was growing larger by the day, this awesome, anonymous presence in her life.

Mattie had been home for two days, but her usual fluffy white hair was still flat on one side, as if she'd been sick or was just up from a nap. Surely, she's taken a shower, Penny thought, but maybe she hadn't washed her hair. This seemed strange as well. Mattie had a streak of vanity Penny found endearing. Now her grandmother appeared depressed. She wasn't taking care of herself, and she couldn't settle down to knit, or to read, or now to eat. Something was up. Something more?

Penny began again. "If I'd known what you were doing with that yarn, I'd have tossed the bag in the trash."

Mattie had drifted back to the cabinet, and now she was busy shifting cans from the front of the shelf to the back. "I know," she said. "That's why I can't trust you."

Trust? Was this about trust? Penny ran a hand across the table and felt grains of sugar roll beneath her fingers. From Mattie's breakfast coffee, she thought. So her grandmother had neglected to wipe the table as well. Since when had that ever happened? And what did it mean? Maybe nothing. "I'm on your side, Grandmother," she said.

"You *used* to be on my side."

"Whose side am I on, then?"

Already, Mattie's patience with this talk was wearing thin. "I don't know," she said irritably. "Why don't you tell me?"

Penny kept her voice even and, as she spoke, brushed grains of sugar onto the floor with the flat of her hand. "I'm on your side, and I'm on my side, and I'm on Delia's side. I don't have to choose. And I don't have to agree with you. I can be on your side whether we agree or not. Whether I go to the wedding or not. Whether you want me to or not. It's my decision, not yours."

She remembered Carl saying something similar a couple of weeks ago. How he didn't agree with his wife, and he didn't agree with the protesters. Even so, she was certain that if she'd asked, he would have said he was on his wife's side and that he was on Penny's side as well. Suddenly, it made sense to her, complete sense. This notion that you had to take sides over issues—it was wrongheaded, destructive. It led to protracted, pointless wars. There were other ways to solve problems besides lining up on opposite sides of a battlefield.

Just now, Penny was starving. She wished Mattie would go ahead and open one of those large cans of soup she'd just shuffled to the back row—chicken noodle, tomato, alphabet—something the two of them could share. She'd have eaten mushroom if her grandmother had set it in front of her. Gladly. Just to share a meal would be such a relief. "How about if you open that can of chicken noodle?" Penny asked. "I've got bread in my apartment. I'll run and get it. We can have toast."

Mattie hesitated, then pulled the can from the shelf. "I suppose," she said. "Let's do it now. The study group will be here in half an hour."

The study group, Penny thought as she crossed the lawn. They must have helped with the booties, so many of them, dozens of pairs in all shades of the rainbow. Tiny little socks for tiny little feet. Even the clumsiest of hands can make a pair of booties. And Mattie's hands were so quick, so cunning with the needles. She must have finished off at least twenty pairs herself. The newspaper had said the sky rained booties—an exaggeration, surely, but if Penny knew her grandmother, not much of one.

According to the article, Mattie had entered the 40th Street clinic carrying her knitting bag and her Bible. For the first hour, no one took much notice of her. She'd pulled out her knitting, and though she occasionally glanced up to watch women come and go, she didn't say a word to anyone. In fact, the clinic receptionist interviewed for the paper admitted that, "at first, the older woman was a comfort to all of us, like having a grandma around." Reading that line, Penny had smiled. Some grandma. Those who noted her presence assumed Mattie was waiting for someone, and so she was. She was waiting for God to give her the word. When all of the chairs were occupied, when about fifteen women were waiting for either counseling or abortions, she went into action. The woman sitting next to her said she heard Mattie make a little huffing noise a few seconds before she got to her feet. "You all right?" the woman had asked, and Mattie had nodded. "She didn't look all right, though," the woman reported. "She looked peaked and strange around the eyes."

The knitting bag had been stuffed with baby booties, and though no one saw her take them out, suddenly Mattie held heaps of tiny knitted socks in every conceivable color, so many that her arms couldn't contain them. As she began to circle the room, booties slipped down the length of her dress and onto the floor, like the petals of exotic flowers. Before the clinic employees could stop her, before the police could arrive and drag her away, Mattie made her way around the room, dropping into every woman's lap several perfect pairs of socks, small enough to bring an ache to even the hardest heart. "For your baby," she said in a quiet voice, looking straight into each pair of astonished, angry, anguished eyes. "God bless."

She'd refused to leave. That much was clear. When the booties had been distributed, she took her seat again and, opening her Bible, began to read aloud from Psalm 113, her voice rising when she reached the verse that reads, *He maketh the barren woman to keep house, and to be a joyful mother to children.* It took three policemen to carry her to the patrol car, and in addition to trespassing, she was also charged with resisting arrest. Reportedly, she'd used her knitting needles to hold the first policeman at bay. And when it was all said and done, Mattie was jubilant.

Sitting in the back of the patrol car, she was moved to sing. She sang hymns all the way downtown, finishing up with "Amazing Grace," and she swore that one of the policemen had joined in on the chorus. At last, she said, she could see the results of her labors, and the newspaper account verified her perceptions: Five of the women in the waiting room were too distraught to go through with their procedures. Several cried and wailed; counselors scurried this way and that while three other women simply slipped quietly out the door, taking their booties with them. "Praise the Lord," Mattie had cried upon seeing them leave. From her perspective, the visit was an unqualified success, well worth the three nights she spent in jail. And on the way home Monday afternoon, she'd had only one thing to say: "We've been going about this all wrong! Boldness is required."

So why is she depressed now? Penny wondered. She got what she wanted, and then it occurred to her—not enough. She wanted more. Maybe that's where the study group came in. Penny grabbed up the loaf of bread and hurried back down the stairs. It was beginning to rain, fat drops falling out of the night sky. Daylight saving time had ended on Sunday, and Penny still wasn't accustomed to the swift descent of darkness. It bothered her—day seemed to break and be gone before she could get a good taste of it. Lingering in the grassy space between her dwelling and her grandmother's, Penny opened her mouth to the rain. It splattered her eyes and ran off her nose, cold and fresh to the taste. She'd always loved the taste of rain; when she was a girl, Mattie used to scold her for the way she "dillydallied in a downpour." Now Penny hoped it would continue all night, that she could drift off to sleep with the sound of rain pelting the glass pane next to her bed.

By the time she straggled back into the kitchen, she was good and wet, and her chance for a quiet dinner with her grandmother was gone. Juanita occupied the chair that Penny had vacated, and little Buck was busy emptying one of the bottom cabinets of pots and pans, jerking them out just as quickly as his little hands could snatch them up, so that the shiny copper-bottomed pots clattered and banged together. He wore clothes for the occasion, a new pair of jeans with snaps on the insides of the legs and a long-sleeved, striped T-shirt.

The empty can of chicken noodle soup stood on the counter. Mattie stirred the contents in a pot over the burner, all the while listening intently to Juanita, who was dressed up herself in black slacks and a white satin blouse. She was clearly upset. Penny slipped in unnoticed with her loaf of bread in hand.

"Your going to jail was the last straw. He says I could end up there too, and then what?"

"I suppose you could," Mattie replied calmly.

"I'm a mother, he says, 'and mothers have no business taking chances with their safety.'"

"Sometimes there are bigger issues. What does God tell you?" Mattie asked, reaching into a cabinet over her head. She took down three bowls and began ladling the steaming soup.

Juanita was on her own track. "Buck doesn't believe in God. Says he won't go to church with a 'bunch of crazies.' I told him, 'Those crazies saved my life. They were there for me when you weren't.'"

Penny cleared her throat. Startled, they shifted in their seats and stared at her blankly. "Should I fix the toast?" she asked.

"Certainly," Mattie replied.

When they were gathered round the table—Buck perched in Penny's lap and gnawing a brown crust—Mattie bowed her head and gave the blessing, ending with an entreaty on behalf of the young women sitting before her. "Fill their hearts. Speak to them, dear God; show them the way." Afterward, they took up their spoons and began to eat. Penny glanced around and noted that there was no joy in it for any of them.

Halfway through the meal, Mattie turned to Juanita. "I don't care what Buck Sr. says," she blurted out. "What does God say?"

"He says come here, talk to you." Juanita shrugged. She looked terribly unhappy. "I love him; I've always loved him." She picked up her spoon and dipped it in the soup. Her head was down, but Penny could see tears dripping from her eyes into the bowl.

"You love God, or you love Buck Sr.?" Mattie asked pointedly.

"Both," Juanita replied. She sounded on the verge of tears. Concerned, Buck held out a wet, gnawed crust to his mother. Here, his expression said, this will make you happy. But Juanita was inconsolable. "You eat it, sweetie," she told him.

Penny had to try and help her. "Does she have to choose, Grandmother?"

"Yes," Mattie cried, bringing down her fist on the table with such force that the bowls sloshed broth. Warm drops splattered Penny's cold wet jeans. "Sacrifices are called for; choices are necessary. God doesn't make it easy, but He makes it possible."

What else was there to say? They finished their soup in silence, small slurping sounds and the occasional shout from Buck the only noise in the room. When the doorbell began to ring and the study-group members filed into the living room, Penny excused herself and cleared the table. Mattie, Juanita, and Buck got up and disappeared into the front room. Penny was drying the bowls when Esther waltzed in, looking entirely pleased with herself. She waved a flyer in the air.

"Can you believe it? Wal-Mart has a big sale on paint. Doesn't usually happen this time of year." She stopped and looked around, a big woman wearing a flowing dark green dress. "Oh, hello, Penny. Where's your grandmother?" Only the year before, Esther had lost forty or fifty pounds and splurged on a whole new wardrobe in bright colors—mostly reds and yellows—but now she was on her way back up the scale. The dreary old fat clothes had made a reappearance; her friends all did their best not to notice.

Penny shrugged. "Guess she went upstairs to comb her hair. It could use a good combing."

Esther dyed hers a dark shade of brown and wore it teased and sprayed, so that it fit her head like a helmet. "You okay, dear?" she asked, squinting in Penny's direction. She called herself "half blind," but she shunned glasses, except for reading and driving. Most often, she left them dangling around her neck, attached to something that looked like a pearl necklace. So much squinting had carved a deep cleft between Esther's eyes, but her skin was smooth, her cheeks flushed.

"Fine, just a little tired. Tell Grandmother I'm going up to bed?"

"Certainly," Esther replied. "We miss you, Penny." Such a kind woman. For as long as Penny had known her, years and years now, Esther had never said a cross word to anyone.

"I miss you too."

The older woman hung back, as though she wanted to say more. Ask her, Penny thought. Esther is the perfect person to ask. She looked back over her shoulder, found a pair of friendly eyes. "Does God tell you to do this?"

Esther shrugged. "Do what?"

"Whatever it is you're doing. This study group. The protests. Knitting the booties."

Esther thought for a moment, her small features going tense with the effort. She wanted to tell the truth, the complete truth. Penny could see that, and it moved her. "It's not God that tells me," Esther finally admitted.

"No?" Penny heard the disappointment in her voice.

Esther shook her head. "Not God, but the next best thing. My heart. You know, Penny, I don't think God speaks to all of us. It's not possible. He doesn't have time. Just think how many of us there are. Billions, right?" Penny nodded, and Esther continued. "But He left part of Himself inside each of us." Here she pushed her glasses to the side, so she could lay a hand across her chest. "When God is silent," she said, "it's our hearts we have to listen to."

Penny wanted to be sure she understood: "Your heart tells you these things are right?"

"My heart tells me, and when it doesn't speak loud enough, your grandmother lets me know." Esther smiled ruefully, but her small face shone. If the Lord lived in any of them, He lived in Esther.

Penny twisted the dish towel in her hands. "Oh, Esther . . ."

The older woman pressed a finger to her lips. Her fingernail glowed pink in the dim light of the kitchen. "Shhh, Penny. It's all right. Our hearts don't always tell us the same thing. You listen to yours."

———————————

BARTON Creek Mall spread out across the hilltop like some ancient walled city, vast, impenetrable, surrounded on all sides by an ocean of a parking lot. Penny rarely shopped at this mall, but when she did, she always felt disoriented and confused by the sheer sprawling size of it. She tended to go in the wrong door, wander needlessly around the concourse, and finish by forgetting where she'd left her van. Driving up the access road late on Thursday afternoon, she got her first glimpse of the huge, hulking exterior. The last time she'd come here, policemen on horseback had been patrolling the lot. As she recalled, it had been the holidays, almost a year ago now, and a group of thieves had been making a game of snatching bags from weary shoppers.

She'd come today to buy Delia's wedding present, which she could have managed quite nicely right on Sixth Street. All she had to do was step out of her shop and into Knickknack Paddywack. Surely, she'd have found something suitable there, a glass vase perhaps or a music box. Delia was easy to please. When Penny had called to tell her mother she'd be coming, Delia had let out a small shriek of delight. "I was so afraid you wouldn't," she admitted. Penny needn't have gone to this trouble on her mother's account. No, to be honest, she was doing it to see Carl Solace again. Her heart had spoken his name, and here she was.

She'd even concocted an excuse to stop at the bookstore. This Sunday, and every Sunday this month, she had nursery duty. She'd decided to buy a few books to read to the children, holiday stories to keep them happy and quiet. This Sunday, especially, she'd be exhausted from the wedding and the long drive home. The wedding ceremony was scheduled for three in the afternoon on Saturday, the reception for four, and by the time dinner was over and the band—friends of Dwayne's—had finished playing, it would be late. Penny didn't expect to get back to Austin until after midnight. Delia had offered to put her up, but Penny had begged off, using the excuse of nursery duty. It was a solemn obligation, she explained. Only emergencies and illness were acceptable reasons for absence.

Halloween was barely over, but already the Christmas decorations were up inside the mall. Huge red and white peppermint sticks dangled from the ceiling above Penny's head, and an enormous tree constructed entirely of red poinsettia plants graced the entrance. Drawn to the plants, Penny stepped up and fingered the broad green leaves of a poinsettia, one of hundreds, all of them brilliant and healthy-looking. But how long would they stay that way? she wondered. The air inside the mall was warm and dry. Before long, the plants would be dropping leaves by the score. The arrangement was gorgeous, Penny thought, but wasteful too. So many beautiful poinsettias could cheer the holidays of the elderly all over the city. Here, busy shoppers hurried past with only a quick glance. Penny might have been the first person all evening to tarry long enough to have a close look.

She located Walton's on a map near the entrance—first floor, straight ahead on the right. Approaching the bookstore, she practiced her words: "I'm so glad to see you. I'm looking for a book." She kept them going in her head as she entered the store. A last-minute decision of no consequence, that was the effect she was hoping for. Don't look at the counter, she told herself, not so much as a glance.

Instead, she concentrated on a huge table of best-sellers by the door, lingering to read and reread the titles—*Insomnia; Interview with the Vampire; Men Are from Mars, Women Are from Venus; The Celestine Prophecy; Nicole Brown Simpson; Debt of Honor.* Aimlessly, she flipped the pages of several books, the words a blur on the page. Finally, she allowed herself a quick glimpse of the sales counter. Two young women manned the registers, both briskly ringing up sales and slipping books into merrily decorated Walton's bags. No Carl. Oh, well, she told herself. Doesn't matter. It's for the best. She was used to disappointment.

Then it occurred to her: He might be elsewhere, back with a customer or stocking shelves. Surely, lots more was involved in running a store besides standing behind a cash register. The books didn't appear magically on the shelves, for heaven's sake. Slowly, she made her way through the crowded aisles. Back in the children's section, she spotted a young woman with a white-blond crew cut pulling books for a lady in a red and white polka-dot blouse. Undoubtedly, the young woman was an employee. Penny blinked and looked again. The dots on the woman's shirt danced, but Carl didn't appear. Lacking the heart even to choose a picture book for nursery duty, Penny turned toward the entrance.

"Penny?" She heard his voice, and when she looked up, there he was, in the middle of the aisle, arms full of children's books, as though he'd been waiting for her. "I thought that was you. How's Buck?" he asked.

"Fine," she replied, nodding quickly. "In fact"—she pointed to the books in his arms—"I'm here to buy books to read to the children in the nursery." She rattled on, explaining nursery duty, the small space, the rowdy children. He nodded, but she could see that he was thinking of something else.

"And the cat?" he said. "I meant to ask about the cat last time I saw you."

"Flash?" Penny replied brightly. "That's her name. She streaks around the apartment like greased lightning."

He grinned. "She's grown, I bet. It's been over a month. . . ."

Penny saw the shadow cross over his face, so she pushed quickly ahead. "Yes, she's getting bigger, too big to hide in my bag these days." Now she remembered to ask about his dog, whose name she couldn't recall. "Your cocker spaniel?" she asked expectantly.

Carl shrugged. "Blind, you know, and old as the dickens. He gets around the house okay, enjoys the simple things—eating, sleeping, a nice long brushing." He stacked the books in his arms onto a nearby table and led her to the shelves of children's books. "What age group are you looking for?"

Later, after she'd chosen the books—*The Grinch Who Stole Christmas, The Snowman,* and several others—after his fingers had grazed hers, once, twice, three times, passing the books to each other, fumbling with the pages, after he'd offered her an educator's discount— "You're educating in the nursery, aren't you?"—she finally got around to mentioning the wedding and her need for a gift.

"My mother and her fiancé. His name is Dwayne."

"Your mother's getting married?"

He sounded surprised. She supposed it was a little surprising, now that she thought of it. Did mothers get married? Hers did from time to time.

"I don't suppose you could find anything for a wedding at a pet store?" Carl went on to say. "My friend has a big sale on. I could walk you over."

No sooner had they darkened the doorway of Noah's Ark than Noah himself swooped down on them, a large blond man in a bright blue turtleneck. He greeted Penny expansively and escorted her into "his domain," which was reminiscent of one of those dollar stores Esther was always dragging her into, merchandise piled high on every shelf. "Noah," Carl said. "This is my friend, Penny."

"I'd have known her anywhere." He was grinning broadly and looking very pleased with himself. "Lovely little slip of a girl. You've captured her, I think." Noah wrapped an arm around Penny's shoulder and squeezed her to his side. "Have him show you his sketchbook," he whispered loudly. "He's done drawing after drawing."

She remembered now. Carl had mentioned sketching her face, how he'd gotten her mouth wrong. The last time she'd seen him, he'd asked her to smile. How could that have slipped her mind? "You've seen Carl's drawings?" she asked Noah.

"Ye-ees, my dear. Our man is an artist. The genuine *art*-icle." Another squeeze.

Penny liked this Noah, but his teasing made her uncomfortable. He seemed to think she was a child, that he could sail these remarks right over her head, like paper airplanes. I'm not stupid, she wanted to tell him.

"Penny's looking for a gift," Carl put in.

"Fabulous. As you can see, we're having a little pre-Christmas sale." Noah waved a hand. Signs and banners hung off nearly every cage and floated from the ceiling. WE ARE 20% OFF, read one dangling from a lizard's cage. TAKE US HOME FOR CHRISTMAS. Penny tried to imagine the look on Mattie's face when she discovered a pair of lizards under her carefully decorated tree. Would she scream?

"Actually, I'm looking for a wedding gift," Penny told Noah.

He glanced at her sharply, then smiled. "Lucky for you!" he exclaimed. "I've got just the thing." Leading her through the store, he warned her to watch her step, pointing out animals of interest as they passed. At last, they stopped in front of a cage of lovebirds. "Perfect, aren't they?" he asked.

So they were. The large cage was crowded with these tiny creatures, fluttering blots of color that set up a nervous chattering at their approach. Some were green with orange heads and brilliant turquoise tails, others an olive green with mustard-colored breasts and gray heads. "We have the Peach-faced and Madagascar here," he told Penny before pressing his big face to the bars and addressing the birds: "Okay, listen up. Which of you wants to go home with this lovely young woman?" Agitated, a burst of birds took flight, swooping from perch to perch. Turning back to Penny, he grinned slyly. "See how excited they are?"

"Lovebirds are part of the parrot family," Carl spoke up. "The name refers to the fact that they mate for life." He was standing just behind her, and as Penny stared at the birds, they blurred in her sight, a palette of colors that bled and blended. "Let me help you choose a pair," she heard him say. She nodded, and he slipped around her and bent over the cage.

Noah ducked out then, after reminding Penny to let him know when she was ready to check out. "Give you a great deal on the birds and a pretty little wrought-iron cage." Halfway up the aisle, he thought better and turned back. "Have Carl introduce you to his friend E.T." he suggested.

As it turned out, E.T. was a parrot, but not the beautiful macaw that came to mind, wild jungle colors and a huge curving yellow beak. This bird's beak was smallish and a dull black, his body bulky and gray. The tail feathers were a bright red, but even here God had scrimped. E.T.'s tail looked as though someone had taken a pair of shears to it, clipped it right up to his rump.

"Hey there, E.T." Carl backed up to allow the parrot access to his shoulder.

"E.T. phone home!" the bird shrieked in reply. Then again: "E.T. phone home!"

"E.T. phone home!" Penny called back. "Can you say anything else?"

In fact, he could. Carl was teaching him a Christmas carol. "I'm dreaming of a white Christmas," he crooned, "just like the ones I used to know. . . ."

The parrot twisted his neck to peer into Carl's face, then joined in, his voice a screechy counterpoint. They sounded like carolers from the state hospital, so funny and astonishing that Penny laughed out loud.

Carl insisted on carrying the cage with the lovebirds to the van for her. When it was snugly situated on the floor of the passenger seat, he reached out and grasped her shoulder.

"So good to see you," he said. Night had fallen, but in the light from the street lamp she could see his face, the strong nose and the curve of his upper lip. Maybe it was the curling hair or the way he smiled, a shy self-effacing twist of the lips, but he reminded Penny of an aging child, a ten-year-old boy with the cares of a forty-year-old man. "Have fun at the wedding," he told her.

"I might have fun," she replied, but her tone of voice suggested otherwise.

"Of course you'll have fun," Carl admonished. "It's a wedding. That's what you go for. To be happy." But Penny saw the pained expression that crossed his face. "Wish my mother would get married again," he said, "but I don't suppose that's likely." He was gazing off over her shoulder, toward the last traces of light on the horizon.

"Does she live in Austin?" Penny asked.

"No, Terrell," Carl said. "My mother lives in Terrell. So does my brother. Dad hides out in a little cabin at Lake Texoma. He's been there so long I hardly know him anymore."

"I've never known my father," Penny admitted in a quiet voice. She'd never spoken about this, not that she could recall. In fact, it had taken her years to realize she must have a father. Everyone has a father, someone at school had said. She remembered now, a boy in a class with her. He was angry about something.

"I'm sorry," Carl said quietly. She shook her head and smiled. The memory came back to her now, and he must have seen it cross her face. "What is it?" he asked.

When Penny hesitated, he squeezed her shoulder. "Okay," she told him. "You're an artist. You'll like this. I was in second grade, I think, somewhere around there. A teacher asked the class to draw pictures of our parents. What was I going to do? I sat there and sat there, but nothing came to mind. I was as blank as my paper. I could draw my mother, but nothing of my father. I couldn't even imagine what he looked like. You'll never guess what I did."

Carl shook his head. "Made him up?" he tried.

She sighed. How could she have forgotten? "No. I copied the boy sitting next to me. I used his parents. Right down to the red bow in the mother's hair." She recalled now how upset he'd been and what had made matters worse: Her picture had turned out better than his. Hers had been neat and colorful—she'd stayed in over recess to decorate the area around the parents' feet with grass and flowers. Their teacher had tacked her artwork on the bulletin board for the rest of the class to see, a painful little triumph that Penny had tried to ignore each time she passed in and out of the room.

Carl reached out and squeezed her shoulder. "All artists are cheats, Penny," he said. "We steal from everybody." Then: "So you've *never* met him?"

Penny shrugged and felt his little finger graze the back of her neck. His hand was large and warm and pleasantly heavy there on her shoulder. "No," she said.

"It's his loss."

"Mine too," she replied. Best to move on to something else, she thought; otherwise, she might start to cry. Penny gestured toward the open door and the birds in their cage. She could just make them out, huddled together for comfort. They hadn't made a sound since Carl had carried them out of the store. "Seems like every time we meet, I bring home some animal or other."

Carl laughed. "That's right," he said.

"It was a good thing," she finished, "your taking me to the Humane Society."

Carl nodded, his eyes locked on hers. "*You* took *me*," he reminded her. They were both silent, remembering the moment. Finally, he spoke. "Well, I better get back to work."

Penny straightened her shoulders and waved good-bye as he loped off into the darkness. She felt a catch in her chest followed by a tug, and that was it: Her heart went with him.

———————

READING the Saturday morning paper on the porch swing, Mattie grumbled about the weather. "Might as well take a boat to Houston, Penny. Might as well drive into the mouth of a hurricane." Though Austin had been spared, Houston had received an unending deluge all through October. Only a couple of weeks earlier, some areas around the city had reported a record thirty inches, and by October 24, President Clinton had declared thirty-five counties disaster areas. Among those, the hardest hit were all in the vicinity of Houston. The San Jacinto River had risen fifteen feet above its banks, and the Trinity had overflowed as well. Twice, Delia had called to verify Penny's arrival time. "Yes," Delia had admitted. "It's been coming down cats and dogs, but the worst of it has moved off to the east. You'll be coming from the west." Not to worry, her mother had said. But as Penny carried her suitcase down the stairs, she couldn't help noting the overcast sky. And unlocking the van, she felt the first fat drop hit her face.

She was loading the birdcage when Mattie emerged from the house with a gift. Stiffly, slowly, her grandmother made her way across the yard, using her carefully laid step stones to make the trip. At first glance, she appeared overly cautious, prematurely old, but truth be told, she'd always been that way. She never had accidents, broke dishes, burned biscuits, spilled milk, or dialed a wrong number. She never missed an appointment, neglected her plants, forgot a birthday, or left a bed unmade. Constant diligence had been both her salvation and her downfall. Being so careful took a great deal of time; her life had become a series of obligations.

"My gift for Delia," Mattie said, thrusting the package into Penny's arms. The box was wrapped in used silver-foil wrapping paper; creases where the paper had been folded and put away crisscrossed the top. Penny knew what was inside: bath towels, hand towels, and a couple of washcloths, the same gift Mattie gave every church member who married. Everyone washes, she reasoned, or everyone should. "Don't forget to give it to her. And give her my best. She's finally marrying Dwayne. Persistence in this one thing, at least."

"What do you mean?" Penny asked.

Mattie didn't answer. She was peering over Penny's shoulder, into the shadowy interior of the van. "Lots of room in there," she said.

"Grandmother, have you met Dwayne? You talk about him as though you know him."

"Of course I've met him," Mattie replied. "You've met him too, though you might have been too young to remember." She waved a hand as though to dismiss the subject, then stepped around Penny to get a better look in the back. "My goodness, look at all this space!" she exclaimed. So much enthusiasm. Until this moment, Mattie had never paid much attention to Penny's pride and joy, except to give instructions on how to park it, flush against the back wall of the garage apartment.

"When did I meet him?" Penny tried again. She was waiting for her grandmother to ask about the birds in the cage. They were right in plain sight, and as soon as Mattie threw open the second service door, they began their nervous chattering.

"It's not my place, Penny," Mattie replied in a curt voice. She didn't seem to notice the birds. "Ask Delia or Dwayne your questions."

She would get nowhere with this, Penny thought, reaching around her grandmother to close the van doors. Obviously, Mattie was in the way, but she didn't step aside, which meant she wanted something. Penny could see it in the set of her mouth, in the way her hands flew to her hips. She wanted something and she wouldn't move until she got it. "Juanita can drive this thing, can't she?" Mattie asked.

"You know she can. She's been sneaking out in the van to visit Buck Sr., remember? You're the one who told *me* about it."

Mattie waved her hand again. "That's all over with," she said. "All right, then. I've made up my mind. It's an inconvenience, and I'm sorry for that, but I'm going to need your van this evening. You'll have to drive my station wagon to Houston." She nodded her head, as though it were a done deal, but Penny wasn't having any of it.

"I'm leaving now," she said. Pointedly, deliberately, she slipped around her grandmother and succeeded in closing one door. "And I'm taking my van," she added. "I've already gassed up, checked the tires. . . . Why do you need it, anyway?"

Mattie rushed ahead with her plans. "It's best you don't know. And don't worry if I'm not home when you get back tonight. I'll be very late."

"You're not even going to tell me why?" Penny was incredulous.

"Let's not dally," she said, reopening the door and grabbing the small suitcase. "The Lord is about to send us a torrent." Penny couldn't argue with that. The sky was dark and threatening, and in the silence of the moment, thunder grumbled above their heads. "You ought to get on the road. This will pass over us, but it's likely to follow you. I'll carry your suitcase and your dress." She looked back over her shoulder and offered Penny her first smile of the day. Suddenly, Mattie appeared downright happy. "You get those birds. They're lovely. I'm sure Delia will have a fit over them."

What could Penny say? What could she do? Once again, her grandmother had surprised her into abrupt surrender. It happened nearly every time. Just when Penny had steeled herself against anger, Mattie made an about-face and turned sweet and loving. One, then another raindrop pelted her cheeks. If God believed in sides, He was definitely on her grandmother's. No denying that. Penny grabbed the wrought-iron cage and rushed with the stunned birds to the dry warmth of the old station wagon.

Rain followed her the entire 163 miles from Austin to Houston. Sometimes, the storm overtook her and pelted the windshield with hard fat drops the wipers barely touched. Except for a brief stretch outside Brenham, Highway 290 was two lanes, and the wind buffeted the old car so that Penny had to fight to keep from crossing the center line. One semi truck after another roared past in the other direction, throwing up sheets of muddy water. Twice, then three and four times, Penny pulled over to let more-aggressive drivers pass. One car honked as it swept by, a plaintive baying that sent chills up her spine. The lovebirds were too terrified to make a peep.

By the time she reached the outskirts of Houston, the rain had diminished to a steady drizzle. Now that it appeared she wouldn't die on the highway, Penny began to think of her mother, marrying on this gray and dismal day. She puzzled, too, over Mattie's comments. "Persistence in this one thing, at least." What did it mean? In her rush to get on the road, she hadn't insisted on an explanation. And why did

Mattie need the van, anyway? Now, passing through the outskirts of Houston, Penny wondered what her grandmother was up to and how Juanita was involved. Surely, she wasn't planning another stunt like the one with the booties. She wouldn't have needed the van for that. Never mind, she told herself. She wouldn't find out until tomorrow, so it was best to put it out of her mind.

Delia lived a few blocks from Rice University, and turning the car onto her mother's street, Penny slowed, not so much to look for a house number as to hunt down the last remnants of a lost dream. The neighborhood was old, how old Penny wasn't sure, fifty years, maybe even seventy-five. But one thing was certain. When these houses were built, they had been the picture of elegance. Some were pillared; others had wraparound porches or a series of gables embellished with gingerbread. And each of them—every single one—was three times as big as Mattie's little bungalow. Back when this neighborhood was new—Penny could well imagine it—black women in white uniforms, heads covered in brightly colored scarves, had arrived early in the morning to cook and clean, then left by bus in the late afternoon. But that was before she was born. By the time she was a little girl, these houses must have been transformed from one-family residences into boardinghouses and student apartments. Penny was familiar with the process. She knew of similar neighborhoods in Austin, some bordering the University, where old sofas had been shoved onto wide porches and the flower beds gone to rack and ruin.

Now proximity to downtown and nostalgic yuppies were restoring the old grandeur. At long last, money had returned. As she scanned the house numbers, Penny spotted a roofing truck parked at the house across the street, another structure being reclaimed. Three workers were jammed in the cab, eating sandwiches and waiting for the weather to clear. Maybe their next job would be her mother's roof, which looked in desperate need of repair. Shingles flapped, and the porch rails leaned. The white, two-story, ramshackle frame house was distinguished only by a pot of purple chrysanthemums on the porch and lace curtains in the upstairs windows. In every other respect, it looked entirely neglected. The front yard was weedy, the sidewalk cracked and uneven. Penny pulled to the curb and stopped.

"Don't do it," she told herself, but already the tears were rushing down her cheeks. Many times as a child, Penny had tried to imagine where Delia might live. Not that her mother had been at this address for all that time, only a year at most, but Penny couldn't remember paying her another visit. Delia had come to see her daughter, not the other way around. At long last, here Penny was, twenty-three years old and landing in her mother's territory. She couldn't help herself; she wilted over the steering wheel and cried. When someone knocked on the passenger-side window a few minutes later, she couldn't bring herself to look up. Oh God, she thought, but it was too late for prayers. Whoever this was would just have to go away. But whoever didn't. Instead, the knocking stopped, and a second later Penny heard the familiar squeak of the hinges, the sound of a stranger opening the door.

"Delia?" Penny kept her gaze averted. Please God, she thought. Let it be Delia.

"No, sweetheart. Delia's upstairs." A man's voice. Then: "It's raining out here, you know it?" With a sigh, he dropped into the seat beside her.

Slowly, very slowly, Penny turned her head, her gaze traveling across the windshield until she found the man sitting in the seat beside her. He was in his early forties, dressed in a pair of baggy jeans with holes in the knees and a brand-new white dress shirt, neatly pressed and starched. Fine brown hair laced with gray fell over his forehead, obscuring wide, dark eyes. His face was narrow, his nose thin and pointed, lending him the intent and soulful expression of a collie. While she watched, he raised one bare foot, propping it on his knee, as though he expected a long wait and wanted to be comfortable. In sharp contrast to his tired eyes, the wet sole of his foot shone pink and new-looking. Small brown leaves and a tiny twig or two clung to the damp skin.

"I'm Dwayne," he said, offering a tentative smile that came and went. He searched her face, looking for something, then, apparently satisfied, he reached into his pocket and pulled out a handkerchief with a flourish. "Voilà!"

Penny smiled faintly and, taking it, began wiping around her eyes. The handkerchief was linen and soft with age. It smelled of licorice. Penny took a whiff and held her breath.

"And you must be . . ." Dwayne continued.

"Penny," she said, letting out her breath in one long rush.

"Pleasure to meet you. Something I can help with?" He glanced over the seat to the birdcage in back. "Would you looky there," he said brightly. "If that's not the prettiest pair of birds I've ever seen!"

Dwayne said he loved birds, that there was no better present for him on the face of the earth. "And I'm gonna prove it to you," he promised as he swung the cage out of the backseat. He minced up the wet walk in his bare feet, carrying both the cage and her suitcase, a small wiry man whose jeans dragged the ground. Penny trailed behind him with her dress in its plastic sheath slung over one shoulder and Mattie's present under her arm. Ahead of her, Dwayne hobbled up the porch steps and crossed to a side door. He limped a little, and it wasn't simply the discomfort of bare feet. Something was wrong with his left leg and maybe with the foot; he favored it, lifting it higher, setting it down gently. Just as the thought entered her head, Dwayne turned and gave her a hard little look. "War wound," he called, as though it wouldn't do for them to have secrets, as though they had to dispense with all of them here and now, in the first five minutes of their acquaintanceship. "I'm a veteran," he explained. "Vietnam, 1970. Lousy goddamn war. Messed me up for years, Penny, and I'm not talking about my leg." He tapped his forehead and grimaced, as though it hurt to the touch. "Guess you heard about it?"

Penny shook her head.

He sighed. "Just as well, probably. Wouldn't improve me in your eyes, that's for sure." He shook his head and threw open the door. "Welcome to the Hanson Manor, Miss Penny."

Her experience with men had been limited, that was true, but still it seemed to her that all by himself and in less than fifteen minutes, Dwayne managed to disprove every conclusion she'd ever drawn about the opposite sex. For one thing, he talked nonstop, a string of words so continuous that they carried her across the living room and into a small dark bedroom, where he took her dress and hung it on a hook before placing the suitcase on the floor beside it. "There, how's that?" he asked. All the while he kept a firm grasp on the birdcage.

First, he told her how the house had been his parents' and now was his. "Wasn't worth a dime when they died," he said, sliding the bird-cage onto a large round oak table in the comer of the living room. "And that's how I liked it." He opened the tiny latch, and the door to the cage swung open. "Come here, birdies." He put a finger in, crooking and waggling it. The birds huddled on the bars at the back, their lovely orange heads ducking and twisting. There was something coy about the way they pecked at his finger before backing away. "But now," Dwayne continued, "the accountants and professors have moved in. Taxes going up. I'll be damned if Delia and me aren't the last white trash for miles around. I suppose that's why we decided to get married. Solidarity and all." He shrugged, withdrawing his finger and latching the door. "I'll try again later. We have to get to know one another." Penny wasn't sure whether he was talking about the birds or her.

Dwayne led her through a dining room and into a warm and well-lit kitchen that had clearly been remodeled with new cabinets and a stainless-steel sink. The counters were lined with shining glass bottles filled with herbs and flours, all of them carefully labeled: GINGER, GIN-SENG, GLUTEN. In alphabetical order, she thought. Hard to believe, but he put Mattie to shame with his gleaming surfaces and the smell of fresh-baked bread in the oven. Penny blinked, reminded herself that all this was real and happening now.

She turned back to him, intent on his narrow features, but he was already directing her attention elsewhere, to one of the three windows that looked out on the backyard. "See there!" he said, his tone triumphant. "Told you I loved birds."

Sure enough, Penny thought. Five feeders—no, six, seven—dangled from tree branches. A handmade birdhouse was nailed to the trunk of an old, hulking oak. Two cement birdbaths shaped like mushrooms sprouted side by side in the middle of the overgrown lawn. In the midst of all the splashing and preening, a dozen or so robins and jays chased off sparrows and made threatening dives at one another, a lovely chaos of activity. Dwayne retrieved a pair of binoculars hanging from the back doorknob and handed them to Penny. "Here," he said, "take a closer look."

She'd just brought them to her eyes and was focusing on the largest robin perched on the far feeder—he was saying that very bird had been born in this yard last spring—when she felt the tears welling up once again. But Dwayne foresaw this, too. Before she'd sniffed once, he handed her his already damp handkerchief. "Mattie . . . says we've met . . . before," she stammered.

"Oh, yes," he told her. "We've met. Course we have. How is your grandmother, anyway?"

"She's fine," Penny told him. "She sends her best. And a wedding present . . . I gave you that, didn't I?"

"You did. She sends her best, huh? Don't get me wrong, sweetheart, but I find that hard to believe. Your grandmother's not one of my biggest admirers." In the silence that followed, he shuffled his bare feet on the hardwood floor, and looking down, she saw them there, pale toes splayed against the dark hardwood floor. It came back to her in a rush.

"I was drowning. . . ." she whispered.

"Yes," he said sadly. "I didn't know if you were too little—"

Penny interrupted. "You pulled me out! It's your feet I remember."

He laughed. "Really? Do you? You remember how I held you upside down and pounded your back?" He whapped at the air in front of him to demonstrate, then shook his head. "Damn, you scared the hell out of us." He gave her a sharp look. "That was all my fault, Penny. Don't ever let your mother tell you otherwise."

She nodded and buried her face in the handkerchief. She didn't understand what he meant by that, but it was enough, enough for now. For the moment, she knew all she needed to know. Dwayne waited patiently, and when she was done with her crying, he led her to the table and set her down to lunch. All that emotion had made her ravenous. She ate everything he put down in front of her, the bread, the freshly made chicken potpie, the fruit salad, all of it delicious, the best food she'd ever tasted.

As soon as she'd pushed away her plate, Dwayne came up from behind and bent over her shoulder. "Your momma's waiting upstairs," he whispered conspiratorially. "Her stomach's been bothering her all morning. Nerves, I guess. Anyway, she refused my lunch. Said she didn't even want to smell it, which might have hurt my feelings if I were a sensitive kind of guy." He chuckled at his own joke, then pulled back Penny's chair and stepped aside while she got to her feet.

"Thank you so much for the lunch," she said. "It was wonderful."

"My pleasure. I love to cook, and it's a good thing because Delia's allergic to the kitchen. Will you do me a favor? Run up and say hello to her? She's a little under the weather, but I know she's dying to see you."

"Is she sick?"

"Nervous, I'd say. Here, let me show you the way."

He led her out the front door, onto the porch, and through yet another door, providing more history on the house as they went. It had been a single residence until he was grown, he said, but when his mother died, his father had divided it into two apartments. Since then, a succession of boarders had come and gone—Dwayne himself had moved in and out several times. For the past year, Delia had been renting the upstairs, and they had no plans to change things after the wedding. "Too much togetherness ruins a relationship," he explained. They were standing at the foot of a flight of stairs covered in mauve carpeting, damp near the entrance and scattered with dead leaves.

A door at the top creaked open and Delia's voice sailed out: "Dwayne, honey. You're talking her head off. When am I going to get a turn?"

"Right now, my bride," he called up to her. Bowing deeply, he muttered an aside. "I better scoot. See you later."

Penny peered up the stairwell, but the door was open only a crack, her mother hidden behind it. Delia didn't throw it open until Penny had reached the top. "Hey, girl!" her mother cried. She was dressed in gray sweatpants and a navy blue Dallas Cowboys sweatshirt, her blond tresses pulled on top of her head in a frizzy knot. In the light from the open doorway, her hair appeared nearly transparent. As a young woman, Delia had worn it loose and curling around her shoulders and it had been the spun gold of fairy tales. Goldilocks, Mattie had called her. Now the color had faded, and years of close work had left deep squint lines between her eyes.

"You okay?" Penny asked as she moved into her mother's embrace.

"Fine, just fine now that you're here," Delia said.

"Aren't you happy?"

"Sure I'm happy. Really happy. Just nerve-racked. This wedding business, it'll make you crazy. Especially when you've gotten it wrong as many times as I have."

"I think you've got it right this time."

Delia smiled. "So you approve, sister?"

Penny nodded vigorously. "I do."

"Hey!" Delia protested, punching Penny's arm. "That's my line!" Then she grimaced and clutched her middle. " 'Scuse me a minute. My stomach's giving me fits. I'll be right back." And she hustled off through the archway.

Penny looked around her mother's apartment, which was noticeably smaller than Dwayne's. The main room—bedroom, workroom—was cluttered but orderly, the sewing machine and cabinet stationed by the window, stacks of fat paperbacks lined along one wall. Delia's library. Penny knew all about her mother's weakness for fantasy novels, most culled from the shelves of musty secondhand bookstores. Mattie no longer allowed them in her house, pronouncing them "the devil's doing." Not that Delia paid her any mind. Witches, unicorns, fairies, ghosts, and assorted goblins—she consumed them by day and conjured them at night. "If I could just remember my dreams," she'd once told Penny, "I'd give up sewing and take up writing." Here, she'd sighed and shaken her head. "I have some wonderful dreams, sister, but they slip away with the first light of day." What Penny hadn't known about was her mother's fondness for white wicker. It was everywhere in the room—bedstead, love seat, footstool—and by the window, a wicker love seat piled with tapestry pillows.

Against the opposite wall stood the only piece of wooden furniture, a dark and imposing chifforobe with an inlaid mirror, and hanging from its door, an elaborate satin wedding gown. "Oh, my!" Penny breathed. The corseted bodice was inset with hundreds of glass beads, and the narrow waist gave way to a voluminous skirt that cascaded over the floor in front of it, wave after wave of shining ivory satin. Wisely, Delia had laid a rug on the floor to protect the fabric from dirt. The dress looked like something pulled from the attic of a castle. Penny couldn't take her eyes off it.

"Surely you don't think I'm wearing that thing!" Delia said, coming up to stand next to her. "I can barely get my arm inside the waist to do the alterations." She placed her hands on her hips and moaned. "Oh, that dress. It looks like something out of a fairy tale, only it's actually a nightmare."

Delia took Penny's hand and pulled her toward the love seat, where the two sat down. "I can see you're under the spell," Delia said. "Girls your age go ga-ga for white satin. I'm not even going to show you *my* dress."

Immediately, Penny turned to her. "No, do," she pleaded. "Please."

Delia pursed her lips and shook her head. "Nope. You'll see it when I put it on, same as Dwayne."

"I remember him," Penny said quietly.

Delia glanced at her sharply, then grabbed a pillow to wrap her arms around. "Tell me."

Penny lifted her gaze to the window. The storm had picked up again, and water cascaded down the panes. "Not much to tell," she began. "We were at the lake."

Delia sighed loudly. "So you remember *that*?"

Penny nodded. "You were out a ways, and I was wanting to be with you." She stopped and forced herself to look away from the window and directly into her mother's warm brown eyes. "I was always wanting to be with you," she said.

Her mother pressed her lips together and squeezed the pillow tighter. "I know," she said. "Go on."

"I don't remember how it happened really, just all of a sudden I was under the water, in this bright sparkling place. So beautiful! And my arms were floating out away from me, like I was flying." She thought for a second. "Dwayne must have pulled me out at the last second. I remember sputtering and choking, me hanging upside down and staring at his white toes."

"Do you remember me screaming?" Delia asked.

Penny said no, she didn't remember a sound.

"It was all my fault. I didn't have any sense back then," she said sadly. "Not a bit." And she drooped over the pillow and hid her face from view.

Penny scooted closer to stroke her mother's temple. Delia's hair was soft and fine beneath her fingers, a pleasure to touch. "It was an accident," Penny soothed. "Everybody knows that. Everybody but you, anyway."

Delia sat up and, sniffling, reached over to a nearby table for a

Kleenex. "You've always been so good," she marveled. "A good baby, a sweet girl. So much better than any of us deserve."

Penny bent her own head to the pillow in Delia's lap and closed her eyes. Far away, she could hear the sound of the rain beating against the glass and closer, much closer, the steady rhythm of her mother's breath.

Chapter 14

THE CANVAS WAS READY. Yesterday, Carl had applied a thin coat of white gesso, just enough to cover his initial painting, which had been merely experimental—trees, rocks, a stormy sky—an unremarkable landscape he'd blotted out. Today, he hardly remembered it. Gone for now, he thought, but maybe not forever. Carl studied the canvas, so purely white it made his heart beat a little faster, and felt a rush of gratitude. If nothing else was going well in his life—if he and Hannah still weren't talking much, if they weren't making love at all—this, at least, sustained him.

He was trying something new, and he'd even come up with a name for it: intentional pentimento. Pentimento referred to the way an old painting sometimes found its way to the surface of a newer one, rising like a phantom. Back when canvas was hard to come by, artists often whited out their less successful pieces and started over. But the old painting wasn't always gone. Sometimes, bits and pieces of it reappeared, the old forcing itself on the new, like the baby's eye in the sketches he'd made in the dark. Using oils and only the thinnest coat of gesso between the old painting and the new, Carl hoped to speed up the process, perhaps even control it to some extent.

He grabbed up a tube of cobalt blue, cradling then squeezing it in his fist. Ordinarily, he was drawn to the uncomplicated, the easy to identify, but today he wanted something ambiguous and changeable. Cobalt blue was between colors, approaching navy but with a sheen of green. Carl dabbed the paint on his finger, then moved to the window. Though the morning was young, sunlight poured through the panes, filling his small studio. Carl blinked and held his finger to the light: cobalt blue—the color of the night sky on certain winter evenings, crystalline bright and velvety dark.

Outside, the lady across the street emerged from her house, a lumpy woman wrapped in her husband's robe, hurrying to snatch up the newspaper off the grass. She did this every morning, rushed out the door and back inside, the only time of day Carl ever laid eyes on her. For all he knew or cared, she ceased to exist the moment she closed the door. Today, though, she deviated from the script. Instead of scurrying back up the steps, she stood at the end of her walk, gawking at Carl's house. Her paper was in plain sight, on the lawn just behind her, but she'd forgotten all about it. What the hell? Carl thought. A moment later, her husband wandered out in striped pajamas. The wind grabbed at the pants material, waving it around his skinny legs like a flag. A cold front had blown in the day before, and the temperature was hovering around forty. The man stooped to retrieve the paper, but instead of returning indoors, found his way to his wife's side and assumed the same befuddled stance. Hugging himself for warmth, the man stamped his slippered feet and stared.

Peering out at his lawn, Carl wondered just what they were looking at. And then he saw. Beyond the big oak, out by the sidewalk, he spied something that looked like a sign, the sort that mushrooms by the roadside in the weeks before a political election. If he craned his neck, he could see a second one and maybe a third as well. What the hell? "Hannah!" Carl called out. "Hannah!" He grabbed a rag to wipe his hands and, returning to the window, noticed that the couple across the street hadn't budged.

Hannah was out of bed and on her way across the room by the time he got there. "Neil?" she asked him, her face blotchy with fear. Carl knew she was expecting the worst where Neil was concerned. They both were. "Neil's fine," he said quietly, taking Hannah by the arm and leading her to the window.

"What is it?" she asked.

He pulled aside the sheers and pointed at the couple across the street. They were just as they had been, a pair of salt-and-pepper shakers, slovenly husband and slovenly wife. From this window, the signs were more visible; he counted four now. "Someone's stuck signs in the yard," he told her. Out in the street, a car was stopping. The driver's door swung open and a man in a suit got out to stare. A few seconds later, a little boy on a bicycle swerved to the curb and he, too, stood rapt, straddling the bar of the bike.

"Why?" Hannah asked.

"I have no idea." Carl was reminded of a certain sci-fi movie. The title escaped him, but he clearly recalled scenes of befuddled, bewildered bystanders lining both sides of the road and gazing intently at something the movie viewer couldn't even imagine, much less see. "We better go out front," he told Hannah. She was hugging her arms to her chest, her shoulders pressed forward like the wings of a bird. "Are you cold?" he asked. He realized now that the house was chilly; he should have turned on the heat. "Let me get you something."

She waited by the window until he returned with a long robe of filmy white material. It didn't look the least bit warm, but she shrugged it over her shoulders and thanked him. "What are they looking at? Do you have any idea?"

"Well, they're looking at the signs. The question is: What the hell do they say?"

On the way up the hall, it began to dawn on him that this was about more than signs; something bigger, more mysterious, had happened. The sun was fully up, but the living room was still dark—not gloomy, the way it could sometimes be on stormy afternoons; no, this looked like nighttime. "What the hell?" he muttered.

Hannah was right behind him. "It's so dark, Carl!" she cried. "Why is it so dark?"

"Hell if I know." His first thought was to throw open the front door; instead, he hurried to the picture window and drew aside the curtains. Hannah gasped. Although the curtains were open, the room was *still* dark; if anything, it had gotten even darker. The glass was covered with black paint, long uneven swatches of darkness. Here and there, it was streaked, allowing a patch of light to seep in. The effect was of being thrust underground, in a cave maybe, or underwater—far, far beneath the rest of the world.

By the time they ventured outside, cars were lined along the curb and people were getting out, singly and in pairs. It looked like the beginnings of a party, only no one crossed the yard to the house and no one was smiling. Instead, these strangers milled about the street, occasionally venturing onto the sidewalk but no closer. They whispered to each other, putting up hands to shield their mouths, leaning in close. None of them addressed Carl and Hannah. His first instinct was to shoo them away. These were gawkers, the ones who stared at car wrecks and followed fire trucks, voyeurs of personal tragedy. But he was too stunned to do more than glare at them. The front door had been doused in red paint, and as Hannah passed, her filmy white robe blew up against it and was streaked with red.

"Murderer?" she said in a low voice. "Is that what it says?"

Carl nodded and glanced about. The garage door, too, was emblazoned with red letters two or three feet tall: B-A-B-Y-K-I-L-L-E-R. All one word. He sidled over and ran a finger across the *R*. This paint was dry to the touch, which meant they'd used different kinds. On the front door they'd opted for slow-drying latex, splashed on to resemble blood. The steps had been splattered, and when Carl glanced down at the sidewalk, he noticed a footprint or two. Evidence, he thought.

"This is about my abortion?" Hannah asked.

He nodded again. Undoubtedly. The signs planted in the yard— cardboard posters affixed to wooden stakes—featured photographs. One was of a fetus, curled and floating above the drying grass, like some sort of transplanted sea urchin. The other was of a baby, cherub-cheeked and round-eyed, pink lips turned up in an innocent smile. Carl couldn't help himself. He stared at the baby, who seemed to stare right back. He recognized that dimpled chin, and the ears too, like delicate shells. He'd drawn ears just like them, hadn't he? Oh God, he thought, oh dear God. Striding over, he tried to jerk it out of the ground, but the stake wouldn't budge, and all he had to show for the effort was a handful of splinters. "Shit!" he shouted, glancing over his shoulder to gauge the crowd's reaction. He thought he saw sympathy, pity, shock, disgust on their faces, but who knew? Not one of them stepped forward to help. Not his wife either. She hadn't moved from her spot in the driveway. Arms wrapped tightly about her chest, she stood blinking in the bright light of morning. When he returned to her side, she still didn't speak.

Carl was standing next to her when the television crew arrived. As soon as the reporter stepped out of the van—he recognized her face from the six o'clock news—he began trying to hustle Hannah back to the front door. How horrible if she ended up on the news this way, stranded in her own front yard, her filmy white gown streaked with red. She'd never live it down, he thought. Never. They'd have to move elsewhere, start their lives over again. And yet she was no help to him. She didn't turn and run. In fact, he had to grasp her arm and jerk her along behind him. Several times she stumbled and cried out against him. "Let go!" she wailed as they reached the porch, but he only tightened his grasp.

"Hurry," he urged, looking back at her. In the bright light of morning, she appeared middle-aged and fragile, all her years and more. "A reporter's here."

"Oh God!" Hannah cried, as though only now, at this moment, had it suddenly become real to her.

The blonde reporter was trailing after them, her stride shortened by a straight skirt. "Hannah Solace?" she called in a breathless voice. How had the news spread so quickly? he wondered. How did this perky little bitch know Hannah's name? "I know this is a bad time. . . ." she conceded as a man with a video cam hustled across the yard, edging up until he was only a few feet to the left of the reporter.

"Get the hell out of here!" Carl shouted before pushing Hannah through the front door. "She doesn't want to talk, and if you were any kind of a human being, you'd turn off the goddamn camera!" And he slammed the door behind them.

Inside, he held his wife, soothed and grateful for even this sort of contact. Hannah sobbed, choking on her grief. "This is horrible," she moaned. "Don't you realize how horrible this is?"

Of course I realize, he thought. It's happening to me too. "It's unbelievable," he agreed. "Have you ever heard of such a thing?"

Hannah shook her head against his shoulder. "Never," she muttered.

Carl wrapped her more tightly in his arms and waited, keeping his eye on the window, on whatever he could make out through the small swatch of clear glass. Figures passed, bright blobs of color that blocked the light. The doorbell rang, once, then again, but he made no move to answer it, and Hannah acted as though she didn't hear it. After several silent minutes, he whispered in her ear. "You better change clothes. I'm going to call the police."

She gazed up at him, her pale face blotched with emotion. "You're right," she said, and then he heard the first hint of anger: "Why aren't they here? Everyone else is."

She pulled away, and Carl went to telephone. The voice at the police station was a woman's, and it was all business, not even a modicum of sympathy. "Sit tight," she told him. And next he learned something new: They weren't the only ones—other houses had been vandalized.

"I'm not talking about toilet paper," Carl said savagely.

"Neither am I," the woman replied. She went on to tell him about the eight others, scattered across town. "It may take a while," she concluded.

After he hung up, Carl dialed Helen. Someone real, he thought. I need to talk to someone real. While he waited for his sister-in-law to answer, Carl listened to the water running in the shower. He imagined his wife's body under the spray, the long red hair gone dark and plastered to her shoulders and back like seaweed. Distracted, he let the phone ring and ring, ten times, then twenty. Finally, Helen picked up. "What is it?" she asked in a strained voice.

She thinks I'm Jimmy, Carl thought. "Hi, Helen," he said. "It's Carl. We have a problem over here."

But her tone didn't change. "I have a problem over here too," she snapped. He could hear baby Shane wailing in the background. There are problems and then there are problems, he wanted to say, glancing again at the black glass in the living room, but he stayed silent and polite until she relented. "I'm sorry, Carl," Helen finally said. "What is it?"

He took a deep breath. How to describe what had happened? He still didn't know himself. "Right now, a hundred people are standing in the street in front of our house." He was exaggerating, and it had the intended effect.

"What?" He could hear the concern in her voice—all irritability gone.

"Television reporters and cameramen are ringing the doorbell." Actually, no one had rung the doorbell in several minutes, but just then the bell sounded.

"Reporters? What's this about?"

"It's about vandalism, malicious destruction of property. You know those subway trains in New York, the ones covered with spray paint? Some gang comes along and uses them to share their bullshit with the world? That's our house now. A big billboard 'For life.' I'm gonna kill that son-of-a-bitch preacher." The asshole with the bullhorn, he thought. Of course. Who else would it be?

"Are you all right, Carl?" Helen sounded far away.

"Carl? Are you out there?" Now it was Hannah calling him.

He put a hand over the receiver. "Be there in a minute, honey!" he shouted. And in a low voice to Helen: "I'm fine. It's your sister I'm worried about. She's taking this hard, Helen. We were out in the yard when the television crew showed up. She was in her nightgown. It was a mess, a horrible mess."

Just then, Hannah called again—a long wailing sound that even Helen could hear.

"You better go," she said. "I'll be right over, as soon as I can get there."

"Thanks," he breathed, and slammed down the receiver.

When he got to the bathroom, he found Hannah stranded in the middle of the bathroom floor, a white towel wrapped around her head. The discarded gown and robe were heaped on the toilet seat, stark white streaked with red, and he rushed to grab them up. He'd throw them away, quickly. It was the least he could do.

"This is so awful, Carl," Hannah moaned. She was hugging her arms to her naked chest, her breasts swelling around them. "How do you think the TV people found out?"

"They were tipped off, don't you see?"

Hannah shook her head and reached for another towel, quickly wrapping herself, as though a cameraman might burst through the door at any second. "Who tipped them off?" she asked him. "They know my *name*. They're standing on my front porch!" As though to punctuate her point, the doorbell rang again. "Go away!" Hannah wailed.

Carl moved in to put his arms around her, but she waved him away and backed against the counter. He waited patiently for her attention, but instead of meeting his gaze, she stared at the blank screen of the little black-and-white TV. Later today, she'd be on it. Was that what she was thinking? he wondered.

"You don't have to talk to them," he told her. "We don't have to answer the door."

"I have to go outside!" Now she turned to face him. "I have to live my life!"

"Calm down, Hannah. You're making things worse for yourself. You're making them worse for me."

They stared at each other in silence. Tears ran down her cheeks. "Are you still mad at me?" she asked in a quiet voice.

"About the abortion?"

She nodded.

Clasping the gown and robe to his chest, he thought hard. This was one of the first times they'd addressed it directly, and for himself, for both of them, he had to tell the truth. "Yes," he said slowly. "I want to forgive you, I want to go on, but I'm not there yet. Not now, not quite. You've got to understand, Hannah. I really wanted that child. With all my heart."

She looked away, back to the blank screen of the television set. "You're on their side, then," she replied in a matter-of-fact voice.

"How can you say that?" Carl asked loudly. "This is happening to me too!"

"Not really." Her tone was icy. Whatever bad happened, it was always eventually his fault. The only way Hannah could accept and manage catastrophe was to assign blame. Blame yourself, he wanted to shout, or blame that asshole with the bullhorn. "This isn't about you, because you're not the baby killer," she finished.

"What shit, Hannah!" He tried to hurl the clothes at her, but they were too light. They unfurled in the air and floated to the tile floor between them. It slipped out then, just slipped out: "I'm not the baby killer. I'm the baby killer's husband."

"I hate you right now," she hissed.

I hate you too, he thought of saying, but he had to put an end to this. It was up to him. "Listen," he began, but he didn't move to comfort her. He stayed put, in the middle of the tile floor. "I shouldn't have said that. Helen's on her way over. The police will be here shortly. You really should get dressed."

Hannah nodded and edged past him without touching, without so much as a glance into his face. He heard her bare feet on the hardwood floor as she ran for the bedroom, then the slam of the door behind her. She doesn't know what I'm feeling, he thought, and she doesn't care. For a brief time, they'd been in this together, but now they were in it apart. He glanced up and found his own gaze in the mirror, saw himself for what he was—a rumpled and befuddled man on the verge of tears. A man standing alone.

Chapter 15

By THE SIX O'CLOCK NEWS, the reporters had coined a phrase for the destruction of property: *paint bombing.* Hearing it, Hannah groaned. Paint bombing sounded like a high-school prank, irritating but essentially harmless, like egging windows or throwing rolls of toilet paper into trees. That would have been bad enough, but the reporter also indulged in a fair amount of speculation. She'd toured the affected houses and, because there were nine, concluded that those responsible had "bombed one house for each month of a woman's pregnancy." She made this ridiculous pronouncement while standing in front of a small white bungalow disfigured with paint. The vandals had worked quietly and quickly, she said, and in the "wee hours" of Saturday morning had managed to hit houses all over town. The report concluded with a map of Austin dotted with red stars to mark the locations of the affected homes. Hannah and Carl's was easy to find, right off Burnet Road, a main thoroughfare. Red Star House #4.

"My house is a tourist attraction," she said out loud. She hoped it wasn't true, and she waited for Helen to say something reassuring. However, her sister wasn't saying much this evening. Helen was holding Shane and staring at the television screen, but her thoughts were clearly elsewhere, probably on Jimmy, who'd called half an hour before to say he'd be late and not to wait dinner. Hannah had been the one to answer the phone, and after Jimmy had made his excuses, he'd offered his condolences as well. That was the word he used, *condolences*, as though someone had died. Damn shame he'd called it, and Hannah had agreed. Damn shame indeed.

"World is full of crazies," he said. "You take your chances walking out the door in the morning."

Hannah wondered how he'd found out. "Did Helen tell you?" she asked.

"Hell no," he replied. "She didn't have to tell me. Got a call on the old car phone. Real-estate-related news, you understand."

She did. On the way to Helen's, Hannah had stared out the window, watching neighborhoods flash by, shopping centers, churches. She'd spotted brick houses, stucco houses, white frames with wraparound porches. Just then she'd yearned for one, any one, a clean, anonymous house to move into. It had occurred to her that this was possible, that she could rent a new house and start over. Leave the furniture behind, she'd told herself. Leave everything behind, the blind dog, the do-nothing husband. The ugliness of such thinking had made her shudder. Don't, she'd told herself. Don't make it worse.

"Do you think we'll have to move?" she asked Jimmy.

"Not unless you want to." His tone had been fatherly and solicitous. What was it he'd called himself? Jackass, that was it. He was a jackass, all right. "If you decide to," he'd continued, "just let me know. I'll be glad to help."

Yeah, she thought now. You'll be glad to help, all right. When a commercial flashed on, Hannah returned her attention to Helen. "Jimmy said he wouldn't be all that late. It really did sound as though he had work to do."

Helen didn't reply, didn't even bother to turn her head. She was perched in a recliner on the other side of the living room, cradling Shane in her lap. He was sound asleep, his little mouth open, his arms limp. He'd drifted off at least an hour before, but Helen hadn't gotten up to put him to bed. She'd just gone on holding him against her breast, as though he might wake up and want to suckle. In her pink sweat suit and fluffy house slippers, a sleeping baby in her arms, she was the very vision of motherhood.

"Okay, Lady Madonna," Hannah said. "Why don't you put the baby down?" If her tone had been slightly more jocular, she might have gotten away with it. But she knew she sounded condescending and irritable.

Helen bristled and clutched Shane more tightly, so that the child opened his eyes and yawned. "Okay, Gloria Steinem," Helen shot back as she struggled to her feet. They were sisters, and Helen would take her in, but that didn't mean she agreed with her. Holding the baby all afternoon long was her way of making that point perfectly clear. When she reached the doorway, Helen turned back. "It's awful what they did, Hannah," she said. "An awful thing, a cruel thing. But what you did was cruel too. Cruel to Carl, cruel to you. You gave him no say in the matter."

Hannah turned from the screen to her sister, who was standing in the doorway now. "Which is why you had to call and warn him?"

Helen nodded. "Like I told you before, it was his decision to go to the clinic. He decided that part on his own."

"You're splitting hairs!" Hannah cried. "What did you think he was going to do?"

Helen pulled back a few steps. "Keep your voice down. You'll wake the baby."

Ignoring the warning, Hannah waved a hand toward the screen. "You might as well go to work for the paint bombers," she said loudly. "You're just like them, interfering in other people's lives. You had no right—"

"*I* had no right? *I* had no right?" Helen interrupted. "What about Carl's rights? He deserved to know. That child . . . that child was as much his as yours."

"Not a child—" Hannah began.

"Yes!" Helen cried, startling baby Shane awake. "A child! If only Carl had been able to get through to you," Helen continued, "none of this would have happened. You'd have been showing by Christmas. We'd have been painting the nursery instead of the front of your goddamn garage." She was pleased with herself, Helen was. Proud of this little speech.

"Joy to the world!" Hannah sang in a bitter voice. "A child makes everyone *so* happy! You've got three of them. So why aren't you happy, Helen?"

"I *am* happy," Helen hissed before padding off down memory lane. All those faces, staring at her from the walls, she wanted them there for reassurance, Hannah realized. They confirmed her view of the world.

Traitors, she thought, going into the bathroom and closing the door. It was a mess. Grayson had left the lid up on the toilet and, worse, he hadn't bothered to flush. Cassie's white tennis shoes littered the floor. Her bath towel, decorated with characters from *The Lion King*, lay wadded beside them. Water cooled in the tub, a grimy soap ring forming around the edge. A rubber duck patrolled the perimeter. Leave it, she thought. Let Miss Priss clean it up.

Hannah was exhausted; otherwise, she would have gathered her things and left. But the truth was, she had nowhere else to go. Over the years, she hadn't done much to cultivate friendships. She rushed through her days, too tired at night to do more than a little reading before bed. And before all this had happened, she'd had no reason to make the effort with other people. She and Helen had gotten along so well. And Carl too. He'd been a good friend to her, the best, really. If she was honest with herself, she'd have to say that he had been an absolutely faithful friend, a good listener, a patient adviser. Only in this case, she hadn't gone to him for advice or support. How could she? It was what he wanted against what she wanted, an impossible conflict of interests. "I really wanted that child," he'd said earlier, "with all my heart." Only now, in Helen's house, surrounded by the detritus of Helen's children, did Hannah see what a betrayal the abortion had been. To him. And yet she was still certain that continuing the pregnancy would have been another sort of betrayal, a greater betrayal, a betrayal of the self. She kicked the towel into the corner, closed the lid on the toilet, then gave herself a quick glance in the mirror. Catching her own eyes, she quickly turned away.

Dinner was a mostly silent affair. In a quiet house, it was amazing how much you could hear. Between the clatter of cutlery, Hannah caught snatches of a lullaby tape playing in Shane's bedroom. At least the baby's happy, she thought, sleeping away this tense evening, too young to understand his father's absence or his mother's unhappiness. Grayson seemed to understand all too well. From time to time, he glanced toward their father's empty chair, then shot quick looks at Helen and Hannah. Otherwise, he and Cassie stayed busy twirling spaghetti with big spoons. Once, Cassie lost a meatball when it rolled over the edge of her plate and onto the table. On another evening, this little getaway would have inspired giggles and jokes, but not tonight. Quickly, before their mother could notice, Grayson intervened, forking the offending meatball for his sister and replacing it on her plate. Helen went on eating her big bowl of salad, all of her attention devoted to spearing tiny squares of cucumber and carrot.

After the meal, Hannah rose to help clear the table—chattering all the while, offering compliments on the food and complaining that she'd overeaten—but Helen only smiled absently. Grayson lugged in the platters and began pouring the leftover sauce into a plastic container. Obviously unpracticed, he splattered the tile wall and white blender with it, and, like a small defenseless animal, went perfectly still. Helen surveyed the mess and sighed. "Be more careful, would you?" she asked. Coming back to life, he grabbed the dishrag and said, "Sorry, Mom." Without a word to either of them, Helen left the room.

"I'll do this," Hannah told Grayson. He tossed her a grateful look, dropped the dishrag in the sink, and ran for his room.

Once the kitchen was clean, Hannah wandered through the silent house looking for Helen. She found her holed up in the back bedroom, a cramped space set aside for sanding furniture and completing crafts projects. Hunched over the table, Helen was busy gluing together pieces of balsa wood and pretended not to notice Hannah's arrival. The two younger children were nearby. Shane surveyed his domain from a walker stationed near the door, and Cassie was camped out in the hall, where she lay on her stomach and scrawled with crayons on butcher paper.

"How about I rub your shoulders?" Hannah asked. Before Helen could reject the offer, Hannah stepped behind the chair and began kneading her sister's neck. Closer now, she could see that the bits of balsa wood belonged to angels—tiny torsos, heads, and wings. "You want to talk about it?" she asked.

Helen shook her head, so Hannah went on massaging the tight

muscles, content with the silence. In a few minutes, she realized her sister was quietly sobbing, dripping tears in the glue, her shoulders quaking. Hannah lightened her touch through this crying spell, glancing around at the children, who played happily on, oblivious to their mother's grief.

After a few moments, Helen spoke, her voice quavering: "I've decided not to do Thanksgiving here this year," she said. "It's too much. Everything. Your house, my house. I want to go home to Tyler." She cradled one of the tiny balsa-wood angels in her palm. It had only one wing; the other lay on the table, next to a bottle of glue. "Will you go with me?"

As a rule, Hannah never went home for Thanksgiving. It was enough, she thought, to return each Christmas. Too stressful to go twice in two months. But she understood why Helen needed the trip, and, really, she was right. How could they sit around the table this year, filling their plates and glaring at each other? The children deserved better, and Harriet, their stepmother, would certainly see to it that the turkey was stuffed, the candles lit, the blessings said.

"All right," Hannah agreed.

"Just you and me and the kids?" Helen asked.

"Yes," Hannah told her. "Of course."

Carl called after the ten o'clock news. Jimmy was still out, and Helen had retreated to her bedroom. When the phone rang, she called out from the end of the hall. "It's for you." Hannah picked it up in the kitchen, knowing who it must be and also why Helen didn't say. Carl was a sore spot between them right now. No use mentioning his name.

After exchanging hellos, both ends of the line went silent. Eventually, Carl said, "I'm sorry."

Hannah knew Carl, knew he'd apologize just to clear the air. That's the way he was. On the other hand, she rarely apologized. Her pride got in the way; that's the way she was. In moments of introspection and self-scrutiny, she could see how arrogant she must look, how cold and condescending. No wonder Helen sometimes called her "the Ice Queen." Always, she promised herself to do better next time, but in the heat of the moment, she failed. And this time would be no different. The most she could manage was a statement of regret: "I wish we hadn't argued," she said haltingly. "I wish I hadn't said those things." The apology lurked there, behind her words. She could only hope that Carl heard it.

"I know," he said simply, then moved on to the late-news coverage. He'd seen it when he got home from work. "What a lame report!" he exclaimed. They discussed the idiocy of it; then he told her about the police visit—a number of polite questions, he said, and quite a bit of hemming and hawing around. "I don't think it's going to amount to much," he admitted.

"What do you mean?"

"The investigation. They've got bigger fish to fry. Murderers, rapists; you have to keep things in perspective."

He was right, of course. She couldn't argue. Carl was so fair, so rational, always ready to step to the end of the line. It drove her to distraction. "So they're going to get away with this?" she said.

"I didn't say that. But don't expect anything to happen right away. Don't expect immediate arrests. They've got to find some evidence or witnesses or *something*. Right now they don't have anything to go on."

"But *we* know who did it."

"Yes," he agreed. "But we can't prove it, now, can we?"

They were quiet again, listening to each other's breath. "I could come home," she offered. She wanted to come home. She could already imagine herself in her Blazer, winding down the dark stretch of Mount Bonnell Road.

"Not a good idea, Hannah. It's bad news over here, people driving by and shouting things out of car windows."

"Saying what?"

"You don't want to know. Just stay put, okay? It'll blow over in a couple of days. I'll drive up there after work tomorrow. Make me a list. I'll bring you whatever you need."

After hanging up, Hannah fixed herself a bed on the couch. Helen had left out a pillow, sheets, and a blanket. She lay down, exhausted and determined to sleep, but even closing her eyes was difficult in her present state of mind. She felt restless and bereft and, after going to the kitchen for water, roamed the house, eventually finding her way into Cassie's room. The night-light revealed a tiny table and chairs, a rocking horse in one corner, a seashell mobile that curved and swayed each time the central heat clicked on. She sat down on the edge of Cassie's bed and breathed in the smells of toothpaste and bubble bath. You'll feel better in a minute, she told herself, and she did. Just as Hannah was carefully raising herself from the mattress, the little girl opened her eyes. "Want to sleep with me, Aunt Hannah?" Cassie whispered.

"I didn't mean to wake you."

"It's okay," she replied. "Mommy sleeps with me too."

"Does she?" Hannah asked, curling up beside her. She wasn't at all surprised. In those long weeks after her mother had died, the longest weeks of her life, Hannah had given up sleeping in her own room and taken up residence in Helen's. She and Helen would curl together in the darkness, Hannah's heart beating against Helen's back, Hannah's hand on Helen's heart.

One night, maybe a week after the funeral, Helen had pitched up in bed and let out a loud agonizing hiss, followed by a rush of words so hushed and hurried that Hannah couldn't make sense of them. Frightened, she'd clasped Helen's small hand. "It's all right, Little Girl," she'd said softly. Little Girl was a pet name their mother had used. Little Girl for Helen and Big Girl for Hannah. Through tone of voice and inflection, Naomi had put her own stamp on these generic names, making them particular and individual, theirs and theirs alone. Maybe it was the use of the pet name that stirred something in Helen's consciousness.

"Momma?" she'd whispered. Her eyes had been wide open and blank, as though she'd gone suddenly blind. "Momma?" she'd screamed, all the while staring straight at Hannah. So this was what was next, Hannah had thought, and in some small kernel of her deepest self, she was jealous. It wasn't fair. She hadn't laid eyes on their mother since she'd died. Not even in her dreams.

"It's me, Helen," she'd said, but her sister was in the midst of a night terror, and no ordinary measures would work to bring her out of it. Speaking to her, shaking her, even slapping her had no effect. And so Hannah had ended up doing the only thing she knew to do, on that first night and all the subsequent nights. It had gone on, she thought now, for nearly a year. As soon as Helen began to thrash and moan, Hannah climbed over the heaving bedclothes and dropped to the safety of the wooden floor. There, she crouched for a minute to come back to herself. Sometimes, Helen's screams started when Hannah was in the midst of a dream, and then the dream itself became tinged with Helen's hysteria. Even with her eyes open, even with her feet on the smooth wooden floor, Hannah would sometimes see the dream unreeling before her eyes, a thing gone wrong, insistently wrong.

The bathroom was at the other end of the long hallway. It was an old house with one of those narrow halls that seemed to close down over you as you walked its length. Hannah would drag her screaming sister by the arms because Helen was too big to carry, and during the long journey down that hall, she would often soothe herself with thoughts of another Helen—Helen Keller and her teacher, Annie Sullivan. She'd seen *The Miracle Worker* with Patty Duke and Anne Bancroft, and she remembered the drastic measures Teacher had been forced to take, how she'd dragged Helen Keller screaming from the table. Sometimes, things that appear cruel are done in the name of goodness, she told herself.

"It's for your own good," Hannah would say when they reached the bathroom, and then she'd let go of her load, allowing Helen's head to knock heavily against the wooden floor. Naturally, the little girl shrieked with pain and indignation. At the time, Hannah had told herself that she let go of her sister to turn on the light, but the truth was, she did it on purpose, provoking Helen to her loudest screams just outside their father's door. Serves her right, she'd think, and I hate his guts, and help me, Jesus—all of them at once and all with the same urgency.

The bathroom was well-lit, a bulb over the sink and one in the ceiling that turned on with the same switch, filling the room with a yellowish glow, more light than the narrow space could contain. The brilliance of the room should have brought Helen to her senses, but it didn't. Light had absolutely no effect on her, though each time Hannah hoped it would, hoped she wouldn't have to go the whole distance. The tub was an old thing, raised up on brass feet, and Hannah had to heave her sister over the side and into the freezing shower. "Come on, Little Girl," Hannah would say. By the time she had them both in the tub, frigid water would have pooled in the bottom, the drain too sluggish to carry it all away. Hannah's toes curled in the icy water, and she'd bend her head away as she held her sister's face in the spray, straining to keep her there until Helen went limp and silent, until Hannah was certain that the fit was finished for another night.

Teeth chattering, wet flannel sticking to their chilled skin, Hannah would peel off Helen's gown, then rub her sister down with a towel. When Helen was good and dry, Hannah would instruct her to sit on the lid of the toilet while she returned to the bedroom to collect their dry clothes. Another trip down that awful hallway, still dressed in the sopping gown and dripping cold water with each step. Often, her father would be standing in his doorway when she passed. His white T-shirt and underwear would glow in the darkness, and if he was smoking a cigarette, there'd be that tiny red ember near his mouth. She'd turn away from him, pretend not to notice his presence, partly out of embarrassment, partly out of anger. He was no help to any of them. By the time she returned, he'd have retreated to the black hole of his grief. She'd hear his bedroom door close and think to herself, Good riddance. On the other side of the bathroom door, Helen would be waiting, naked, a small, shivering bundle of flesh. Together, they'd dress and return to bed, huddling together for warmth and comfort, going off at last to a peaceful sleep.

This time when Hannah awakened it was Cassie sitting up in bed. The little girl was sobbing and clutching a lumpy stuffed animal to her chest. "Stop it, stop it," she chanted.

Groggy and befuddled, Hannah reached out and touched the child. "Stop what?" she asked. "What's wrong?" Then she heard the noise on the other side of the house, a scuffling followed by the sound of someone pounding on a door. Hannah looked to the dark doorway and back to the child, who'd ceased her chanting and was listening alertly. Before Hannah had the presence of mind to stop her, Cassie had crawled to the bottom of the bed and scrambled over the end board. "Cassie!" Hannah called. Sighing, she got up to follow.

The hallway was L-shaped, and as Hannah neared the intersection, she could see that the lights were on in memory lane. Cassie was just turning the corner, her flannel nightgown humped up over her underwear, the flattened animal dangling from her hand. "Cassie, come back!" Hannah cried, realizing what lay ahead. Hurrying now, Hannah heard the frame scraping the wall, then the glass shattering. She started to run, imagining Naomi's picture crashing to the floor. That's what had happened; she was sure of it. Turning the corner, Hannah nearly stumbled over Cassie. The little girl was standing stock-still and staring straight ahead. At the other end of the hall, her parents were engaged in a knockdown drag-out fight, but one that was entirely silent. Their mouths were shut tight, as though they had a pact: We can do what we want to each other, as long as we do it quietly. Jimmy was forcing his way into the bedroom, and Helen was struggling to keep him out. Her face was scarlet with effort and rage, wet with tears. The framed photograph of Naomi lay on the floor by the bedroom door, the broken glass glittering on the carpet.

Hannah let out a little moan of regret, then bent and scooped Cassie into her arms. "It's all right, sweetie," she whispered, holding on tight. The lies we tell to children, she thought. Nothing was all right, and Cassie could perfectly well see that. The little girl squirmed, then screamed. "Daddy!" Cassie shrieked. "Mommy!"

Helen's startled face appeared in the doorway. "Cassie, baby," she cried. Then, "Move, Jimmy!"

He did as she asked, allowing her to push past him. One strap of her red nightgown had slid down her arm, and strands of copper hair stuck to her wet cheeks. As she stumbled down the hall, all those eyes in the photographs watched her progress, the unblinking stares of grandmothers, fathers, aunts and uncles, and at least a dozen versions of Helen herself. But she was blind to them. No good pushing her into a shower tonight, Hannah thought. Her sister was wide awake and well beyond all that.

Part

III

Chapter 16

THE WOMAN ON THE PHONE was sniffling. She was calling long distance from Dallas, and from the sound of her voice, Penny guessed she'd been in the midst of an all-out cry only moments before. "You delivered the balloons for my grandson's birthday," the woman explained, "and I thought they were charming. You were so nice."

"Thank you," Penny replied. She was only half listening. With the receiver crooked between her ear and shoulder, she was busily stripping the bottom leaves off a bunch of yellow pompon chrysanthemums. Holding one up to the light, she pronounced it fresh and full. The chrysanthemums would hold up well. So far, most of the delivery looked to be in good shape, with the exception of the baby's breath, which appeared to have been soaked in water, tiny wads of white for blooms.

"You probably don't remember," the woman continued, "a little boy of six, and a dozen of his friends. Just a few months ago, back in May."

"I'm sorry," Penny said. "I do lots of birthday parties." It wasn't much of a response, but she couldn't muster anything more. As usual, the flower market had delivered first thing Monday morning, only Juanita hadn't shown up for work. Even with two pairs of hands, they were often taxed to clean the flowers and get them into the cooler by midday. Alone, Penny would have to work straight through—no breaks, no lunch, no small talk with customers.

The woman from Dallas wanted flowers, of course she did. People ordering flowers were often at their absolute worst—grieving, guilty, depressed, distraught—whereas people ordering balloons were mostly happy. Juanita had a whole spiel on this subject. According to her, the flower business catered to "a bunch of emotional basket cases." Juanita thought Penny should forget about flowers and concentrate on balloons, and this morning's mess made her wonder. Flowers *were* a lot of trouble. But she couldn't worry about that right now. She couldn't worry about Juanita, or the scene in the nursery on Sunday morning, or the streaks of paint on the floorboard of her van, or any of the myriad mysteries of the past weekend. Myriad mysteries, she thought. It sounded like something from one of Dr. Bill's sermons.

"They're for my daughter," the woman was saying. "She's been the victim of a crime. Oh, you must have seen it on the news. Awful stuff. Just awful."

"Yes, ma'am," she agreed, though she didn't watch television, didn't even own one. "What kind of flowers would you like?"

"Daisies are her favorite. Do you have daisies?"

"Just got some fresh this morning." Penny glanced down the table to where several bunches of daisies lay waiting to be cleaned. "I can mix in some montbretia too," Penny told the woman. "Bright orange. Perfect this time of year. Shows off the white of the daisies. And some yellow and rusty-pink pompon mums? How's that sound?"

"Nice," the woman replied. "Perfect. Just nothing red. Do you have any pretty vases? I don't mind paying extra for something that looks like crystal." A note of hope had crept into this woman's voice. That's part of what kept Penny in flowers. Just talking about them could make a person feel better.

They discussed prices while Penny cut stems, whacking through the woody bark with one sure squeeze of the scissors. These days, she was practiced and confident, not at all the same girl who'd gone to work in a neighbor's shop for minimum wage five years earlier. That girl had been tentative and scared, but she'd learned quickly. No matter how mundane the task, she'd found a way to take pleasure in it. Something done well, Mattie had taught her that. And this: Nothing comes easily, certainly not knowledge or skill. Now, all that hard work later, Penny had her own shop and a woman from Dallas calling because she wanted *her* flowers, *her* personal touch. Those were things worth waiting for; they were important, even on a day like today.

"When can you deliver them?" the caller asked. "I want Norma to have them as soon as possible."

The flowers would arrive today, Penny reassured her, though it might be late afternoon. Her assistant hadn't shown up for work, she explained. "What shall I put on the card?" Penny asked.

"*You'll make it through this, Norma,*" the woman dictated. Penny wrote it down in her careful, loopy hand. "*Love, Mom.*" After hanging up, she dialed Juanita again and listened to the phone ring fifteen times before resigning herself to getting through the day alone.

Fortunately, Monday's deliveries were light. Most of the balloons went to office parties downtown. Two of her Flowers from the Sea arrangements had to be delivered to houses in Northwest Hills. Aside from those, she had only to take Norma her flowers in South Austin. By the time Penny headed across the river and in the direction of Norma's house, the light was waning on a gloomy, overcast day. Dead leaves scuttled across the intersection; carried by gusts of wind, they gathered at the curb in growing piles of brown husks. Gazing through the windshield, Penny couldn't help feeling a little sad. She supposed it had something to do with the upcoming holidays. Thanksgiving and Christmas were observed quietly in Mattie's household; sometimes it was just the two of them taking part. This time of year, Penny was always reminded of her own solitary place in the world. Festivity required people, lots of people, the more the merrier. Didn't Delia and Dwayne's reception prove that?

It had taken place at the American Legion Hall, a barbecue chicken dinner followed by dancing to a band called The Old Timers. The crowd had grown to fill the hall, and these were the sort of people who knew how to have a good time—lots of whooping, hollering, dancing, and beer drinking. Midway through the night, Dwayne had dragged Penny out on the dance floor. They must have been a sight, she thought. The only dancing she'd ever done was square dancing in gym class, and Dwayne, well, he was hindered by his "bum leg." For him, dancing was a sort of rhythmic limping, accompanied by a waving of arms. "A drunk hula dancer," Delia called him. Pretty soon, Penny had found herself copying him, bobbing gently when he did, the two of them going up and down together, like a pair of old men in a boat. Once she'd gotten the hang of it, she'd enjoyed dancing, and they'd kept it up for hours. It had been nearly three in the morning when she'd finally pulled into Mattie's empty driveway.

The rain had followed her home from Houston, stalling for more than a day. Now and again, fat drops popped on the windshield. Though the temperature was almost sixty, the world outside looked wintry, everything brown and dreary. To cheer herself, Penny glanced over at the vase of flowers strapped into the seat next to her. Into the flurry of white Shasta daisies she'd slipped a half dozen orange mont-bretia and a scattering of yellow and rusty-pink mums. The mums were muted in color, while the daisies and montbretia were brilliant, the perfect complements. Altogether, the bouquet seemed to glow in the last light of evening. Lovely, Penny thought. Just looking at the bouquet made her feel better, and she hoped that it would do the same for Norma, whoever she was.

Off and on as she drove across town, Penny admired her creation, but it only served as a partial distraction. Just as often, her eyes would stray to the smudge of red paint on the gray upholstery—high up, where the back of someone's head would rest—or to the streaks of black that marred the floorboard. Or to what was most obvious, the two blurry red fingerprints that smeared the radio dial. And the worst of it wasn't even visible from the driver's seat. Inside the left back door, two long splatters, one red and one black, arced away from each other. They were reminiscent of a child's first attempt at artwork, an oddly colored rainbow gone awry, only this wasn't artwork. In the space of a day, Mattie and Juanita had made a mess of her service van, the only thing in the world Penny could truly call her own, and the baffling part was, they'd refused to explain. They wouldn't tell her why or how or what it all meant.

The van had been missing in the early hours of Sunday morning—that in itself had been strange and a little unsettling—but when the alarm went off at seven A.M., it was *still* gone. Astonishing. Such a possibility would never have occurred to her. Standing at the window, she'd stared out at the spot where her van should have been, everything swimming before her eyes—the expanse of gravel, the lacy branches of the mimosa, the neighbor's chain-link fence. She'd thought of calling the police. They would know what to do. But in the end, she'd simply climbed into the station wagon and driven to Gospel Fellowship, hoping to find the answers there.

Sure enough, she'd discovered her van parked in the small gravel lot in back of the church, the only vehicle there. Inside, the seats and floorboards were covered with trampled newspapers, all of them smeared with red and black paint. The back was strewn with paint-can lids and more newspaper. For a minute or so, Penny had simply stood and taken it in. Then she'd set to work cleaning up as best she could, gathering armloads of newspaper and hauling them to the Dumpster on the other side of the lot. Walking back and forth, gravel crunching beneath her feet, she'd thought, "How dare they?" and "What in the world were they doing?"

It had been well after eight o'clock when Penny let herself in the back door of the church with a key they kept hidden above the casing. The paint on the casing was all but worn away, and as she felt for the cold grip of metal, her fingers pressed into soft wood. Everything's coming to pieces, she thought. The building that housed Gospel Fellowship was old, and for years the upkeep had been spotty. She knew the history: Originally constructed back in the twenties, the building had housed a small but devoted Episcopal congregation. Back then it had been nothing more than a modest chapel over a basement. The basement was divided into three small rooms and a janitor's closet, the latter of which now served as the nursery. Penny unlocked the door and headed down the stairs.

The nursery still bore signs of its former service as a janitor's closet. A nearly square space, the only natural light came from a rectangular window near the ceiling. Heavy metal shelves lined one wall, stacked now with jigsaw-puzzle boxes and old games: Chutes and Ladders, Barbie, Cootie, Candy Land, most missing an essential piece or two. On the opposite wall, big hooks, screwed into the walls for mops and brooms, held particleboard cutouts of Disney characters, oddly arranged, so that Donald and Mickey appeared to be fighting. Recently, Dr. Bill had improved the space by patching together a crazy-quilt carpet, cutting and piecing a variety of remnants, then notching them to fit like a puzzle. To complete the decor, he'd hung a Dutch door, painting it an orangish-red, exactly the shade of the Campbell's soup can. The result was garish but undeniably cozy.

Generally, they kept the nursery locked up tight, but on Sunday morning the door had stood wide open, and as soon as Penny had stepped inside she discovered Juanita, asleep in the rocking chair. Her first thought was to shout and jolt her awake, but she couldn't bring herself to do it. If only Juanita had looked like a grown-up, Penny might have chastised her as one. But she appeared childlike in every way: in her posture, slumping, openmouthed; in her clothing, paint-splattered jeans and canvas sneakers; and even in the very circumstance of her repose, the rocking chair of a toy-strewn nursery. Often enough, Penny had noticed the way children drop off to sleep, abruptly and without regard to time or place. Any stroller or stretch of floor will do. And here was Juanita, her long dark hair hiding one side of her face, looking just like them.

Nearby, Buck slept under a yellow blanket in the old white baby bed, eyes squeezed shut, bottom lip curled under, that shock of black hair spread out over the worn pink sheet. But wet, she realized, soaked through, his diaper, his sleeper, the sheet under him. The ammonia smell of urine hung in the air above the bed, such a strong stench that Penny drew back. He slept peacefully enough now, but the hair on the back of his head was matted from tossing and turning. He'd had a long night, and he'd obviously spent all of it here. Why? Penny wondered. Why had he been in the church all night? Where had Juanita been? It had something to do with the van. Of that, Penny was certain. Just as she was turning away, Buck whimpered and, opening his eyes, gazed directly up at her. "Poor little fellow," she whispered, reaching down to caress his cheek and rub her fingers in his matted hair.

He needed to be cleaned up and fed, but Juanita slept on. Fortunately, Buck's diaper bag hung from one of the posts of the baby bed. Penny slung it over her shoulder and, with a sigh, gathered the heavy baby into her arms, holding him out just enough so as not to ruin her dress. She carried him down the hall, shouldered her way into the tiny rest room, and got to work. Not knowing what else to do, she peeled off Buck's sleeper and soggy diaper and set him in the sink. The water wasn't nearly as warm as she would have liked, and the brown paper towels were scratchy. Buck was indignant at this treatment, slapping at her hands and shrieking as the water pooled around his belly. "It's okay, Bucky," she kept saying.

When Penny returned with him, two more children had arrived, but Juanita was still asleep. A little boy in a red bow tie played nearby on the rug, quietly erecting a tower of blocks. Seeing his mother, Buck began to wail. Juanita shifted a bit, turning her shoulder to the door. She seemed determined not to be disturbed. What kind of mother are you? Penny wanted to ask, but abruptly, she knew the answer: Juanita was the same kind Delia had been, one who wasn't finished with her own childhood, or even with high school for that matter, ill-prepared but well-meaning, making it up as she went along. "Juanita!" Penny cried, all out of patience.

Startled, Juanita sat bolt upright in the rocker and rubbed her eyes. "Why are you shouting?" she asked.

"Bucky here wants a bottle. He was soaking wet. I had to bathe him in the bathroom sink."

"Thanks," Juanita said, then, seeing the disapproval on Penny's face, she shrugged dramatically. "It's no big deal, you know. He's like that every morning. I've tried putting two diapers on him, even three. It makes no difference."

"And my van? What about that?"

Another shrug, smaller this time. "Nothing," Juanita replied in a hard little voice.

"My van is a mess!" Penny shouted, startling the children on the floor, who looked up at her with expectant faces. "What were you doing last night?"

Juanita got up then and took her baby, quickly settling him on her hip. "Calm down," she said to Penny. And to Buck: "I've got a bottle for you in the fridge." Then, maneuvering around children and toys, she made her way out of the room. That was the last Penny had seen of her. Juanita didn't return to the nursery all morning, and Penny couldn't very well leave her charges to track her down. On Sunday evening, Mattie hadn't answered her door or her phone. And this morning, Juanita hadn't shown up for work. They were shutting her out.

Three or four blocks from Norma's house, Penny ran into unexpected traffic, a line of cars several blocks long, all of them waiting to turn onto Stassney Lane. "For heaven's sake," she sighed, glancing at her watch. Already, it was after four. The traffic was always bad this time of day, but a backup like this one spelled an accident or something unusual. Taking a right off Stassney Lane and entering the humble neighborhood of small brick houses and worn-looking winter lawns, Penny began to suspect that the cars in front of her were all headed for the same destination, some garage sale maybe, though it seemed an odd time for that. Not until she made the same turn as the rest of them, onto Salem Hill Road, did Penny realize that they were *all* on their way to Norma's. And the reason began to dawn on her. "Please God," she prayed as she passed clots of bystanders and a line of parked cars. "Don't let this be true." But it was true. The red brick dwelling was trimmed in white—shutters, front door, garage door— and all of it had been splattered with red and black paint.

Pulling her van into the driveway, Penny was confronted with the word BABYKILLER, splashed in red across the garage door. Huge, wavery letters written in Juanita's handwriting, or maybe Esther's, or Mattie's. Had to be. The proof was right here inside Penny's van. She glanced down at the smudged red fingerprints on the radio dial. Evidence, she thought. In their haste, they'd given it to her, forced it on her. Her heart pounded; her head throbbed. She knew she should get out, make her delivery, be on her way, but she couldn't move. Part of her wanted to drive away, part to confess, part to sit silently and weep.

An older man dressed in overalls and a white paint cap was working on the front porch, ignoring the traffic jam on the street behind him. His stiff posture conveyed disdain for the drivers of these trucks, vans, cars, even a stray motorcycle or two. No matter how unruly, no matter how rude, he wouldn't dignify them with so much as a glance. He even declined to look Penny's way. Instead, he bent methodically to the can of paint, dipped his brush, and brought it up swathed in thick white. His movements were slow, and although Penny couldn't tell for sure, she thought he might be trembling. She sat in the driver's seat and watched him swipe paint across the letter *M*. She could only read the first three letters—M-U-R—but she knew the word.

Penny took a deep breath. "Be strong," she whispered. Then she got out of the van and edged around to the passenger door, where Norma's flowers were strapped into the seat. Like the man on the porch, she studiously avoided the stares of passersby. A circus, that's what it was. Tears welled up behind Penny's eyes as she struggled with the seat belt. Leaning across, she discovered one more long streak of red paint on the underside of the passenger's seat. Don't you cry, she told herself. Don't you dare cry. Starting up the walk, holding the vase of flowers in front of her chest, Penny called out, "Hello there!" Her voice sounded bright and brittle in the cool November air.

The man whirled about, his pained, suspicious expression giving way to a fleeting smile. "Flowers," he sighed. "How nice." Penny climbed the steps, and the man reached for the knob, throwing open the marred front door. "Looky here, Norma!" he called. "Your favorite flowers." He stepped aside and motioned Penny ahead of him. "Sorry about this mess," he murmured. "The police told me to leave it alone, but I can't."

"*I'm* sorry. I'm *so* sorry!" Penny blurted. The old man stood patiently, nodding his head and waiting for her to step through the door. "This is so terrible!" she went on. "I wish there were something I could do. . . ."

He patted her on the shoulder. "Not your fault," he said. "Thank you for coming by."

Thank her? She was the last person he should thank. She thrust the vase of flowers in his hands. "Why don't you give them to her?" she managed to say.

The 7-Eleven on Stassney Lane had a pay phone out front, but Penny couldn't hear much over the din of traffic. Not that it mattered. She hadn't called Juanita to listen. "I should have you arrested!" she yelled when she heard Juanita pick up. "I should hang up and call the police! I have evidence. Do you hear me?" She was shaking, her words running ahead of her thoughts. "I can't believe you did this to me!" she wailed. Immediately, she regretted those words. They'd done nothing to *her*, really. Norma was the real victim, Norma and her family. To shame them this way, to humiliate them before the world seemed very nearly evil to Penny. "If only you could see the pain you've caused," she said, but Juanita was already gone. The line was dead.

By the time she pulled into her parking spot behind the garage, the sky was fully dark, and she'd sunk into a weariness the likes of which she couldn't recall. Tomorrow, she told herself. I'll sort this out tomorrow. On the way home, she'd imagined climbing into bed without changing her clothes, without brushing her teeth, crawling under the covers and sinking into oblivion. But as she approached the stairs, her eye caught the glint of metal reflecting off a street lamp. Dr. Bill's Harley was parked in Mattie's driveway, and the lights were on in Penny's apartment. They're waiting for me, she thought.

On her way up, she glimpsed them through the window: Dr. Bill was slouched in her red armchair, his legs thrust out in front of him, the tips of his shiny black cowboy boots pointing toward the ceiling. Hearing her step, his expression went from bored to expectant. He sat up straight and jerked off his ball cap, raking fingers through his hair. The gesture spoke to her, told her what she needed to know. Whatever he might say in the coming minutes, whatever he might do, he still cared. Mattie was farther away and harder to read. She perched on the bed, shoulders thrust back, knees pressed together, hands in her lap. She'd even dressed for the occasion, in navy slacks and a long-sleeved print blouse. Minus the jacket, this was the same outfit she'd worn to church last Sunday. Serious business, Penny thought, official business. No wonder Dr. Bill took off his cap. He was here to bring one of his own back to the fold. I'm the lamb, she thought, the lamb that's strayed. Bah, she wanted to say. For a second, she considered standing in the doorway and bleating at them. It was exactly what they deserved, the sort of thing Delia would have done without thinking.

But not Penny. She let the screen door slam behind her. Mattie flinched, but Dr. Bill seemed not to notice; his attention was on Penny. He kept his head down as she entered the room but looked up at her, peering out from under his eyebrows, his expression interested, even friendly.

"Hello," Penny said.

Mattie started to get up, but when Dr. Bill remained sitting, she sank back onto the bed. From under the bed frame, Penny could see

Flash's eyes, fluorescent green orbs, peering out at her. A friendly face, just when Penny needed it most. She cracked a small smile, which Mattie registered. "Nothing's funny here, young lady," she said.

"I'm not laughing," Penny replied quietly, then: "What are you doing here?"

"What are you doing, Penny?" Dr. Bill's tone was conversational, even soothing.

"This is my apartment. I'm *supposed* to be here."

"It belongs to me," Mattie corrected her.

Penny's anger flared. "I should have known," she said loudly. "Nothing is mine. *Nothing.* It's all yours because I'm yours. Is that what you think? Is that why you thought you could use my van to do your dirty work? What's mine is yours?"

"What's yours is God's," Mattie replied. She didn't even have to work at it, Penny realized. The answers were immediately available to her. "We're doing God's work, and if you had any sort of gratitude, you'd be helping us." Mattie paused; her eyes burned with indignation. "The very idea of turning us in, of calling the police. It's purely evil, Penny. I'm surprised at you, really I am."

"Now, Mattie." Dr. Bill lifted himself out of the red chair and crossed the room to Penny. For a second, she thought he meant to embrace her, but he kept his hands clasped behind his back and circled her twice before stopping directly in front of her, blocking her view of Mattie. "What's your favorite book in the Bible, Penny?" he asked.

Taken off-guard, she gave the first and only true answer to his question. "The Book of Ruth," she said. She'd loved the story since she was a child. Her first image of Ruth had come from an illustration in a book of Bible stories: a beautiful young woman gleaning in the fields of Boaz, her skirt gathered in her arms, her hair hidden by a burgundy veil. For a long time, Penny had thought Boaz was a place and not a person.

He nodded slowly. "Knowing you, I would have guessed that *Whither thou goest, I will go. . . .*" He sat back on his heels and waited for her to respond.

Finally, she forced herself to speak. "*Where thou lodgest, I will lodge: thy people shall be my people, and thy God my God.*"

Dr. Bill nodded again, in the way of a teacher satisfied with his student. "Just so, pretty Penny." He took a step closer. He was near enough now to kiss her. "What I most admire about Ruth," he said, "is her obedience to God."

Obedience to God? Penny thought. How dare he use scripture to trap her into doing his will! Not God's will, his own and Mattie's. "I've never thought of Ruth that way," she said after a moment. "As far as I can tell, the Lord wasn't a large consideration for Ruth." There, she'd said it, something shocking but honest. Ruth's behavior had always been a mystery to Penny. Even reading between the lines, she couldn't find anything to explain Ruth's apparent selflessness. The woman seemed never to think of her own happiness.

Dr. Bill took a step back, allowing a glimpse of Mattie's face, which appeared pained and a little sad. It occurred to Penny that her grandmother might have carried this sadness for years without ever sharing it. Mattie could express her disappointment but not her sadness; she could speak of her anger but not of her love. Penny returned her gaze to Dr. Bill, who didn't look the least bit pained. In fact, she could see that he was enjoying himself. "Go ahead," he challenged her. "Finish your thought."

Penny took a deep breath. "It was Ruth's love for Naomi that took her to Bethlehem, her obedience to Naomi that sent her into the fields to glean. Naomi advised Ruth to go to the threshing floor, bade her to lie at Boaz's feet. What did the Lord have to do with any of this?"

Dr. Bill's answer was immediate. "The Lord spoke to Naomi."

Penny's answer was just as quick. "But not to Ruth."

"No," Dr. Bill agreed, "not to Ruth."

"So what if Naomi was wrong? What if all those things weren't God's will at all? How was Ruth to know?"

Dr. Bill was clearly surprised. He hesitated, and in that instant, Mattie took over. "Enough of this!" she cried. She leapt off the bed and strode over to Penny, grabbing her granddaughter by the arm and jerking her toward the window overlooking the side yard. "You think I don't know God's will?" she cried. "Maybe I don't. But I do know when something *isn't* God's will. I know the work of the devil when I see it."

"Mattie," Dr. Bill interrupted. He was just behind them now. "Mattie," he said again, but she was not about to stop.

"Can you see the rose of Sharon?" she asked. The night was clear, and the street lamps bathed the yard in silvery light. Penny could just make out the lithe little tree, a bundle of shadows in the side yard. It had been there for as long as she could remember, and for nearly that long she had loved the grayish-green leaves and purple flowers.

"Yes," Penny said. She had no idea what was coming, but suddenly she was frightened. Her grandmother's grip was tight, and Penny could feel a tremor running through the older woman's fingers.

"I planted the tree to mark the spot," Mattie said, then stopped and waited.

The silence grew until Penny was forced to fill it. "What spot?"

"The place where my grandbaby nearly died." Mattie's voice was trembling.

"Are you talking about me?" Penny asked. She was the only grand-child as far as she knew, but the world had gone topsy-turvy. She wouldn't have been surprised to hear that Delia had a sister, and that the sister had a child, two or three children even. Just now anything seemed possible.

"I'm talking about the day your mother dragged the ladder out of the garage and climbed up on the roof." Mattie pointed at the glass, stepped closer until she could poke at it with her fingertip. "I was in the kitchen cooking dinner. It was raining outside, late October. I heard this scraping and what sounded like footsteps on the roof."

"Mattie, don't," Dr. Bill tried again.

She turned on him. "You're trying to protect her, aren't you? Always trying to save her feelings, and for what? So she can turn on us?" Dr. Bill sighed, a huge exhalation Penny felt as a breeze on the top of her head. Mattie took up the thread of her story again. "At first, I thought it was only a squirrel or a cat, but then God put a thought in my head: It's your daughter up there. Just like that, not *my* daughter, but *your* daughter. I was terrified! Sure enough: When I ran out, Delia was leaping, already in the air. For a second, I actually expected her to fly." Mattie gazed through the window, and she looked so sad that in spite of everything, Penny's heart went out to her.

"But she didn't." Even now, Mattie sounded disappointed. "In-stead, she landed right down there. Hit the ground hard." She brought a hand to her chest and took a deep breath. "Broke an arm. Wailed all the way to the hospital. Crying for Dwayne, who'd just been sent to Vietnam. That was before the Supreme Court legalized baby killing, you see. Delia had to jump off a roof. Wouldn't you know it? She had to do something crazy."

Penny went still inside. She'd suspected, of course she had, but now she knew: Her mother hadn't wanted her. That was bad enough. But here all these years she'd had a perfectly good father, and they hadn't bothered to tell her. Didn't they think she cared? "Why didn't you tell me?" she cried. It was too much for one day. Her legs went out from under her, and with Mattie still gripping her arm, Penny sank to the floor.

Chapter 17

NEVER MIND ABOUT preparing the surface. Carl knew what he *should* do, knew it as an artist and as a homeowner. Preparing the surface was critical if you wanted your work to last. Canvas required preparation, and so did a garage door. He'd read what the *Consumer Reports Buying Guide* had to say about the eight steps to a perfect paint job. He'd even gone so far as to dig out the '93 edition, but then he'd forgotten to take it to Wal-Mart when he went to buy the paint. Standing before a long row of cans—paint as far and high as the eye could see—Carl had drawn a complete blank. He couldn't recall a single one of the recommended exterior latexes. Luckily, an old guy in paint-splattered overalls took pity on him and told him what to buy, pointed a wavering finger. "That stuff there," he said, "it'll cover anything." Problem was, the paint *didn't* cover. One coat didn't begin to fix things.

Before dawn on Friday morning, Carl had hauled himself out of bed, toted the paint out to the front of the house, and spread a few newspapers in the driveway. The sky had just begun to flush with first light, but it was still plenty dark outside, dark enough to need headlights and flashlights, too dark to tell the difference between black and red. Not that it mattered. These were emergency measures. He was slinging paint at the problem and hoping it would go away. Almost a week had passed since the vandalism—the police had taken four days to get to their house, to finish taking samples and photographs and fingerprints—now something had to be done. Which was why he didn't prepare the surface or even wash the damn door. He just wanted to get it done and done early, before people started driving by on their way to work.

Brushing on the first coat, he was impressed with the coverage. One quick swipe seemed to do the trick, but he of all people should have known better. Around seven, he took a coffee break; when he returned, the black letters were already swimming back to the surface, grayish now but still perfectly legible in the full morning light, BABYKILLER, all one word, as though it were someone's name, a rap artist maybe, or a serial murderer.

Carl had to laugh, a small private chuckle that tasted bitter on the way out. It struck him that the vandals had provided him with the perfect example of intentional pentimento. He'd slather on another coat, and yet another, but someday, some chilly winter morning in the future, another man would hurry out to raise his garage door and discover the word there, come back to haunt the new owners: BABYKILLER. (Already, Carl noted, he was imagining the house in the hands of others.) Naturally, the new owner would take it personally, apply it to himself or to his wife. Find a way to make it stick, just as Carl and Hannah were doing.

As he stood and studied the garage door, Carl avoided looking at the brick. If anything, the brick was worse. There he might have made some headway, if Hannah hadn't gone berserk. Late Tuesday afternoon, while he was still at work, she'd rummaged in the garage and found the plastic jug of gas for the mower. Filling one glass jar after another, she'd managed to slosh a full gallon across the front of the house. Presumably, she'd imagined that the gas would take care of it, that it would melt away the paint or some damn thing. An anxious neighbor had called the bookstore to let Carl know. He'd assumed it was the woman across the street, though she hadn't bothered to identify herself, just launched into aimless explanation, beginning by telling him that she'd seen him several times at Walton's, that she was a romance-novel addict, and ending with this: "Your wife is throwing gasoline on the front of the house. You don't suppose she's gonna set a match to it, do you,

Mr. Solace? I'm worried, you see, because it's awfully dry this time of year."

Carl had left immediately, but by the time he got home, the damage had been done. The bricks had absorbed the liquid, soaking it in, the red darkening to the color of dried blood. It was hideous really. His house looked like the set for a horror movie, or the scene of a multiple murder. Horrendous. Something had to be done. Right then and there, he'd forced himself to look closely, to prioritize the list of tasks. First things first: Get rid of the graffiti. He'd promised himself to buy paint and to cover up those horrible words as soon as possible.

Inside, he'd found Hannah slumped against the kitchen counter, a glass of wine in her hand. "You're home already?" she said. "I was planning to be good and drunk when you got here." By the sound of her voice, she was already halfway there. Still, she was entirely steady as she opened the cabinet and took down another glass. "Now that you've seen what I did," she said over her shoulder, "you'll probably need some wine as well." He nodded, though beer sounded better. In his book, wine was for celebration, beer was for solace. Solace, he thought. Carl and Hannah Solace. What a joke.

"I'm home because a neighbor called," he'd explained. "The woman across the street was looking out the window. She was afraid you were going to burn down the house."

Hannah sighed, but she didn't seem surprised. "Well," she said, "I hadn't planned to, but now that it looks so much worse . . . maybe torching it *is* the best idea." She poured his wine, finishing off the bottle, and handed him the glass.

He tossed back a quick gulp that left him choking. What was he thinking? Tears burned at the corners of his eyes. Hannah stepped closer and brushed his cheek with her palm. "I'm sorry, Carl," she said. "I'm so sorry." He knew she was apologizing for more than the gasoline, but for how much more he couldn't ask. Both of them were so fragile right now; if they were to misunderstand one another and argue, they might shatter.

"Some of the teachers won't speak to me," she said, "and others won't stop patting me on the back. It's only been a few days, but I don't think I can take much more of this."

He'd suggested that she soak in the bathtub, that she take her glass of wine with her, and his as well. Now that he knew the situation wasn't desperate, he had to get back to work. Holiday season, the place was a zoo. "But the situation *is* desperate," Hannah had replied. At the time, they'd pretended she was making a joke. He'd seen her to the bathroom before hurrying out the door, and he'd kept his head down on the way to the car.

Now, confronted with the mess he'd made of the garage door, Carl realized that throwing the gasoline had been impulsive, something Hannah had seized on when she pulled into the driveway. He knew how she felt: positively frantic to have this in the past. His quick trip to Wal-Mart and this morning's episode of painting in the dark: What were these if not more desperate measures? His actions might not have been quite so rash, but the end result was the same. The garage door looked like hell, and short of ripping it off the runners or plowing through it with the front end of the Blazer, there were no quick solutions, no easy cover-ups.

By the time Hannah emerged for work on Friday morning, Carl was in the midst of applying a second coat. This time around, he was determined to cover the entire door and not just the offending word. He had to. From the corner of his eye, he watched as she made her way down the steps then hesitated on the sidewalk. She looked unsteady this morning. Was it his imagination? She seemed to lean forward in her high heels. He wondered how old she'd be before she saw fit to give the damn things up.

She sidled in beside him and surveyed the door. "Thanks for trying," she finally said.

He made a face. "Not much better, is it?"

"No. Not much better." There wasn't anything else to say. She shrugged and headed off for her Blazer, which was parked out in front, but before getting in she turned back. "Listen, Carl," she said. "I've decided to go to Tyler for Thanksgiving. Helen's asked me. She says she needs to get away, and God knows I do too."

He couldn't help himself. "And what if *I* need to get away? Does it ever occur to you to ask me along?"

"We don't do that, Carl. We've never done that."

It was true. Holidays, they tended to split up and go their separate ways, he to Terrell and she to Tyler. But that was at Christmas and sometimes Easter. On Thanksgiving, Hannah and Helen rarely went home; Carl couldn't even remember the last time. Generally, they got together at Helen and Jimmy's for a leisurely dinner and a Cowboys game. It was a tradition, or the closest thing they had to one. Why go messing with it at a time like this? Why go off and leave him alone, a public spectacle of one? In his opinion, the least Hannah could do was to suffer along with him.

"Do you think I want to sit here by myself, in this house? Give thanks for this fucking mess?" He had a paintbrush in hand and, without thinking, he used it to gesture, slinging beads of perfect white onto the driveway. What the hell, he thought as he saw them fly. Not much could make matters worse here. Certainly not a little white paint. Hannah edged farther away.

"You should go to Terrell," she suggested. "See your mom."

Carl knelt on the newspapers and balanced the paintbrush on the rim of the can. "And how can I do that?" he asked coldly. She really was living in her own little world, he thought. "Neil's at the vet's. Remember?" He waited for her to speak, but she didn't. Finally, he stood and faced her. She looked stricken, which made Carl regret his tone if not his words. He couldn't blame her for forgetting. They were trying not to think about Neil, who was having unexplained seizures.

Two days before, Hannah had let him out in the backyard to do his business, and when she'd returned, she'd made a horrible discovery: Neil, lying splayed in front of the steps, his legs stiff and useless, his body bloated and his head so small. That had been Carl's first thought. Has his head always been this small? The dog was paralyzed, just like that. How shocking that must have been for him. Out there doing his business like on any other day, and—whammo!—all he could move was his neck. They'd rushed him to the vet, who'd had no explanation, no words of advice. "Let me keep him for observation," he'd said. "Run a few tests." Poor Neil was back in a cage. If Carl regretted anything he'd done in the past few months, it was leaving Neil at the Humane Society.

"So is Jimmy going?" he asked.

"What do you think?" Hannah replied.

She was right: stupid question. Dinner at Helen's was entirely out of the question. Hannah had confided in Carl about the fight and the affair with Cecile Barbone. Which meant Carl would as soon hit Jimmy as look at him. No decent man could cheat on a woman like Helen. Jimmy didn't deserve what he had, three nice kids and a wife who took pains to make him happy. Just the day before, Jimmy had called to offer his services with the cleanup, and Carl had turned him down cold. "Look—" Jimmy started, but Carl interrupted—"I don't want to hear it, okay?"—then slammed down the phone. His brother-in-law hadn't called back.

"So Jimmy and I get to eat pork and beans for Thanksgiving? I know what Jimmy did," he said, "but what did *I* do?"

Hannah took a quick look around. He could read her mind: Arguing out in the front yard, this was what they'd come to. What difference does it make? Carl wanted to ask her. They could strip down and run naked around the neighborhood. Everyone already knew their business. The protesters had chosen the cruelest possible tactic, to make of them a living and public example. "I have to get away!" Hannah cried. "It's nothing personal."

"Damn straight it's personal!" he shot back. This much he was sure of: If you squinted and looked closely, everything, absolutely everything, would turn out to be personal.

Hannah waved a hand toward the house. "What do you think? Have the police just given up?"

They hadn't heard a blessed word all week. Given up, he thought. No they haven't given up. To give up suggests an initial expenditure of effort and energy. You have to *try* before you can give up. "No one's dead here, Hannah. No one's raped or kidnapped. We got a little paint tossed on the front of our house. Big deal. That's what they're thinking."

"How do you know? Did they tell you that?"

"They don't have to tell me. I watch the news at night. One awful tragedy after another." He shook his head sadly. "If we want this solved, we'll have to solve it ourselves."

"Well, we *know* who did it!"

"But we can't prove it."

Hannah threw up her hands. "I can't solve this, Carl," she cried. "I can barely live with it." Her purse strap had slid off her shoulder and into the crook of her elbow, leaving her big leather bag dangling a few inches off the ground. Hannah's shoulders hunched from the weight. First the paint bombing and then Neil. She wasn't her usual strong, upright self; that much was obvious. He wouldn't have been surprised to see her topple over into the grass. Times like these, his mother used to say, you find out how deep your roots are. Maybe Hannah's weren't as deep as he'd thought.

"Let me work on it," he said. "You better get going, hadn't you?" She nodded and waved good-bye. Carl returned to the painting. He wasn't sure he could solve the crime, but he did know how to begin. And he knew where.

The first time he'd visited Penelope's Balloons and Bouquets, Carl had expected a small room filled to overflowing with vases, baskets, and dried flowers. Lots of knickknacks and doodads, plenty of cutesy clutter. He'd been wrong, though. The front of the shop was one large room, sparsely furnished, a half dozen small tables scattered across a broad expanse of hardwood floor. Penny must have spent time scouring garage sales, coming away with spindly little tables that now held sample arrangements. The middle of the floor was empty space, covered only by a braided rug of orange, brown, and gold. Last time he'd been here, the rug had been hidden by a playpen and a scattering of plastic toys, but today there was no sign of the baby. The room was quiet. Too bad, he thought. He'd have enjoyed a quick game of toss the toy, and the baby's presence had made it easier to converse. If in doubt, discuss the baby. He saw how it must work in many marriages, how it might have worked in his own.

Looking around, Carl noticed the ornate fireplace and mantel at one end of the room, the single calla lily in a glass vase on its hearth. In a previous lifetime, this shop had been someone's master bedroom, he realized. People had slept here, made love here, maybe even died here. Now the space was occupied by a young woman zealot who created flower arrangements and inflated balloons, too busy and beautiful and devout to doubt anything but her own ability to get it all done at the end of the day. He'd come to vent his anger, to knock over a few of these spindly tables, maybe to make her cry. On the way over, all that had seemed right and good. An eye for an eye. After all, Hannah had cried, hadn't she? Carl had even shed a few tears. Why not Penny?

But now he hesitated in the doorway. Breathing in the smells of greenery and flowers, he asked himself whether the mess at his house could really be Penny's fault. Here in her shop, he had trouble believing it, despite her alliances, her placards, and her prayers. Much as he wanted to be angry with her, at heart he believed in her goodness. He had only to think of her face as she'd turned to him in the Humane Society, all those cats milling about her feet. Releasing the animals was something she'd done instinctively, an act of kindness. Could a person like that inflict intentional pain? He didn't think so. Still, he suspected that she knew something, and the longer he stood in her doorway, the more convinced he became that the proof of her goodness would be in what she was willing to tell him.

He stepped quietly through the doorway, relieved not to hear a buzz or a jangling bell. No need to alert her to his presence, not yet anyway. He was hoping for one long look at her before they had to speak. He wanted time to read her expression, to see what her face said. For several long minutes, he wandered about the front room, gazing at the arrangements, stroking the silky length of the calla lily's white trumpet, marveling at the perfect symmetry. When ten minutes had passed, he began to wonder if she'd gone off and left the door unlocked. He was due at work in another half hour and hadn't much time to spare. He approached the counter, cleared his throat, and called her name, once and then again. "Penny?"

"Yes?" Her clear voice rang out from the workroom. A few seconds later, she appeared in the doorway, wiping her hands on a towel. Her baggy overalls and yellow and white striped T-shirt made her appear even younger and smaller than she was. She could have passed for a girl in junior high. "Carl," she said, sounding surprised. She looked tired, he thought, in the way of the very young: tousled and pale, a bit dazed.

"Are you all right?" he asked.

She shrugged. "It hasn't been an easy week."

It was a vague statement that might mean anything. He pushed on. "Where's Buck?"

"His mother isn't working for me anymore." She said this stiffly, distantly, while wringing the cloth in her hands. Maybe she wasn't so much tired as distressed, he thought.

"So, how was the wedding?" he asked, casting about for a way to reach her. "Did your mother like the birds?" And then it came to him, a realization so sudden and startling that he reached out to grab the edge of the counter. Penny had been in Houston on the night of the paint bombing. Of course she had. Why hadn't he thought of it before? It let her off the hook entirely. He smiled broadly, relieved.

Penny moved to the counter so that they were standing face to face. "My *father* liked the birds," she told him, smiling shyly.

"Your father? You said you'd never met your father," he said. "That you stole someone else's father for the drawing you made in elementary school."

She nodded eagerly. He could see it in her face, her pleasure. "Yes." A note of joy crept into her voice. "You won't believe it, really. Turns out, my mother married my father. Just now, last weekend. I had no idea when I talked to you. . . ."

Carl nodded. How would it be, he wondered, to meet your daughter for the first time when she was all grown up? Such a lovely young woman, and here you'd missed her entire childhood. How could you ever reconcile yourself to such a loss? And how could you explain it? "How did you find out?" he asked.

The phone rang then, startling them both, and Penny excused herself to answer it. He listened and watched while she took down an order for a dozen balloons, writing the information on an order pad, careful to ask the caller's preference about any number of things: color, size, time of delivery. Once or twice she glanced up at him, but he couldn't read her expression. This time around, she seemed much more complicated. But, then, her life was more complicated too. She'd gained a father since they'd last met.

"I'd love to talk," she said, when she hung up, "to get a cookie and sit out on the grass, but I'm running behind. No help, as you can see." She waved her hands to indicate the empty room. "I was getting ready to load the van."

He didn't want to leave, nor did he want to say why he'd come. It seemed completely beside the point now. "I've got a few minutes," he lied. "Why don't you let me carry a few things."

She smiled, clearly pleased. "Are you sure? Don't you need to get to work?"

"I can be a little late."

Penny's service van was parked on a slope at the back of the building. To load it, she carried the arrangements out a window and down the fire escape. It was easier and faster, she said, than going out the front of the building and walking all the way around. With the van doors wide open, she could jump directly from the stairs into the back. She insisted that she did it every day, whistled down those narrow, rickety stairs and back up again. Carl was amused and a little amazed. "That might work for you," he said. "But I'm twice your size. I could get down that thing in an emergency, but—"

"It'll be fine," she assured him.

When he stepped onto the fire escape for the first time, Carl was holding a dozen balloons in one hand and a bouquet wrapped in paper and cellophane in the other. Spread out in front of him was a vista of treetops and pitched roofs, and off to his far right, the eastern edge of the Austin skyline. The wind picked up as he began his descent, threatening to pull the strings of the balloons out of his grip. "You sure about this?" he called to Penny. She nodded and waved him down, meeting him at the bottom step, taking the balloons and quickly anchoring them to a metal pipe on the floor of the van. "Bring me more!" she called. And so he did. For his last trip, Carl picked up a dozen roses in a green glass vase. These were headed for a nursing home off 35th Street, and Penny wanted them in the passenger seat. "Maybe you'd better carry them through the house and out the front door," she suggested.

"Fine," he replied, relieved not to have to brave the fire escape again. On the way down, he drank in the lovely, uncomplicated crimson of the flowers. "These are gorgeous roses," he said when he reached the van. He was happy now, truly happy for the first time in over a week.

"Thank you," she called from the back. "Why don't you strap them into the seat?"

He opened the door, settled the vase in the seat, then leaned around for the belt. He'd have seen the paint regardless—his eye was too practiced, too keen to miss a slash of orangy-red on a background of gray—but the deep crimson roses only made it all the more obvious. Immediately, his mind went to the red paint on his front door, to the word MURDERER. No doubt about it. They were a perfect match.

"Goddamn it," he muttered, then louder: "Goddamn you!"

"What?" Penny cried. Her head and shoulders appeared over the top of the console, and, suddenly, they were face to face, so close he could have kissed her. Her brow was furrowed, her mouth open; he could see the pink slip of her tongue. Carl gave her a good long look before drawing back and wiping his hands on his pants. He wanted to hit something, the vase of roses, the side of the van, Penny's smooth cheek. He'd believed in her; that was the worst part.

"Who do you think you are?" he asked. "Destroying people's lives this way?"

"What? I don't know—" she began, but the words died away as she glanced from the roses to the streak of red on the passenger seat. He could see it dawning on her, reality settling in. She closed her eyes. "Not your house?" she whispered.

"My house," he replied.

From Penny's shop, Carl drove straight to the mall. On the way, he tried to sort out his feelings, but he was numb and utterly confused about what to do next. She'd begged him not to go to the police, not to put her grandmother in jail. "I don't know if you can believe this," she'd said, "but my grandmother is a good person."

"If she's *good*, how could she do such a thing?" he'd asked.

"It's because she doesn't know you."

"That's what I mean," he'd insisted. "I'm a stranger. My wife's a stranger. Why do they want to hurt us this way?" She didn't have an answer, not for that question or for his next one: "What do you expect me to do? Just pretend I never saw this?" He'd pointed a trembling finger toward the paint and watched as she'd slowly turned her head away.

He was nearly an hour late to work. He ran from the parking lot to the store, bursting through the entrance out of breath, only to find his favorite employee, Ruthanne, draped over the counter, in deep conversation with her punk boyfriend. Not a customer in sight.

"What happened? You run everybody off?" Carl asked.

It was a distinct possibility. All by herself, Ruthanne could make a person skittish. She wore garish color combinations—stripes with plaids, polka dots with madras, that sort of thing—and her white-blond hair in a buzz cut. As if that wasn't enough, she sported a nose ring. The day she'd swaggered in to fill out an application, Carl had had no intention of hiring her. But he'd been taken in by her smile and her warm laugh, by the way she nodded her head while listening, eager for communication and contact. She was a good kid, no matter what she looked like. The boyfriend was another matter. Carl wasn't the least bit sure about Mike, who had a taste for leather and combat boots.

Carl had just slipped in behind the register and was in the midst of checking the sales tape when the boyfriend reached out and grasped Ruthanne's arm. "Better shove off," he said, kneading her skin with his fingers. Carl couldn't help noticing a tattoo of a nasty-looking spider on the back of his hand.

"Not much business this morning?" Carl asked.

Ruthanne shrugged. "Not really."

"Couple of old ladies were in a while back," Mike offered. I thought you were leaving, Carl wanted to say. But he could see that the guy was in the mood to share. "They were taking a trip to Europe, all by themselves."

"We're talking *old* here," Ruthanne emphasized. "One woman was using a cane."

"So, should they stay home, in a rocking chair, where they belong?" Carl heard his tone, sarcastic, even mocking.

Ruthanne looked surprised and a little hurt. Carl had never talked to her this way before, and, clearly, she didn't know what to make of it. She furrowed her eyebrows and tried again. "That's not what we meant," she said.

"Yeah," Mike put in. "You've got us wrong, man."

"Sorry," Carl said. "It's been a rough day."

"We understand," Ruthanne replied, nodding in that slow, solemn way of hers.

"Don't mention it," Mike agreed. He let go of Ruthanne and reached a beefy arm over the counter to squeeze Carl on the shoulder. The spider was inches away from Carl's face. It was all he could do not to swat at it. "Must be a tough time," Mike went on. "Heard about your house. Sorry, really sorry, man."

Carl shrugged, resigned to the fact that everyone, absolutely everyone, must know about him. Was this how famous people felt, stripped bare?

"Any idea who did it?" Mike asked.

"I think so," Carl ventured.

"What do the police tell you?"

Another shrug. "Nothing." He thought again of Penny, how she'd asked him to leave it in her hands. "I'll put a stop to it; you have my word," she'd promised. "Nothing more will happen. Dr. Bill will listen to me. I know he will." If he'd needed proof of her goodness, he certainly had it. Before he'd left, Carl reached across the seat and touched her face, ran his fingers over her soft cheek. He'd left her crying, just as he'd imagined. Only he hadn't felt vindicated or satisfied, only miserable for both of them.

"Hey, ya listening?" Mike asked, squeezing Carl's shoulder again. When Carl nodded, the guy leaned in as close as the counter would allow. "I know what I'd do," he whispered. "Certain situations, the police just don't know where to start. You have to take things into your own hands." He smiled, a sly little crack of the lips.

"What are you talking about?" Carl asked, shaking off Mike's grip.

"I'm talking payback time," Mike said.

Carl was taking a deep breath, trying to think what to say, when Lydia waddled onto the scene. He was truly happy to see her. "Lydia!" he cried.

"Hey, Carl!" she crowed, obviously delighted at his reception.

"How's Trish?" he asked. He'd never been very nice to Lydia; more than anything, he'd tolerated her conversation, pretended interest in her pouty daughter, Trish. Secretly, or maybe not so secretly, he'd felt safe and superior. The worst might happen to her, but *he* was safe. And now look at him: He was a victim on the six o'clock news.

"Fine," Lydia said, nodding her head proudly. "She's got a pass for Thanksgiving. Be home for a whole day and a half." She nodded again, and Ruthanne nodded along with her, as though this wasn't news to her, as though she and Lydia were friends. Who knew? Carl thought.

"And how are you?" Lydia asked.

"Getting along," Carl lied. He would have liked to tell the truth to someone, but it wouldn't have been Lydia, who had a mouth and a pulpit for spreading the news.

"Gotta be getting along myself," Mike said, punching Carl's arm, a short hard blow that actually smarted. "Remember what we talked about."

"Sure," Carl said, turning away.

As Ruthanne showed Mike out, Lydia sidled up, taking his place at the counter. "Got a little news I thought you'd want to hear."

He braced himself for yet another intrusion into his privacy. But this time the gossip concerned Noah. Someone from the management office had stopped by the Nut House for a bag of chocolate-covered pretzels and leaked the latest casualty: Noah was behind in his rent, at least four months and maybe more. "Looks like the Ark is going down," Lydia said, shaking that little cloud of gray hair. Carl could see that some small part of her was pleased—someone else had it worse than she did.

"You shouldn't repeat such things!" he cried. "What's Noah done to you?"

"I just told *you*!" Lydia replied. "I thought *you'd* want to know." She backed up a step and crossed her arms across her sagging chest. Now her face sagged too.

"I do want to know," he agreed, "I do," and before he could stop himself, he apologized. She looked so unhappy; he just couldn't bear to see another miserable face.

Carl waited until closing time to visit Noah. Walton's filled up toward midafternoon, and they stayed busy all the way through to nine. He might have slipped away for the odd half hour—no one would have begrudged him that—but the truth was, he just didn't have the heart for it. All evening, he kept telling himself that Lydia might be mistaken, that she might have gotten her facts wrong. But he knew, too, that Noah had never been much of a businessman. He didn't have the disposition or the discipline for it. And the location of the pet store didn't help matters any. It was off the beaten path, down a side hall, wedged between a maternity shop and an eye-care center, one of those joints that advertises glasses in one hour and delivers them in a week.

Approaching the pet store, Carl could see that it was still lit up. Noah himself was out in front, unrolling one of his hand-lettered banners. He looked tired and rumpled. His blue jeans were a little short in the stride, revealing red socks and penny loafers.

"Hey there," he called when he saw Carl. "It's Friday night. Don't you have a life, you pitiful creature?"

Carl shook his head.

"No? Well then, grab this." Noah handed Carl one end of the banner and a roll of masking tape. When they had the sign affixed to both sides of the entrance, Carl stepped back and read it. NOAH'S ARK IS SINKING FAST, it read. EVERYTHING MUST GO!!

"What's this?" he asked, following Noah into the store.

"Bankruptcy, my friend. If you haven't noticed, it's *au courant.*"

"Shit."

Noah nodded and plopped down on a stack of unpacked boxes. Here he was, going out of business, and he didn't have all the merchandise on the shelves. He had to unpack it so he could lose his shirt on it.

"Shit," Carl said again.

"Ahh, yes," Noah agreed. "It's shit all right. Shit is an undeniable part of the business. Poo-poo, doggy-do, dung. Little hamster pellets. Even the reptiles have to relieve themselves. It's a universal function."

"Isn't there something—"

Noah interrupted. "To be done? Certainly. And you're just in time to see me do it." By the entrance, Noah had amassed a jumble of cages: a wrought-iron birdcage full of parakeets; a tank of white mice; and six plastic boxes, each containing a fat, healthy tarantula. "These parakeets are so shy," Noah complained. "It was hell to get 'em together." Carl counted five parakeets lined up on thin wooden perches, lovely, Easter-egg-colored birds in shades of pale yellow, turquoise, and mint green.

"I'm so glad you're here," Noah said, handing Carl the birdcage, which was surprisingly heavy. "Now you can give me a hand. Come on."

"What are we doing?" Carl asked, but Noah was already striding ahead, carrying the glass tank of white mice and heading for the middle of the concourse. When they arrived at the fountain, the spot where the old men tended to congregate, Noah set the tank on a bench and rushed back to the pet store. "Put the cage down," he called back to Carl. "Come on. Get a move on."

Carl assumed they were organizing a sale. Each trip back, he expected to help Noah haul a heavy, fold-out table. Tomorrow morning, some winsome high-school girl would show up to run things, exchanging the little creatures for a few wrinkled dollars, dropping the money in a shoe box. On the last trip he finally asked: "What time's the sale start?"

"What sale?" Noah asked.

They were carrying a huge plastic bucket of crickets—thousands of hoppers meant for the gullets of hungry reptiles. When they reached the spot where the cages were gathered, Noah bent and, spreading his penny loafers wide, dumped the crickets onto the white linoleum floor. They scattered in an instant, a splash of dark brown and black, like thousands of moving splotches of paint. "Go forth and multiply!" Noah cried. Carl was too stunned to speak.

Next, Noah bent to open the little wrought-iron doors on the birdcage, but he couldn't get the parakeets to budge. "Come on," he whispered, crouching next to the cage and wiggling one finger through the open door. The parakeets resisted, bunching themselves on the far end of the perch. "Damn!" Noah cried. Undeterred, he moved on to the tarantulas, lining up the cages across the floor. The doors were on top, so he turned each box on its side. The tarantulas weren't the least bit reticent. No sooner were the lids swung up than the creatures extended hairy legs to probe the openings, rushing forth all at once, as though for a race.

"Noah!" Carl cried.

"What?"

The tarantulas had taken off in different directions. Two headed for Foley's, one rushed off in the direction of the food court, and two more disappeared under nearby hosta plants. That left one unaccounted for. Carl glanced down around his feet, half-expecting to find a pair of hairy legs inching up his Rockports. Nothing. Where the hell did the damn thing go? "People will be hurt," Carl complained. He thought of Lydia behind the counter at the Nut House, a tarantula edging its way up her support hose.

Noah looked up, clearly disgruntled. "I'm surprised at you. First of all that you'd give a shit, and second of all that you'd be so misinformed. Like any other asshole who happens into the store. Really now, Carl. Tarantulas have never hurt a soul, not a human soul any-way. Their bite's less toxic than yours is."

"And what about the rest of these animals? How are they going to make it?"

"They'll be fine," Noah reassured him. "Better than they were at the Ark. The birds will nest in the trees and feast on popcorn, the crickets will set up shop in the planters, and the tarantulas, well . . . they'll scurry about in the dead of night and scare the hell out of the security guards." He threw up his arms and grinned. "Before you know it, they'll be one big happy family!"

"You're sure?"

"Oh course, I'm sure." Noah stood and wiped his hands on his jeans. "I'm not just doing this to get back at the big, bad management. No indeed. This is also an act of contrition, my friend. All these years of making my living off poor, dumb creatures, it's the least I can do."

Carl was ready to be convinced. He *wanted* to be convinced. The tarantulas were entirely gone, the crickets well on their way to new destinations. This began to be exciting; it began to be fun. Noah dumped the tank of mice, and they scurried out in pursuit of the crickets. Or so it seemed. One big happy family. Yes, it looked that way.

"My turn!" Carl cried, but glancing about, he saw the cages were all empty. No more animals to release.

Then the bravest of the parakeets edged out the open door and took to the air. Noah and Carl turned their faces to the arched plexiglass roof. Heavy white clouds massed in the dark sky, but inside the mall it was light and warm. This is just a larger cage, Carl thought, but what of that? For her, this building was limitless. He watched as she soared above their heads, a brilliant patch of yellow, twisting and turning, like a bright fall leaf caught in an updraft, dizzy with grace and liberty.

Chapter 18

DURING CAFETERIA DUTY, Hannah hovered in a nook behind the double doors of the dining room. The vantage point was excellent. She could scan the entire room and, if she craned her neck, even manage a glimpse of the hallway through the far doors. Today was typical: long lines at the pizza counter and the snack bar; clusters of kids hunched over tables, shaking open bagged lunches; a few slackers leaning against the walls, feigning fatigue in a pathetic attempt to look cool. She heard the hum of talk, bursts of laughter, and the occasional screech of protest from one of the girls. General, ordinary mayhem. The periods were carefully staggered to give the kids just long enough to eat, but not a minute more. Any extra time, and they would use it to create mischief. Most often, lunch periods passed without a hitch, but Hannah tried to stay close at hand, just in case.

Two boys skulked past:

"I don't have any homework."

"Yes, you do. He writes it on the board. Didn't you check the board?"

"He should *tell* us."

"Duh. I guess he thinks we can read."

Only two feet away, but Hannah might as well have been invisible.

They passed without so much as a glance in her direction. Teenagers were like animals who couldn't sense your presence unless you were moving. Usually, she could stand still for long periods of time—doing so was part of the challenge—but in the last week, the heels had been giving her trouble. Occasionally, she wavered, and the observant ones caught on. "Hey there, Dr. Solace," the well-socialized kids would say. The rest merely dropped their gaze, clearly afraid that she knew too much about them. The truth was, she could hardly tell them apart. They dressed alike, sheared their hair alike, talked alike. Sometimes she even had trouble discerning gender. Most wore baggy jeans and T-shirts. Some of the boys sported long locks and pierced ears, and a few of the girls actually shaved their heads and swaggered.

Just now two girls were passing right under Hannah's nose.

"I just hate that girl, don't you?" said one.

"Totally. Everyone hates her." Hannah strained to see the girl in question but couldn't manage it without moving.

"Then why is she so popular?" the first one asked.

They shrugged in unison as they took their place in line. Hannah yawned and checked the time.

"Your secretary told me I'd find you here," a man's voice said.

Startled, she turned to discover Gabe Faber standing just to her right. She flushed, indignant. How long had he been there, watching her watch? "What can I do for you, Mr. Faber?" she asked briskly.

"You eat lunch?" His manner was more relaxed than the last time she'd seen him, and so was his attire. He was wearing jeans—creased and a dark shade of navy, maybe even brand new, but jeans nonetheless. A green polo shirt revealed well-developed biceps and broad shoulders. Once again, she couldn't help noting this man's appeal, nor could she keep from him the fact that she'd noted it. It was infuriating, really, the way he was on to her and the manner in which he let her know it, with just the briefest of smiles.

"No, I usually eat lunch in my office. . . . So, what can I do for you, Mr. Faber?" A public servant she was, and determined to please.

"You can go to lunch with me, Dr. Solace," he returned. "We'll whip over to one of those places on Barton Springs Road. Your choice. I'll have you back in forty-five minutes."

"I have a meeting at two," she said, pretending interest in a squabble taking place by the back doors. It wouldn't amount to anything; she could see that, but she wanted to appear disinterested where Mr. Faber was concerned, even uninterested, if that was possible. The better part of her wanted to turn him down flat—she could still do it, just change her mind—but curiosity and an empty stomach lobbied against it. She was starving. Hannah paged another of the assistant principals to take her place, then made a big show of introducing Gabe as Erica Faber's father. None of this escaped his notice. The smile showed itself again before fading into something like pleased self-assurance. Maybe she could spill something on him, Hannah thought, near the end of the meal, of course.

After they were seated in his silver Infiniti, Gabe asked where she'd like to go. Hannah was in the mood for Tex-Mex and suggested Chuy's.

"One of my favorites," he said.

"It's close," she replied.

"So it is." He drove fast. Five minutes later they were getting out at the restaurant. She began to relax, even to enjoy herself.

While waiting for their enchiladas, they chatted about the upcoming Thanksgiving holiday. Gabe boasted of the Thanksgiving dinner he was fixing for a group of friends: tamale stuffing and green beans with almonds, a pecan pie made with bourbon and molasses. All the while he ticked off the menu, Hannah took care to look skeptical, though the details were convincing. "I haven't always been a cook," he admitted. "When Angela and I were married, I left the meals up to her. You know, the typical male/female divisions of labor. I was a chauvinist, the whole nine yards. But I've learned better over the years. I like to cook. I'm a good cook, better than Angela ever was, frankly."

"My husband cooks," Hannah admitted. "And he's better at it than I am." She didn't know why she opened herself up this way, and she regretted it almost immediately.

"What does your husband do?" he asked.

"He's a visual artist," she said, then added for veracity's sake, "and he manages a bookstore." She didn't say "at the mall." Let Gabe think Barnes & Noble or that big one on Sixth Street. She shifted in her seat uncomfortably. Carl was right about her. She wanted her own liberation, but she couldn't tolerate his. She needed him to be an achiever, 1950's style—a doctor or, God forbid, a lawyer—and he wasn't, wouldn't ever be.

She kept her eyes away from Gabe, choosing instead to stare out the window at the cars whizzing down Barton Springs Road. She remembered when this same street had been one lane each way, going to nowhere but Zilker Park. Now it led to Mopac, an expressway. Day and night, the traffic was heavy. The establishments that had sprung up on either side of the road were trendy and upper middle class. No more trailer parks, no more bike shops or barbecue stands. No more 1950's, Hannah told herself.

The waiter arrived with plates resembling platters, enough enchiladas to feed her entire office. Gabe took a large bite of his and chewed with a serious air. "Well, I promised a quick lunch," he said, "and I'm determined to keep that promise. I want to start with an apology for that phone call a few weeks back. I get on a high horse, and damned if I can get off it. I know these past weeks have been difficult for you, and that makes me doubly appreciative of your efforts on my daughter's behalf."

She flinched a bit at the reference to her "difficulties." Did absolutely everyone know? she wondered. Efforts on my daughter's behalf, Hannah thought. Was he talking about the AIDS test again? Lovely, the way he could shine an entirely different light on it when he cared to. Before, her "efforts" had been a "breach" of something or another. She considered reminding him of this but decided to let it pass with a brief smile of her own. Something more was coming, she was sure of it, and a glance at her watch might hurry it right out of him. She wiped her mouth, sighed, and checked the time.

Sure enough. Gabe took a sip of water, then cleared his throat. "Dr. Solace, Erica is over three months pregnant."

Hannah was just bringing a chunk of enchilada to her mouth, and she carefully put down the fork. "I'm sorry," she said. "I really didn't know." Poor Erica, she thought, then: He must think I held out on him, conspiring with his daughter to keep him in the dark. Otherwise, what was the point of all this? She braced herself, but Gabe waved his hand.

"None of us knew, Dr. Solace. May I call you Hannah?"

She nodded. He was preoccupied now, leaning over the table in her direction; another inch or two and the front of his green polo shirt would be covered in chili and cheese. "Watch out," she said, gesturing toward his plate.

He pushed it away and talked while Hannah ate. Among other things, he told her about Erica's call to his ex-wife. "Angela likes to think she's still a girl herself. The idea of being a grandmother made her burst into tears." Gabe gave a derisive little snort. "I have to hand it to Erica. She knows how to get to you."

This was true, Hannah thought. Erica was as intuitive as any adult, and canny with her questions. It hadn't taken her any time to find Hannah's weak spots. Likely, she'd inherited this ability from her father, who seemed not to miss a thing. Hannah was finishing her rice when Gabe came to the point.

"I was hoping you could talk to her," he said.

"Talk to her?"

"Yeah. Make her see the light. March her down to the clinic again, if necessary."

Hannah's anger was instantaneous. "What do you think I am?" she asked, shoving her own plate aside and sitting up straight. "Some sort of spokesperson for abortion rights? If my privacy hadn't been violated, you wouldn't *know* about my abortion. Speaking of breaches, Mr. Faber. This whole conversation is a breach of good taste."

He blinked several times, then pursed his lips. "I see," he said. "So you think Erica should have this baby?"

Hannah shook her head. "I didn't say that, did I? It doesn't matter what I think. This is Erica's decision, and it will make a woman out of the girl. Nothing either of us can do will spare her that transformation." Hannah hesitated, sliding her hand up and down the chilled, wet glass in front of her. "If she wants to talk to me, I'll be glad to listen, but I won't advocate for abortion. That would be wrong of me, completely wrong."

"Wrong? Really? I must say I'm surprised."

"Why is that?"

"An assistant principal advocating teen pregnancy—"

"I'm not advocating anything, Mr. Faber. That's the point. If I could keep teenagers from getting pregnant, I would, but that's not my job—that's up to their parents."

"I see." He reached up to smooth his hair, took a turn at gazing out the window.

Hannah had no idea what was going on in his head, whether he was considering her words or merely waiting her out. In any case, she had to say it: "You're not nearly so liberated as you think you are. It's one thing to stuff a turkey, quite another to be there for your teenage daughter."

He leaned forward and his eyes narrowed to slits. "But we let her live, now, didn't we? We didn't do away with her in the womb."

Hannah winced, but she was ready. "No, you didn't," she said. "But in the here and now, you seem determined to do away with your grandchild. I don't see that you have any claim to the moral high ground." Suddenly, she felt nauseous and swallowed hard.

Gabe Faber rose from his chair and motioned toward the door. "Once again, you've overstepped," he said, a slight tremor in his voice. "I don't think either of us has an appetite for any more of this. We'd better get back to work."

Hannah got to her feet and, with the back of her hand, smoothed the wrinkles in her skirt. "Yes," she said, striding ahead of him to the door. "I have to leave town in a few hours. I had no business having lunch with you in the first place."

ALL the way to Tyler, Helen hunted angels. "We'll never get there at this rate," Hannah complained. "It's already four o'clock." Austin to Tyler was a three-and-a-half-hour drive. With kids it would take longer; tack on a few more stops at junk stores, and they might not arrive until midnight.

"Which means the stores will only be open another hour or so," Helen replied. "Indulge me, will you?" Without waiting for a response, she turned her blue Voyager up the hill toward a huge Victorian house big enough to get lost in—two turrets and a wraparound porch. All the junk in Texas could be crammed between those walls, Hannah thought. "I really need an angel," Helen muttered, as though the desire were as simple and straightforward as the need for a drink of water or a nap.

"For the top of the tree?" Hannah inquired. She had one at home, a porcelain angel with a hollow skirt that would probably do the trick. Maybe they could skip the junk-store junket.

"Not a decoration. This is for me. Remember when we were kids, those eight-balls that told your fortune? You asked it a question and turned it upside down to get the answer?" Hannah nodded. She remembered, all right. Helen had carried the damn thing around the house for weeks. The slightest decision had necessitated a consultation with the ball. "Remember?" Helen asked again. "It helped me make up my mind. I need something like that now. A grown-up version."

She parked along the curb behind a red pickup truck, opened the door, and leaned over the seat for her purse. "Please don't make fun of me, Hannah. You can think it's crazy if you want to, but just don't say it, okay?" She jumped out of the van and onto the yellowed grass. "I'll be right back. Shane and Cassie are sound asleep. Promise, no more than fifteen minutes."

"Yeah, right," Hannah muttered. She wished *she* could sleep, but she was wide awake and irritated. Angels, for heaven's sake.

The kids had only just gone off. Five minutes into the trip they'd begun to fuss—Shane to shriek and Cassandra to complain about Shane's shrieking. (At the last minute, Grayson had stayed behind with his father.) Hannah had been surprised when Helen flat-out ignored the children's pleas for attention. For a few minutes, the noise was deafening, but shortly after they got on I.H.-35, the kids exhausted themselves and drifted off to sleep.

Helen was as good as her word. She was gone less than ten minutes. "Nothing there," she announced as she hopped back into the driver's seat. She'd joined a support group—what sort she didn't say—and many of the women in it were angel watchers. They went about their daily lives like everyone else, she said, except they kept an eye out for angels. Feathers floating in the air, an unexplained brush on the shoulder, flickering lights—all signs of a celestial presence. Until now, ordinary, run-of-the-mill Christianity had been enough for Helen. So Hannah could hardly believe what she was hearing. "It sounds goofy, I know," Helen admitted. "But it's kind of comforting too."

Once they were back on the highway, she explained the procedure for hunting angels, and Hannah did her best to keep a straight face. The angel was supposed to beckon to her. She'd feel drawn in one direction; her skin would go prickly—that sort of thing. Nothing had beckoned in the Georgetown castle. She'd stood in the doorway for a moment to get her bearings but hadn't been able to decide which way to go. So she'd wandered aimlessly, up and down the stairs, through the kitchen and living room and then back out again. "I didn't get a reading from anything." Hannah thought of angel Geiger counters but didn't say a word. She didn't have to. Helen cut her sister a quick look. "The women in my group would hate you."

Hannah shrugged. "I'm sure they would. Hating me is trendy now."

Helen grabbed a bag of sour-cream-and-onion potato chips from the backseat and opened them. "Poor Hannah," she hissed, jamming her hand in the bag. "Let's start a poor Hannah club."

"For someone who believes in angels, you're downright nasty." Hannah noted that Helen's nails were bitten down to the quick. The salt from the chips would sting.

"Sorry," Helen conceded. "Let's just be quiet for a little while, why don't we?"

Fine, Hannah thought, settling back in her seat. They weren't an hour out of town, and already she regretted this trip. All signs pointed to a hellish weekend, and she still hadn't recovered from the lunch with Gabe Faber. Not to mention Carl and Neil. She felt bad about leaving her husband, even worse about leaving her dog. Two hundred dollars in tests had not resulted in a diagnosis or a cure. He could move again, but barely so. He was old, the vet said. He might improve; he might not.

Now, as she left him behind for a few days, Hannah realized that what she wanted was simple: She wanted Neil to get better or she wanted him to die. This interim stage was torturous, hauling him out the door and down the back steps, holding his leg up so he wouldn't pee all over his fur. In the middle of the night, she awoke to his moans in the darkness; even in his sleep, he suffered. She couldn't stand to hear it. In fact, she didn't mind being awakened in the night or even the times when the dog's aim was off and he wet on her hand. She could get used to that, but she couldn't reconcile herself to the lack of hope, or to the sense that they were biding their time, waiting for it to be over. On top of everything else, it was just too sad to bear.

An hour passed quietly, the tension in the van dissipated, and when they stopped in Lorena for gas and another Diet Coke for Hannah, the children were still sleeping. Amazingly, they'd snoozed through their mother's jerky turns and sudden stops, all of which had given their aunt a violent case of car sickness. On her way to the bathroom, Hannah spotted a sign taped in the service-station window. Hand-lettered in a crude calligraphy, it advertised a small antique store across the street. She could only hope that Helen would miss it.

No such luck. By the time Hannah emerged from the bathroom, Helen was chatting with the mammoth man behind the counter. Everything he wore, including the ball cap on his head, was several sizes too small. It looked as though he'd been standing in that very spot, eating continuously for several months, until he had slowly outgrown his clothes. "The wife owns the shop," he was saying. "Just a small operation."

Hannah waited behind Helen to pay for her Coke. "Surely it's not open now," she said. According to her watch, it was after five. "Tomorrow is Thanksgiving." Hannah had never cooked a Thanksgiving feast in its entirety, but it seemed to her an awesome undertaking. She assumed it was necessary to start the day before, maybe even the week before, especially if you were married to a man the size of this one.

"If a customer happens along, the wife opens the door," the man said. "We don't have no time clocks around here." He looked pleased with himself, but not half so pleased as Helen.

A sign perched above the porch read IDA'S JEWELS AND JUNQUE, and as soon as they drove up, a tiny woman appeared at the door, presumably Ida herself, wiping her hands on a dish towel. Sure enough, Hannah thought. She's busy cooking. But Ida was clearly happy to show Helen inside. Hannah opened her Diet Coke and sat back. In a few minutes, the sun would be down. Already, the town was lost in long shadows. The day had been overcast, nothing at all to brighten the miles of brown fields and small leafless trees. Winter was no time to travel in Texas. In the springtime, a trip down a Texas highway could be a colorful affair, thanks to the efforts of Lady Bird Johnson. Every April, the medians and drainage ditches burst into bloom with blue-bonnets, Indian paintbrush, black-eyed Susans, red poppies, and laven-der thistle. But in winter, the countryside was bleak, and travelers had to console themselves with conversation. Something in short supply this afternoon, Hannah thought.

Helen stepped out a mere fifteen minutes later, clutching a wrinkled brown bag to her chest. Ida waved good-bye from the open doorway. The two of them looked so cheery that Hannah's spirits were lifted as well. "I found it!" Helen exclaimed as she climbed back into the driver's seat, so delighted with her purchase that she forgot all about lowering her voice. The children stirred but didn't wake. Once they got back on the road, Helen pressed the bag on Hannah, urging her to open it. The angel was run-of-the-mill, a handful of white porcelain with gold wings, blue eyes, and a tiny blot of red for lips. If anything, the angel's lips appeared pursed, as though she was disapproving or apprehensive. Hannah thought the figurine completely unremarkable and was tempted to say so until she turned to her sister, who said, "Isn't she pretty?" Her face was all anticipation, and now that she looked so happy, Hannah realized how downhearted she'd looked be-fore.

"She's perfect," Hannah lied, careful to say "she" and not "it." Angel watchers probably had a rule about that.

"Yes, she is," Helen replied, her voice calm now. "And I just know she'll help me figure things out."

"What things?" Hannah slipped the figurine back in its bag and under the seat. Now that the angel was taken care of, she hoped they could have a real talk.

Helen glanced back over her shoulder to the two children strapped into the back. Cassie was still snoozing, but Shane was in the midst of his wake-up dance, stretching his arms and rubbing his widened eyes. He wore a wrinkled, disgruntled expression, more like an old man's than a baby's, and his hair was tousled, a wad of brown flax on the top of his head.

"Whether to divorce Jimmy, for one," Helen said, lowering her voice still further. "There. I've said it. The D word. Are you surprised?"

Hannah *was* surprised and hurt too. So the angel watchers had heard of this before she had? "Why can't you talk to *me* about Jimmy?" she whispered back. "I'm your sister. Why won't you let *me* help?" At least I can offer a response, she thought, which is more than that dime-store piece of junk can do.

"I'd have to start so far back," Helen replied, keeping her eyes on the road. "I mean, you know some things—the bad things, mostly. You know about the luna moth and . . . the fights. But you don't know the rest of it. There's so much I've never told you."

"What?" Hannah asked. "What haven't you told me?"

"Lots of things, the things that don't fit."

"Don't fit what?"

"Who you think I am, who you think Jimmy is."

Much as she wanted to protest, Hannah supposed it must be true. She'd assumed a life for her sister, the one she'd wanted her to have, and not just the good parts but the bad parts too. If Helen was to be blessed with a beautiful house and children, those blessings had to be balanced by a brute of a husband. Hannah herself got the sensitive man. What Helen had confided about Jimmy over the years had simply worked to confirm Hannah's preconceived notion of him. Or maybe she'd only registered the things that confirmed it. That was possible as well. She'd begun to question her image of Jimmy on Halloween night, when he'd confessed to her in the parking lot. It had occurred to her then that Jimmy saw her much more clearly than she'd ever seen him.

"I wish you'd talk to me. If I'm all wrong about you, then tell me, Helen."

"You're all wrong about me, Hannah."

It had to be a joke, but it didn't sound like one. "Really," Hannah insisted, turning in her seat to face her sister. "I mean it."

"Me too." Helen kept her eyes on the semi truck lumbering up ahead. "We have parts to play, the people in your little world—"

Hannah snorted. "That's not fair, and you know it."

Helen snorted back. *"I wish you'd talk to me,"* she mimicked. "Do you want me to talk or not?"

"Yes, by all means, talk."

"I'm not just a deluded little housewife, and you're not just a big bad assistant principal. Jimmy *is* a philandering bastard, but he's more than that, Hannah. How can I talk to you about Jimmy if you won't see the whole person?"

Oh, I've seen the whole Jimmy, Hannah thought, but she kept her mouth closed. She knew what her sister was saying, and she knew Helen was right: Jimmy wasn't his infidelity any more than she, Hannah, was her abortion. Simple as that. She stared out the side window. It was dark now, but she could make out the shape of a barn hulking off to the right, a line of barbed-wire fence bordering the thin strip of highway, and, beyond all that, a stand of trees at the top of the next hill, hundreds of gnarly branches grasping at the sky.

Their family home, an L-shaped red brick, was situated midway along the Tyler Azalea Trail, a five-mile route that wound through a section of the city famed for something other than roses. Although the streets were dark and deserted in late November, springtime found them congested, the scene of a small festival. For two weekends in late March and early April, the area was overrun with tourists, some on foot but most in cars, all of them craning their necks for a better view of the thousands of azalea bushes in all shades of pink, salmon, lavender, red, and white. The Lambert house featured white azaleas, a whole hedge of them running along the west side of the property. And azaleas were the least of it. By east Texas standards, the yard was a jungle. Dogwoods, magnolias, and crape myrtle, all of them planted by Naomi and all featuring white blooms. Years after her death, it became clear that she'd overplanted, planted too close, that the yard could do with a little more color, but no one had the heart to thin it out, certainly not her widower. A few of the bushes had been choked out, but most of the trees had prevailed, spreading their limbs and intertwining until they completely blocked the view of the house.

Low branches scraped the roof of the Voyager as Helen pulled into the driveway and a moment later their father opened the front door and stepped out onto the porch. He must have been watching from the window, Hannah thought. She was touched. In the yellow porch light, she could see George Lambert perfectly: a tall, narrow-chested man with spindly arms and legs. He wore a navy blue jogging suit, the sort that looked to have been cut from a parachute, a leisure suit for the nineties. Seeing her father surrounded by so much darkness gave Hannah pause. He looked old, didn't he? But he waved broadly, using his whole arm and cutting a wide swath through the air. "Helen!" he shouted, then, "Hannah!" He stood and waited for them to get out of the van.

"So he finished the porch?" Hannah asked Helen as she opened the door. The original had been nothing more than a concrete slab, good enough for the rest of them, but Harriet had wanted something grander, more gracious. He'd seen to it, building her a wooden porch that spanned the house. A pair of high-backed rockers and concrete planters graced either side of the front door. The effect was inviting and genteel, distinctively southern.

"The porch was finished back in June," Helen replied. "You think that's something, wait till you see the kitchen." Hannah had lost track of all the home improvements. It had been nearly a year since her last visit. Too long, she thought, watching Helen slip from off the driver's seat and hop to the ground. "Hi there, Daddy!" she called.

Helen's voice set their father into motion. He hurried down the steps and across the flagstone walk. He was just as Hannah always remembered him, a man in waiting, the kind of person who's more comfortable reacting than acting. If those around him didn't make the first move, he didn't know what to do with himself. His lifelong occupation as a pharmacist had only reinforced this tendency. People handed him slips of paper, and George filled their orders promptly, efficiently, rarely making a mistake. But years of counting pills had left him stooped and perpetually squinting. He'd never smiled easily, and now when he grinned, he appeared to be wincing, as though happiness hurt.

Here he comes, Hannah thought, opening her arms to the obligatory hug. He slipped in close, giving her one of his loose, one-armed embraces, the ones where he scooped her up and let her go. It reminded Hannah of a dance step, something her father might have learned at Arthur Murray and adapted for day-to-day life. He did enjoy dancing. In fact, that was the way he and Harriet had met, two lonely people taking dance lessons. "Hannah," he said when the hug was finished. "It's good to have you home."

"Glad to be here," she replied, realizing that she meant it.

After escorting Helen and her children inside, George rushed back out, just as Hannah was lifting the suitcases out of the van. "I've got them," she called, waving him back.

"Let me haul them," he insisted. "Don't go treating me like an old man."

"You're *not* an old man," she said.

"No," he agreed, "not quite yet."

But he carried the bags slowly, his shoulders hunched against the weight. Hannah trailed after him, a clothes bag over her shoulder, watching as her father shuffled across the wooden porch in his gray boot-style house shoes. The left one was run over at the heel, and he turned out his right toe, so that one foot pointed in a slightly different direction. He slid his feet rather than lifting them. Economy of movement, Hannah supposed. Did he still manage the waltz, she wondered, and if so, was his step lighter when he danced?

Crossing the threshold, she took a deep breath. The hallway's hardwood floor was still the same rich reddish-brown from her childhood; she knew every plank of this floor by heart. There it came, the pain of the familiar. Hannah stood still for a moment and let it pass through her, knowing that resisting would only make it worse. With age, she'd expected the pain to fade, become a throb rather than a thrust. But that had yet to happen. At last she managed to speak, though she sounded a little breathless. "Where's Harriet?" she asked.

"You'll find her in the kitchen," George said before retreating down the long hall.

Hannah smelled green beans cooking with salt pork and something sweet, maybe a pumpkin pie. They'd skipped dinner, making do with potato chips, fruit, and Diet Coke. Now Hannah was ravenous. Harriet was bustling about, rushing from the cabinets to the refrigerator then back to the center island. Her concentration was so complete that Hannah was able to sidle up to the doorway of the kitchen and linger there, unnoticed.

Helen had warned her about the kitchen; even so, Hannah was stunned by the transformation. All during her childhood, the room had been dark and dreary. Three of the four walls had been covered in a fake-wood paneling accented with wallpaper that featured a forest scene, all dark greens and browns. More like a cave than a kitchen. In honor of their five-year anniversary, George had remodeled and gone to the opposite extreme. Now everything was white: the cabinets, the appliances, the tile floor, even the paneling. It was positively brilliant, light reflecting off every surface. I'll need sunglasses to sit down to breakfast, Hannah thought. The new kitchen featured an oblong center island with open shelves where Harriet could display her collection of cookie jars. Animals were her weakness. She had dogs, cats, rabbits, ducks, horses, cows, pigs, even an elephant rearing its trunk. All of it was so unfamiliar, the remodeled kitchen and the new wife bustling about inside it. Over five years had gone by, but Hannah still thought of her stepmother as new, partly because George had been a widower for more than twenty years and partly because Hannah and Harriet had not become friends. That, Hannah supposed, was her fault. Harriet had always been friendly enough.

Their father had married his new wife in the same Methodist church Hannah and Helen had attended as children. All during the ceremony, Hannah had kept her eyes on Harriet, who'd resembled nothing so much as a middle-aged porcelain doll: her pale face splotched with blush, her off-white satin tea dress a little too large in the shoulders and waist. She looked dowdy as a bride, but she'd been a beauty in her youth, the 1951 Rose Queen, which amounted to being a sort of royalty in Tyler, Texas. Occasionally, Hannah still heard her father refer to his wife as "Queenie."

After the wedding had concluded and the few guests dispersed—Carl and Jimmy heading outside for a breath of air—the four of them lingered in the foyer, where the air was heavy with the scent of roses. Lacking a suitable number of guests, Harriet must have decided not to lack for flowers—lovely lush arrangements were everywhere. Since childhood, the smell of flowers had made Hannah nauseous. Looking on as Harriet thanked the minister, Hannah had felt worse and worse. Keeping her eyes trained on the heavy oak doors that led outside, she'd been about to excuse herself when her father said something to the minister: "Harriet, Hannah, and Helen," he'd joked. "I've always been partial to women whose names begin with *H*." They'd all laughed dutifully, Helen stepping in to give him a hug, but Hannah couldn't move. Her heart was whispering something. Until then, she hadn't known that a thought could originate in the chest, but this one beat inside her. Hannah tried to get it out; she intended to fill the whole church with three syllables: NA-O-MI. Instead, she'd bent and vomited, yellow bile spewing out of her mouth, splashing the parquet floor and the tips of their shoes. Even now, it humiliated her to think of it.

Sighing, she raised a hand to tuck back a few stray hairs. Harriet was busy flouring the counter, a white apron tied around her lavender sweat suit, her hair a froth of white. Flour dust rose in the air around her face, and, waving a hand to clear the air, she caught sight of Hannah in the doorway. "Hello, dear," she chirped, a hint of surprise in her voice. Hannah knew her stepmother was thinking that it isn't polite to simply stand and gawk. She was right, of course. Wiping her hands on her apron, Harriet bustled forward to offer Hannah a hug. She, too, wore the cloth house boots, only hers were decorated with a rash of pink satin bows.

"How was your trip?" she asked, shaking her head in sympathy, as though Hannah had just flown in from New York or Fiji. Harriet hated travel; even a weekend of shopping in Dallas was more torture than pleasure for her. Being away from her house and living out of a suitcase left her feeling "unmoored." That was the word she used, and Hannah supposed it came from one of those gothic romances Harriet was always reading. Her stepmother's aversion worked out well for Hannah—visits to Austin were few and far between.

"The trip was fine," Hannah said, returning the hug briefly before taking another step back into the shadowy dining room. Part of her wanted to keep her distance, but Harriet was not one to brook a retreat. Instead, she plucked up Hannah's sleeve and led her into the warmth of the kitchen and over to the island where a cookie-making command center had been set up. A huge pancake of dough had been rolled out in the middle of the counter, and spaced around it were tiny glass bowls filled with candy dots, chocolate shavings, colored sugar, red hots, and tiny silver candy balls. A children's paradise.

"I thought Cassie and I would make angels," Harriet said, beaming. She didn't have grandchildren of her own, and she was the sort who yearned for children to fuss over. Harriet's one daughter was in her thirties but still single, a hairdresser in Dallas. Hannah had only met her once, at the wedding five years ago. She opened her mouth to inquire about the daughter but drew a blank on the name. Lola, she thought, or Lucille. An *L* name, something dramatic and old-fashioned. Later, she'd ask Helen to jog her memory.

Helen arrived in the doorway just in time to overhear. "What did you say?" she asked.

Harriet wheeled about. "Helen!" she sang. "Where's Cassie? I have us all set up to make angels!"

"Cassie's asleep," Helen replied. She didn't seem to notice Harriet's crestfallen expression, but Hannah did. At the news, their stepmother's pillowy face sagged. "You're making angel cookies?" Helen whispered.

"I know it's more Christmas than Thanksgiving, but . . ." Suddenly, Harriet seemed too drained to complete her sentence. Her makeup had collected in the pockets beneath her eyes and in the lines around her mouth; she'd probably had it on since early morning. To-night, after her little disappointment, Harriet's face resembled a smudged pastel. Carl came to mind; Hannah imagined his blunt finger rubbing at the lines of her stepmother's nose and mouth, making her look soft and dreamy.

"No, it's perfect, really," Helen was saying as she wandered over to the center island. "Very thoughtful of you."

"So how about if you two girls help me?" Harriet asked, her voice bright again. "In the morning we'll have a nice surprise for Cassie."

Helen nodded and, with a little sigh, picked up the angel cookie cutter. "I'll make the first one," she said. Tears leaked out of the corner of her eyes, but if Harriet noticed, she didn't say anything. She simply watched as Helen shoved the tin angel into the dough and pressed it down with the flat of her hand, muttering, "This one's for me."

When the first tray came out of the oven, Harriet poured four glasses of milk. "Hannah, dear," she said. "Will you go get your father? We don't want him to miss his chance at a hot cookie."

Hannah found him in his bedroom, curled up on the edge of the bed, quietly asleep. It looked as though he'd sat down for a moment to collect himself and, finding that sitting didn't refresh him, decided to put his head to the pillow. Hannah drew nearer. In many respects, her father had aged well. Though stooped, he was still lean and strong enough to haul heavy suitcases. But his skin was stretched thin now and appeared slightly transparent. Even in the dim light of the lamp, she could see a blood vessel beating at his temple, the flower-shaped age spot blooming on one cheek. His white hair was so sparse it didn't cover the freckled skin of his scalp. It hurt to see this. Over the years, Hannah had felt many things when it came to her father, a welter of conflicting emotions, but one of them was surely love.

So still he was, so silent. For a second, Hannah wondered whether he was breathing. Did people die this way? Did they begin an ordinary task only to stop breathing when they finished it? She supposed it happened, an instantaneous giving up on life. It would be a pleasant enough way to die, no time to prepare but no time to be fearful either. Not that she was ready for him to go yet, not that she would be. He was only sixty-six, after all; he'd retired just last spring. Kneeling there beside him, she assured herself that he was indeed sleeping, peacefully. If she hadn't been so close she'd never have heard his moan, a low keening sound, the force of which was very nearly physical. The memory it prompted was inexplicable to Hannah but that only made it all the more real. Why had she slipped into her parents' room when her father was asleep on the bed? What had she been up to? The shadowy room had been cluttered with dark and heavy furniture then, just as it was now. And her father had been curled up asleep at one edge of the neatly made bed. She could even see the bedspread, a tan chenille with fringe that brushed the floorboards.

Hannah had headed for the closet. Silly, really, for a twelve-year-old to think her dead mother might be hiding in the closet, but that was it. Somehow, she'd expected to find her there. She'd crawled into the dark space on her hands and knees and encountered her mother's high heels, all of them standing at attention in a long neat row: red, black, tan, navy, and gold. Like Hannah, Naomi had had a weakness for impractical shoes. The closet was a long narrow space, and gangly Hannah had been unable to avoid the shoes. As soon as one had toppled, the others went over too, like bowling pins at the alley they went to on Friday nights. Hannah had stopped in her tracks and waited, sure the noise would awaken her father. He'd always been such a quiet man, but since the accident he'd become unpredictable. She pictured him lunging into the closet after her, grabbing her up by the collar of her dress and dragging her out. She'd frozen then, waiting for his response. But all he did was moan, an odd strangled sound that took little Hannah's breath away. The sound permeated the room, but he didn't wake.

Safe, she'd thought, moving again, scrambling over the tops of her father's patent leather shoes, her palms slipping off the toes and onto the gritty floor. She made her way to the back of the closet and reached up for a cotton skirt—sweet-smelling and familiar. Pressing it to her face, holding it over her own mouth, she'd sucked in its smell. Once or twice, she'd choked on her tears, but she went on with it, sobbing and kneading the material until the skirt came off the hanger and settled about her head. There, in the darkness, surrounded by the fragrance of her mother's perfume, she'd curled up and slept.

Sometime later, she'd awakened to her father's moans. Would he never stop? But now she knew what to do. Hannah emerged from the closet and tiptoed to her mother's vanity, to the mirrored tray lined with bottles and an atomizer of Jungle Gardenia. Naomi had shown Hannah how to hold the bottle in the air in front of her, squeeze the little rubber ball and—quick as a wink—duck into the scent. "Just a whiff is what you want," Naomi had told her. "That's why you spray it in the air and not directly on your skin." Her mother had always done it for her, but this time Hannah tried it herself. Squeeze and duck, quick as a wink. It was a blessing, that scent. It brought her mother back.

One puff in the air above her father's head and he went peaceful and still, so silent and calm that the young Hannah's heart had clutched. Don't die on me, Daddy, she'd thought, kneeling next to the bed to watch him breathe. And he hadn't died, or at least most of him hadn't. She'd sat back on her heels and watched over him as he slept, just as she was doing now. Such a long time, Daddy, she thought, nearly thirty years. You'd think we'd be over it.

Harriet cleared her throat, and Hannah looked up to find her step-mother standing in the doorway. "Oh dear," Harriet said. "He's gone off again." Framed by the molding, she looked smaller and lumpier than she had in the kitchen. Or maybe it was only the contrast. Naomi had rarely stood still, almost never sat down. She was a little brown bird full of a mysterious energy. And for a few moments there, she'd been very nearly alive again.

"He's been this way ever since he stopped working," Harriet explained, edging into the room. She wrung her hands, then rubbed them on the apron. "Stopped sleeping at night and started snatching little naps in the daytime. I'm afraid when he drives, for fear he'll just drop off at the wheel."

Hannah got to her feet. Her knees were stiff, her back tight. She could no longer make a car trip without feeling the effects immediately afterward. Next week, she'd be forty. She joined her stepmother in the hall. "Has Dad been to the doctor?" she asked.

Harriet motioned for Hannah to follow. When they were in the kitchen, she answered the question. "I was hoping you could convince him. He doesn't like to see the doctors here in town. Knows them all and is afraid of disappointing them by getting ill. And you know how he hates the pills." Hannah nodded. This was true. He never took prescriptions himself, though he swore by them for everyone else. Harriet reached out and patted Hannah on the shoulder. "He has such respect for you, Hannah." She meant it as a compliment, but it felt like a slap in the face. Respect was something best done from a distance. Hannah felt so weak she had to lean against the white wall.

Harriet didn't notice or pretended not to. "You ready to turn in?" she asked.

"Yes," Hannah replied. "But can you wait to lock up until I get something out of the car?"

"Certainly." And reaching out, Harriet patted her on the shoulder.

The angel was still wrapped in her bag under the driver's seat. Hannah carried her in and said good night to her mother-in-law, who was waiting by the door. Entering her old bedroom, she didn't bother with the lights. She knew the layout by heart: the antique-white canopy bed in the middle of the room; the matching dressing table and stool against the far wall; and the eyesore, a scarred and rickety walnut dresser pressed to one side of the bed. The antique-white set had included a matching dresser, but they'd only been able to afford the two pieces. "We'll come back for it," Naomi had promised. A gift for Hannah's thirteenth birthday. "See if it doesn't come before you know it."

Now Hannah eased into a wooden rocker in the corner and secreted the angel out of its sack. She'd brought it in for Helen, or so she'd told herself, but she held it for herself. Rocking in the dark, she fingered the cool, smooth outlines of the angel's skirt, the pert little lips and round halo, until at last she went off to sleep.

"I wish Carl were here," Hannah said. It was midday, and she was spooning creamy mashed potatoes from a large pot into a big blue serving bowl—enough potatoes to feed the whole block—and contemplating the picture it made. Carl would have appreciated it, mounds of snowy potatoes in a sky blue bowl, visions of Norman Rockwell.

"Me too," Harriet replied. "What's he doing today?"

Hannah shrugged, realizing she didn't really know. Still in his studio, she supposed. When she'd left the day before, that's where he'd been. She'd knocked once and called out her good-byes, but he hadn't answered, or at least she hadn't heard him. Still mad, she'd thought then. Now she wondered whether he'd have turkey and dressing at Luby's cafeteria or whether he'd bother to leave the house at all. Probably not. Likely, he'd make do with opening a can of soup. That would be just like him. He loved preparing food for others, but he rarely bothered for himself.

"He's such a sweet man," Harriet began. She was about to say more when the phone rang and she hurried from the stove to answer it. "Hello, Jim-my." She lingered on the name, to alert Hannah, no doubt. The edge in her stepmother's voice made Hannah wonder how much Helen had confided. Or was it possible the older woman had simply guessed the problem? After all, Harriet had been around the block a few times. In fact, if Hannah remembered correctly, infidelity had ended Harriet's first marriage. "Just a minute," Harriet was telling Jimmy. "I'll ask Hannah to check. Helen might have taken Cassie outside. It's a beautiful day here."

Which wasn't the least bit true, Hannah thought, glancing out the kitchen window. Dark clouds were bunched overhead; now and then, the sky spit a few cold drops at them. Over breakfast, George had predicted a dousing of sleet. "Good thing you girls aren't planning to head back until tomorrow," he'd said. "We're all safe and snug here." Then he'd winked at his wife. "And Lord knows we won't be starving anytime soon."

On her way down the hall, Hannah admired her stepmother's tact.

Harriet had managed to be solicitous of Jimmy's feelings while still offering her daughter-in-law a way out. Helen was in the living room, reading a book to Cassie while Shane rested in his grandfather's arms. They looked so peaceful together that Hannah stood and watched for a moment. What would Helen do if she divorced Jimmy? Go back to nursing? Could she support the four of them on a nurse's salary? If she got child support she probably could. And, for all Hannah knew, Helen might get alimony as well. With the help of a good lawyer, she might seize a healthy chunk of Jimmy's wages every month. Most of the benefits of Jimmy without the jackass himself. It sounded like a good deal to Hannah. She wondered if Gabe Faber handled divorces. For a second, she imagined the scene, Gabe Faber sinking his teeth into Jimmy. If anyone could do it, Gabe Faber could.

"Helen," Hannah finally said. "You have a phone call."

Helen looked up. "Who is it?" she asked.

Hannah mouthed Jimmy's name. Helen shook her head emphatically. Cassie tugged on her mother's sleeve. "Read, Momma," she ordered.

Hannah returned to the kitchen.

"Nope," she said. "Tell Jimmy he just missed them."

Harriet nodded and turned back to the receiver. "Oh dear," she put in smoothly. "Hannah tells me they've gone out, and we'll be having dinner as soon as they get back. How about if I have her give you a call later on?" She listened, a small worried smile on her tiny pink lips. They were a little like the angel's lips, Hannah thought now. "I will, thank you," Harriet said into the receiver. "You too, dear."

"Well," Harriet said, hanging up the phone and turning to Hannah. "Shall we get this on the table?"

Whenever Hannah ate at Harriet's, she always had the sense that a number of other people had been invited, that this was more than a meal, that it was, in fact, an occasion. Today, her stepmother was serving ham *and* turkey, sweet *and* mashed potatoes, cranberry relish *and* cranberry salad. Followed by heaping bowls of green peas and creamed corn, hot rolls, and a relish tray. There was hardly room on the long table for their plates and place settings.

They were all dressed for the celebration: Hannah in a white silk blouse and brown wool slacks, Helen in a dark green crinkle dress so enormous Cassie could hide beneath it and giggle. The little imp had been doing just that before dinner, much to the amusement of her grandfather, who wore a white dress shirt and a thin navy blue tie. He might have been on his way to church or sitting down to dinner with company. They *were* company, Hannah realized, or at least she was. She was a visitor, a welcomed guest, but a guest nonetheless. Harriet wasn't quite so dressed up as her husband. Of course, she'd been cooking all morning, rushing from stove to refrigerator to the dining-room table and back again. Her face was flushed from all the activity, her brown pantsuit a little snug but flattering.

As soon as everyone was seated, Harriet offered grace, a no-nonsense version she launched into without warning. "Holy Father," she began. Hannah bent her head and closed her eyes. Back when she was a girl, she'd given God her best shot. Right here, at this very table, she'd closed her eyes before every meal and offered up a fervent little prayer. She'd wanted to believe—after all, heaven was her only chance at seeing her mother again—only she'd never quite managed it. Even now she'd have been willing to welcome God into her life, if only He'd have made His presence felt. Except it seemed He was squarely on the other side, the mascot of the pro-lifers. Not fair, she thought now. Not fair that they get to claim Him for themselves.

Harriet had just said "Amen" when the phone rang again, an abrupt jangling that made them all jump.

"Must be God," George quipped, but no one laughed.

Cassie leaned over her plate and tried to get a glimpse of the phone ringing in the kitchen. "Does God call on the phone?" she asked.

Harriet frowned as she slipped out of her seat to answer. "George, please," she said reprovingly. She was gone for several minutes, and they all sat and waited, not wanting to eat without her. Instead, they passed the relish tray. Finally, Harriet appeared in the doorway, just as Helen was spooning cranberries onto Cassie's plate. "I'm sorry, Helen," Harriet said. "I can't put him off this time. Would you like to take it in the bedroom?"

Helen didn't look up, just shook her head. Then she spoke to Harriet in a firm voice meant for her husband: "Tell him we've started dinner," she said. "I'll call him back when we've finished. If he tries to

argue, just hang up. *He's* the one being rude." Harriet did as she was
asked, returning quickly to the table with a plate of rolls, as though the
trip to the kitchen had been about food and not adulterous husbands.

They ate quietly for the next few minutes, but as soon as Cassie had
finished her mashed potatoes, she began to scoot off the telephone
books. Hannah was sitting on the other side of her, and she reached out
to try and hold the squirming child in place. Let your momma have a
moment's peace, she thought, but what she said was, "Sit here and
finish your good dinner."

"That's all right, Hannah," George put in. "Cassie, why don't you
come down here and sit on Grandpa's lap?"

Immediately, the little girl slid off the chair and under the table,
emerging with a sly grin on her face. The soles of her dress shoes
clattered on the hardwood floor as she scampered to the other end of
the table. When she was settled in her grandfather's lap, he bent his
head to her ear.

"Do you suppose Grandma made pumpkin pie?" he asked in a
whispery voice meant for all of them.

Cassie nodded her head. Earlier in the day, Harriet had taken the
little girl on a tour of the desserts: apple pie, pumpkin pie, chocolate
layer cake, and, of course, the angel cookies. "Pumpkin pie is made
from jack-o'-lanterns," she announced.

"So it is," George replied, smiling over Cassie's head and looking
directly into Hannah's eyes. "I heard that once, a long time ago."

How could she have forgotten? She could see it so clearly now, the
palm of her own small hand, no bigger than Cassie's, full of flat white
pumpkin seeds, the pulp still clinging to them. She'd wanted to plant
the seeds, but her mother wouldn't hear of it. "I've just gotten the yard
the way I like it," she said. "You think I want some enormous vine
crawling over everything?"

She'd grabbed Hannah firmly by the wrist and led her to the
kitchen trash can. Hannah could see it all in her mind's eye, she and
her mother hunched over the garbage. "Throw those away," Naomi
had insisted, but Hannah was stubborn. She'd closed her fingers into a
fist, refusing to give them up. The seeds had seemed magical to her, full
of potential, like the ones in "Jack and the Beanstalk." By the time

George had happened onto the scene, Naomi was prying the little fist open finger by finger. Hannah no longer remembered what he'd said, only that he'd soothed them both and led Hannah into the backyard. They'd found a narrow strip of soil between the back of the garage and the fence, and he'd dug it up with a trowel before instructing Hannah in the fine art of seed planting. "A little bit of fertilizer goes in with 'em," he'd told her, taking care to pack some of the meat of the pumpkin around each seed. Hannah had covered them up. If she remembered correctly, the plants had come up just before the first hard freeze.

"Dad," Hannah said. "I was thinking of those pumpkin seeds you planted with me after Halloween one year. Wasn't I about Cassie's age?"

He nodded and smiled again. "I wondered if you remembered. I think a few waited to come up until the following spring. I seem to recall a vine emerging from behind the garage, inching its way across the grass." He shook his head and laughed. "Your mother wouldn't have liked that a bit."

"Did we get a pumpkin out of it?" Hannah asked.

He shook his head. "Couldn't say. I do know there's a line of white rosebushes out there now," he added. "And that I have hell pruning them every year."

Harriet sat nodding at the other end of the table. "Such a shame," she said. "Those roses just go to waste hidden back there. Not a soul to see them."

"Wonderful dinner," Hannah offered.

Harriet flushed with pleasure. She'd just started to list the choices of dessert when the phone rang again, that persistent shrill buzzing. "Well, for heaven's sa—" she began, her words dying away. It wouldn't do to appear exasperated, her expression said.

Hannah rose from her seat and folding her napkin, laid it beside her plate. "Let me get it this time," she said, giving Helen a significant look. On the way to the kitchen, she decided to treat her brother-in-law as she did recalcitrant teenagers, no questions asked, no excuses accepted. When she picked up the receiver, she didn't even bother to say hello. "This is Hannah, Jimmy," she announced.

"Hannah," Carl said. "I'm glad I reached you." She was so surprised to hear her husband's voice that she almost missed what came next: Neil had taken a turn for the worse, and Carl had rushed him to the nearest vet emergency clinic. He paused then, expecting a question from her, but she waited him out. She knew what was coming. "I had to put him down, Hannah," Carl finally said. "He was suffering. If you could have heard him moan. I know you'd have done the same." Hannah closed her eyes. Carl breathed into the receiver and waited. "Hannah, did you hear what I said?"

"I heard you." She was fighting back the tears. "I just wish I could have been there."

"Me too," Carl agreed.

———————

THE two sisters made the drive back to Austin in companionable silence. Helen pulled into Hannah's drive and helped her bring her things inside. Keeping her eyes on the sidewalk, Hannah managed to avoid the mess on the front of her house, and Helen didn't say a word about it. After she'd hugged her sister good-bye, Hannah rolled her suitcase to the bedroom. Carl was at work. The house was so silent, she thought, no skittering on the hardwood floor, no welcoming bark. She put her things away, and, without really intending to, wandered into the dining room and peered out the picture window. There it was, the pile of fresh dirt under the mimosa tree.

Already, the sky was darkening, marking the close of another day. Hannah opened the back door and stepped out onto the porch. The air was fresh; earlier, it had rained here. She took a deep breath, then another, and a moment later, found herself standing before Neil's grave. Carl had piled the extra dirt in a mound. Last night on the phone, he'd told Hannah they could smooth it out later, and in the spring they'd patch the grass. A year or two from now, they wouldn't know it was there. It had sounded like the right thing then, but now Hannah realized it wasn't what she wanted.

Looking directly at that barren patch of earth opened up something inside her. Maybe she'd plant flowers here, she thought, create a border with stones or bricks, make a memory instead of blocking one out.

That was what she'd done wrong all these years. She'd tried to avoid the pain, to look the other way and pretend it wasn't there, and in the process she'd shut herself off from the rest of life. She wouldn't do that anymore. Hannah made herself that promise, and as the last light faded from the sky, she told Neil good-bye.

Chapter 19

On the first of December, Penny pulled into the alley at dusk, and rather than go upstairs, stood in Mattie's yard and watched her neighbor Henry stride gracefully up and down his pitched roof. Penny was awed by his agility, but she was also a little frightened for him. She'd always been scared of heights. Even on elevators, she felt compelled to hold her breath.

Just as she was turning to go inside, he surprised her by calling out, "Wait, Penny! You're just in time to see the lights." He was finished and ready to come down. Now Penny noticed the wooden ladder leaning against the side of his house, Mattie's ladder, old and rickety, distinctly unreliable.

"Wait yourself!" she cried, and hurried across the yard to hold it for him.

The wooden rungs creaked and groaned as Henry descended, but fortunately, he was a small man. "This is yours," he said when he reached the ground.

"I know," she replied, smiling. "It's been in our family for generations."

He hoisted the ladder over his shoulder, and Penny hurried ahead to open the garage door. The garage was old, built with double doors that opened out, only one of which still moved willingly. She rarely ventured inside; Mattie either. No one had parked a car here in years. It was a cavelike space, musty and mysterious, not much more than four walls and a dirt floor; the only light came from a naked bulb screwed into a socket in the ceiling. Penny took a deep breath and waded into the darkness, waving her arms in front of her face and above her head, searching until she felt the string graze her fingertip. She yanked it and squinted against the glaring yellow light.

Henry strolled in behind her, replaced the ladder against the far wall, and, leaving, called over his shoulder, "Hurry. I'm about to throw the switch."

"I'll be right there," she promised, and reached for the string. One hard pull and the light blinked out, but not before she glimpsed the ladder, back in its place against the far wall—dusty, discolored, and missing the bottom rung, a fixture in the dark garage for as long as Penny could remember. And longer, much longer, she thought now.

Although she'd wanted to deny it, she'd known the truth of Mattie's story as soon as she'd heard it, known it in her bones. For weeks, she'd been imagining the specifics and replaying them in her head as she went about her daily tasks. In the room that had been Delia's, the room Penny herself had lived in as a child, a full-length mirror hung behind the door. Penny had pictured her mother standing before it, raising her white nightgown above pale, pudgy knees, above the yellow knotting of hair between her legs, up, up, all the way to her waist. One morning, she must have discovered a slight rounding of her belly, proof positive that her mother's fate was on its way to becoming hers as well, a legacy of sorts. The ladder would have been waiting for her, and once Delia had hauled it out to the side of the house, the rest would have been easy. . . .

"Penny!" Henry shouted. "Get out here, Penny!"

She stumbled out of the dark garage just in time to see the strings of red lights blink on next door, transforming her neighbor's house into a fairy cottage. A few minutes later she heard the phone ring inside her apartment, but Penny simply ignored it. Likely, it was Dr. Bill. This past week, he'd called several times to "check in," the last time on Tuesday. He wanted to come by, he said; they needed to have a serious talk. "Some things," he told her, "can't be discussed over the phone."

"What things?" she'd asked. "Us," he'd replied. Penny hadn't felt up to discussing "us"; she made excuses. "I'm tired," she'd said on Tuesday. "Let's wait."

When the phone finally went silent, she climbed the stairs and went inside for Flash, who darted out from under the bed and into her arms. What had she done before she had Flash? Penny wondered. Bundling the cat into her arms, she returned to the porch and settled on the top step, enjoying the peaceful evening, cool but not cold, perfect with a warm little cat in her lap. The huge bowl of dark sky rose around her, so that she felt small and contained. She'd been sitting there for at least half an hour when the familiar noise of a motorcycle engine filled the air, and the beam of a headlight swung across the yard. Dr. Bill pulled into Mattie's driveway and cut the engine. He'd arrived, then, determined to have their little talk.

He came striding around the corner with his head down—no baseball cap tonight—and started up the stairs. She couldn't see him well, but she could feel the force of his step reverberating in the wood underneath her. Flash burrowed more deeply into Penny's lap.

"Hello, there," she called out.

"Penny!" He stopped, mid-flight, clearly surprised.

"I wasn't sure you saw me," she said.

He shook his head. "No, no, I didn't. I didn't know if you'd be home."

"I just got here," she lied, surprised by how easy it was.

"Working late?" He took another step, gentler this time.

"Juanita quit, you know. It's hard, running things by myself." All this was true enough.

"I'm sorry, Penny," he said. "I talked to her. I really did. I told her she should go back. I thought maybe she had." It was too dark to see his expression, but she didn't need to. His voice told her all she needed to know. Juanita wouldn't be returning.

She stood, gathering the cat against her chest. "I'm really tired, Bill."

He gestured to the house next door. "Nice lights," he commented.

"Yes," she said. "I've been sitting out here enjoying them. It doesn't seem like Christmas until the lights go up."

"You know, you could wrap this railing in red and white, make it look like a candy cane." He shook it for emphasis, sending a tremor through the staircase. Flash huddled deeper into her shirt. "Better yet," he said, "we could do it together."

"I've been getting home late every night. Really, there's no time."

He gripped the railing and leaned toward her. "Let me in? Just a little. Please?"

Rather than softening, Penny felt herself turn hard inside, and her words sounded it—small stones she tossed at him. "Why are you asking me now? The way I remember it, you let yourself in."

"I'm sorry. Will you give me a few minutes. Please?"

She didn't answer, but she opened the door and waited for him to duck inside. In the light, she could see he was wearing blue jeans and a festive-looking red and white flannel shirt. He carried his Bible, a tattered, black leather-bound copy.

"Can I sit down?" he asked.

She nodded and watched him settle on the edge of the bed. He sat forward, with his elbows braced on his thighs, and he held the Bible out in front of him, as though he might pitch it in her direction. Penny curled into her red chair across from him, pulling her feet up under her and glancing about for Flash, who hovered near the door, eyeing the space under the bed.

She motioned to the Bible. "So. You're back to convince me I'm wrong about Ruth?"

He shook his head. "Absolutely not. That's not it at all." He sighed, clearly miserable. "I'm here to *see* you. Aren't my feelings perfectly obvious?"

"No," she replied.

"Well then, let me just tell you." He took a deep breath and looked directly into her eyes, holding her with his gaze. He spoke slowly and deliberately. "This is me, Bill, speaking: I care about you, Penny, and because I care about you, I want you to understand why I do what I do. I want you to *agree* with me and be my ally, but if that's not possible, I at least want your understanding."

"Are you talking about the paint bombings?" she asked. "Because I don't agree—"

He shook his head. "No, no," he said impatiently. "That was your grandmother's idea. I wasn't even there."

"But you knew about them?"

"Yes," he agreed. "I knew about them."

There were things she wanted *him* to understand. "I don't believe in violence," she said.

"Neither do I," he replied. "But violence doesn't care if we believe in it. Like it or not, it's all around us." He hesitated, then went on. "So, do you think that violence can work for good?"

"No," she said immediately. It seemed like an easy question, but he smiled at her from across the room and pursed his lips. He must be trying to trick me again, she thought. She was about to say so when he spoke.

"Penny, Penny, my perfect little pacifist. If only the world were as simple and good as you are."

She felt stung. Simple and good? He made her sound like a child. "Am I a child to you?"

"No!" He stood up and paced the floor in front of her, still grasping the Bible in one hand. "That's not what I meant! Do you deliberately misunderstand me? Why is it I can get through to everyone else but never to you?"

"Jesus says we should love our enemies," she told him stiffly, feeling like a young girl in Sunday school. How could she love someone who made her feel so small?

He stopped his pacing and stood directly before her. "And so we should." He went on in a calmer voice. "But loving doesn't vanquish them. I ask God every day to help me love that Stecker woman. My jaw still aches when I eat, and I haven't managed love. I haven't even managed forgiveness. But no matter how much love I send her way, she's going to sacrifice her grandbaby if she has a chance. Their skins are thick, Penny. Their hearts are hard. Not like yours. Not like you."

"You don't really know me," she said.

"I *do* know you. I look in your eyes and see everything I need to know."

Penny raised herself out of the chair and went to him. Taking his free hand in both of hers, she looked up into his dark eyes. "You've got to stop this," she said. "You've got to stop, Bill. You're ruining people's lives."

"Ruining people's lives?" he echoed. "You want to see ruined lives?"

He led her to the edge of the bed and sat down beside her. While she watched, he slipped a well-worn photograph from the back of his Bible and held it out. Penny hesitated, then took it, placing it in her lap and peering down at the image. Her fingers trembled, her vision blurred. For a few seconds, she couldn't see a thing.

"You all right?" Dr. Bill asked.

She nodded. "Fine. I'm fine."

"So what do you see?"

She squinted her eyes and studied the grainy black-and-white photograph. "Hands against a white background?"

"Yessss. A pair of hands. Go on."

Penny stared again, and when she spoke, her voice cracked. "In the hand . . . there's a little curled creature?"

"Yessss. And how does it look, this creature?" Dr. Bill bent over her, casting his shadow over the photograph, but it didn't matter. Penny knew what was there. It was etched in her memory.

"Cold," she responded. "And old. Very old."

"Old? An old life?" he asked.

She looked up at him, her eyes streaming tears. "Yes," she replied.

"And what's the creature doing, Penny, my darling?"

"Sucking . . . its . . . thumb."

"Yes, that's right. Now look back at the pair of hands cradling the creature. The left one, the middle finger. Do you see the large, dark mark on the fingernail and the cut just underneath? Where it looks like the doctor hit his finger with a hammer?"

Penny nodded.

Dr. Bill sat back and folded his arms across his chest. When Penny looked over at him, he wore a pained, distant expression, as though he was giving up a hateful secret. "Every night I sleep with that photograph under my pillow. Every night I ask God why He didn't take the finger or the whole hand. It could have happened—a bigger accident. But I've finally realized that accidents aren't God's province. Accidents are up to us."

"What are you saying?"

"We're His creatures, but He doesn't make us His puppets. He allows us the freedom to make mistakes." He pulled back then, until he

316

could look into her eyes. "You've made a few mistakes lately, haven't you?"

"I make mistakes every day," Penny said evenly. "We all do."

Sighing, he rose to his feet again. For a minute or so, she watched him pace the small space in the center of her apartment. Occasionally, he performed this same little ritual during Sunday sermon, simply pushed away from the podium and walked back and forth before his congregation, head down, hands hidden inside the sleeves of his robe. What did it mean? Penny had wondered more than once. Was he too confused, too disgusted, too heartbroken to go on? He never explained or justified or apologized. He simply took up where he'd left off, which is what he did now. Returning to her side, he gathered her hands in his and squeezed them tight. "Who am I to talk about *your* mistakes? I'm really here to ask your forgiveness for mine."

Forgiveness? For what? she wondered. "Forgiveness is up to God," she told him.

"I'm asking you," he said softly. "Forgive me, Penny, for not protecting you."

She shook her head, baffled by the quick turn their conversation had taken.

Reluctantly, he spoke: "I didn't know about your father."

She felt herself go stiff. "I don't want to talk about that."

But he continued. "I didn't know about your mother either. That she . . ." He paused and glanced back, toward the window. "I wouldn't have agreed to be here," he told her. "I wouldn't have agreed to stay. She had no business beating you up with all that." His voice rose, the minister in him taking over. "None of it, do you hear me, Penny? *None* of it was your fault. You know that, don't you?" He squeezed her hands, then carefully placed them in her lap. "You have to believe me."

"I believe you," she said, but he didn't hear her.

"I know what it's like," he went on, pacing the floor again, "how much it hurts. 'What sort of worthless person am I,' you ask yourself, 'if my own father doesn't want to know me?' "

"But you know your father," Penny put in.

"Now I do," he answered, "but when I was young . . . well, I saw him a few times. My stepfather was in the Air Force, and we kept moving—from Shreveport to Alamogordo, from Alamogordo to Salina. My dad, my real father, was back in Louisiana, not much money, not much initiative. He thought about calling me, about getting in the car and driving to see me. That's what he says. Only it didn't happen. I was twenty when he got around to looking me up. Hated the son of a bitch, despised the sight of him. But I'd had my fill of menial labor, and he promised help with college. Wanted to make amends, he said. I never planned to love him, but it happened." He shrugged and stopped in front of her chair. "Wait and see. You might end up loving your dad too."

"I already love him," Penny admitted.

"What?" Dr. Bill sounded incredulous.

It surprised her too, how quickly it had happened. But then, she'd started loving Dwayne before she knew who he was. "If you knew him," she said. "You'd understand."

Sighing, Dr. Bill sank down beside her and wrapped her in his arms. He smelled of soap and leather. She heard him whispering in her hair, thought he said, "You're my angel."

"You don't understand," she protested.

"Oh yes, I do." He kissed the top of her head. "I understand you, and I love you."

Chapter 20

THE APARTMENT BUILDING was compact and tasteful, a modest four-story structure perched on one corner of West Sixth Street and West Lynn. Each apartment came with its own slab deck enclosed by a low stucco wall, one deck stacked on top of another, like unpainted wooden blocks. At ten o'clock at night, the drapes were still open on some of the patio doors, showcasing elaborately decorated trees. Carl could see lots of white walls and, off to his left, a deck jammed with people. The evening was just cool enough to be pleasant, and when he rolled down his window, swells of "O Holy Night" drifted into the car, followed by a burst of civilized laughter. Ken and Barbie are having a Christmas party, Carl thought. Ironically, the building was just down the block from Penny's shop. Hannah might get a yen for flowers and stop in someday. Carl could imagine the two of them smiling at each other, Hannah remarking on the freshness of the roses or some damn thing.

From his vantage point in the parking lot, he couldn't see her place. If he were to drive up West Lynn, he'd get a passing glimpse of her deck and patio door, enough to tell whether the lights were on inside. Not that he needed to do so. He knew she was home. Her Blazer was parked directly across the lot. Ten o'clock on a Saturday night: Do you know where your wife is? Carl's wife was in her tasteful and anonymous studio apartment. No mess, no muss. No blood on the brick, no pastel dust path down the hall. Part of him wanted to leap out of his car and bound up the stairs to her studio, pound on the door until she opened up. "Are you happy now?" he might ask her. "You'll never guess what I'm about to do." If he were to confess his plan, would she try to talk him out of it, or would she egg him on? Hard to say. Lately, her behavior had been completely unpredictable.

Take moving out, for instance, he thought as he started the car and rolled slowly out of the lot. Now, that had been a real kick in the teeth. No advance notice whatsoever. He'd come home from work late last Saturday night—during holiday season he worked till close on weekends—only to discover that Hannah was gone. She'd packed all her clothes, leaving behind the furniture and the mess, along with a note that invited him to Sunday breakfast at Grandy's. Fool that he was, he'd shown up at the allotted hour, sat across from her in a booth, eaten cinnamon rolls and slugged back coffee while Hannah swore up and down that the apartment was just a short-term fix, a getaway, someplace she could think. Too stunned to be angry, Carl had asked if she was still upset about Neil. She insisted that wasn't it. Their dog had been suffering, and she was grateful to Carl. He'd been braver than she; he'd done the hard part, and now that it was over, they were better off, especially Neil.

Carl didn't believe her. She might *say* he'd done the difficult and right thing, but Hannah needed someone to blame. He hadn't lived with her all these years without learning at least this about her: She didn't and couldn't accept that death was the inevitable outcome of life. For her, death was an outrage, an injustice. But they were at a restaurant, and he was determined not to make a scene. "Well, then," he'd said. "What about E.T.?" Carl had moved the parrot into the house only two days before Hannah moved out.

"I don't know what you see in that bird," she'd replied, taking a bite of egg and chewing before she went on. "If you ask me, he's bad-tempered and ugly. But I didn't move out to get away from him."

E.T. was Carl's now. "Either you take him or I have to sell him," Noah said. Even his beloved mother's house was on the market. *Every-thing must go* was his newest mantra. Noah was going too, moving to San Francisco. "Make a clean start." Evidently, the relationship between Noah and Harry was over as well. Carl didn't have the heart to ask, but he did take E.T. off Noah's hands. At first, he'd tried keeping the bird in the bookstore, but E.T. was bereft, and a bereft bird is a bad bird. When small children stuck their fingers through the bars of his cage, E.T. couldn't resist pressing their pink appendages inside his sharp beak. Even before Ruthanne pulled him aside to show him her own swollen thumb, Carl knew he'd have to take E.T. home. He'd expected a showdown with Hannah, but she'd barely reacted when he'd carried in the crated bird. She'd followed him into the studio and watched quietly as he put together the cage. Removed and distant, he'd thought then, and how right he'd been. What difference if he brought home a gila monster or a potbellied pig? In her head, she'd already been gone.

"So why did you leave?" he'd asked as they finished up their breakfast.

"The house," she said. "Looking at that house every day was killing me."

"But you left me too," he'd replied. "And looking at that house every day, looking at that empty house, is killing *me*."

Now, waiting at a stoplight a few miles from home, Carl turned and peered into the window of the car idling next to him. Sure enough, he spied a married couple or what passed for one: a man driving, a woman sitting beside him, both of them staring through the windshield, not speaking. No need to talk. They'd said it all a hundred times already. Now they'd reached the stage of communing without words. To the uninitiated, it might look like boredom, Carl thought, but often it felt like bliss. The lives of the long-married were made up of such moments: eating together, sleeping together, driving home together, much of it done gracefully and quietly, like a dance without music. Had he lost all that forever, then? The rest of the way home, Carl felt good and sorry for himself. He gazed out at the Christmas lights wrapped around tree trunks and light poles. "By God," he said aloud to an empty car. "I'm going to do a little decorating of my own."

But he had hours to wait until his own lonely holiday festivities could begin. To fill them, he brewed a pot of coffee and sat down on the dirty hardwood floor to watch a movie. He needed a little distraction, and Jimmy Stewart's *It's a Wonderful Life* was just getting under way. Hannah managed to see it every Christmas season, and Carl generally sat beside her on the sofa, dozing off about halfway through. He wasn't sure he'd ever gotten to the end of the silly thing. This year, Hannah would have been proud of him. He stayed awake for the tremulous finale and, in spite of himself, cheered for the downtrodden George Bailey. Lucky man, he thought. If we all had a guardian angel, the world would be a better place. Closing his eyes, Carl pictured Hannah sobbing into a Kleenex on the other side of town. When it came to old movies, she was endlessly sentimental. He'd never quite understood how she could cry for flickering black-and-white heroes and heroines, yet stay so stony-faced when it came to him.

At 1:30 A.M., he began his preparations, slipping on dark slacks and a black silk shirt Hannah had given him for his last birthday. Truth was, he never wore black, a fact that should have been perfectly obvious to his wife. "Try something different," she'd told him, but the suggestion had left him feeling deflated and depressed: Try to *be* something different. That's what he'd heard. Now Carl shrugged the shirt over his shoulders, not even bothering to cut the tag, which hung down his back and tickled the skin between his shoulder blades. "I'm trying something different, Hannah darling," Carl muttered as he strode to the front door, stuffing a knit ski mask into his back pocket. A dozen cans of paint were waiting in the car.

Before he'd gone out to buy, Carl had learned a thing or two about paint. Water-based enamel—that was the ticket. The beige-colored brick at Gospel Fellowship would absorb the stuff, suck it up like a sponge and be hard as hell to get out. Carl had taken all the necessary measures and more. First, he'd bought just two cans at a time—one color in each place—black, red, and something of his own, purple. He had to add his own touch; after all, he wasn't one to simply give as good as he'd gotten. But purple paint was hard to come by. He'd spent all Friday morning driving around town, filling the trunk and then the floorboard with gallon after gallon. No one would remember him, but just in case, he'd worn a gray Dallas Cowboys stocking cap pulled down over his forehead, and while he waited in line, one can cradled in each arm, he'd grinned from ear to ear. He'd looked like a man anticipating a well-earned chore, which is exactly what he was.

Gospel Fellowship was in a residential neighborhood, and when

Carl was within six blocks of the church, he flipped off his headlights. He didn't intend to be seen, nor did he intend to stay long. He figured he could come and go in less than an hour. The hardest part would be hauling the paint, and he'd come up with a way to lighten his load. Reaching the church, he spun the steering wheel until the front tires bumped up over the curb and onto the sidewalk. The car coasted to a stop in front of the double doors to the chapel.

Eight spotlights lit the front and sides of the building, and the first order of business was to take them out with a baseball bat. The first one popped and shattered as he smashed it, creating much more noise than he'd anticipated. Carl's heart beat wildly, partly from exertion—he was in lousy shape—and partly from fear. He'd been planning this escapade for days, but he hadn't allowed himself to consider what might happen if he got caught. He couldn't afford to worry about it now either. Instead, he did his best to break the lights quickly, racing from one to the next, the ski mask stretched over his face and sticking to his skin, sweat from his forehead soaking into it until it was all he could do not to rip the damn thing off.

Within minutes, the area around the church was doused in darkness, and he saw no sign of reaction from neighboring houses. Too bad it had to be done blindly, he thought, dropping the bat in the trunk and grabbing the first two cans of paint. He would have enjoyed watching it go on—the sloshing motion and the resulting pattern. To see the paint as it washed over the church would have satisfied him twice, once as a man seeking vengeance and again as an artist curious about methods and results. The front of the church was a canvas of sorts, a wide empty space. He thought of the mural painters, covering the walls of churches with graceful figures—Michelangelo lying prone on a scaffold, sweating and gasping as he worked his magic on the Sistine Chapel ceiling. Fra Angelico, Raphael, da Vinci, all of them masters. He knew and revered them, but he didn't delude himself. What he was doing now, this was no magic. This was mischief. After allowing himself one long sigh, he got down to work.

Beforehand, he'd wondered whether the day after would be a terrifying mixture of anxiety and regret, whether he'd pace his living room, waiting for the police to screech up and haul him away. Until now, he'd

never realized how little trust he had in law enforcement, how antago-
nistic and suspicious he was. I'm worse than Ruthanne's boyfriend, he
thought, as he fixed himself a cup of coffee the next morning and
turned on the television. No local news yet. Just Charles Kuralt inton-
ing, "Sunday Morning," and a real-estate magazine. Idly, he sat down
and watched the houses screen past, taking note of square footage and
selling price. Housing prices were going up again, which meant the
worst of the real-estate crisis was over. For years, brand-new high-rise
office buildings had stood vacant while FOR SALE signs rusted in front
yards all across the city. But at long last, things were turning around. It
was a good time to sell, and Carl couldn't help wondering how much
they'd get for this place, once it was cleaned up, of course. He realized
that it didn't kill him to consider it. Only a few months ago, it would
have been unthinkable. He supposed a house in disarray is easier to
shrug off. Witness Hannah, who'd shrugged it off pretty damn easily.

Even so, he knew it would take time and money to ready the house
for the market. He surveyed the whole of the living room, the early-
morning sunlight rendering it all clear: the dust that coated the coffee
table and the entertainment center, the dark tracking of chalk ground
into the hardwood floors. They would have to be stripped now. How
much would that run him? He thought of Hannah's rent, which was
eating up the money they might have used for repairs. The insurance
would cover the sandblasting, but it would be weeks before they got the
check. He got up and poured another cup of coffee, then sat back
down, flipping through the channels once more. Nothing doing. No
local news. It was maddening.

He wanted to see the church, he realized; in fact, he *needed* to see it.
This proprietary feeling was wholly unexpected. No wonder criminals
gave themselves away by showing up at the scene of the crime. The
enforced anonymity was maddening. A crime was an accomplishment
of sorts, and something in him ached to take credit. No one must
know; everyone must know. The feelings were positively schizophrenic.
Before long, Carl had worked around to a sort of compromise: He'd
dress and make a quick drive by. He had to go in to work, anyway;
might as well leave a little early. What harm would it do? They couldn't
pin it on him because he drove down the street, could they?

Carl doubted they could pin it on him at all. He'd been careful; he'd thought it through. Yesterday afternoon, he'd washed the paint cans in the backyard to get rid of fingerprints, and last night he'd worn gardening gloves. Now the paint cans were gone, disposed of in Dumpsters around town. Paint came right off if you caught it quick enough, and God knows he'd been quick. He was home free, he told himself, but just to be doubly sure, he showered again.

By the time he pulled out of the driveway, clouds were rolling in from the west, a mass of dark boomers portending heavy rain. They'd had very little rain over the summer and fall, one sunny hot day after another until the monotony of it became depressing. Bravo for the storm, Carl thought. He was satisfied that the paint on the front of the church was dry, so let it rain. The first drops hit the windshield on the ride across town, but the sky didn't open up the way he expected. Heavy gray clouds eased across the face of the sun, and the world went dark, the landscape and road dimming until car headlights blinked on all around him. Lightning crackled every minute or so, accompanied by a rumbling thunder. As he turned onto the street he'd visited the night before, sheets of rain dropped out of the sky. This might have been a scene from a bad movie—the storm being God's comment on his conduct. Fuck God, he told himself. If Dr. Bill is God's ambassador, the two of them have it coming.

Even in the semidarkness, that first glimpse of the church astonished him. The large oaks along the street hid most of the building, but Carl caught a flash of red and purple as he turned the corner and made his way slowly around the block. After passing the church twice, he eased the Mazda forward and parked as close to the building as he could. Other cars already lined the street along both sides, so he couldn't get within a block. Just as well. One good look and his heart had jumped in his chest. Through the blur of the wipers, he studied the front of the church, pondering it as though it were a work of art he'd labored over. It *was* possible to construe this as artwork, he decided, a late Morris Louis or something, the colors separated into broad stripes across the canvas. People had done worse. It depended on the eye of the beholder. Artwork or terrorism, you be the judge. Either way, the paint wasn't spread as widely as he might have wished. Still, he'd completely covered the front door and the area around it, and he'd managed to get one bucket of black all the way up to the rose window in the center of the chapel.

He'd hesitated to splash the window, the one thing about the church he truly admired. Three times this past week, he'd driven slowly around the building, deciding where to put his efforts, how to approach the task. Once, on a Wednesday evening, the doors had stood open and he'd chanced a quick peek inside. The chapel had been empty, and he'd gotten a good look at the stained glass. It was a nondenominational work of art, religious only in its devotion to pattern, color, and attention to detail. The wheel was divided into twelve spokes, each ending in a smaller circle. Kaleidoscopic in design, some parts resembled snowflakes while others resembled leaves or the petals of flowers. The colors were various, though red was certainly primary. He'd seen lots of blue too, the color of the summer sky, and yellow, rich and yolky. Purple and orange appeared as well, and at least two shades of green, early spring and late spring. All this he remembered; all this he'd blotted out. No rose light would wash over this congregation, not for a long time. Today, it would be dark as night in there.

Carl didn't see Penny coming. She appeared mysteriously—stepping out of the bushes or emerging from the shadows of the yard across the street—opening the door and climbing silently into the passenger seat, as though it had been prearranged, as though he were a husband or a boyfriend picking her up from work. She looked weary, something about the way she grabbed the door handle and jerked it closed. And he could hear her breathing, deep and a little ragged, like a sick person or someone coming off a crying jag. She was soaked to the skin, that wispy hair plastered to her scalp, so that her eyes looked all the larger in her pale face. She sat forward in the seat, back straight, knees together, a good girl's posture. Rather than look at him, she gazed straight ahead at the church.

"I knew you'd show up," she said. Her teeth were chattering. "This is awful. Don't you realize how awful this is?"

Carl was silent. Although he saw no point in proclaiming his innocence, he didn't intend to admit guilt either. No comment, he thought.

"Awful," Penny whispered.

"You've made that observation," he said tightly. Perhaps it *was* awful from some perspectives—Penny's, for instance—but he preferred not to consider that right now. Before she'd gotten in the car, he was working around to viewing the mess as a work of art, and he needed to maintain some hold on that angle. "You're freezing." He leaned forward and, switching the heat to high, busied himself with directing all the vents toward her. "There. Is that better?"

She nodded, but kept her arms pressed to her chest. "Don't you see this makes it worse?" she asked. "I told them they were wrong, and now I'm telling you. This is wrong, Carl."

"It's all wrong," he said flatly. "Only sometimes you're not left with a choice."

He saw now that Penny wasn't dressed for church. She was clad in baggy jeans and a long-sleeved flannel shirt that clung wetly to her. A heavy gold chain around her neck disappeared inside her shirt. While he watched, she fiddled with it, fishing with her fingers for a cross that hung between her breasts. She balled it in her fist and began yanking it along the chain. The car was so quiet he could hear the little grinding noise as she wrenched it back and forth. Her lips were pressed tight, her eyes fixed on the floorboard.

"You always have a choice," she said.

"What's this?" he asked, trying for a tone of gentle mockery. "What's this I hear? Talk of choice from a pro-lifer? They'll kick you out of the church for that, girlie."

She managed a little laugh. "That's pretty much what's happening." Then she turned her face away, to the side window.

"What?" he asked. "What are you talking about?"

But she didn't answer, just went right on with her train of thought. "God always offers more than one path. It's up to us to choose the right one."

"And what if all paths lead to hell?" Carl asked. In conversations like this one, he couldn't help playing the skeptic. Hell, he *was* the skeptic—he'd just vandalized the house of the Lord, for Christ's sake. He didn't believe in God, and there was no looking back now.

Penny turned her face to him. "They don't! They just don't, Carl." She'd used his name, and she was absolutely certain of her convictions. He was grateful, so grateful for both.

The rain fell steadily. Outside the chapel, people continued to gather; most huddled under umbrellas. The women favored bright colors and the men black. It was an interesting tableau, Carl thought, the shifting umbrellas in the foreground, the shocking splashes of paint on the beige brick church, and above all that, a dark and troubled sky. He tried to memorize certain details, the man at the paint-splashed door, for instance, standing like a sentry, holding it open for the women to slip gingerly through.

"Nothing good is going to come of this," Penny told him. She ran the cross along the chain again, back and forth, back and forth.

Carl reached across the seat and closed his hand over hers. "You're going to break that."

Her hand was small and soft, a warm living thing in his grasp. He wanted to groan with the pleasure of it, the unexpected rush of energy passing between them. Already, he'd forgotten the vitality of another life in his hands, the way he yearned to feel another pulse in order to be sure of his own. She was talking, but all he could hear was the blood inside his head.

"Carl, look!" Penny cried, wresting her hand from his to point through the windshield. He turned to see Dr. Bill sweeping up the sidewalk toward them, dressed in a black robe and black cowboy boots. The wind and rain blew the robe back, plastering it to his chest and forcing it between his legs. Out there in the weather, he looked like something from the Old Testament.

"Drive, Carl!" Penny cried. "For God's sake, let's go!"

Carl shifted into gear, but Dr. Bill was already alongside and reaching for the door handle. Carl spun the wheel and the car jerked away from the curb. My God, he thought. Am I going to run him down? Still, he pressed his foot to the gas and they sped up the street. His heart pounded while Penny screamed at him, "Go! Go! Hurry up!" It was crazy, really. You'd have thought the man could wave those arms into black wings, that he was about to take flight in pursuit. Before turning the corner, Carl glanced into the rearview mirror. Dr. Bill stood in the middle of the street, a black figure shrinking into the distance. Even from so far away, he looked stricken and, suddenly, Carl knew why. It wasn't his church he was heartbroken over; no, it wasn't his church at all.

"Shall I take you home?" he asked gently, when they were a mile or so away.

"No," she said. "I can't go there, not right now."

"How about my house, then?" he suggested. "You can dry your clothes. Have a cup of coffee. I need to go to work in an hour or two, but I have time to drop you by somewhere, wherever you want to go."

She glanced over at him, her brow furrowed. He knew what she was thinking.

"My wife's moved out," he said simply.

"Oh, Carl," she breathed. "I'm so sorry."

"Me too," he said. "Maybe it's not permanent. We don't know, really."

They were halfway across town before he spoke the words: "He's in love with you, isn't he? Dr. Bill, I mean."

Penny nodded but kept her face turned away. Her hair, almost dry now, had curled into tendrils that reminded him of ivy—vines and tiny leaves. Several strands slipped under her collar, and he could imagine them sending out feelers, wrapping delicately around her small breasts. No wonder he's in love with you, Carl thought. I may be in love with you myself.

When they reached the house, he hurried her up the paint-splattered sidewalk. He'd given the garage and front door several coats of paint, but the brick still looked like hell. Carl could see that Penny was taking it in. "Your wife moved out because of this?" she asked, waving her hand to indicate all of it, the whole bloody mess.

Carl shrugged. "That's what she said, but it's never one thing, you know?" He unlocked the door and ushered her inside, though his impulse was to rush her right back out. The exterior of the house might be an embarrassment, but it wasn't his fault. The interior surely was. "I'm sorry," he said. "This isn't the way I live. It's just the way I'm living right now." He'd left the television blaring; the real-estate magazine was long over, and a football game was in progress. Carl hit the power switch, and the room lapsed abruptly into silence.

Before Penny could question the plan, he strode back to the bedroom and returned with one of his heavy robes. He had at least three of them. His mother and Hannah's stepmother liked to give him robes for Christmas, though he never wore them. "If you'll put on the robe and give me your clothes, I'll toss them in the dryer." He kept his tone light and cheerful. Any minute, he expected her to panic and run for the door, to realize she was consorting with the enemy. And she did want to protest. Carl could see it on her face, but he gently showed her to the bathroom. Once the door was closed, he sighed deeply and turned away.

The studio was directly across the hall, and he couldn't help looking in and taking note of E.T. But the sight of the cage made him feel guilty. He'd been ignoring his new pet ever since he'd brought him home. It was no sort of life for the bird, staring all day at a bunch of fake flamingos when he'd had a whole cadre of real friends at the pet store. Carl wandered into the studio and over to the cage, where E.T. appeared to be sleeping. The bird had a large bare spot above his left wing. If you didn't know better, you'd have thought he was molting, but Carl knew he was plucking himself bald.

"Hey there, buddy," he said. E.T. gave no response. "Want to get out and take a spin around the house?"

Carl opened the cage door and, with some prodding, managed to get E.T. to step off the perch and onto his wrist. By the time Penny emerged from the bathroom, the bird was inching up Carl's outstretched arm. Penny crossed the hall, holding the bundle of wet clothes against her chest. The robe swallowed her. She looked like a small child dressed in her father's clothes.

"Hello, E.T.," she said. She stepped closer, offering her index finger.

"E.T. phone home?" The bird sounded plaintive. Carl thought of Noah's Ark, empty now, a dark space that looked larger after all the merchandise and cages had been carted away. Lydia reported that a Hallmark store was taking up the lease.

Penny heard the bird's distress. "What's wrong?" she asked.

"He's lived in a pet store most of his life, people in and out, other birds and animals. He's bored and lonely, I guess."

"Poor bird," Penny said.

She dropped the bundle of clothes on a chair and inched closer. She was barefoot and mincing on the seeds and shells that E.T. had scattered. This place is a pit, he thought. Old paint rags hung over every available surface, all of it dusty and cluttered. The yard flamingo had toppled off his Styrofoam pedestal, and he lay now on the floor, as if shot. Maybe a dozen canvases lined the room. Lately, Carl had taken the trouble to line them up, using all the available floor space. The pieces he'd done in pastel were taped to the wall, helter-skelter, some of them crooked.

"Sorry," Carl said, waving a hand as though to make it all disappear. "Ever since Hannah moved out, I can't seem to get it together."

"Did she take your dog?"

"No," Carl said. "Neil died a few weeks ago. He had to be put down."

"Oh," Penny sighed. "I'm so sorry." She glanced around, taking it in. "These are wonderful, Carl."

He was pleased, though he suspected she was trying to make him feel better.

"Do you paint every day?"

"Lately. I'm on a streak. Can't stop painting. That's the way it is sometimes."

She moved over to the right wall, where the new work was clustered. These paintings were mostly of children, done in acrylics, using photographs from old copies of *Life*, snapshots of himself and his brother Buddy as boys, and, most recently, one of Hannah's mother, Naomi, when she was a girl. Penny stopped directly in front of this one.

"Who's this?" she asked.

Carl shrugged. How to explain Naomi, someone he'd never met, a dead woman who'd exerted a presence in his life for over seventeen years? "Hannah's mother," he said simply.

He'd recreated the image just as he saw it, Naomi squinting into the sun, her hand up in a tentative wave. She'd been a cute kid with a biggish nose, long hair done up in lopsided pigtails. He'd rendered the photograph faithfully, in black and white. Then, when the picture was complete, he'd taken his widest brush and X'ed through the whole thing with a shimmering shade of lavender. He recalled what Lydia had said about lavender—that it's a moody color. And this was a moody painting. The image of Naomi hadn't been entirely lost. It could still be seen, vaguely, in the spaces around the X, and even through the sheen of color. Carl cocked his head, trying to get a glimpse of his art through the eyes of another. Moving or morbid? He had no idea what Penny might be seeing. Nothing to cheer her up, that was for sure.

He stepped over to her, seeds cracking and busting under his Rockports, and taking her by the arm, tried to lead her away. "Come on. Let's get out of here."

She shook him off and continued studying the canvas.

"This is just shit," he said.

She wheeled about. "Don't ever say that about your work!" she cried. E.T. screeched and tried to fly off Carl's shoulder. "I'm sorry," Penny said. She raised a hand, as though to soothe the bird.

"Nothing to be sorry about," Carl replied. He wasn't sure what to do, so he went with instinct, folding her into his arms, a small, warm thing he pressed to him with such force that he expected her to cry out.

She didn't; she was entirely silent. After a few seconds, her arms rose from her sides and wrapped around his waist. She felt entirely different from Hannah. Always, Hannah had responded to his embrace as a sort of entrapment, like cats he'd held that resisted from the inside, a tension he could feel, even as they lay in his lap and allowed him to stroke them. His pleasure in their company was tainted because he knew that they were only humoring him, that their real desire was to be set free. His wife was the same, always guarding herself, always asserting her autonomy.

But Penny's body seemed to melt into his. He could barely feel her breathing; already, her breath had synchronized with his. My God, he thought, what would it be like to make love to this woman, someone who wanted to be close, the closer the better? He felt himself stirring and willed it to stop. This wasn't the time, though his body yearned for it, to hold her against him, skin to skin.

"Are you okay?" he asked.

She nodded, her head moving against his collarbone, her face burrowing into his shirt. He raised his hand to stroke her hair, feathery and fine, thin enough that he could feel the warmth of her scalp against his palm. "Don't worry," he whispered. "You'll see. It's going to be all right."

Chapter 21

Mrs. Pilsner was back in the hospital, and Hannah had put off visiting for as long as she could. Today was the day. As she left her apartment, it occurred to her that flowers would be nice, something cheery. The day was dreary, mostly overcast and with a chilly wind. The local florist she'd spotted just down the street was closed on Sundays, so her only choice was a grocery store. She stopped in at H.E.B.'s on her way across town, expecting to grab up the obligatory cellophane-wrapped bouquet, only to discover a garden. "My goodness," she breathed. Buckets brimmed with long-stemmed white gladiolus, yellow lilies, purple iris, and a multitude of other blooms whose names she didn't know.

What to get for Dorothy Pilsner? Hannah barely knew the principal's wife, but on the few occasions they'd met, she'd found her to be pleasant and obliging, the sort of woman who seems as interested in you as she is in herself. A rarity, in other words. Wouldn't it be nice, she thought, to truly please Dorothy? Perhaps to guess her favorite flower or some such thing? Hannah picked up a stem of white stock and, bringing it to her nose, breathed in its spicy scent. For an instant or two, the smell released her from her daily rounds. I need to get away somewhere, she thought. And yet, she'd already done that, hadn't she? Moved out of her house and into a strange, clean building. Every night, she went to sleep surrounded by four white walls, not a thing on them, which was just the way she wanted it. Even so, getting away had a cost. It had left her unmoored, as her stepmother might say, cast adrift in the odd limbo land of the suddenly single, and at the worst time of the year.

Hannah browsed through the buckets, admiring the lilies and gladiolus, dusty-red roses and deep-blue iris. So much choice made the decision difficult, but at last she settled on an orchid with two tongue-shaped green leaves and one creamy white bloom, its center shot through with veins of red and purple. Picking up the plant, she had the sense of discovering something rare and beautiful, and she carried it carefully to the front of the store.

Seton Hospital was only a few blocks from Highland Mall, and Hannah planned a little Christmas shopping after the visit, anything to stay out of her oh-so-silent apartment. She parked in front of the hospital, which looked more like an office building than anything else, and took the elevator up to the sixth floor, Oncology. Mrs. Pilsner's room was at the end of the hall. Hannah hesitated outside the door, both hands wrapped around the green plastic pot. For a few uncertain seconds, she studied the silky white flower dangling upside down from a long thin stem. It appeared so fragile.

"Can I help you?" a woman's voice called out.

Startled, Hannah looked up to find a big busty nurse wearing pastel-printed scrubs and a huge smile striding toward her.

"I'm here to see Dorothy Pilsner," she said, moving aside while the nurse knocked briefly then called out, "Dorothy, better cover up, darlin'! You've got a visitor!"

"Is Mr. Pilsner here?" Hannah whispered.

"Harry's always here," the nurse replied. "The man is one of the most devoted husbands I've ever met. We should all be so lucky."

Hannah nodded. "I know," she said. "He's my boss."

"You're lucky too, then," the nurse remarked as she swung open the door. "Visitor!" she sang out.

Hannah stepped inside and was immediately struck by the scent of raspberries. "Smells good in here," she remarked cheerily, taking her cue from the nurse.

Mr. Pilsner was seated at the end of the bed. He looked up and smiled. "It's this lotion," he explained, waving a pale hand toward a pink plastic bottle half hidden in the sheets. "She just loves a good foot rub." He held one of Dorothy's feet in his lap and, as Hannah watched, ran his long fingers under the arch and around the ankle, caressing and kneading. Dorothy's toes were lacquered a bright red, oddly incongruent with the white sheets and Mr. Pilsner's tan khaki trousers. In fact, the foot itself seemed disconnected, as though it didn't belong to the woman in the bed, who bore no resemblance to the Dorothy Pilsner Hannah remembered. Part of the problem was the wig she wore, a synthetic mop of brown that covered her forehead and curled up around her cheeks and eyes, which were pinched shut. The woman in the bed looked diminished, on the verge of disappearing. A prickling dread made its way up Hannah's spine. She held still and waited for it to pass, wishing all the while for the reassurance of Carl's presence. He was better with people than she was, warmer, more accepting.

Trying to look relaxed, Hannah glanced around. As hospital rooms went, this one was pleasant enough, sunny and not too cramped. A well-worn, blue-upholstered recliner fit between the bed and the wall. Hannah took in the stack of computer printouts beside the chair, several travel magazines, a Tom Clancy novel.

"How's it going?" Mr. Pilsner asked in a low voice.

"Fine, I guess," she whispered. "We miss you. How are you holding up?"

A little shrug followed by a squeeze of his wife's foot. "As well as can be expected. No need to whisper, Hannah. She's the devil to wake up these days."

"You look good," Hannah told him. It was true. His pale skin had a peachy glow, and he appeared rested, though Hannah couldn't imagine that he was getting much sleep in that chair.

"Strange, isn't it?" he said. "I look at myself in the mirror, and I think, Why aren't you dead, man?" He shook his head. The word *dead* reverberated in the room. Hannah glanced toward Dorothy, who appeared asleep, breathing with a little panting sound.

"I'll try and wake her in a minute," Mr. Pilsner promised.

"No need," she told him. "I can always come back."

He shook his head. "It doesn't matter when you come. These days, she's nearly always asleep. The morphine knocks her right out. Problem is, we've got to the point where we need it all the time. If we're not sleeping, we're in misery." He shrugged and looked at Hannah, noticing for the first time the orchid she clutched to her chest. "How beautiful," he said. "Here, let's put it where she can see it." Carefully, Mr. Pilsner tucked his wife's foot back beneath the sheets before turning to clear the bedside table. Hannah placed the orchid where it could be seen from the bed. The flower quivered, then went still.

Mr. Pilsner put a hand on his wife's shoulder and shook her gently. "Dot," he said, once, then again a little louder. "Dot?"

She opened her eyes, blinking them into focus. "Yes, dear?"

"Hannah's here to see you."

"Han-nah," she breathed.

She makes my name sound lovely, Hannah thought, like a gift. Suddenly, it was all she could do not to cry. "Hello, Dorothy."

"Hannah's brought you a gift," Mr. Pilsner said, pointing to the orchid.

Obligingly, his wife turned her head to admire it. "Isn't that lovely?" She brought a hand from beneath the sheet and reached for the plant, fingering the bloom with trembling fingers. "It won't get enough light here," she told her husband. "Let's put it over on the glass shelf." She watched him carry it to the window, then drifted back to sleep.

"She can't help herself," Mr. Pilsner explained.

"I understand," Hannah replied.

He couldn't help himself either. Already, he was returning to his station at the end of the bed. While Hannah watched, he pulled his wife's foot into his lap and squeezed another dollop of lotion into his palm. "It'll be Christmas break before you know it," he said. "I'm not sure I'll be back after the holidays."

"Take whatever time you need."

"Afraid it's not a matter of that anymore," he replied sadly. "All that's behind us now." He looked up at Hannah, his eyes shining. "Dot and I have been married for over thirty years," he said. "For better, for worse. To look at us, you might think this is the 'for worse' part, but somehow it's not." He bent and kissed the top of his wife's foot. "At least not for me. I've never felt closer to her. Just wish it wasn't almost over."

When Hannah got ready to leave, she put a hand on his shoulder and asked him not to get up. "I can show myself out," she said.

"You'll give Carl my best, won't you?"

"I will," she promised as she backed out of the room.

For some time, she sat in her Blazer in the hospital parking lot and concentrated on the heat of the sun as it penetrated the windshield. She stared at her hands gripping the steering wheel, at the blue lacing of veins visible just under the skin, and eventually turned her gaze outside, on the bare trees bordering the street and the cars passing in and out of the lot. She listened to the sound of her breath going in and out and felt terribly alone. "You silly fool," she muttered to herself and, turning the key in the ignition, backed slowly out of the space.

She was grateful for the hustle and bustle of the mall. To be swept up in a crowd, to be simply another face in a sea of faces, it was exactly what she needed. For a while she wandered in and out of stores, picking up music boxes and baskets full of soap and empty picture frames, content to run her fingers along the edges of things. When at last she got down to the work of shopping, she went through the list quickly— a Humpty Dumpty cookie jar for Harriet, a computer golf game for her father, a basket of goodies for the two of them—gourmet coffee beans, smoked salmon, imported crackers.

That done, Hannah remembered Carl's mother, who was about the same age as Dorothy Pilsner. I'll buy something nice for Inez, she thought, something I can wrap and put in the mail this week, perhaps sign the card *Love, Carl and Hannah.* In the past, Hannah had never bothered to pick out a gift for her mother-in-law. Carl took care of his own relatives, and she evinced so little interest that he rarely even bothered to show her what he'd bought. This year, she was determined to change her ways. At Dillard's, she picked out a costly silk scarf, a brilliant swatch of gold and blue splashed with wine red, and chose a gold tulip pin to go with it, tucking both into a small gift box. While the salesgirl rang up her purchases, Hannah imagined her mother-in-law calling Carl the following Sunday. Wouldn't he be surprised when she thanked him? "The most thoughtful gift I've received in years,"

Inez might say. To which he would make a stuttering reply, "I'm—we're so glad you liked it."

It was after eight by the time Hannah unlocked the door to her apartment and let herself inside. She'd managed to kill the whole day and had only an hour or two until time for bed. Most evenings she sat on the rented brown couch of her anonymous living room, the television on for company, waiting for someone to call. Generally, no one did. Her new answering machine went days without taking a message. To be sure it worked, she'd called herself from the high school and left a message, "Hello, Hannah." Sad to say, messages from herself had become the extent of her communication with the world. Several times this past week she'd managed to feel good and sorry for herself. Not tonight, though. Visiting the Pilsners had put her own woes into perspective. And, happily, as soon as she walked in the door, the phone began to ring. Carl, she thought. Her heart lifted; she dropped her bags and dived for the phone.

"Did he do it?" Helen asked. No hello or how are you, just this odd question.

"Do what?" Glancing down, Hannah noticed her machine was blinking. Four messages, a windfall. "Did you call earlier?"

"I've been calling off and on all day." That in itself was surprising. Helen hadn't been calling at all. In the first place, she disapproved of Hannah's move, but there was more to it. On their return from Tyler, Slick Jimmy had talked himself back into his wife's good graces, and in the same breath, he'd talked Hannah out of them. He'd confessed to the affair with Cecile, among other things, and begged for another chance. Of all people, he credited his sister-in-law with his born-again-husband status. It had all started, he said, with the talk they'd had on Halloween night. As a consequence of this revelation, Hannah was on Helen's it'll-be-a-cold-day-in-hell list. "You didn't say a word to me about seeing Jimmy at the high school," she'd fumed. "All that time we spent in the car together, driving back and forth to Tyler, and you never even mentioned it!" It had been over a week since they'd talked; Hannah was thankful for the sound of her sister's voice. "Tell me, Hannah—I'm dying to know."

"What? Know what?"

"You haven't heard, then? Where have you been?" Helen cried. "Where the hell have you been all day?"

"Well, let's see." She ticked off her day. "Seton Hospital to see Mrs. Pilsner, Highland Mall for Christmas shopping, then I stopped in at Luby's for dinner. Just got home."

"So you haven't seen the news?"

"No," Hannah said, a note of irritation creeping in. "What is it?"

Finally, Helen explained herself. It was on the news, she explained, the lead story, all about the paint-splattered chapel of Gospel Fellowship. "You remember that blond woman who came to your house?" Helen asked. "The reporter? She was out in front of the church, giving all the details. 'No one's been arrested yet,' blah, blah, blah. You should see it, Hannah. Red, black, and purple paint, big honking stripes up the side of the church! Someone knew what they were doing, and it just occurred to me that my brother-in-law—"

"Have you talked to Carl?" Hannah interrupted.

"I tried, but he wasn't home. I thought . . . I thought maybe you were out together."

"No. He was at work, but he should be home by now." Hannah was thinking. "Don't say a word to anyone. You hear me? He could go to jail."

"So you think it was him? This is so crazy, Hannah—"

"Helen. Just sit tight, okay? I'll call and let you know."

Twenty minutes later, Hannah pulled into the driveway of her old house. Except for the light in the studio, the place was dark. She'd decided not to warn Carl that she was coming, and parking the Blazer in front, she felt her resolve draining away. Maybe she should have given him a chance to prepare himself. What if he wasn't pleased to see her? He could be so cold, Carl. As she stepped off the sidewalk and into the grass, Hannah took a deep breath and clenched and unclenched her fists. The blinds in his studio were open, as usual. It never occurred to him to want or need privacy. He went about his business and assumed others went about theirs. "Some people don't have any business," Hannah had told him more than once. To which he'd simply shrugged: "That's their problem."

Now she edged into the square of light on the lawn and peered into the window. Carl stood directly in front of her; only the panes of glass separated them. He was dressed in a pair of old gray sweatpants, but his smooth chest was bare, and it seemed he'd lost weight these last few weeks. She couldn't see his expression, but his posture was relaxed. He held up a small paintbrush as though it were a lighted candle and stared at the canvas in front of him. He'd always been able to fix his attention on one thing to the exclusion of everything else. For a few minutes, Hannah concentrated on sending him her thoughts. I'm out here, Carl, only a few feet away. Look up! Look out the window! After so many years, shouldn't he sense her presence, feel her stare? But no—she realized she could stand here all night, grow moss on her back. The bird in the cage next to him would be more likely to take notice than Carl.

Hannah returned to the porch to ring the bell. It felt strange, pressing the buzzer on her own front door. After what seemed a long time, the porch light went on, and he opened the door. "Hello, Carl," she said. She was aware of the thickness in her voice, the tentative way she was standing, one foot on the top step, as though braced for flight. "Can I come in?" she asked. "I thought we should talk." So cautious, so mannerly. She hardly recognized herself. Or him either. His face looked thinner too, his eyes more recessed.

He hesitated, still holding the brush, then without a word stepped back to let her enter. The living room was dark, but she recognized the smell. There was a hint of lemon in it and something bitter, like the scent of geraniums, overlaid with the odors of the artist—the turpentine and gesso and sweat. Hannah breathed it in, relieved for the smells of the familiar.

"Hold on a minute," Carl said, turning back down the hallway to his studio. Alone in the dark living room, Hannah reached over and switched on the lamp. The room was orderly; he'd done some housecleaning since she'd left. Dusted? She ran a fingertip over the surface of the end table; it came away clean. A bulky-looking machine stood in the middle of the floor. She circled it a couple of times and decided it must be a sander. Was he getting ready to refinish the floors? In a minute, Carl returned, drying his hands on an old towel.

"You all right?" she asked.

He shrugged. "Maybe, maybe not. What time is it, anyway?" She looked down at her watch.

"Nearly ten."

"Well, good." A wry smile crossed his face, something she recognized. "I guess you're just in time to see the news."

So she had her answer. Even so, she couldn't quite believe it. Driving over, Hannah had considered all she knew of Carl and decided someone else had to be responsible. The Carl she knew simply wasn't the vengeful sort. He'd always been so patient, so forgiving of her tantrums and of his parents' shortcomings. So ready to see the other person's perspective, to let bygones be bygones. He wasn't especially brave either, and committing a crime like this required a certain sort of courage, didn't it? Carl had avoided the draft by going to college, and as soon as the war was over, he'd abruptly stopped taking classes, halfway through a master's degree. Such a waste, she always told him, but nothing had ever seemed to matter that much to him. By nature, he was easily contented, or so she'd always thought.

The "paint bombing" of Gospel Fellowship was the lead story. Sitting beside Carl on the sofa, Hannah felt her attention divided between the screen and the expressions flickering across her husband's face—puzzlement, satisfaction, and then, at Dr. Bill's appearance, contempt. The newswoman speculated that the vandalism was an act of retribution, and in the brief interview a harried-looking Dr. Bill agreed. As soon as the minister appeared on the screen, Carl mumbled, "Fight fire with fire, right, asshole?" So angry, Hannah thought; it was a side of him she'd rarely seen.

"My God," she said when the segment was over. "I'm still in shock. Helen called about eight to ask if you'd done this, and it was the first I'd heard of it." She slapped her forehead with the heel of her hand. "I told her I'd find out. She's dying to hear. She thought it was you, but I told myself no. I would have bet no, Carl."

He'd been staring at the screen while she spoke, but now he turned his gaze on her. His beautiful blue eyes were dark and serious, piercing really. It was all she could do not to look away. "See," he said, "you really don't know me, and what's worse, you don't know yourself. You think living with someone for years makes you an expert, but it doesn't, not unless you pay attention. You haven't been paying attention, Hannah."

She flushed but was determined not to be angry. "I've been paying attention," she protested.

"To other things," he said. "Not to me."

She bit her lip. "There's some truth to that," she replied haltingly. "But—"

"But what?" he interrupted. "Things are gonna change now that you're living across town? I find that hard to believe."

"The apartment's temporary. It's just for a month or two. I'm lonely, Carl. I miss you."

He turned and searched her face. "Do you?" he asked.

"Yes. We've been together so long. . . . I've been thinking how important that is." She reached out to touch his arm; then, before he could pull away, she leaned over and put her lips to his cheek. "Thank you," she murmured.

Carl sighed and turned his mouth to hers. She'd always enjoyed the way he kissed, slowly but insistently. Back when they'd first met, all that passion had been downright frightening. Now she knew to trust it. It was what she loved the most in him, this great excess of feeling. They kissed like school kids, long and lingering, Hannah running her fingers up the length of Carl's arm while he cupped her face in his hands. They held back like school kids too, afraid to touch too much, to go too far. Afraid the other would say no. Finally, Hannah slipped a hand around his neck and ran her fingernails lightly over his shoulder blades, something that often made him shiver with pleasure. He moaned. "Aren't you cold?" she whispered.

"Not now," he whispered back.

He took her hand and led her down the hall to the bedroom. They didn't turn on lights, but even in the darkness Hannah could sense the mounds of discarded clothes on the floor. When he laid her down on the bed, she felt something hard press against the small of her back. A magazine, a sketchbook? She wasn't sure. She took a deep breath and tried to drop into it. This was all so familiar—this house, their room, the man in her arms—but it was strange too, like returning to her old bedroom in Tyler and her father's careful embrace. She knew by heart how these things felt—or rather, another Hannah knew them, the Hannah she'd been twenty years ago, ten years ago, two weeks ago. To move backward, to slip into the old skin, even one shed so recently, was it still possible?

They undressed quickly, Carl shedding his sweatpants, Hannah her jeans and blouse, as though both of them sensed that hurrying was important. She knew that if either of them were to think about what they were doing, one might back away. Immediately, Carl bent his head to her breasts, his mouth to her nipples, sucking and kissing, his blunt fingers cupping them in a way that thrilled her. From the very beginning, he had loved her breasts. The first time they ever made love, back in college, he'd moaned aloud when his mouth touched her nipple. Now he did it again, a low groan of contentment that released her, moved her in a way nothing else could.

Just before Carl entered her, as he rolled over and covered her with his body, Hannah put both hands on his shoulders and pressed down hard, digging her fingernails into his flesh. It was an old move, but they both felt the difference. She was rougher tonight, insistent on giving back a little of the hurt she'd felt on the couch. I know you, she thought. I know you, you bastard. How dare you say I don't? He held still for an instant before thrusting inside her; her hips rose to meet him. "I know you," she murmured. "I know this." It was true; she knew it as well as she knew anything in this life. Carl didn't answer; she wasn't sure he heard, and in another moment she no longer cared. She locked her feet at the small of his back and held on tight. On dark nights, sex could carry you away, and Hannah wanted to be taken— over a long distance, far enough so it would take all night long to return.

The next morning, he had to shake her awake. She opened her eyes to the naked sight of him. Seeing him standing over her—his long legs and torso, long arms, and long, thin cock—she recalled the time she'd discovered some nude sketches Carl had done of himself, distorting his body lines, elongating them, like a painting by Goya. Did you do this on purpose, she'd wanted to ask, or is this really the way you see yourself?

"Good morning," she greeted him, smiling shyly, and reaching out to touch the inside of his thigh. She was naked too, under the sheets, and aroused.

He leaned down; those blue eyes gazing into hers. "One thing," he said softly, stroking her hair. "One thing you have to understand. What you saw last night on TV—I didn't do it for you."

Hannah pulled away, curling into the sheets and blankets. "I know you didn't do it for me, Carl," she said stiffly, but that wasn't exactly the truth, and both of them knew it. He turned and left the room. Afterward, she couldn't force herself out of bed. For some time, she lay motionless, hoping he'd come back and say something to release her. She heard a few noises from the kitchen—Carl making coffee—then his steps in the hallway. Maybe he'd carry in two cups, she imagined, hand her one, say something nice.

Instead, he turned in at his studio and closed himself inside. She heard his voice from behind the door—comforting, lulling sounds. He's talking to the bird, she thought. He'd rather talk to the damn bird than to me! Remembering the way she'd cried out to him in the darkness, she wished she could take it back. She felt embarrassed and vulnerable, as though she'd given herself over to a stranger. You're right, she thought. I don't know you at all.

It was a little after seven-thirty when Hannah pulled into the high school's side lot, which was set aside for teachers and staff. She whipped the Blazer into the space reserved for her—ASST. PRIN. #1 spray-painted in white on the asphalt—and quickly checked her makeup before getting out. Hugging her leather briefcase to her chest, she crossed the half-empty lot to the building. Good thing her apartment was close by, just across the river. She'd barely had time to shower and put her hair up. Pressing a suit was out of the question. She looked rumpled, yes, but otherwise presentable.

Inside, the dark halls were strangely silent. The first bell rang at eight, but lots of students arrived early, some to socialize, others to finish homework and conduct last-minute meetings. Most teachers, on the other hand, showed up at the very last minute. It was written into their contracts these days, the last to arrive, the first to leave. She glanced around the main hallway, checking her watch—7:40 already.

Something was wrong. Ordinarily, the more-dedicated teachers would have been taking off their coats and getting ready for the day, calling back and forth to one another, loitering in the halls in small knots and sipping coffee.

Halfway to her office, Hannah spotted someone approaching from the other end of the hallway. "Clendon?" she called. "Is that you?" He scuttled forward, waving his arms wildly, looking for all the world like the Scarecrow in *The Wizard of Oz*. "What is it?" she asked.

"Dr. Solace," he cried. Such a formal man; he treated her with a deference she found both endearing and aggravating. When he reached her side, he patted her shoulder, a gesture of consolation that froze Hannah where she stood. "You don't know, do you?" he said. "I think you'd better follow me." He took her hand and led her down the center hallway to the main doors. As they approached, Hannah could see that a crowd had gathered at the entrance outside, so many people they blocked the light. "What in the world are they looking at?" she asked Clendon.

"Excuse me," he called, pushing through the doors. Faces turned in their direction, some strange, others familiar. A murmur arose. "Here she comes," Hannah heard. Then someone pressed in close and whispered in her ear: "Hold your head up. Don't let 'em get you down." Hannah couldn't place the voice, and when she turned to look, whoever it was had melted into the crowd.

"What is it, Clendon?" she asked, a little frightened now, but he was in front of her and didn't turn around.

Even after they'd shouldered their way to the front steps, Hannah still couldn't see what the fuss was about. Too many people, too many cars. In the few minutes since she'd arrived, the traffic out front had increased. Students were being dropped off at the curb, just as they normally were, but this morning parents weren't pulling away and kids weren't bounding up the walk to the building. Instead, everyone clustered at the edge of the sidewalk, milling about with wide-open eyes and gaping mouths. Oh dear God, she thought. Surely it's not happening again.

"What's going on?" she asked aloud. She could hear the tremor in her voice.

"You don't want to know," someone muttered.

"Bunch of religious assholes, Dr. Solace," a boy called. "Don't pay any attention."

"Oh, no," Hannah whispered.

Clendon put an arm around her and drew her up on a wide brick ledge a few feet above the top step. In a second or two, Hannah found her balance and focused on the scene below: a small procession of six women and one man marching up and down the front sidewalk. The man was Dr. Bill. Hannah recognized him immediately. He was wearing a baseball cap pulled down over his eyes and a pair of snug black jeans. The slight swagger to his walk infuriated her. Just who did he think he was, a rock star? Hannah thought. Each of them hoisted placards: One shouted the word SHAME in big red letters; another read ABORTION STOPS A BEATING HEART. For a moment, Dr. Bill's sign was blocked from view by the crowd of teenagers gathered on the lawn. But as he strode past, she could see it clearly, the message blocked out in letters even the most illiterate student could read: HANNAH SOLACE KILLED HER BABY. She thought she might faint. She grabbed Clendon James's scrawny shoulder and held on tight.

"Has anyone called the police?" she finally asked.

A whole group of her colleagues had gathered on the steps, most of them teachers from the main floor, including Dorothea Blerin, the music teacher, and Hannah's secretary, Janet. Ever efficient, Janet nodded. "They're sending out a couple of patrol cars, but they've already told us—there's not much they can do."

"You mean"—Hannah squeezed Clendon's shoulder until he flinched beneath her grasp—"this is going to continue? There's nothing we can do?"

"I'd say what's done is done," Janet replied in an even voice. She went on squinting into the bright sunshine, not looking Hannah's way. "And I'd say it's pretty horrible, all right."

Hannah's face smarted. Humiliation didn't cover what she felt; she couldn't think of a word that did. Bending down, she slipped off her heels and, in her stocking feet, jumped from the ledge to the top stair. "Excuse me," she said again and again. "I'm sorry. I have to get by."

Once she was in her office with the door locked, Hannah thought of calling Carl, but no sooner had she picked up the receiver than she put it down again. How could she call him? What would she say? She pushed aside a stack of papers and let her head sink to the desk. She wanted to cry; crying would have been a relief, but for the moment she was beyond tears.

Shortly before nine, she slipped out of her office, still in her stocking feet. The last thing she wanted to hear was the authoritative click, click, click of her high heels. What a racket I made, she thought. Who did I think I was fooling? Thankfully, most everyone was in class now; for the most part, she had the dark hallways to herself. She found an empty classroom on the second floor, a science lab overlooking the school's front lawn. By the time she reached the bank of windows, police cars had arrived and officers stood on the sidewalk, talking to the protesters, who had halted their inane marching but were still hoisting signs. All except Dr. Bill. He was arguing with the officer, who must have confiscated his sign and was at present holding it away from him. After a minute or two, Dr. Bill jerked off his baseball cap in frustration and tossed it to the ground. He began yelling, his mouth open wide, his gestures so expansive that the patient policeman had to back up to keep from being hit. Was he talking about her, then? Hannah wondered. Was he this mad at her? Then it dawned on her: his church. He was furious about what had happened to his church, and somehow or another, he'd decided to blame her. How did he know? How on earth did he know?

Now the officer shifted his stance, swinging the sign around so that it was directly in her field of vision. HANNAH SOLACE KILLED HER BABY. Seeing it a second time and in another's hands was even worse somehow. Hannah felt the classroom expand around her, the four walls stretching back and back, the windows moving out and away, until she seemed to be standing on the very edge of the earth, absolutely on the edge and utterly alone. She took a breath and held it in her lungs. Relax, she told herself; you're doing the best you can. Then she gripped the windowsill and held on.

An hour later, the same policeman stopped by her office. He was still the picture of patience, a short, freckled fellow who insisted on calling her ma'am. He told her the protesters were gone for the day but that he couldn't make guarantees. "I don't think they'll be returning," he said with a little shrug, "but I couldn't say for sure." She wondered if he was always this abashed or if the school building did it to him. Maybe he was just embarrassed for her, though she'd have thought he'd be beyond all that by now. He went on to tell her that Dr. Bill had nearly managed to get himself arrested, not for his slanderous sign but because he had threatened an officer. "We gave him the choice of leaving or going to jail." He looked pleased, as though Dr. Bill's temper were the solution to all of their problems. No, no, no, Hannah wanted to tell him. It's the cause.

She'd just gotten back to work when Mr. Pilsner phoned. "Oh dear, Hannah," he said. "I wish I were there to give you a hug. Has someone given you a hug?"

"Certainly," she said. Clendon had given her a hug, she thought, or at least he'd put an arm around her.

"Dorothy says not to let them get you down." He paused and Hannah heard him say, "What, honey?" Another long pause as he listened to his wife then repeated her words: "Life is too precious. You hear that, Hannah?"

"I hear," she said. "How did you find out?"

A hesitation. "An old friend called. A school-board member, as it happens."

Hannah sighed.

"Yes, I guess there'll be a meeting, but don't you worry. You've done nothing wrong, Hannah. Nothing. Best thing you can do is take the rest of the day off. Go on. Get yourself home."

Hannah thought about it, remembered her empty apartment and all those blank walls staring at her. "No," she said. "That would just make it harder to come back tomorrow." She couldn't tell him the truth, that she'd given up her home and her husband and wasn't sure how to get them back again. At the moment, that seemed the worst thing, the very worst thing of all.

The afternoon was uneventful. No one else came to her office, no one except Janet, who carried in all sorts of busywork, forms to be filled out, letters to be written. The two of them managed not to look at each other and, except for the stray word or two, not to speak. Finally, the last bell rang for the day. After the parking lot emptied and the outer office went quiet, Hannah began to breathe easier. She hadn't realized what an effort it had been, sitting up straight in that chair all day, typing words into her computer.

She was packing her briefcase to go home when she heard a tentative little rapping on the door. If she sat still, whoever it was would go away, she thought, but out of habit, out of sheer resignation, she called out, "Come in." Her heart lifted at the sight of Erica, who stepped halfway into her office.

"Come in, Erica," Hannah said again. "I'm glad to see you." It was true. She felt this girl's presence as a sort of gift.

"Dr. Solace, how are you?" Erica asked. She stood back, nearly against the door she'd closed behind her. She was wearing black stretch pants, a man's blue work shirt that hung nearly to her knees, and a battered pair of Doc Martens. Hannah noticed the ponytail was gone. Now Erica sported one of those spiky haircuts that had cropped up in the halls recently. Any shorter and it would have been a crew cut. It shouted rebellion, but Hannah had to admit that the severity of it was becoming to Erica, accentuating her angular cheekbones and heavy-lidded eyes.

"Fine," Hannah said, then dismissed the word with a pained expression. "I've been better," she admitted.

"I wanted to talk to you," Erica said earnestly. And as she came closer, Hannah realized it wasn't just the hair that had changed. Erica had undergone a metamorphosis in the last couple of months, putting on weight in her hips and legs—not much, really, but enough to take her the distance from girlhood to womanhood. It saddened Hannah to see it. She leaned over and flipped open the top of a small cooler she kept under her desk. "Want a Diet Coke?"

Erica waved away the offer. "Nix on the caffeine," she said. "Nix on the NutraSweet." Yes to the pregnancy, Hannah thought. So would Erica tell her today, and if she did, should Hannah mention the lunch with her father?

"Is it okay if I sit down?" Erica's tone was absolutely deferential.

"Certainly," Hannah replied, waving toward the little metal chair in front of her.

Erica sat down on the very edge of the seat, legs spread out in front of her for balance. "Lots of kids are really sorry for what's happening to you," she began.

"And lots aren't, right?" When Erica opened her mouth to backtrack, Hannah put up a hand. "Forget I said that. Okay?"

The girl shrugged. "You know, Dr. Solace. There are always jerks, wherever you go. Last summer, in California, I was expecting crowds of cool people."

"And you didn't find them?"

"No-o-o." She drew out the one-syllable word and shook her head. "But the thing is, you don't always know who's cool and who's not— not right away, anyway. It's like what you've been told all your life." Here, she made a self-deprecating face and her voice went singsong. " 'You can't judge a book by its cover.' Only we can't help it. We're drawn to what's beautiful on the outside."

"So there were things you liked about California?"

"You know the thing I liked best about it?" Erica asked. Hannah took a sip of Coke and waited for her to go on. "My baby brother. Isn't that the weirdest? I mean, while I was there, I resented him like hell, but after I left, well, I start missing the little bugger."

Hannah nodded.

"All of a sudden, I realized how *cool* he is." She pressed her lips together and shoved her chin out. With that spiky hair, the expression looked defiant, but Hannah knew that Erica was trying to keep from crying. "He'd wake up in the morning, and he'd yell for *me*. Someone else would be holding him, and if I walked by, he'd reach for *me*." She smiled broadly.

"So you still miss him?"

Erica's face crumpled. "So much," she managed to say; then she got up and turned away. Hannah wondered if Erica had told her father about Stephen and whether his knowing would make matters better or worse. It depended, really, on where Gabe was with his ex-wife. If he still loved her, the very idea of Stephen would only infuriate him. If not, it might make things easier between them.

Erica was studying the painting on the far wall, the three children on a country road, and Hannah sensed that the girl was working her way toward a confession. Waiting for it, Hannah's heart grew heavy.

"I've decided to have my own baby," Erica finally said. "I'm already four months along."

Hannah sighed. It was a relief, really, to have it out in the open. "Oh, Erica. It's not my business, but you know—"

Erica interrupted and held out her hand. "Don't explain. Don't apologize. I know how bad my timing is, but I just had to tell you. Right now. I couldn't wait. It's all I've been thinking about all day." She offered Hannah a rueful smile. "You remember the surfer I told you about."

"Of course." Hannah recalled their trip to the health clinic. It seemed so long ago, but not that much time had passed. Erica was pregnant then and she was pregnant now, hardly even showing yet.

"For the first couple of months," she went on, "I didn't know anything was different about me. I mean, I've never paid much attention to my body. I'm in it, but I'm not in it. By the time it dawned on me, I was home from California and missing Stephen something terrible. In love with a baby. Isn't that the worst?"

Hannah had been holding her breath, and she let it go then, in one long rush. "Have you told your father?" Of course, she knew the answer, but it seemed the right question to ask. And she was hoping, hoping Erica and her father had made some progress since the lunch at Chuy's.

Erica smirked and nodded. "Now, that sounds more like the old assistant principal talking, Dr. Solace. Yeah, I told him. He's taken to calling me 'the unwed mother.' 'So, what's the unwed mother want for breakfast?' Shit like that."

Hannah shuddered. She could just hear him.

"As though it's the worst thing you can be." Erica stopped for a second, took a long ragged breath. "See, I don't understand it. You have an abortion, Dr. Solace, and that's the worst thing. 'Selfish,' they say, 'so selfish.' And I *don't* have one," Erica continued, "and that's the worst thing too. I'm simplifying, I know, but so are they. Is it age? At your age, any baby should be a blessing. At my age, no baby should be? Is it being married? Anybody who's married should want a baby, and anybody unmarried shouldn't? Where'd all these rules come from?" Erica seemed to want to say more, but suddenly the energy was gone. She slumped in the metal chair, trembling.

Hannah rose from her desk and edged around. She hesitated, then knelt beside the chair and wrapped her arms around the girl, whose small frame shook, as though she were cold to the bone. "Shhh," Hannah whispered, drawing her close. "Use your head. . . . Use your heart. You don't have to follow their rules, and you certainly don't have to follow mine."

Chapter 22

IT TURNED DARK SO EARLY in December. Penny couldn't get used to it. She left for work before dawn and drove home long after dusk. The days were short, the nights long and lonely, her only consolation the sky above, black and shining. Often, her last deliveries were made in the pitch-dark, and in the past few weeks she'd taken to carrying a flashlight in the van to guide her up a strange sidewalk or an unseen set of stairs. Thursday evening, she turned into the dark alley behind her apartment and gasped in surprise. "My goodness!" she whispered. In her absence, her little garage apartment had been transformed. From a distance, she saw what appeared to be a blazing line of red and white stripes ascending into the nighttime sky. As she came closer, she could see that hundreds of twinkling red and white lights had been wrapped around her railing, row after tight row, just how many strings she couldn't guess. Boxes and boxes, she supposed. The door and windows had been decorated as well, the door in red, the two windows over the stairs in white.

For some time, Penny simply stood in Mattie's yard and stared. No one had ever taken such trouble over her—she wanted, first of all, to be grateful—but enchanting though it was, she couldn't take much pleasure in the sight. Climbing the stairs to her apartment, bathed in a glow of red light, Penny could even name this act for what it was: a labor of love. But unlocking the door, she realized that it was also an apology for their last encounter, and something more as well—an intrusion, Dr. Bill's way of staking his claim. He wouldn't let her go easily. But, then, she already knew that.

It had been late Monday afternoon when Penny learned about the high-school protest. She'd been making deliveries when it was reported on the radio news. Distracted and distraught, she'd slammed on the brakes too quickly at the next light, propelling a dozen red roses out of the vase and directly into the windshield of the van. Petals had exploded in the air, covering Penny's lap with blots of red and ruining the bouquet, so that she'd had to return to the shop. The rest of the day had been torturous. She could think of nothing except Dr. Bill and what she wanted to say to him. Finishing work well after dark, she'd driven across town to the little RV park where he lived. It was after nine by the time she found his trailer, late for an unannounced visit, but she knew that this couldn't and wouldn't wait. As soon as he opened the door, she blurted the words: "I can't see you anymore. And I'm not going back to your church."

He didn't seem surprised. "Come in," he said, showing her to the couch. His shirttail was out, and he was in his sock feet—the black cowboy boots lay discarded by the door. Otherwise, he was dressed, down to the thin red tie he often wore for special occasions. "Go ahead and say what you want," he told her.

He listened quietly while she talked, and when she was finished he said, "Don't do this. Please don't. You can be angry. I can live with your anger. But don't cut yourself off from me."

"You've got to leave that poor woman alone," she told him. "First her house, now her work. What are you thinking of?"

"Hannah Solace?" He began to pace in front of Penny, five steps each way, caging her where she sat. "Hannah Solace?" he repeated. "I have no intention of bothering her again. That's over." He stopped and let the room go silent before he asked the question. "So," he said, "did . . . did her husband send you?"

"No," she replied. "Absolutely not. Carl has nothing to do with this."

He laughed, a small, bitter sound. "Let's be honest, shall we? Carl Solace has *everything* to do with this. Do you know how much that hurt, seeing you with *him*? Good God, Penny! What was I supposed to think?"

"I don't care what you think." She got to her feet and pushed past him. He didn't try to stop her, but just as she was about to open the door he spoke again:

"Has he . . . Have you been with him?"

Startled, she turned back and searched his face. He looked wary and a little wounded, but above all, he looked curious. He wasn't trying to hurt her; he was serious. "I can't believe you're asking me that," she said. "Now I'm certain I never want to see you again."

"Penny, come back!" he'd called from the doorway. "I'm sorry!"

The Christmas lights cast a soft pink glow over the interior of the apartment—across the table, the bed, the floor, and especially the sunrise-colored walls. The effect was otherworldly, magical; Penny couldn't help wishing she had someone to share it with. She couldn't help thinking of Carl either, wrong though it was. He was an artist, she told herself; surely he'd appreciate it more than anyone else she knew. And she knew so few people anymore. By and large, the ones she'd thought she knew had turned out to be strangers. And the strangers had turned out to be relatives. Sighing, Penny slung her canvas bag onto the table, then knelt on the floor, scooting forward on her knees until she could scoop up the cat.

When the phone rang a few minutes later, she hesitated before answering. What would she say if it was Dr. Bill? Should she just hang up once she heard his voice? Would she be able to do that? Better not to answer, she supposed, but in the end she picked up the receiver and said a tentative "Hello."

"Hey, little sister," Delia said, happily. "What's up?"

Penny was relieved to hear her mother's voice. "Well, my house is decorated for Christmas. I came home and it was all lit up."

They'd been talking more lately. In fact, Delia had called only two days before. As it happened, the protest at the high school had made the Houston paper, and naturally, Delia had read the story carefully. Although the accompanying picture was blurry, one of the women looked exactly like Mattie. When Penny confirmed her suspicion, Delia had been awed. "Wow!" she'd said. "Momma is obsessed."

Now she asked whether Mattie was in one of her decorating frenzies.

"No," Penny said. "I don't even think she's put up a tree."

"Who then?"

"Dr. Bill."

"No way!"

"Monday night I told him I didn't want to see him anymore. Tonight I come home and he's covered my house in lights." She pulled the cord across the room and, pressing the cat to her chest, dropped into the red chair. Flash startled then relaxed, curling into Penny's lap.

"Gosh, Penny. You've been keeping me in the dark here." Delia sounded a little hurt. "I didn't know you were *dating* Dr. Bill."

"I'm not," Penny said quickly. "At least I'm not anymore." Her eyes went to the lone window on the far side of the apartment, the only one left undecorated. From where she sat, it looked like a rectangle of darkness, a black painting hanging on her rose-colored wall. Unreal, unlikely. "Well," she said, "there's a lot you haven't told me either."

"Like what?" Penny heard the edge of indignation in her mother's voice. "Ask me. I'm not hiding anything."

She took a deep breath. "Why didn't you tell me about Dwayne? Why did I have to find out from Mattie?"

"I'm so sorry, Penny. I promised him I'd tell you before the wedding and made him swear *not* to tell you. I wanted to, I meant to, but the words just wouldn't come. We were having such a good time; I was afraid of ruining it."

"So where has he been all this time? Why does it take twenty-three years for me to meet him?"

"Well. He went off to Vietnam while I was still in high school. Came back and got married to someone else. Gosh, we went years without seeing each other. Then we had that one disastrous day at the lake. It's all ancient history now, but for a long time it was damn painful." She went silent for a few seconds before picking up the thread again. "He wants to get to know you, Penny. He wants to make up for lost time. That's why I'm calling. We're hoping you'll come for Christmas. He's taught the birds some tricks, honey. Wait till you see."

Bird tricks, Penny thought. She's still trying to divert my attention. Kaleidoscopes, bicycles, beautiful dresses. It won't work this time. "Twenty-three, Delia. That's a lot of lost time."

"Yes," her mother replied. "What can I say? Year after year, I kept telling myself that you weren't ready to hear about it, that you'd ask when you wanted to know. The truth was, I was chickenshit. It runs in the family. Momma was the same way with me. My entire childhood I went around thinking I was the second case of Immaculate Conception. That was me, Jesus's half sister."

"I wish you wouldn't say things like that."

"Sorry, sorry. Little Miss Devout. I keep forgetting. Anyway, I must have been twelve or thirteen when I discovered I wasn't the least bit special. That I was a little bastard, just like the rest of the world thought. Found the proof of it in Momma's closet."

"What'd you find?" Penny had searched Mattie's closet a couple of times, but they were halfhearted, timid attempts she'd cut short out of guilt.

"Oh please! Don't tell me you've never seen the letters. Don't you ever snoop, little sister?"

"Not really, or at least not well."

"You *are* a better person than I am. But if you want answers, you're gonna have to wallow in sin like the rest of us. Go on. They were in a shoe box behind the garment bag last time I looked. Go find them," Delia urged, "then call me back."

Her mother was on the verge of hanging up, but Penny wasn't finished yet. "What about the ladder and the roof?" she put in.

"Whoa! Hold your horses. One revelation at a time, please."

But Penny wouldn't be deterred. "Did you do it?"

Delia sighed. "She told you that too?"

"Yes." Penny bent her face to the cat's back to brush away the tears.

"It had nothing to do with you," Delia breathed into the phone. "I didn't even know you, honey." Here her voice dipped and then deepened. "Why did Momma tell you all this? What's with her?"

"She was really angry—" Suddenly, Penny was too dispirited to go on.

"At you? I can't believe that. She's adored you from the minute you were born. I've often thought you were Momma's *real* daughter. That the best thing I could do was to stay out of the way."

For an instant, the far window filled with light before going black again. Mattie had just pulled into the driveway. She was home again. Penny could feel the tension humming in the air around her, or maybe it came from inside her, friction from a divided heart. "It wasn't the best thing," she said.

Delia was silent for a long moment. "Of course it wasn't," she agreed. "I can see that now. But you have to believe me, Penny. At the time, it was all I knew how to do."

Two days passed before Penny was able to slip into her grandmother's house, but on Saturday afternoon she came home from work to find Mattie's car gone. Where her grandmother had taken off to or when she'd be back Penny had no idea, but she couldn't wait another minute. She had to take the chance.

The house was quiet and dark inside; all the shades were drawn, as usual. Passing through the living room, Penny couldn't help but note that the Christmas tree still wasn't up. December 17th, she thought. Christmas was only a week away, and Mattie hadn't done the first thing about it. The tree was something they'd always shared, buying it in the parking lot of a nearby grocery store, tying it to the top of the station wagon and hauling it home, the branches lapping over the roof and waving as they whizzed down South Congress. Mattie tended to choose tall, thin trees—six feet or more—and the job of trimming generally took all evening. They started with the bottom branches and worked their way up, finishing with a gaudy red and silver star that bobbed gently on top. The tree was so clear in her memory that Penny could almost see it standing in the empty space before the living-room window. Sighing, she turned to the stairs.

Like all the closets in the old house, the one in Mattie's bedroom was musty. Once or twice over the years, the roof had leaked, water seeping in through the ceiling of the bedroom. Mattie had repaired the mess and painted over the water spots, but the smell of mold was something even a fanatical cleaner couldn't abolish. The scent of talcum was just as strong, and the sweet smell of it made Penny want to sneeze. Mattie had a fondness for talcum, using it instead of deodorant, dusting under her arms and between her breasts after her bath. As a little girl, Penny had observed her grandmother through a crack in the bathroom door, watching as the older woman patted powder into her secret places. She was beautiful then, Mattie was, with full, pear-shaped breasts and a small waist. Sometimes, when she finished her toilet, Mattie would stand admiring herself in the mirror, a small smile playing around her lips.

The letters were right where Delia had said they'd be, stashed in an old Hush Puppies box. The hanging bulb cast an uncertain yellow glow over the small stack of envelopes in Penny's lap. She picked up one and ran her tongue across the strip of old glue, found it rough and still vaguely sweet. Hurry up, she told herself. You're stalling. Her hand hovered over the small collection. Finally, she chose the one with the oldest postmark, June 30, 1954. The plain white envelope spilled its contents, two thin sheets of paper that whispered as Penny unfolded them. Though the stationery had yellowed slightly over the years, the ink fading to a watery blue, the handwriting was still perfectly legible, a careful, rounded script, with lots of billowing loops. Instead of dotting her *i*'s, the writer had drawn perfect little circles that hung like balloons in the empty air over each line.

June 29, 1954
1711 Allen Avenue
Lubbock, Texas

Mattie dearest,

Once again, the Lord has seen fit to spare us. A fair-sized tornado swept through last evening. I was sitting at the kitchen table mashing potatoes when the light turned. You know how it does, the way the sky darkens to that sickly green color, and the air goes so still you want to scream. And me all by myself! Your daddy was in town, down at the bank. I couldn't help but wish for you, dear. In the worst moments, you always know what to do. Like your daddy, and it's a good thing. Me, I freeze up. "Kill me if you must," I said aloud, not exactly a prayer but the best I could do under the circumstances, and returned to cooking dinner with trembling hands. By the time your father drove up, I had the chicken sizzling in the skillet and was busy setting the table. You would have been proud of me, Mattie. This morning Rosie called, said the storm went west of us and killed three fellows in the back of a pickup truck out near Levelland, not one of them a day over twenty. He gives and He takes away.

I hope it's pretty in Austin, lots of sun and a cool breeze, good weather for gardening. Tell me something, Mattie. Does your aunt Lucy work out in her garden at night? More than once, she's told me she does her best work by flashlight. Says it's nice and cool after dark, all the kids in bed and out of her hair. Is it true? Check on her, will you? When we were girls, Lucy was such a fibber. I never know when to believe her.

Is she being nice, Mattie? It's a kindness she's doing, but Lucy needn't hold it over your head. Let me know if she does. You made a mistake, but it's the kind of trouble lots of girls get into. If you shake our family tree, all kinds of bad fruit will tumble out. Shoot, if you look close enough, none of it's perfect, a bruise here, a peck hole there. Hold your head up. As the preacher says, none of us escape unscathed. Not that you're bad fruit, honey. That's not what I mean.

But here's what's troubling me, Matilda. Lucy says you won't listen to reason, that you're turning a deaf ear to all talk of arrangements. Don't be foolish, please don't. You've such a stubborn streak, so I know I have to talk plainly. Keep this child and your daddy will never let you in the house again. What will I do? My only girl lost to me. Take pity, Mattie. Think of your mother. And think of the child. I can't say more, but go back and reread this passage. Take it to heart.

Lately, I've been wishing I'd had a second girl, a younger sister for you. Growing up, you seemed enough, all I could want, but now you're away, I realize the mistake I made. Another girl in the house would have been good for you. Maybe I wouldn't have doted on you so, and maybe I wouldn't be so lonely now you're gone.

As it is, I am looking for a job, if you can believe that. The

Piggly Wiggly needs a cashier, and I went in yesterday and filled out an application. A woman I know up at the church, her husband manages there, and she gave me the tip. He's a nice enough man, wears a bright red bow tie and sits very straight in his chair. He didn't seem disappointed that I hadn't worked all these years. Said it's not true that you can't teach an old dog new tricks. "Old dogs learn pretty good," he said. You'll be glad to know that I didn't correct his grammar. Am I an old dog, Mattie? I don't feel like one, except sometimes late at night, when my hip aches and the world seems to be closing down around me.

Can't wait till you come home. I dreamed last night we were both working at Piggly Wiggly, only here's the funny thing. Mr. Hernandez wasn't my boss, you were! You were wearing a white dress shirt and a snappy little bow tie over your best dress, the one I made you for graduation. I'm glad you made it through to graduation. I thank the Lord for that.

Write soon and promise you'll talk to the preacher and whoever he brings round. Others know best in this matter. Trust, Mattie, you simply must.

Love to you,
Momma

So it's true, she thought. Her eyes scanned the page. *Take pity, Mattie,* she read again. *Think of your mother.* For maybe the first time in her life, Penny was truly aware of her grandmother as a separate being, someone with her own history, her own foibles, her own destiny to attend to. Rereading bits and pieces, she was struck by all that had never occurred to her, chiefly that her grandmother had been a child herself once and that she'd learned her lessons the hard way. To be sent away from home when she was still a girl, to be locked out of her house, abandoned by her parents. It was so unfair. How she must have mourned them, especially her mother. In all their years together, Penny couldn't recall Mattie ever speaking the words *my mother,* and yet the letter made her seem like such a kind and funny person, so open with her feelings. When Mattie was younger, she must have been more like her mother, Penny thought. Then, as she'd aged, she'd closed down, locked herself up and tucked away the key. Penny's eyes returned to the final lines. *Trust, Mattie,* her mother had implored. *You simply must.* But Mattie had chosen to keep her own counsel. And if she hadn't, Penny realized, I wouldn't be here today.

She'd just slid the letter back into the envelope when she heard a noise downstairs, a scraping sound accompanied by the hard-soled clack of Mattie's shoes. A prickling fear ran up Penny's spine and, fumbling, she gathered the envelopes in her lap and dropped them back into the box. "You can do this," she whispered to herself, but the sound of her heart beating in her ears was louder than her words. Even so, she got to her feet, tucked the box under her arm, and started down the hall.

"Who's up there?" her grandmother called out. Penny could hear the dread in her voice. It said everything: I'm an old woman alone. Don't hurt me.

"Hello, Grandmother!" Penny called.

She arrived on the landing before Mattie had time to react. Her grandmother had just hauled in a tree, and the noise upstairs had arrested her in mid-act. She stood frozen in the entryway, her arms wrapped about the branches, panting from exertion. The fear of an intruder lingered on her face, but in only an instant, fury overcame her fear. "What are you doing?" she cried.

For a second or two, Penny considered lying. She could say she was looking for something else, anything to save her from this confrontation. But here she stood with the box of letters under her arm. The least she could do was tell the truth. "I'm sorry," Penny said, her voice level and surprisingly clear, "but I had to look. Delia told me about the letters. I think I have a right to know."

Mattie propped the tree against the door to the coat closet, then returned to the head of the stairs, hands on her hips. "Right to know?" she echoed. "Then why not ask? Don't you owe me the respect of a simple question? Must you nose around in my private papers? Haven't I taught you better than that?" She didn't wait for a response. Instead, she turned away and dropped heavily in the nearest chair. The springs complained of her weight, and Mattie sighed, a deep exhalation that conveyed exhaustion and resignation and loneliness. Penny had never seen her grandmother at such a loss.

Coming halfway down the stairs, far enough to have a clear view of her grandmother, she called out, "Who was my grandfather?" Her voice was loud, louder than she'd intended. "His name, I mean. I'd like to know his name."

Her grandmother was silent, as though she hadn't heard. Penny cleared her throat to repeat the question, but Mattie spoke up: "I heard you. Can't you come sit with me?" she complained. "Is it necessary for you to stand up there and yell down at me?"

"No," Penny replied, hurrying down the last of the stairs. "No, of course not."

She sank to the floor beside her grandmother's chair. Mattie was still breathing hard, and the front of her white sweatshirt was covered with thin green needles. The pungent smell of pine filled the air around them.

"Mr. Lyndon Abernathy," Mattie said, her eyes on the opposite wall. "That was your grandfather's name. He was married to my third-grade teacher, Miss Sarah. Knew both of them most of my life. A betrayal, pure and simple. I was only seventeen, but old enough to know better. *Thou shalt not commit adultery.* How hard is that to understand?" She faltered. Penny wondered then if her grandmother would cry, something she couldn't remember seeing. "Loving him was the hardest thing I've ever done, and the easiest too," Mattie went on. "Mr. Lyndon Abernathy. Back in the early seventies, Delia tried to look him up. Wanted to know her father, she said. I suppose she told you."

"No," Penny said. "She didn't."

"Well, she should have. Could have saved us both this trouble and embarrassment. He's dead now, or so I hear. I saw him only once after my little girl was born. One time." Penny heard the wistfulness, and it took her breath away. To love this much and be denied, she could hardly imagine it. "Mr. Lyndon Abernathy. I always thought of him that way. Could never settle myself on just Lyndon. A big mistake, a terrible sin. Luckily, few knew of it. But of those who did, only my mother could forgive it."

"God forgave it," Penny put in.

Mattie was silent. "Maybe," she finally said. "But I've never repented. Can God forgive what we don't regret?"

Penny didn't know the answer. "Did you love him that much?" she asked.

"I loved *Delia* that much. And, yes, I loved him too. It was wrong of

me to love him, but I couldn't help myself. Over the years, I've wondered why. Why him? Why not someone my own age? Why not someone who didn't have a wife? Sarah was a good, simple woman. She
didn't deserve a mosquito bite, much less a small-town scandal."

"I thought you said not many people knew."

"A few did, I said." Mattie sounded offended. "What difference
does it make how many?"

Delia had made a quip about married men when Penny confessed
her feelings for Carl Solace. "It's in our genes," she'd explained. Until
now, Penny hadn't fully understood, but the flippant way her mother
had dismissed the matter had disturbed her. It was a relief now to hear
the pain in her grandmother's voice. To recognize the sin but not regret
the love, this was a harder way to live in God's presence and something
Penny could respect.

"I've missed you, Grandmother," she said.

"I've missed you too." But Mattie had something else on her mind.
She leaned forward in the chair, bracing herself with a hand on either
knee. "Don't you see now why I want you to love him? Can't you find
it in you to care for him?" Rather than reply, Penny lowered her eyes to
the shoe box and the jumble of envelopes inside. "If you could have
seen him the other day," Mattie went on. "He was over here all afternoon putting up those lights."

"For a while I *thought* I could love him," Penny told her. "I thought
if it were your will or God's will, then I could just give myself over to it.
Trust you. Trust those who know best. One day, though, I realized it's
not even *my* will. Love's more mysterious than that." She picked up the
box and held it out to her grandmother, who hesitated before accepting
it.

For a few seconds Mattie studied the contents, then tentatively
reached in and shuffled the envelopes with her fingertips. "It's been
years since I've seen these," she said. When she looked up again, her
expression had softened, and her eyes swam with the past. She's crying,
Penny thought. Placing the box on the floor between them, Mattie
leaned forward and took her granddaughter's chin in her hand. "You're
right, Penny," she said softly. "Love can't be forced or bought or bar-
gained for. It comes on its own terms. Of all people, I should have
remembered that."

Chapter 23

WHEN THE PHONE RANG, Carl had just assembled the ingredients for Sunday breakfast—a big plate of scrambled eggs sprinkled with sharp cheddar and green chilies and a soft, warm tortilla to go with it. Weekends, he brewed a big pot of coffee, and he planned one last cup with his food. By then, it would be black and bitter, nearly scalding, and he'd take it in sips, between bites, like medicine. Carl was ravenous and sore through the arms and shoulders and hips, stiff and starving and utterly satisfied with himself. Operating a sander was more work than he'd thought it would be, but the grain he'd uncovered was gorgeous. Inspecting the living-room floor in the morning light, he'd admired the way the wood glowed from inside. It looked alive, the wide planks curving under his feet, as though he were standing on the back of some huge, gleaming beast.

He waited until the third ring to pick up, guessing it would be an employee calling in sick. Today, he would have to be hard-nosed. It was only a week until Christmas, seven short days, and he needed all the help he could get, whether sniffling, snorting, or hobbling about on crutches. He picked up the receiver and spoke in a stern voice: "Don't even think of calling in sick."

"It's me," Hannah said. "I didn't wake you, did I?"

"No, no, I've been up for hours." Carl heard the surprise in his voice. He certainly hadn't expected to hear from his wife this morning. They hadn't spoken for nearly a week, not since the evening of the high-school protest. As it turned out, he'd been one of the last to know. Like most everyone else in Austin, he'd seen it on the ten o'clock news.

Shocked, he'd done the only thing he could think of: jumped in his car and started over to Hannah's apartment. Not until he was halfway there had he begun to consider what he might say, and surprisingly, nothing much came to mind. Nothing substantial, anyway. All that was really important he'd determined to keep for himself. He didn't trust Hannah anymore, a discovery he'd made on the night they had sex. Although he hadn't expected to, he'd held back—watched the two of them going at it and felt little or nothing—even as she'd moved beneath him and, crying out, let go. Where the high-school protest was concerned, he might say, "I'm sorry it happened," but he refused to say, "It's all my fault." To do so would have required confessing his connection to Penny, something he was unwilling to do. Hannah would never have understood it—no reason she should; he barely comprehended it himself. In the end, he'd swung a U-turn and, returning home, called her on the phone, like every other chickenshit. He wasn't even sure now what they'd said to each other, only that it had been painful and unsatisfactory and vaguely dishonest on both sides.

"Hannah, are you okay?" he asked now. Unlike his employees, she *did* sound sick, congested, fatigued, in her own little universe of pain. He waited for her to tell him she had a fever—Hannah was prone to fevers—and that she needed to go to the doctor.

"You're still my husband, aren't you?" she said instead.

Such an odd question. He was tempted to be hard with her, to remind her of any number of things, starting with their wedding vows. "I don't know what difference it makes," he began.

She interrupted. "Please, Carl. Let's don't start fighting."

He sighed. "All right," he said. "Of course I'm still your husband." These were the words she needed to hear. Hannah made a low moaning noise, a kind of keening. It scared him, that sound. He tried to think what more might have happened, what else they might have lost. Wasn't most of it already gone or nearly gone? "What is it?" he asked.

But Hannah couldn't say. She was crying. Carl glanced about, his gaze landing on the gray tile counter; the three white eggs; the perfect, rounded lines of the turquoise Fiesta bowl; and the orangy-yellow hunk of cheddar cheese warming on the wooden chopping block. There was a sameness and a saneness about these things that calmed him. I could paint this as a still life, he thought, and others might find comfort in it too. "Life Must Go On," he might call it. "Why don't you come over and have some breakfast?" he asked Hannah.

She couldn't, she said. She had a funeral to go to, and she'd called to see if he would accompany her. What could he say? Funerals frightened him, but they frightened her more. He knew that. "Please, Carl. I need you with me."

What could he do but promise to be there, in her parking lot, in an hour or less, to take them both to get some breakfast and then to the service? "It's at a funeral home on Burnet Road," she told him. "I have the address." As soon as he hung up, Carl dialed Ruthanne and asked if she would come in early for him. Rashly, he promised her Christmas Eve off. After she'd agreed to help him out, Ruthanne asked who'd died, and Carl had to admit that he had no idea. Even a woman with a buzz cut and a nose ring was shocked by this little revelation. "Jeez, boss," she said. "I think you better find out."

When Carl tried Hannah's number again, her answering machine picked up. He stood and listened to his wife's voice instructing him to leave a message, but there were certain things you couldn't or shouldn't say into a tape recorder, and "Who died?" certainly qualified. He hung up and began getting ready. All the while that he replaced the eggs and cheese in the refrigerator, inspected his dark suit for spots, stood under the warm spray of the shower, wrestled with his tie, Carl tried to think who his wife might be mourning. And came up entirely blank.

As he pulled into the parking lot of her apartment building, Carl glimpsed Hannah waiting in the passenger seat of the Blazer. It was her hair that caught his eye, the gleam of reddish-gold in the diffuse winter sunlight. He was reminded of the wooden floor at home, which gave off that same warm red hue. For a split second, he imagined Hannah lying naked across the wooden floor, her long pale legs crossed at the ankles, that glorious mane spread out around her head, a flaming aura. What a magnificent painting that would make, he thought. After parking the Mazda next to her car, he sat still for a few seconds, bringing it into being; then, as he put the final touches on it—a slight blue tint to the skin at her neck, green eyes with gold flecks—he let the picture go, recognizing it for what it was, something else that was never meant to be.

Carl got out of his car and straightened his jacket before climbing into the driver's seat of Hannah's big red vehicle. The keys were already in the ignition, and after he'd settled himself behind the wheel, Hannah turned and leaned in, offering him a quick little peck on the cheek. "Thank you for coming," she said.

He shrugged and considered making a joke along the lines of "Anything to get out of work," but that was all wrong for this occasion. "You look lovely," he offered, which wasn't really true. The black wool suit didn't flatter her. Dark colors washed out her complexion and overwhelmed her fragile beauty. Her hair was pulled back in a rather severe French twist, accentuating the thinness of her face and the pink skin around her eyes.

"Do you want to go to Grandy's?" she asked.

He thought of their last breakfast there, after Hannah had moved out. "I never want to set foot in Grandy's again."

She considered that. "All right," she finally said. "How about the Nighthawk?" The Nighthawk was an Austin institution; they made the best biscuits in town, and Carl loved a good biscuit. He couldn't argue with the Nighthawk.

"Fine," he said. He hesitated, afraid to ask, but if he didn't do it now, when would he find out? At the service itself? "Hannah," he said gently, reaching out to touch her elbow. "Whose funeral are we attending?"

She looked startled, then distressed. "I'm sorry," she said. "It's Dorothy Pilsner's. She died Wednesday evening. I guess I just thought you knew. I don't know why . . . maybe because she asked about you the last time I saw her." Hannah stared out through the windshield at the stucco box balconies. "In fact, I think it was the last thing she said to me. 'How's Carl doing?' Something like that."

"And you told her I was busy paint-bombing churches?" He wanted to make her smile, but as soon as he said it, he knew he'd misstepped.

She turned her face away. "That's not funny," she said.

"You're right," he agreed, and leaned over to start the car.

On the way to the restaurant, Hannah was quiet and Carl spent the time trying to call up a mental picture of Mrs. Pilsner. He assembled frosted blond hair and small features, a scarf at the throat, but he wasn't the least bit sure of this picture. He might have been confusing Mrs. Pilsner with someone else, another woman of his mother's generation. You ought to pay more attention, he told himself.

The Nighthawk was crowded but they didn't have to wait. A hostess led them through the dark restaurant to a booth with well-padded burgundy seats. Hannah slid into her side and immediately opened the menu, propping it in front of her so that Carl couldn't see her face.

"I wasn't trying to upset you, Hannah," he said.

"I know," she muttered from behind a wall of plastic.

A waitress who looked alarmingly like Carl's vision of Mrs. Pilsner—frosted hair and all—appeared to take their order. Carl decided on a western omelette while Hannah opted for French toast. He smiled to himself. Though she often denied herself the calories, she adored anything she could drench in syrup. It was one of the things he loved about her, that someone so no-nonsense, someone so elegantly thin, could crave a batch of greasy bread topped with liquid sugar. The incongruity of it gave him hope, made Hannah human and vulnerable. His wife was ordering a child's dish, he thought, and it came over him in a rush, the reason for this huge aching sadness.

"I don't really remember Mrs. Pilsner all that well," Carl said after the waitress had brought their coffee. "We went to their house for dinner, right? A couple of years ago?"

"Yes," Hannah said. "It was a dinner party. Mr. Pilsner had received a service award, and we went there after the ceremony. I'm not sure exactly. It might have been two years ago last spring. Before Dorothy got sick."

"How well did you know her?" he asked.

She shrugged and sipped a little coffee, but just as she was about to speak, the waitress arrived with their plates. Carl took an experimental bite of his omelette then watched while Hannah dribbled syrup onto her stack of French toast, swirling the little pitcher over her plate, once, twice, then three times around. Finally, Carl couldn't help but laugh. "Whoa, Hannah!" he cried. "The toast is going to float right off your plate." She gave him a peeved look and put down the syrup.

A moment later, he tried again. "But you must have known her a lot better than I did."

She looked up, still chewing. A drop of syrup gleamed in the corner of her lip. "Well," she said. "Only a little better. Dorothy came by the office occasionally, brought cakes for people's birthdays, cookies for holiday parties." Hannah gazed at him across the table, her green eyes brimming. "Why are you asking all these questions?"

"I'm trying to remember. We're about to attend her funeral, after all."

She grabbed her napkin and dabbed at her eyes. "You think I'm too sad, don't you?"

"No!" he replied, a little too loudly. "I just want to understand *why* you're so sad."

"Dorothy was a very nice lady, Carl." She looked down at her food and, as though suddenly disgusted with it, shoved the plate away with the flat of her hand, so hard that it hit the basket in the middle of the table, spinning it. One biscuit lifted off the top and landed in the middle of Carl's omelette.

"I'm sure she was." He fished out the biscuit and proceeded to butter it. "I wanted another one anyway," he said, and dishing on the apple butter, smiled across the table at his wife.

"Don't you see, Carl?" she went on. "It's so unfair, the way she had to die."

"I do see," he said, and reaching across the table, gently squeezed her hand.

They'd been lucky as a couple, Carl thought. In seventeen years of marriage they'd attended only two other funerals together, one for Hannah's paternal grandfather and another for a San Marcos school teacher killed in a car accident. The school teacher's funeral had been gut-wrenching, though he hadn't really known the woman. She'd been a colleague of Hannah's, and she'd left behind three small children and a husband so bereft he'd spent the entire service with his head in his lap. Every time someone lifted him into a sitting position, he gazed about for a few bewildered seconds before collapsing into a heap again. All the marrow had seeped out of his bones, and despite his own best efforts, despite the constant attention of others, he'd simply folded in on himself. Parking the Blazer in the lot of the red brick funeral home, helping his wife out of the passenger seat, Carl thought about grief and how, if you let it, it will suck the life right out of you.

He took Hannah's hand and, together, they walked up the sidewalk to the entrance of the funeral home, a carbon copy of the others he'd visited over the years. When they stepped over the parquet threshold, their feet sank into soft carpets, and a solicitous woman in a navy dress swept forward to guide them in the right direction. The atmosphere was intended to be gracious, even luxurious, but Carl felt oppressed by it. Since when did churches give up on death, he wondered. Why did they turn it over to the professionals to be packaged and handled? Death should be better than this, he thought.

The funeral home's chapel was small and dimly lit, over half full when they arrived. Carl recognized a number of the faces: teachers, secretaries, and from the looks of it, even a few students and their parents. Mr. Pilsner stood at the front, erect and dignified in his black suit and flanked by two grown children, one of them a young woman, the other a young man. Both wore glasses and had the same flushed cheeks and blond hair. Both bobbed their heads as Carl shook their hands, thanking him for coming with the same words and inflection. The siblings resembled each other so closely they might have been twins, but they didn't look like their father nor did they call up the specter of their lost mother.

When Hannah reached Mr. Pilsner, the principal pulled her into a long hug. His large hands gripped the small of her back, and he drew her in close, murmuring words into her hair. Mr. Pilsner's embrace was unexpected and slightly embarrassing, but more surprising to Carl was Hannah's response—she surrendered to it, wrapping her arms around the principal's neck, cocking her chin on his shoulder. They resembled stranded dancers arrested in the midst of a slow number. Before letting her go, Mr. Pilsner shuddered a little, then stepped back and turned to Carl. "Thank you for bringing her," he said in a heartfelt voice and, as though he couldn't help himself, threw out his arms and drew Carl into a hug as well.

Hannah began to weep as they started back down the aisle to their seats. For most of the service, she cried, and during all of it, he kept an arm tightly around her shoulders, feeling wave after wave of grief pass through her. Poor Hannah, he kept thinking, poor little girl. He wished there were something he could do, some way he could give Naomi back to her. Surely that's what all this crying was about. Near the end of the eulogy, Carl's thoughts turned to his own mother, who'd called the night before to thank him for the scarf and pin she'd received in the mail. "I'm going to wear them to church on Christmas Day," she'd promised in her proud-mother voice. For a bewildered minute or so, he'd tried to tell her there must be some mistake. Buddy must have sent it. "No, no," she insisted, finally retrieving the card to read it aloud. Only then did Carl realize he had his wife to thank.

Squeezing her shoulder, he leaned in and whispered a few appreciative words. She nodded and, turning her head, managed to give him a teary smile. Will I be this bereft when my own mother passes away? he wondered. He glanced toward the front of the chapel, where Mrs. Pilsner's children sat side by side in the front pew. Though he couldn't see their faces, their shoulders were straight and still. They appeared composed. No, he thought. None of them would ever be as heart-broken as his Hannah. He remembered that afternoon at the Methodist Student Center, how he'd looked up from his work on the mural and laid eyes on her for the first time. "You have such a lovely face," he'd told her, "perfect for the Madonna." Back then, he'd assumed it was Hannah's beauty that had made her perfect; only now, as he dabbed at her wet cheeks with his handkerchief, did he realize that it was, and always had been, her sadness.

Chapter 24

THE CARROT CAKE FOR CHRISTMAS was Helen's idea, something warm and sweet. "And good for him," she said over the phone. "Full of carrots and raisins and nuts. Naturally nutritious. You can do this."

"I'm not much of a cook," Hannah said. She needed persuading.

Helen was up to the task. "If you want to make him something, I suggest baked goods. It's Tuesday evening already. Christmas is Sunday. You don't have time to knit a sweater."

"Not to mention the fact that I don't knit."

"Well, you could pick it up, if you put your mind to it. Your attitude sucks, Hannah, but there's no reason you can't learn to be crafty."

Hannah sighed into the receiver. "Not by tomorrow. Carl asked me to stop by on my way home from school. He's made me something for Christmas. That's what he said."

"So you want to make him something too?"

"Yes. Don't you think it's a good idea?"

"Of course. Handmade gifts are always best because you put something of yourself into them." Helen launched into a speech on the subject and finished by promising to walk Hannah through the cake-baking experience. "I have the perfect recipe," she said. "I'll read you the ingredients. Go to the grocery store; call me back. And don't worry. A smart dog could make a carrot cake," she said, "that is, if he could get his paws around a grater."

"Very funny. I don't have a grater." When Hannah had moved out, she'd brought very little with her in the way of kitchen utensils. "Honestly, I didn't plan on being gone very long. I took my clothes and not much else."

A short silence on the other end. "All right, then," Helen went on. "They have graters at the grocery store. Pick one up. And pans too, if you don't have them."

Hannah ended up putting more of herself into the cake than she'd intended. It wasn't easy, holding the receiver to her ear while she sifted—read *mixed*—the dry ingredients. ("No one sifts anymore," Helen maintained.) While she cracked the eggs and stirred in the vanilla, Hannah put down the phone, so the first real mishap didn't occur until she was grating three cups of carrots. "Ouch!" she screeched.

"Good God, Hannah," Helen complained. "You're going to burst my eardrum. What happened?"

"I grated my knuckle," Hannah said. "I think I bled on the carrots. What should I do?"

"Are they orange or red?"

"They're orange."

"Then keep going."

And so she did. An hour and a half later she lifted the two cake pans from the oven. Excited, she dialed her sister again.

"How do they look?" Helen asked.

"Great! Like a cake." The two halves had risen evenly, and the tops were a deep rich brown, confettied with orange, exactly as her sister had described.

"Don't try to take them out of the pans until they're cool," Helen instructed. "And for goodness sake, be gentle. If they break apart, use the frosting to glue the pieces back together."

"I see," Hannah said, still admiring her work. She touched a finger to the middle of one and was gratified by the firm texture. "I did it, Helen!" she cried.

CARL had been very clear about time. He was working a split shift—he'd be home at two-thirty but had to be back by five. Knowing that high-school classes let out at three, he'd asked Hannah to stop by the house at three forty-five, which would give them nearly an hour to visit. "Will that work?" he'd asked. "I don't see why not," she'd told him. But the why not was Erica Faber, who waylaid Hannah in the hallway as she was rushing out of the building. "I can't talk now," Hannah tried to tell her, but Erica pleaded for just a few minutes. Which turned into half an hour. Whipping through traffic, Hannah hoped Carl would be understanding. She planned to tell him the whole story over a pot of coffee and a slice of cake. "I don't think I've told you about Erica," she'd say. Embroidering the picture, she imagined their dinner table set with the butter-yellow Fiesta plates and cloth napkins. Domesticity pure and simple. She was hungry for it, she realized, positively ravenous.

Pulling up to the front curb, Hannah noted that the sandblasters had paid a visit since she had. The brick looked good as new now, better than new, really. The doors and trim wore a fresh coat of white paint; the leaves had been raked, the walk swept, and the shrubs under the windows all clipped to the same height and width. Whatever remained of the incident—a few paint splatters on the concrete—was underfoot now and easily overlooked. While walking up to the house, Hannah glanced down only once, and all she saw—all she allowed herself to see—was the toe of her brown suede heel against a background of gray.

She carried the foil-covered cake in both hands. The top was festooned with cheap red and green bows, which barely stuck to the foil. Hannah wished she could rip them off and start over. The closer she got, the more she regretted the whole impulse toward homemade. Who did she think she was, baking a cake? Not Hannah Solace, that was for sure. Hannah Solace selected her cakes at fancy bake shops, the kind with glass counters and employees in starched aprons, the kind where they slipped your chosen confection into a crisp white box and sealed it shut with shiny gold stickers. Hannah's gift rested on a plastic dinner plate, the same one she'd scarred chopping the walnuts, and the cake felt heavy and unwieldy in her grasp.

Carl stood waiting for her inside. "Be careful," he said as she crossed the threshold. "I've just refinished the floors."

"They're beautiful!" she exclaimed. "My God, you've been busy, haven't you? Everything's so spic and span!"

"Thanks." Carl looked pleased. He took her by the elbow and led her through the living room and into the kitchen, where Hannah thrust the cake into his hands. "Merry Christmas!" she said.

"You baked this?" She heard the incredulity in his voice. No wonder. This was her first cake, the first of their marriage anyway. "Wow, Hannah. You've been busy too."

She shrugged. "No big deal." But they both knew it was.

She must have had a faraway look on her face, because Carl smiled. "What is it?" he asked.

Hannah was tempted to tell him. Last night, in the midst of baking, she'd picked up an egg and cradled it in the palm of her hand. Suddenly, she'd recalled baking a chocolate cake with Naomi—the cracking sound of eggs hitting the glass bowl, the puzzle of inserting beaters into the old upright mixer, the pleasure of spinning the mixing bowl on its stand. At the time, she'd thought of telling Helen; now she considered telling Carl. But, finally, she couldn't tell anyone. She was afraid to share memories of her mother, most of which seemed suspiciously sentimental, spun from episodes of *The Donna Reed Show* or *Father Knows Best*. If she were to utter them aloud, she might hear the falseness in them, watch them dissipate then disappear. Better to keep them to herself. "Nothing. Why don't you make some coffee?" she suggested.

"Good idea," Carl said. While he filled the pot with water and measured the grinds, Hannah offered to get the plates from the hutch and cut the cake. "Hold on," he called as she headed for the doorway. "It may be hard to get into that hutch right now."

She could see that for herself. Evidently, Carl had moved his studio. The dining-room table had been shoved against the back door, the easel situated in front of the window, so that the back leg was flush with her hutch. Carl appeared to be in the midst of a large pastel. Although she couldn't see the work itself, she could see the clothes pins holding the paper, the debris of chalks all around. This time, he'd covered the area around his easel with newspapers. "What's this?" she asked. "You've

376

moved your studio." She glanced back over her shoulder and caught him staring at her, his expression troubled or fearful. Something. She couldn't quite read it.

"Whoa!" he said. "I'll show you that in a minute. We don't have much time, and I want to give you your present. Come on. It's back in the bedroom."

On the way down the hall, Hannah stopped in front of what had been Carl's studio. The old door was gone; in its place was a new screened one. The light from the bare window poured into the hallway. "Carl," Hannah breathed. "Have you taken leave of your senses?"

He was beside her, a sly curve to his lips, more smirk than smile. "What senses?"

What senses, indeed? He'd hauled out most of the furniture, though the old desk was just where it had always been, cleared of jars and tubes and wadded bits of tissue. Now the surface was spotted with bird droppings. The plastic flamingo had been caged in, and the wooden flamingo with it. She'd been proud of those gifts, and now here they were, targets for bird poop. The floor was covered with a drop cloth; she was relieved to see that, anyway. Two perches extended from one wall, and a small galvanized trash can stood just under them, a round hole cut into the side to provide the birds with a hideaway. Yes, birds. Hannah spotted a white cockatoo hunched on the windowsill. She turned and gave her husband a bewildered look.

"That's Mildred," Carl said.

E.T. rested on the top rung of the desk chair. He appeared to be asleep, head tucked under his wing. She'd never understood Carl's fascination with the parrot, his very apparent affection for the creature. To her mind, birds were not like dogs. They weren't lovable companions. In fact, they weren't companions at all. Something about them seemed alien, even slightly hostile. And little as she cared, Hannah couldn't help despairing when she saw them in cages or sitting on perches, wings clipped so that they looked like old men in jackets with empty sleeves. If a bird was meant for anything, it was flight. "Two birds?" she said.

"Three," Carl admitted. "There's another cockatoo hiding in the trash can. I figured they'd be happier if they had their own space. At first I gave E.T. too much freedom," Carl went on. "He wrecked things. Freaked Helen out too. She came over one evening, and you should have seen her face. Told me it was unsanitary to take meals with animals." Hannah knew all about it. Helen had stopped by and caught him at the table with E.T.

"She called me," Hannah said, laughing in spite of herself. It was the first real laugh she'd managed in over a week. "She said it was like something you'd see in a Fellini movie: a man and his bird sitting across the dinner table from each other." Hannah always fell asleep in Fellini movies. Naturally, Carl loved them. "She told me it wasn't like you." Carl was smiling. Hannah felt so fond of him just then, so glad of his company. "You know what I told her?"

"No, what?" Carl said.

"I told her it was exactly like you." Hannah faltered, and her laughter threatened to turn to tears. " 'That's where you're wrong,' I said. 'It's exactly like him. He's becoming himself, now that I'm not around to keep him in check.' " She waited for him to reach out to her, but he kept his distance, his arms folded across his chest.

To hide her disappointment, Hannah turned away. Until now, it had not seemed quite real to her, this room. It was like something he'd staged, an elaborate practical joke to make a point. But this change was for good. He'd drilled holes in the walls and taken the old door off the hinges. The arrangement looked permanent. "We'll never get a buyer for this house," she said. "Not without taking a loss. Did it occur to you to consult me, Carl?"

"Actually," he said, "I've decided not to sell—"

She interrupted. "You've—"

He held up a hand. "Let me finish, Hannah." She didn't recognize the steely voice. "I'm not moving. Why fix up the place for somebody else?" He hesitated, then went on. "You didn't ask me a thing when you left. Left me with the paint and the reporters and—" He started to say something more; instead, he waved his hand in front of them to clear the air. "But I'm not mad anymore, really. It turns out to have been a good thing, a really good thing. It shocked me, brought me back to life." He smiled at her, a forced smile but a smile nonetheless. "Come on. Time's a wasting. I want to give you your gift."

He'd staked his claim in their bedroom as well. Whatever space she'd occupied was gone now. He'd taken it, used all of it, stretched his arms from one end of the house to the other and declared it his own. Canvases were propped against the walls, long lines of them, two deep in some places. She recognized at least half of the work, but the rest was new. Much of it depicted children from the fifties and sixties, his childhood and hers, and the details spoke to her: canvas high-tops, frilly dresses and net petticoats, patent-leather shoes, hula hoops, and wooden baseball bats. Scarred knees, missing teeth, and wavering smiles.

"These are wonderful," she said.

"Thanks," he replied. He opened the closet door and retrieved another canvas. "Close your eyes," he instructed, "and keep them closed until I say."

She could hear him coming closer, feel him standing directly in front of her. It was all she could do to stand still, to keep her eyes closed. She felt wobbly, a little dizzy. She wanted to sit down on the bed, rest for a minute. It had been a long day, a long week, a long year. "Can I open them?" she asked.

"Not yet," he said. "I want to tell you something first. I didn't paint this to give to you, but when we were at the funeral on Sunday, it occurred to me that you should have it. Don't react too quickly, all right? Just look at it a minute. Just think about it."

"All right," she said, and opened her eyes.

He was standing about five feet away, backed up against the foot of the bed and holding a canvas up in front of his chest. She could see that he was nervous about her reaction. He was biting his lip, and it made him appear boyish. "It's your mother," he said.

She nodded. She'd known that immediately. He must have used a photograph, but if so, Hannah didn't recall it. Maybe it was one of Helen's. The original must have been in black and white, as was the painting of a young girl, a grinning tomboy with lopsided pigtails. The realness of it took her breath away, but what made it clearly Carl's work was the lavender X that intersected the canvas, obscuring the image without obliterating it. She could still see her mother between the lines and even through the gloss of color. He'd gone and done it; he'd captured the paradox of loss, at least what Hannah knew of it. No one was ever gone completely, just enough to make you ache. Hannah's mother would always be with her, a shadowy presence she could neither claim nor relinquish, neither quite remember nor ever quite forget.

"What do you think?" he asked.

She stepped forward and took it from him. "It breaks my heart," she said.

He leaned in and kissed her forehead over the top of the canvas. "I'm so glad you like it," he said.

"I didn't say I like it," she replied, tears springing to her eyes. "I said it breaks my heart."

"Close enough." He stroked her cheek. "I think the coffee's ready." She nodded and let him take the canvas back. "I'll put it in your car," he said.

While he was outside, Hannah wandered into the dining room, drawn toward the pastel on the easel. From the very beginning, she'd been attracted to Carl's work. Initially, she'd been impressed by the mastery he'd achieved over his hands, over color and line and form. Later, she'd realized that those things came with practice, with the sheer investment of time, and admirable though they were, his skills lost their power to awe her. What continued to surprise her was the emotion, the way he was able to invest his feelings in his art. She thought it was an act of bravery, to express yourself so openly.

Carl had always said that chalks were a good medium for the human form. The first time she'd heard about the beauties of pastels, he'd been drawing her. Now she saw that he was drawing someone else. The figure in the picture was small and slight—half-woman, half-child. Her brown hair was short and wispy, her eyes almond-shaped, her chin narrow and pointed. She was lovely in an old-fashioned way, with an expressive face that looked straight out at the viewer. She wanted something she didn't yet have, and Hannah knew what that something was. The face might be unfamiliar, but the desire stood out plainly. This woman was as open with her emotions as Carl himself.

She heard him come back in and turned in time to see him disappear into the kitchen. Had he seen her? she wondered. Had he even looked her way? Hand over her mouth, Hannah gazed at the half-finished pastel. The young woman's pose verged on the sentimental, but the starkness of the lines and the sad expressive face redeemed it.

Wearing blue jeans and a simple white blouse, she sat in the middle of a wooden floor—theirs, Hannah realized—knees pressed to her chest, bare feet flat on the floor. She might have been a little girl waiting for story hour to begin. At her hip, boxed lines suggested the figure of a cat. Where had she come from? Hannah wondered. How had this happened?

She told herself to breathe, to take the air in and let it out. Why she should be so shocked, she wasn't sure. Carl was a handsome man. In restaurants, she'd seen women's heads turn to follow him, and she'd sometimes teased him about flirting. Typically, his response had been puzzled, even a little hurt. "I'm not flirting," he'd insist, and she knew it was true. In all the years of their marriage, she'd never seriously worried about Carl's fidelity the way Helen had to worry about Jimmy's, checking his pockets when he came home at night, questioning the scratches on his back or the stray, sweet scent about his face. Carl was another sort of man altogether. His heart was something Hannah had been in full possession of, as though he'd handed it over in a box for safekeeping. Only now, this very minute, did she realize he'd taken it back and left her empty-handed.

"Hannah?" he called to her from the doorway. "Are you getting the plates?"

"Yes," she answered, sidestepping the easel to her hutch. She meant to open the glass doors and grab two plates, to carry them into the kitchen and pretend if she could. But he'd known her too long and must have heard the distress in her voice. He came out of the kitchen to check on her, but she couldn't meet his eyes. "Were you going to tell me, then?" she asked. She leaned her head against the glass doors and was comforted by the gentle shifting of her plates inside.

He didn't respond immediately. "Not much to tell, really."

"Yes, there is." She straightened slowly and stepped in front of the easel again.

"Well, okay, something," Carl admitted, "but not what you're thinking. She's religious . . . sort of a holy person, Hannah. And she's very sad right now. . . ." His voice died away. The living-room floor, open and shining, was a vast space between them, growing wider and longer by the moment.

"Are you going to introduce me?" she asked.

"What?" His voice was startled.

"Not really," she answered, keeping her tone light by an act of will. "I just wondered about her name." It was strange, she thought, to have to be so tactful. He was her husband still, after all, but she couldn't ask questions or demand answers. She would have been more forthright with any stranger.

"Penny," Carl told her. Then, as though once wasn't enough, as though he wanted to brighten the air with the sound of her name, he said it again: "Penny."

"Carl," she began, her voice a little croaking sound.

"Oh, Hannah." His words were steeped in regret. The worst thing of all was sympathy. She'd always thought so. He was moving toward her; in a second, she'd have to bear his touch.

She held out a hand to stop him. "I have to go," she said. "Please, please, just let me go."

He stood back and let her pass.

The sun was setting when she pulled up in front of the church. Gospel Fellowship was a neighborhood church, surrounded by white frame houses. The building had the same lines as the Methodist churches of her childhood, with a showy front hiding the no-nonsense, no-frills brick structure just behind it. That was the Methodists for you, always putting on airs, pretending to be something they weren't. All the comforts of religion without any of the inconvenience. In adolescence, Hannah had flirted with Catholicism. Give me a religion with some backbone, she'd told Helen, but when push came to shove, she'd remained a Methodist. It made sense, she thought now. All the comforts of marriage without any of the inconvenience. Wasn't that her to a T?

She recalled from the news reports that Gospel Fellowship had been in the building for just five years. It was a mess now; Carl had seen to that. The front of the church was entirely covered in red, black, and purple paint. He couldn't have been much more thorough if he'd used a spray gun. She felt a thrill of shame and satisfaction at the desecration. It *was* a desecration. She knew she didn't have the guts for such a thing. Carl did; Carl had. Always, she'd considered herself the more courageous one, the one who'd put herself through graduate school without a penny of help from anyone, the one who'd pushed and shoved to get the job she wanted. It hadn't been easy; it still wasn't. In her mind, she'd been charging ahead while Carl lagged behind. If she hadn't dragged him into the present by force, he'd still be hanging out in the sixties. Truth be told, she'd always believed he lacked nerve and imagination when it came to managing his own life. Now she wasn't so sure. Maybe her view of things had been too simple. She was beginning to realize that there are all sorts of ways to push and just as many means of holding back.

Hannah opened the car door and stepped out onto the quiet street. Not a soul in sight. Those who were home from work were busy inside, windows closed, televisions glowing. Not an old man rocked on a porch, not a child peddled a trike, not an aimless dog wandered the perimeter of the yard. The neighborhood was entirely deserted. While she looked around, a string of blue lights blinked on at a house across the street. Still, no sounds. Finally, as she stood listening to the silence, a motorcycle sped up the street behind the church. She blinked and stepped onto the sidewalk, released from her reverie. The engine roared, then abruptly fell silent. Moments later, she wondered if she'd imagined it.

The yellowed grass closest to the building was splattered with purple, black, and red. The paint would remain until spring, she thought, when the grass began to green and grow. A few mowings and it would be gone. But for now, she could tell exactly where Carl had stood and sloshed the cans, moving a few feet each time he changed colors. The pattern repeated, over and over, across the front of the building: purple, black, red, purple, black, red. Methodical, orderly, achingly thorough. Paint shot up the side of the building and near the top exploded open into a wide V shape.

Hannah had seen the church on TV and Dr. Bill standing in front of it. They weren't going to try to clean the brick, he'd told the reporter. Not now. For the time being, it would remain as it was, "a reminder of death and destruction" until "the abomination of abortion is vanquished from our land." Who did he think he was, she'd wondered, some sort of Old Testament prophet? At the time, she'd worried that Carl had played right into Dr. Bill's hands, but now she wasn't so sure. Carl had rendered the front of the church into a huge abstract painting. To her mind, it was some of his best work, anger manifested, an eye for an eye. Don't fuck with me, it said, or I'll give as good as I've got. It was pretty good, she thought. What he had, what *she'd* had, was pretty damn good.

She was turning away, about to retreat back into her Blazer, when a man's voice spoke to her from the steps of the church. "Well, well. What have we here? Hannah Solace has come calling?"

Startled, she whirled back. In what was left of the light, she saw him standing there, a tall man in jeans and a white shirt, elbows jutting out, hands stuffed into his pockets. He descended a step at a time in her direction, and it was all she could do not to run. She was frightened, she realized, and completely alone. "Dr. Bill, I presume," she managed to say, wrapping her arms around her chest and forcing herself to meet his gaze.

He continued striding toward her, not stopping until he was about fifteen feet away, close enough so she could see something of his face, the deep-set eyes, long nose, and prominent chin. "What are you doing here?" he asked, reaching up to brush back the hair from his forehead.

He's wondering how he looks, she thought. It surprised her and gave her back her presence of mind. A handsome man, she realized, and vain, like her. It seemed impossible, this thought. Like her? How could that be? How could he, Dr. Bill, have anything in common with her? Slowly, reluctantly, he stepped forward until he was close enough to extend his hand. "About time we met, don't you think?"

She shook her head, refusing to shake. No, she thought, I won't touch him.

He drew back and slipped his hands in his pockets. "Well, if you don't want to talk, you better head on home." He jerked his head toward her car.

Hannah's anger was immediate: "Why should I go home? You can invade *my* life, *my* house, the school where *I* work, but I show up on your sidewalk, and *I* should go home? Thanks to you, I don't have a home to go to. You've ruined it! You've ruined everything!"

"Bullshit!" He spat the word. "I've driven by your house. Looks pretty good to me. How's my church look? You want to talk about ruined?"

She ignored the question. "Why is this so important to you?" she asked. "You don't know me! You wouldn't have known my child! What difference does it make to you?"

"*In whose hand is the soul of every living thing and the breath of all mankind?* Job 12:10. Is it in *your* hands, Hannah Solace?" His voice rose and fell. A private sermon, she thought. That's what I'm getting here. But she wouldn't let him off so easily.

She felt brave enough now to move in his direction, one step, then another. "Is it in *yours*, Dr. Bill? Be a real human being for a change, why don't you? It's easy to hide behind God, to spout Bible verses and carry placards. You don't have to think. You don't have to feel. God tells you what to do, is that it?"

"I do God's will," he said quickly, "when I can, when I know it."

For a few seconds, she tried to stare him down, but he wouldn't look away. "Here's what I don't understand," she said, inching closer, until she could see the fierce concentration in his eyes. "If it's God who pulls the strings, if He sends one car slamming into another, if He dries up the rain and lets the children starve, if He puts a child in my womb"—Helen's word, *womb*. She smiled a little as she said it— "didn't *He* lead me to abort the pregnancy? Isn't it *His* fault?"

Dr. Bill shook his head. "It's your fault, your husband's fault, my fault." He hesitated, then plunged ahead. "I'll tell you the truth, Hannah Solace. Once, a long time ago, a woman I loved got rid of my child. Washed it out of her and came home empty. 'I'm clean now,' she said. Clean. Clean. I was angry and self-righteous, but it was *my* fault. I didn't love her enough, and she knew it. And you didn't love your husband enough, now, did you?"

"That's not fair!" Hannah cried. "That's not true!"

"What is true, then? You tell *me*."

She stepped back and spoke the words haltingly. "My mother died when I was twelve years old. She was on her way to the grocery store when a man in a white truck slammed into her car. They said she never knew what hit her." Dr. Bill kept his eyes on her face. He's listening, she thought. "Did God make that happen?" she asked. "Was it punishment? Who was He punishing, then? My mother? Me? My father? Do you see how tangled it is, how impossible to understand?"

He nodded. That's all, just nodded.

"Say something!" She lurched forward, grabbing for his arm and clutching at the sleeve. When he tried to pull away, she held on tight. She wouldn't let go, not until he told her what she wanted to know. She could feel his warmth beneath her fingertips. He was skin and muscle and bone, just like she was. "Tell me!" she demanded. "I need to know."

"I don't have the answer," he said quietly. "You know as much about God as I do."

"What?"

"You heard me. You want a real human being? Okay, then. Here it is: I don't know what to tell you. I'm floundering and failing just like you are. All I know is this: I've finally found someone I *can* love enough. Someone I *do* love enough. I'm begging you. . . ." She could hardly hear the words, though he was so close now he could have kissed her. "I'm begging you to move back home. Go back to your husband."

"I can't." She was whispering too. "I wanted to go home today—but he's in love with someone else."

Dr. Bill closed his eyes and turned his face to the night sky. "Penny," he said, softly, once, then again—"Penny"—filling the air around them with the sound of it.

When the doorbell rang the next morning, Hannah was stretched out on the couch, asleep. In her dream, she was standing onstage at school, a new principal addressing a senior assembly, as proud and excited as her audience. Fearful too. She could see the tension in their faces, that mixed expression seniors wear the whole last half of the year, part yearning and part panic. She'd been warming to her subject—whatever it was—when the bell rang and the students rose from their seats and began filing out. "Wait!" she'd cried. But they were already marching single file into adulthood, and not a damn thing she could say or do would protect them. She rushed off the stage and into the aisle, but all she could see were the backs of their heads, the determined set of their shoulders. She grabbed at one of them; for an instant he turned and stared blankly in her direction. She was dumbstruck by the discovery: This was Carl. He was one of the seniors—which meant she must be one too. How was this possible? she wondered. She was one of them and yet not one of them, the only one staying behind. "Carl?" she cried, thinking he might answer to his name, but he pulled away from her and was gone.

The doorbell rang again, and Hannah sat up, bewildered. For a moment or two, all she could see was the blue of Carl's eyes. Nothing in this room of rented furniture—tasteful and durable—was at all recognizable. The television still flashed images, but the movie Hannah had been watching last night was long over. Now an exercise program was in progress; a lithe woman in purple tights attempted a complicated yoga position. "You beginners should wait on this one," she was saying, her voice calm and reflective, as though she were doing nothing more strenuous than sitting in a chair.

"Who is it?" Hannah called from the other side of the door. Her head ached and her eyes felt swollen.

"It's Erica," came the girl's voice, haughty but diffident. Hannah smiled in spite of her aching head. "Didn't you say eight o'clock?"

"So I did," she mumbled, wrapping her robe around her. She'd intended to be dressed and packed by eight, but oh well. Erica would just have to wait.

She stood outside the door, hemmed in by her suitcases. "Nice luggage, my dear," Hannah said, bending to collect the small case in front of the door. It was new and unabashedly feminine, a tasteful floral upholstery. Erica wore a dress too, a first as far as Hannah could remember. It was black and short as the dickens, but the flounce around the hem gave it just a touch of little girl.

"A gift from Daddy." Erica swept into the small living room, leaving the two larger cases on the landing. "His girlfriend helped pick it out. You'd think I was going off to college."

Hannah had been thinking precisely that. She nodded, "Actually, yes."

"Funny, huh?"

"If you say so." She glanced at the two large cases. "Don't you want to bring those in?"

Erica shrugged. "Aren't we going soon?"

"Not as soon as I had hoped. But you're not in a big hurry, are you?"

Erica had been studying the room, but now she turned to Hannah. "Dr. Solace, are you okay?"

"I've been better," Hannah said. "But I'll live. What about you?"

She shrugged again. "I don't know. It'll be weird, being away from home, but I'm looking forward to meeting the other girls. They have a tree up. They make all their own decorations." She looked pleased, a little wistful.

"What about after the holidays?"

"I'll go to school during the day. At night, we cook meals together. It sounds like fun, don't you think?"

"One big slumber party?"

Erica nodded. "Yeah," she said. "Something like that."

Hannah considered. She had to tell the truth. "It won't be all fun."

"Sure. I know. But they help you make plans for afterward too. They don't put you down for your choice."

Hannah reached out and laid a hand on Erica's narrow shoulder. "I'm glad you asked me to take you," she said. "It means a lot to me."

"Me too," Erica replied, leaning in to give Hannah a quick kiss on the cheek. Together, they returned to the landing to carry in the suitcases; then Hannah headed for the kitchen to fix coffee while Erica sat down to watch the yoga program.

The pans from the carrot cake were still in the drainer. Hannah kept her eyes away from them as she measured instant coffee—decaf for Erica—and poured water into the pair of matching cups Helen had given her for Christmas. Red cups ringed with white hearts. They looked like Valentine's Day. Carrying them into the living room, Hannah discovered Erica stretched out on the floor. For a second, her mind flashed back to that day last fall when she'd discovered a pair of legs— Erica's legs—sticking out from beneath the stall door. What a mess. At the time, Hannah would not have bet much on the girl's future. Now she'd have bet her whole life on it. What had changed, then? Was it Erica or was it her? Was it circumstances or the way they responded to them?

Hannah wasn't sure. Some things you have to know before they happen, she thought. When you buy a puppy, for instance, you have to know that the puppy will grow old and die before your eyes. Surely there must be some exception, you might think to yourself, knowing all along that the exception lies in the other direction. That some puppies never reach old age. They run in front of cars or choke themselves on their leashes or some damn thing. That it's the same with a marriage. Standing before the judge or minister, you have to know that your chances are no better than fifty-fifty. And yet you march down the aisle as though it's a foregone conclusion that yours will be happily ever after. No doubt about it. You have to live that way, betting that you'll be the exception, that you'll defy whatever laws you need to in order to survive—no, more than that, in order to be happy.

This morning, Hannah's dog was dead, and so was her marriage. She hadn't managed to slip through any cracks. She knew that, and yet as she sat down on the couch, she couldn't help feeling the smallest stirring of hope. After all, here was Erica, following along with the woman in the purple tights, doing the moves no beginner should attempt. As Hannah watched, holding her breath, Erica wobbled a bit before finding her center. A few seconds of uncertainty passed, and the girl's movements became controlled and graceful, the only sound the small puff, puff of Erica's breath. And then it happened: First, her legs left the earth, next, her back. Soon, her whole body stretched straight as a post toward the ceiling, defying the laws of gravity. Her dress slipped up and settled around her shoulders, revealing black leggings. Except for the rounding of her belly, Erica was one narrow line pointing straight to heaven. It looked damn uncomfortable, but Hannah could see Erica's grinning face. This was no pretend smile; this was for real.

"Look, Ma, no hands," Erica managed to say.

Hannah set her cup of coffee beside Erica's so she could clap. "Bravo!" she cried. And then again—"Bravo!"

Acknowledgments

THIS BOOK took seven years and seven drafts to complete. While writing it, I moved from one state to another, changed jobs and agents and editors. I was living in Iowa when I began the book, and am first of all indebted to the Iowa Arts Council for a grant providing summer support. That same summer, in August 1993, I was the Margaret Bridgman Fellow in Fiction at Bread Loaf Writer's Conference. My thanks to the conference and to my recommender, John Irving, for continued encouragement and support. In addition, I'm grateful to Mark Watson, June Cunningham, Rosalie Cushman, Ned Leavitt, and Kip Kotzen for inspiration and advice during the early stages of the manuscript.

In the process of writing and rewriting the novel, I conducted interviews with helpful strangers and made inquiries of friends and relatives. I am indebted to the staff of the Des Moines Planned Parenthood; to Paul Robert Miller of B. Dalton Books in Ames, Iowa; to the librarians at Des Moines Area Community College; to Assistant Principal Patty Smiley of Emporia, Kansas; to Teresa Wells and her cocker spaniel, Muffin; to Clay Campbell of Albuquerque, New Mexico, and Roxanne McKee of Austin, Texas, for their legal advice; to florist Susan Sutton, owner of Apple Blossoms in Albuquerque; and to my brother, Sonny Oard, who knows all about paint.

My colleagues and students at the University of New Mexico have been a consistent source of support these past five years. I'm particularly beholden to Patricia Clark Smith, Carolyn Meyer, Nancy Gage, Julie Shigekuni, Louis Owens, Mary Beth Folia, Erin Roth, and Holly Romero-Pérez. And I'd be remiss not to acknowledge my long-distance support system: Jonis Agee, first, last, and always; Sandra Scofield; and Marly Swick, all wonderful writers and valued friends.

I am forever grateful to my agent, Kim Witherspoon, who took a chance on this book and on me at a crucial moment. Thank you, Kim, from deep in *my* heart. Because Kim believed in my novel, I've been blessed with two of the most exacting and intelligent editors in New York City—Susan Kamil and Carla Riccio. Carla, how to thank you for all those hours of discussion on the phone, all those margin notes and tactfully phrased attachments, one chapter at a time, one draft at a time?

Finally, to those three wonderful guys at home—Teddy, Corey, and Devin. Thank you for being there, every day, without fail. I love you more than I can say.

About the Author

SHARON OARD WARNER is the author of *Learning to Dance and Other Stories,* and the editor of an anthology, *The Way We Write Now: Short Stories from the AIDS Crisis.* She directs the Creative Writing program at the University of New Mexico in Albuquerque, where she lives with her husband and two sons. This is her first novel.